IT CAN'T RAIN THIS HARD FOREVER

THE SEQUEL TO *PATTIE'S BEST DEAL*

DAWN DITTMAR

Sunshine Publishing

NOTE TO THE READER

Thank you for reading this sequel, *It Can't Rain This Hard Forever*. As anxious as I was to get it out into the world, if you've been waiting for it, you already know, it didn't just happen overnight. In any case, I had fun writing it and I hope you will have as much fun reading it. *It Can't Rain This Hard Forever*, like its predecessor, *Pattie's Best Deal*, is a novel. A story. A work of fiction. As a result, the content, including all the names, characters, incidents and conversations contained herein are fictitious creations that stem from my imagination and which I wove into a story. They are not expressly based upon nor should they be implied to portray the characters, actions or conversations of any real persons, either living or dead. Any apparent resemblance to same is unintentional and coincidental, not to mention downright fantabulous. Although certain public places are mentioned in passing, their descriptions are not intended to reflect their characters.

The only exception, is the "Nor'easter", which was an actual blizzard that started innocently enough on a fairly mild Saturday in December of 2003. It lasted through the night and plastered the entire North Eastern Seaboard with record snowfalls. As of the printing of this book, it remains the most severe and largest twenty four hour snowfall New York State has ever witnessed.

Dawn Dittmar
Spring Lake, New Jersey

"There is no crueler tyranny than that which is perpetuated under the shield of law and in the name of justice."

—Charles de Montesquieu

I dedicate this book to my late twins,
Jason Dittmar and Paul Dittmar,
who only lived for one day.

ACKNOWLEDGMENTS

To everyone who is reading this sequel, *It Can't Rain This Hard Forever*, I hope you are enjoying it. Cracking open that first set of "fresh from the printer" books is an emotional experience I can't even begin to describe. And as the author of this work, naturally I played an important part in its evolution from a raw manuscript to the final book you are now holding in your hands or reading on your Kindle. Having said THAT though, I did not create it in a vacuum. *It Can't Rain This Hard Forever* could NOT possibly have come into existence without the love, support, friendship and skill of many truly wonderful people. What is that saying? "Writers' debts accrue over time?" And while it's true I can in no way actually acknowledge every contribution in as much detail as I would like to, I am going to do my best to try.

First and foremost, my deepest and most heartfelt gratitude goes to my loving Higher Power, for inspiring and guiding me through each and every phase of each and every draft and revision. (And believe me, there were many.) A special thank you for showing me the way and for reminding me how beautiful life can be.

To Archangels Michael and Gabriel, thank you for your protection, strength, guidance and continued enthusiasm.

To my gifted friend John Salvi, a Super Scorpio,

Exemplary Artist and Prince Extraordinaire, who always manages to spur me on, prompt my progress and tirelessly answer every single one of my countless (yet crucial) questions and there were scads of them, ranging from General Science, to DNA, to Visual Arts, to why (and how) people cry, as well as to questions about wedding protocol. And that doesn't include the "what ifs", which are so numerous, they would severely try the patience of any lesser mortal. To you John, an especially sincere and heartfelt thank you. Oh yes and thank you for helping me maintain my sense of humor and for our conversations and chats. You helped and advised me in the beginning and you are still doing it. Thank you.

How can I ever properly thank you, Will Duff, for your wonderful friendship, help, encouragement, continued inspiration about the character of Ryan Pilgrim and other matters, including your support in exploring venues in the book with me AND last (but not least), your constant technical assistance? You are an integral part of this book, just as you were an integral part of *Pattie's Best Deal*. I find "the strange world of technology" confusing at times, but you always find a way to figure everything out so I can get back on track again. I never ask you "HOW" you do it. That would be like asking a magician to reveal his secrets. All I know, is that you truly have the patience of a saint and I am extremely grateful you are in my life.

To my dear, late husband Walter, my one true love, words cannot adequately express how much I miss you. Every. Single. Day. Thank you so much for giving me a lifetime of love, friendship, compassion, encouragement, motivation and happiness and also for selflessly and enthusiastically supporting me and believing in my dreams. Thank you also for always having encouraged me to write. My grief over your loss is mitigated by the knowledge that you are still helping me and cheering me on from across the veil. Memories of you and the happy times we shared together will live as long as I breathe. May God rest your soul.

To my remarkable grandparents, Dolph and Margaret, who raised me from the time I was nine days old and whose memories I revere to this day, a sincere and special thank you not only for arousing my love of literature, but also for assuring me from a young age that I could write. And most importantly, thank you for instilling a set of values in me that, to this day, include both idealism and moral integrity. The two of you and Walter had everything to do with helping me become the person I am today.

To Jackie Slevin, thank you for editing this manuscript. I sincerely appreciate it. You are a talented editor, astrologer and writer yourself, as evidenced by the Daily Guides and Love, Money and Health columns you write for "Horoscope Guide Magazine" and of course, your own book "Finding Success in the Horoscope". I have gained a lot of insight from you on so many levels.

To Michelle Argyle of Melissa Williams Design, thank you for turning my manuscript into a "REAL BOOK" with your amazing graphic prowess AND for designing such a beautiful cover. Because of your loving creativity, artistic talent and excellence, *It Can't Rain This Hard Forever* turned out to be gorgeous!

To Michael Duff, a special thank you for your wonderful enthusiasm for my work. I would also like to thank you and Will for having hosted a book signing for *Pattie's Best Deal* at The "Bethel Mail Service," in Bethel, Connecticut and for the celebration afterwards.

To Rita Maggio, Maribeth Pelly and everyone at "Booktowne" in Manasquan, I would like to thank you for hosting my book signing for *Pattie's Best Deal*.

To Jean Lobasso, I am extending gratitude to you, for your skills and willingness to edit and proofread various early drafts of this manuscript.

To Sue Vernon, many thanks for inspiring me with your knowledge of Jersey City and for exploring its waterfront with me. I appreciate it.

To Linda Piazza, I am sending you a special shout out for having so generously given me some special assistance at a time when I needed it.

To Robby T. Grady, I appreciate your insight into various aspects of the people, places, situations and institutions in Westchester County.

To Corinne Pandelo, thank you for your support, encouragement, companionship, friendship and dinners during this process.

To Photographer Irene M. Zagorski, thank you for capturing my personality on the back cover photo! I love it!

To Holly Corbella and the Bellas, I would like to thank you for having me as a guest on your TV show.

To Genelle Jackson, thank you for your comments regarding various general medical treatments.

To Pam Bush, thank you for your editing and proofreading input during this sequel's infancy.

To Dawn Wells, thank you for your input regarding various general hospital treatments.

To my students, private clients, workshop attendees, loyal readers and friends who bought, read, reviewed or helped me in any way with *Pattie's Best Deal*, a special thank you from the bottom of my heart for your help and support and also for continuing Pattie's journey with me now. I am sending my many thanks, deep appreciation, blessings and love to you all.

PURGATORY

CHAPTER ONE

OVER THE RIVER AND THROUGH THE WOODS

THANKSGIVING NIGHT 2003

Pattie Anwald stood outside her boyfriend Jordan Armstrong's rental car, wheezing and shivering in the rain. She was completely disheveled from head to toe. Her jaw was swollen, her normally pretty face was a hideous mess from her smeared make up and her jet black hair hung down her back in matted, water logged tangles. Jordan hurriedly helped her out of her wet trench coat and folded her into his Burberry raincoat. Since she was frail, petite and delicate boned and he was tall, she found herself practically swimming in it and the weight of it pressed her damp clothes against her. As a result, she felt chilled to the bone. A shudder passed through her.

Jordan opened the passenger's side door and tenderly helped Pattie slide onto the seat, but the pressure on her tailbone caused her to wince and cry out in pain. She carefully shifted her weight to alleviate as much of the discomfort as possible. As Jordan closed the door, she sat perched on the edge of the seat, gnawing the fleshy part of her lower lip between her teeth. Her entire body trembled, as she viewed the night through the fog and the heavy drum beat of rain that clattered against the windshield.

Jordan closed her door and when he got in on the driver's side, Pattie turned to him and smiled. He smiled back at her. Then he started the ignition and cranked the heat, defogger and windshield wiper as high as they would go. It didn't help much. She wanted to thank him for saving her, but her throat was too sore. The minute she started to speak, she broke into a coughing fit, which continued intermittently for the duration of the ride.

As Jordan drove, he peered through the fog for signs that would lead him to the hospital, but as the weather got worse, it occurred to him that he was driving right into the heart of the storm. He didn't mention it to Pattie, because he didn't want to add to her worries. By the time pulled up in front of the entrance to the emergency room, it was raining cats and dogs. He kept the engine running, turned the distress blinkers on and got out of the car. He ran around to the passenger's side, opened the door and tried to pick Pattie up in his arms to carry her inside. She fussed and fumed so much, he dropped his arms and gingerly held her around her waist. Even though he barely touched her, she flinched. Even the slightest amount of pressure on her body felt like torture to her. As a result, he backed off, gently took hold of her hand and walked with her as she took slow little half steps. And although the walk was a short one, it felt to Pattie as if it took forever. The cold wind whipped around her wobbly legs, causing her to shiver and cough once again. She felt lightheaded, dizzy and weak.

The emergency room was chock full of people. The overhead lights were so bright they washed out Pattie's pale skin tone, making her look almost like a ghost. Jordan's dark brown hair had curled into a wet unruly mess and because he had given his jacket to Pattie, his clothes were rain soaked. And at that point, he too was shivering.

The intake clerk looked up, glanced at the two of them and raised an eyebrow. She asked Pattie for her health insurance card and identification. She spoke in broken English and her indiscernible accent was so thick, anyone could have cut it with a knife. Pattie looked around, wide eyed and confused. Her enormous, unfocused pupils indicated she was in shock. She shook her head and stared blankly at the clerk. The moment she tried to speak, she broke into another coughing fit. She waved her hands frantically, while the clerk scowled and waited.

Jordan finally explained that although Pattie had both health insurance and a driver's license, she simply did not have her wallet with her.

The clerk shook her head. There was something odd about the couple in front of her. She didn't understand how someone could even leave their house without their wallet.

Jordan offered to guarantee payment of Pattie's bill, if it meant she wouldn't be turned away. The clerk nodded, asked Jordan for HIS license and health insurance card and photocopied them. Then she handed him a surety to sign. He read it, signed it and returned it to her. She witnessed it, made a photocopy of it and gave him the copy. He folded it and put it in his pocket, while the clerk entered Pattie's name and birthday into the hospital's computer system. Afterwards, the clerk pointed to a sea of hard, plastic, orange chairs that had been bolted to the floor in rows and told Pattie to take a seat and wait until her name was called.

Jordan walked her past the candy, soda and newspaper machines. Still trembling when they finally reached the seats, Pattie gingerly sat on the edge of one of them in order to prevent its rigid hardness from aggravating the pain in her tailbone. Jordan pulled his car keys out of his pants pocket and pointed to the exit. She nodded and gave him the thumbs up sign. He kissed her on the cheek and disappeared.

No sooner was he gone, when a hobo in damp layers of filthy, tattered, moth eaten rags lumbered up to Pattie. Although there were many empty seats, he heaved himself into the chair next to her and slouched. She noticed his shabby shoes were so caked with filth, she couldn't even tell what color they were. She was also conscious of several smells emanating from the man. His breath smelled like beer and the dried vomit that was stuck to his beard, but his body smelled so rank, she couldn't even identify what it was. In her mind, she summed it up as something unwholesome. She shuddered and wanted to turn away from him, but at the same time, she didn't want to appear rude.

Since it's a cold, rainy Thanksgiving, he probably just wants to get admitted, so he can eat a hot turkey dinner and a spend the night in a warm bed, she thought, just as she began another round of coughing.

After she stopped coughing, she still felt terrible. Her head throbbed, her throat burned, her eyes hurt, her skin hurt. Even her hair hurt. She took a deep breath and prayed she wouldn't start coughing again. Then it occurred to her. THIS was the worst she had ever felt in her life. She pressed the palms of her hands to her burning forehead and tried to reconstruct the series of weird events that had literally gotten her underwater in a dark deserted place and from there right to where she was sitting. But she couldn't remember anything. Nothing at all came to her. And it felt strange.

After what seemed like an interminable wait, a nurse's aide appeared with a wheel chair. She called

Pattie's name. When Pattie raised her hand, the nurse's aide rolled the wheelchair up to her seat, helped her into it and whisked her off to an examining room, where Pattie waited and coughed some more.

Meanwhile outside, Jordan circled around the parking lot until he finally found a space. He turned the engine off and decided to call Pattie's best friend, Ryan Pilgrim. He dialed information and requested they give him Ryan's telephone number in Manhattan. Information only had two numbers associated with the name Pilgrim. One was a residence for Arthur J. Pilgrim and the other was a business number for Pilgrim's Hardware Store. Both were listed at the same address in Chelsea. Jordan chose Arthur's number. Fortunately, Ryan picked up the call on the second ring. He told Jordan how worried he was about Pattie. When Jordan asked why, Ryan explained that Pattie had been expected there for Thanksgiving dessert and coffee, but she never made it. What worried him more was the fact he hadn't heard from her and had not been able to get in touch with her.

Jordan let Ryan know he had found Pattie near the Katonah Reservoir, injured and in a state of shock. Then he explained how he had driven her to Downstate Hospital and that they needed Pattie's health insurance card and Driver's License, but she didn't have her wallet with her. Ryan offered to call Pattie's parents. He said if they found Pattie's wallet he would retrieve it and bring it up to the hospital. Jordan accepted the offer. Ryan explained that either way, he'd be calling in a while from his brother Zachary's phone, because he had lost his own phone at some point during the day and still hadn't found it. Although Jordan thought that was a bit too much information, he nevertheless thanked Ryan.

Pattie's beefy, muscle bound, younger brother Lou was in a bad mood. He walked into his parents' circa 1958 style kitchen, in their large, antique Brownstone on West Twelfth Street. He had just returned from bringing a turkey dinner to Justin, one of Pattie's young clients. Justin had been admitted to Bellevue Hospital earlier that evening. Unable to shake off the memory of the fight he'd had with Pattie earlier in the day, Lou walked over to the refrigerator and opened the door. Just as he reached in to grab a bottle of beer, the old, red, dial telephone on the wall sprang to life. He turned and picked up the call. His hooded grey eyes were at half-mast and he scowled as he barked into the receiver.

Ryan sighed, identified himself and cut right to the chase. He immediately asked Lou whether he knew where Pattie's wallet was. Lou went into a tirade about not being his sister's keeper. And he added that he didn't understand why Pattie felt compelled to ask Ryan to call the house for her all the time, instead of simply letting her place "her own damn phone calls".

Ryan explained that Pattie was in the emergency room at Downstate Hospital.

"Hang on," Lou snapped.

He dropped the receiver and let it dangle on its long curly cord. Ryan heard it bang against the wall several times, while Lou returned to the refrigerator to get his long awaited beer. Lou twisted the cap off the bottle with a vengeance and flung it into the black plastic ashtray on his mother's cheap Formica kitchen table. Holding onto the neck of the bottle for dear life, he swilled down a gigantic gulp and walked into the dining room, where his parents, Chet and Edie were huddled miserably at the mahogany dining table.

Edie looked drunk, as she stared into the bottom of her jumbo sized margarita goblet. Chet simply looked exhausted. Without saying a word to either of them, Lou walked past them and made his way over to the sideboard. He carefully picked his way through the shards from the mirror he had smashed earlier that afternoon and zeroed in on Pattie's wallet. He gingerly picked it up and rifled through it to make sure her insurance card and driver's license were there. When he found them, he stuffed them back into the wallet and crammed the wallet into his back pocket. Chet watched his every move and sniffed when Lou headed back into the kitchen.

Lou picked up the receiver and asked Ryan "Where in Holy Hell", Downstate Hospital was. Ryan told him it was somewhere up in Westchester County. He promised to print out directions and suggested Lou pick him up so they could drive there together. Lou agreed, hung up and took another swig of his beer. Without saying another word, he and his bottle were on their way out the door. As soon as Chet heard the door slam, he sniffed again, looked into his wife's bloodshot eyes and shook his head.

"Just for once, I'd like to know what the hell is going on under my own roof," he said.

Edie nodded and lifted her goblet.

"I'll drink to that," she brayed, in her slurred voice.

And she did. Deeply.

CHAPTER TWO

SOUTHBOUND TRAIN

Thanks to the overhead heat lamps at the railway station in Katonah, Willie Hudson's clothes were almost dry by the time he boarded the Northbound train. He was grateful to be on the train and away from the foul stench of the aging human waste that had accumulated in the station. It had made him feel very queasy.

A few minutes after he took his seat, the conductor showed up. Willie asked him the best way to get to Moriah, New York. The conductor gave him such a long winded explanation of what he had to do, his head spun. He found it hard to process all the information, especially when it sounded exactly like double talk to him. He was annoyed that in order to travel north, he had to get off the train, go south to One Hundred Twenty Fifth Street in Manhattan and then take the Hudson line train back North to Yonkers, so he could then pick up the Amtrak line. None of it made any sense to him. It seemed as ridiculous as having had to climb the stairs at the Katonah Station only to descend another flight of stairs, just to get onto the platform. In addition, he really didn't relish being back in New York City, after having gone to such incredible lengths to escape from it in the first place.

He scowled, shuddered and scratched his head. When he was finally on the train bound for New York, he dug in his wallet and handed the conductor the five dollars he had pilfered from Leland LeRoux's corpse. The conductor took the money and waited a few more seconds for Willie to hand over the rest of the fare. Willie just stared at him. When the conductor realized that no further money would be forthcoming, he handed Willie a ticket, along with a bill for the balance of the fare and an envelope. He instructed Willie to use that envelope to mail in the balance, at his earliest convenience. Willie nodded absently.

CHAPTER THREE

HOSPITAL SONG

Pattie's face was pinched from trying so hard to focus on the nurse's name tag. "Kitty" helped her change from her ripped, soggy clothes into a hospital gown. Even though the gown was clean and dry and Pattie was warming up, she still continued to shiver and wheeze.

Kitty stuck a thermometer in Pattie's ear, delicately removed the smeared makeup from Pattie's face and scrutinized her. Most of the black, blue and green smears across her swollen jaw were bruises, rather than makeup. Kitty also noticed the nasty bite mark on Pattie's left shoulder, the splotches that covered Pattie's neck and chest and the scratches that ran the length of Pattie's thighs. Pattie also had a bump on her head, near her temple. Kitty touched it lightly with her index finger and Pattie flinched. When the thermometer beeped, Kitty removed it, frowned and shone a light in Pattie's throat. That triggered yet another coughing fit. Kitty waited for the outburst to stop, took Pattie's pulse and finished the examination.

Afterwards, Pattie lay back on her pillow and tried hard to breathe. There was a knock on the door. Kitty turned, saw it was Jordan and pushed him out. She closed the door and locked it. Jordan knocked again, but Kitty ignored him and turned back to Pattie.

When Pattie asked in her hoarse voice, why Kitty wouldn't let Jordan into the room, she ended up punctuating her question with a coughing fit, which made her feel as if ground glass was ripping her throat apart. Plus her ribs began to hurt from coughing so hard and so often. Kitty noted Pattie's temperature of one hundred four and waited for Pattie to stop coughing.

You're in bad shape, with a high fever, torn clothes, a black and blue mark on your face, a bump on your head and what looks like a human bite mark on one of your shoulders. On top of all that you've got scratch marks running down the length of your thighs. Did I miss anything? Anyway, I don't know about you, but when I see someone come in here in this condition, I begin to suspect they underwent a trauma. None of these things just happen all by themselves." Kitty said.

When Pattie didn't respond, Kitty opened Pattie's chart and wrote, "Possible Domestic Abuse." Then she took out a camera and photographed every one of Pattie's injuries.

"Anyway, by law I need to ask you whether anyone is hurting you."

When Pattie shook her head, Kitty tried to stare her down.

"Well what about HIM?" Kitty said, as she gestured with her head at the door.

Pattie frowned and shook her head again warily. Kitty looked at her with a jaundiced eye and shrugged.

"Anyway, please step down from the table and stand on the scale so I can weigh you," she said.

Pattie got on the scale.

"You're one hundred eight pounds."

Kitty recorded Pattie's weight in the chart, snapped the chart shut and helped Pattie back onto the table.

"Dr. Rogers will be in to see you as soon as he can," she said.

She left, taking the chart with her. She placed it on the shelf outside the door. As she walked down the hall, Jordan approached her, but before he could even utter a word, she put her hand up like a stop sign, breezed past him and made a beeline for the telephone at the nurse's station.

About five minutes later, The Patient Advocate tapped lightly on Pattie's door. Since Pattie had already fallen into a light doze, the knock woke her. She opened her eyes and rubbed them.

The Patient Advocate slowly opened the door. She stuck her head in and smiled sheepishly at Pattie.

"Hi, I'm Deb, the Patient Advocate."

Pattie frowned and groaned. She was disappointed it wasn't Jordan.

"Could you please do me a favor? Go out into the hall and ask my boyfriend Jordan to come in here and join me. Because—and don't think I'm not annoyed about this, but Kitty took it upon herself to kick him out against my wishes," Pattie croaked her request.

It was a real struggle for her to squeak out all those words. The pain stabbed her deep in her throat, but in spite of that she sounded almost manic.

Deb nodded in what she hoped Pattie would interpret as an empathetic manner. Yet at the same time, she managed to ignore everything Pattie said and barreled right up to the examining table.

"Well, after all, our only goal is to ensure your health and safety, by providing you with the best possible care. We know how awfully difficult it can be to break the silence sometimes."

Before Pattie could even respond, the doctor knocked and let himself into the room. Deb blocked his path and asked to speak to him out in the hall.

"What's going on?" The doctor whispered.

"Well, she's injured, not to mention soaking wet from head to toe. And she's chock full of scratches, bruises and bitemarks. Plus, she sounds hysterical. Anyway, Kitty is convinced her boyfriend abused her," Deb whispered.

The doctor shook his head.

"Scratches and bitemarks? Are you kidding me?" The doctor asked, incredulously.

Deb shook her head.

"Do we have any proof the boyfriend is even the one who did it?"

Deb shook her head again.

"Well, wait until I've examined her. Then afterwards, maybe you can go back in there and try to get her to confide in you," he whispered.

Deb nodded and left. The doctor knocked on the door again and walked in. The first thing he noticed was Pattie's remarkably white pallor.

"I'm Dr. Rogers," he said, mechanically.

Without even waiting for Pattie to answer him, he opened her chart, read Kitty's notations and broke into a frown. Then he closed the chart and washed his hands. He began the examination by looking at Pattie's eyes. After he observed how severely her pupils were dilated, he rechecked her temperature. While he waited, he wiped off his stethoscope with alcohol and applied it to Pattie's chest. It was so cold against her feverish skin, she nearly jumped off the table.

"Try to take as deep a breath as you can," he said.

She tried, but she broke into paroxysms of coughing. He staggered backwards, ripped the stethoscope out of his ears and waited for her to finish. Then he tried again to measure her heartbeat and assess the condition of her lungs. He walked behind her, listened to her lungs from the back and then returned to the front of the examining table. One by one he inspected her injuries. Even though he tried to be gentle, she winced at his every touch. He pulled the thermometer out of her ear and checked it. Pattie broke into yet another series of coughing spasms and shook her head vehemently.

"Tell me what happened."

Pattie shrugged.

"I don't remember. But can you PLEASE arrange to have my boyfriend Jordan join me as soon as possible? And for God's sake can you get me some cough medicine?" She croaked.

He nodded and patted her on her good shoulder.

"I don't know how to tell you this, but you have pneumonia, along with a whole host of other problems. So, I can't in good conscience release you in your current condition."

Pattie knit her brow.

"What are you saying? That you're going to admit me? Because I'd actually prefer that NOT happen. I'm REALLY not a very good patient," she said, in her hoarse voice.

Dr. Rogers smiled at what he sensed was comic understatement.

"Even though I have no trouble believing you, I'm still recommending we admit you. My immediate game plan is to clean out the wound on your shoulder, order an alcohol rubdown, as well as X rays of your chest, jaw, lower spine and skull. And since you can't remember anything, I'll also need some blood work to provide me with as much information as possible. That way I can come up with a viable treatment plan for you. And if you insist on your boyfriend being here, I won't stop him, but I should at least warn you that he might catch your pneumonia."

He opened a bottle of hydrogen peroxide to clean the bite mark on her shoulder. The minute it touched her open flesh, she screamed hoarsely and tears filled her eyes.

He apologized.

CHAPTER FOUR

PICTURE ME IN A HOSPITAL

As promised, Dr. Rogers admitted Jordan into the room. Pattie's eyes lit up at the sight of him. She smiled warmly, even though she was still wheezing and shivering. The bite on her shoulder still stung. Jordan pulled a chair up close to the bed, sat and gently took hold of her hand.

"I guess there's no easy way to bring myself to tell you this, but my father and his wife died in a terrible plane crash."

Pattie gasped and tried to clear her throat.

"Oh my God. I'm so sorry for your loss."

He squeezed her hand lightly.

"Thank you. I'll stay with you for as long as I can tonight, but tomorrow I'll have to leave for Scotland in order to sort things out."

Pattie squinted.

"Am I remembering this wrongly or was there also some wedding you were supposed to attend in Florida?" Pattie asked.

Jordan nodded.

"Yes. My friend Clint is getting married and I was looking forward to being there. I hope he'll forgive me, but I just won't be able to make it."

A phlebotomist knocked, came in and took Pattie's blood. Jordan held her hand through it and when the time came for her to go to radiology, he went with her. When her tests were complete, an orderly notified her that her admission papers had come through. He strapped her onto a gurney, wheeled her down the hall and onto the elevator. When they arrived at her new room, Jordan was still by her side. Shortly thereafter, Ryan and Lou rushed in. Ryan was wearing a lamb lined suede jacket. He kissed her on the cheek and she smiled.

"Gee, you look good," she said.

Lou stepped in between Pattie's bed and Ryan.

"What the hell is going on? What am I supposed to tell Mom and Dad when I get back home?" Lou asked.

She shook her head, put her hand up to halt him and tried to clear her aching throat.

"Look, Lou. Don't ask me any questions, OK? Because I have no memory and I have no voice. All I know is that I'm freezing, in a lot of pain and I feel filthy from head to toe. In short I'm a mess and that's all I'm going to say," she said.

Lou tensed up. She could tell he was annoyed, but

she didn't care. He pulled her wallet from out of his pocket.

"Here," he said, as he handed it to her.

She removed her driver's license and insurance card and gave them to Jordan. Jordan nodded and headed for the Admitting Office, just as a nurse with wire rimmed glasses and gray streaks in her hair came into the room. She was carrying two intravenous bags the doctor had ordered for Pattie. Her nametag read "Suzy." Suzy asked Ryan and Lou to step outside for a few minutes. She drew the curtain and proceeded to prepare Pattie for the drip. Not wanting to watch, Pattie rested her head on the pillow and shut her eyes. Suzy stuck the back of her hand with the IV needle and she winced.

"I'm sorry that stung just now," Suzy said.

Once everything was in place, Suzy pulled the curtain back, invited Lou and Ryan to return and left. Pattie looked at the bag, then at Lou and Ryan. Then she leaned back on her pillow.

"I know you can't talk, but there is something I have to tell you. Do you have a client named Justin Edwards?"

Pattie looked at him and nodded.

"Well, I want you to know I rescued him earlier this afternoon."

Upon hearing Justin's name, Pattie smiled. Her eyes filled with tears of relief.

"Oh my God, that's wonderful. I can't wait to hear

the details. Because every day for the past six months, I prayed for that kid," Pattie said, in her hoarse voice.

Lou filled her in on the details and said he was safely recuperating in Bellevue Hospital.

"Wow. When I get out of here I'd love to go see him and of course my other former juvenile clients, Bonnie and Thomas."

"They're all up in that place. I forgot the name."

"Beau Rivage?" Pattie squeaked the words.

"Yes. They're all up there and they're all doing fine," Lou said.

She closed her eyes and let the drip do its work. When Jordan returned, she reopened her eyes and squinted. He gave her the thumbs up sign and handed her license and insurance card to her.

"Everything's all taken care of," he said.

She pointed at her nightstand.

"Thank you. Can you put my wallet in that drawer there?"

Jordan nodded.

"Lou, when you were looking for my wallet, did you happen to come across my phone, moon pendant, ring or watch?" She asked, just as Jordan closed the drawer to the nightstand.

Lou looked down at the tops of his Brogans and shook his head.

"No, but I'll replace your phone for you as soon as you get out of here."

"Why would you want to do that?" She asked.

But before he could answer her, she went into another coughing fit and punctuated it by clearing her aching throat. Suzy popped her head in the doorway. She was holding a sea sponge, a plastic tray, a bottle of rubbing alcohol and a plastic cup with a teaspoon of Promethazine mixed with codeine to suppress Pattie's cough.

"It's time to get your fever down and clean you up. I promise to stay away from your shoulder. Anyhow, gentlemen, visiting hours are over," she said.

Jordan was the first to respond. He nodded, gave Pattie a quick peck on the cheek and said good bye. Lou did the same and Ryan squeezed her arm lightly. As soon as they left, Suzy handed Pattie the cough suppressant, which she drank. Then Suzy got to work on Pattie's alcohol rub. She finished up by adding an ingredient to the piggy back in Pattie's IV to make Pattie sleep. Pattie closed her eyes. A few seconds later, she felt woozy. Eventually she felt as if she were floating somewhere between the floor and the ceiling. She nodded off and obtained refuge in twelve hours of dreamless sleep.

CHAPTER FIVE

BLACK FRIDAY

While many Americans enjoyed "Black Friday," as a Shopping Day, April Higgins and her husband Kyle didn't exactly have that luxury and neither did their staff. Running Beau Rivage, a halfway house for neglected and delinquent adolescents, actually meant they never got a day off. Even though it was still early on that grey, red, Black Friday, April was in a bad mood. Thomas Amissah, one of her teenage residents, had woken up in the middle of the night to sneak into the kitchen and polish off all the leftover pumpkin pie. He just got finished vomiting and now April was looking for their Janitor, Willie Hudson to come and clean up the mess. When no one could locate him, April decided to look for him herself. After all, that seemed like a better alternative than dealing with the vomit. She stormed downstairs to the basement of the huge Brownstone on Riverside Drive. She ran down the hall that led to Willie's quarters and banged frantically on his door. She waited a few seconds, but when Willie didn't answer, she used her passkey. She unlocked the door, opened it gingerly and peered into the room. When she realized he wasn't there, she began to worry. She carefully tiptoed into the room, turned on the shade-less forty watt floor lamp and nosed around.

The room was chilly, but somehow clean and orderly. In fact, calling it Willie's "quarters" was a bit pretentious, since it was actually only a windowless walk-in supply closet with a makeshift cot, a dresser that someone had painted a fake maple wood brown color more than a decade ago and a clothes rack. April ran her hand across the top of the dresser and rubbed her finger in the scar from an old cigarette burn. Willie had stood an oversized flash light at the foot of the cot. An old sink was mounted against the opposite wall. Underneath it was a bucket that housed a dry, sour smelling mop and some cleaning supplies. A buffer, a sander, a plunger and a space heater lined the wall next to it. At the far end was a toilet and a narrow shower. The few janitor's uniforms and some non janitorial clothes Willie had were still hanging on the rack. April fingered them as she walked past them and breathed a sigh of relief. If his clothes were still there, it meant he must still be around. However, her relief turned to annoyance, because it still looked as if she wouldn't find him in time to clean up the mess. She sighed, reached for the bucket and mop and carried them upstairs.

CHAPTER SIX

AGAINST THE WIND

Having successfully dodged the green slime on the platform at the Amtrak Station in Yonkers, Willie stood and shivered in the frosty air. He looked at the potted plants and artwork that was being displayed to revitalize and regentrify what had formerly been known as "The City of Gracious Living." He wondered why it had descended into hell in the first place and why efforts were even being made to resurrect it. Like with so many other things that day, he just didn't see the point. As soon as the Amtrak "Windstar" slowed down, he threw the envelope and the bill for his unpaid train fare onto the track and chuckled as the train ran over it. He waited for everyone else to board, then he slithered in behind them. Every car was already crowded. Willie noticed an old man dozing. Suddenly the old man woke up, blinked and looked around. He practically jumped off the seat and ran out, just as the doors were about to close. Willie elbowed his way over to the newly vacated spot, plopped down and immediately regretted it.

After having waited most of the night to finally dry off after his dive into the Katonah Reservoir, he was enraged to find himself sitting in a puddle. He let out a groan, slid forward and sat on the edge of the seat. The elderly woman next to him shifted and opened her eyes.

When the conductor came to collect Willie's ticket, Willie preempted him, with an earful about the deplorable conditions on the train, all the while pointing at his pants and gesticulating, as if he were speaking American Sign Language. The conductor waited for Willie to stop yelling. Then he merely shrugged and repeated his request for Willie's ticket. Finally, the elderly lady next to Willie handed the conductor her ticket. He took it, walked to the front of the car and called the police on Willie. The elderly lady smiled at Willie dreamily and went back to sleep. Willie sat there, fuming in his clammy, cold pants as he waited for her breathing to indicate she was asleep. He looked around furtively to see if anyone was watching him. When he was confident no one was, he slowly opened her purse, slid his fingers down and lifted her wallet out. Then he hurriedly stashed it in his pocket, stood and walked to the car behind him. He mingled in the aisle with several people who were standing there, because there weren't enough seats in that car. When the train pulled into its next stop at Croton Harmon, he checked to make sure the coast was clear. When it was, he ducked into the bathroom, pulled the wallet out of his pocket and took out the cash, which amounted to three hundred sixteen dollars.

He stashed the money in his pocket, threw the old lady's wallet down the trash chute and slipped out of the bathroom, just as a group of people boarded the train. He decided to use them as a shield in order to avoid having the conductor spot him. He muscled his way through the crowd, walked to the car behind him and ran headlong into another conductor. When the conductor asked Willie for his ticket, Willie shook his head. The conductor asked Willie where he was going. When Willie told him Port Henry, the conductor charged him seventy nine dollars and informed him the fee included a surcharge for buying his ticket while aboard the train, instead of at the ticket window.

Willie whistled at the expense, deftly peeled out four twenty dollar bills and waited impatiently for his dollar change. Unable to get a seat, he remained standing until the train reached the next station at Poughkeepsie. He noticed the farther upstate he got, the fatter and more pasty faced the people looked. Their hair was thinner and stringier and from the oldest men right on down to the daintiest three year old girl, they all seemed to be wearing plaid jackets, jeans, baseball caps and sneakers. Bound and determined not to endure the indignity of being on his feet all the way to Port Henry, he stood in the center of the car and waited for the first person to get up. He prodded and jostled everyone standing between him and the seat and when he got there, he plunked himself down. He remained there until two o'clock that afternoon. When the train pulled into the station at Port Henry, he stepped out onto the platform and looked up at the dreary, low hanging charcoal colored sky. The air was wet and he suspected it might rain or snow any minute. He walked off the platform and scanned the Adirondacks that formed a panorama around him from every direction. He breathed in the clean, fresh, mountain air and began to make his way up the dirt path that led to the main road. He walked past the Senior Center where his mother in law, Zirca, happened to be at a Weight Watcher's meeting. When she spotted him through the window, she made a double take.

Why that Dirty Son of a bitch, she thought to herself.

Nah. It just can't be, she said, shaking the idea out of her head.

When he reached the main road, he lifted his thumb to hitch a ride. An old looking red Tahoe pickup truck came to a stop and the driver invited him to climb aboard. They rode for a few miles past the many streams and foot paths that dotted the mountain roads.

"Oh man I remember them streams," Willie said.

The driver chuckled.

"People joke about them until it rains or snows. Then they realize how them little streams can turn this area into one great, big flood zone."

Willie nodded and grinned.

"I know, but it snows damn near every day, don't it?" He said, wondering why everyone didn't just leave, the way he did.

Eventually, they reached a brick building in a relatively flat part of town and Willie announced it was his "getting off point." The building had been constructed as a school in 1920 and it sat in right in the middle of what had originally been developed as a trading post in 1793. Willie's parents had even gone to school there. But, because of the "Baby Boom" in the 1950's, the town built a new set of schools. They painted the bricks on the original school building red and they painted the trim white. Then they converted it into a mixed commercial and residential building. In fact, the smallest of the storefronts on the first floor actually served as the town's one room Post office. And Willie and his wife had lived in one of the apartments on the second floor. That is, until the day Willie left.

Willie smiled, thanked the driver and hopped off the truck. The driver smiled back, waved his hand affably and drove away. Willie looked around. Country music was blasting from someone's window, but he couldn't place whose. In spite of his history with this building, the truth was, he hadn't actually given it a second thought in the past seven years. On the day he left town, he swore he would never return. And yet, here he was. Life could be weird sometimes. He walked up to the door that led to the apartments upstairs. Surprised to find it unlocked, he opened it, stepped inside and looked for the name "Hudson" on the roster. He couldn't believe his luck. There it was! Phoebe must still be living in Apartment Five.

He pulled out his wallet, took a deep breath and removed the diamond earring from his ear. Leaving only twenty six dollars in his wallet, he stuffed the diamond and the remaining cash in the toe of his sock. Then he grinned from ear to ear as he climbed the stairs and strode down the hallway.

CHAPTER SEVEN

THE PRODIGAL HUSBAND

Phoebe Hudson was standing behind her nine year old son, Shane. He was pointing at the screen on their secondhand laptop, in order to show her the electronic game he was hoping to get for Christmas. He was hoping to explain how it worked before their connection cut out. In the mountains, the Internet was spotty, at best. Willie sauntered through the door and let it slam behind him. Phoebe and Shane jumped and looked up. Shane squinted and scratched his head, while Phoebe tried to suppress a gasp. Of course she recognized him right away. Her eyebrows shot up, her mouth hung open and her mascara fringed blue eyes popped. The stabbing twinges in Phoebe's solar plexus warned her of an impending disaster, but she couldn't pinpoint exactly what it would be. She fought off a feeling of having just been sucker punched.

Willie looked Phoebe over from head to toe. His expression disarmed her, but in spite of that she met his gaze. When he was done sizing her up, he shifted his focus to Shane. He grinned as he gave himself a mental pat on the back for producing a son who looked so much like him. Then his cold blue eyes boldly scanned everything in the living room, as if he were still King of the Castle. His first and most important observation was that there were no signs of another man on the premises. And that fact strengthened his bravado. He figured, as Phoebe's husband, so long as he never got violent, she'd have a hard time convincing the authorities to throw him out. For the most part, the furniture was cheap but orderly and the curtains and matching slipcovers were homemade, but decent. The two most expensive items in the room were the aquarium and the beautiful Himalayan cat who walked into the center of the room, sat and blinked at him.

In spite of the stubble on his face, his disheveled condition and the fact he was seven years older than when he disappeared on Phoebe and Shane, he was still tall, good looking and in great shape. But that's as far as it would go. She'd be damned rather than ever pay him that or any other compliment. The scars caused by his sudden abandonment, which she mistakenly thought were healed over, were now once again ripped wide open, like fresh, new wounds that cut her right down to the bone.

She told Shane to go outside and play. She said it without taking her eyes off of Willie. Shane looked up at her and she nodded in confirmation, but still kept her gaze fixed on Willie. Shane gave the stranger a final once over and reluctantly left, taking his sweet time. When he was finally out the door, Phoebe put her hands on her hips and shook her head.

"Willie, I have to say, I think we'd all be better off if you would just turn around and go right back to whatever rock you crawled out from under," she said, in a voice dripping with venom.

He shook his head.

"Well, maybe YOU'D be better off. On the other hand, maybe you wouldn't be, though. Anyway, who cares? Because the one thing I know for sure is I sure as hell wouldn't be," he said, as he walked past her. His eyes darted back and forth between the cat and the aquarium, as if he were watching a tennis match.

"I have to say, after all the great places I've been, the grinding poverty that runs rampant in this one horse town never ceases to amaze me. I actually think people are better off in Appalachia," he said.

She squared her shoulders, made herself as tall as she could and thought his gray Janitor's uniform with the strange stain around the crotch revealed every-thing she needed to know about what he'd "seen". She almost wanted to laugh at the name "Willie" stitched over his left front shirt pocket, but she didn't. Her heart sunk when he walked over to the couch and sat.

He reached into his pocket, pulled out his wallet and made a point of emptying it in front of her. He unceremoniously slapped the twenty six dollars and

Pattie's unwrapped ring and moon pendant onto the coffee table. She rolled her eyes.

"How classy. Not even a box," she answered.

"Don't be so ungrateful," he snapped.

She walked over to the coffee table, scooped up the items and inspected them.

"Give me one good reason not to be. You left me without any warning seven years ago and you return with this stuff? Anyway, it's witchy looking. By the way, does the no good broad you stole it from, even know it's missing yet? Wait a minute. I've got an even better question. Does she even know YOU'RE missing yet?"

He sighed. It was all coming back to him. The reason he left. It wasn't because Phoebe didn't understand him. It was actually because she DID understand him and all too well. But being reminded that Pattie Anwald was dead put a smile on his face. He didn't answer Phoebe. Instead, he picked up the remote control, turned on the television and channel surfed.

Phoebe turned on her heel, headed for her bedroom and locked herself in. She walked straight over to her closet, opened it and knelt. She reached on the floor for the back right hand corner of her closet until she felt the metal strong box she kept hidden there, behind a stack of shoe boxes. She picked it up, opened it and pulled out the leather pouch that was next to her Christmas Club Savings Passbook. She placed the jewelry inside the pouch, next to the cheap wedding band Willie had given to her. Then she picked up her copy of the divorce decree she had obtained against him six years ago. She ran her fingers over the seal and then checked the balance on her Christmas Club. It was ready to mature and just in time for her to get Shane that game he wanted. She slid the strong box back into place and stashed the passbook, the pouch, the decree and the twenty six dollars in her handbag. Then she put it on the floor of her closet and pushed it into place, next to the strong box.

CHAPTER EIGHT

THE FROST IS ON THE PUMPKIN

Because the temperature had plummeted over-night and the "frost was on the pumpkin", Phoebe put on her warmest coat, a second hand goose down car coat she had picked up at a local thrift shop. She pulled her hand bag out from the bottom of her closet and tiptoed toward the front door, with Shane right behind her. Just as she tried to walk past the couch where Willie had spent the night, she turned to Shane and put her index finger over her mouth. She needn't have bothered, since Willie was watching their every move. He may have been lying down, but he was hardly asleep. His eyes may have appeared closed, but they were open just wide enough to see everything that was going on. He stirred, pretended to wake up and opened one eye completely. Then he pulled the light summer weight thermal blanket close to him, tucked it around himself and demanded to know where they were going. He did all that while continuing to lie there. When she said she was bringing her mother to the doctor, he managed to prop himself up on one elbow. He scowled, shook his head and refused to believe doctors actually saw patients on Saturdays.

"Well, they do when it's Urgent Care."

Willie pointed at Shane.

"Well, does HE need Urgent Care too?"

Phoebe shook her head.

"No. Actually, he's going out to a pancake breakfast that was planned weeks ago."

Shane flashed a happy grin, but when he caught the tightness around Phoebe's mouth, he didn't say anything. He was smart enough to sense that something was wrong, but he wasn't sure what it was.

"Well, it really riles my ass that HE gets invited out for a Happy Meal or whatever the hell and meanwhile I gave you jewelry, not to mention my last twenty six dollars and here I sit, being left alone to freeze to death or starve to death. Whichever comes first. Because THIS piece of crap is the only thing you could spare to cover me with. You know, I froze my ass off all night and I still haven't thawed out," he said, as he shook the thermal blanket.

"So, while you're out, make sure you pick up SOMETHING for me to eat, for God's sake, along with at least one six pack of beer," he added.

Making every effort not to lose her cool, Phoebe kept her mouth shut and nodded. Once she and Shane were out the door, they hurried over to her rusty, mint green colored, '91 Ford Falcon and locked themselves in. Just as she always did, she prayed it would start. Then she snaked her way up the mountain via the dangerous curves and sharp turns on Windy Hill Road. When she finally reached Shane's best friend's house at the top of the mountain, she and Shane got out of the car and knocked on the door. When Shane's best friend's mother answered, she looked surprised to see Phoebe and Shane standing there. Phoebe took the liberty of telling Shane to go inside. Then she bit her lip, fished in her wallet and pulled out the twenty six dollars Willie had given to her. Then she asked her friend to treat the boys to a pancake breakfast. The other woman pushed the money away.

"Sure, but you don't have to pay me to do it," she said.

Phoebe shook her head and thrust the money back at her. The woman shrugged and stuffed the money into her pants pocket. Times were tough and she didn't need to be asked twice. Phoebe thanked her, got back into her car and carefully made her way to the other side of the mountain, so she could visit her mother.

CHAPTER NINE

FRONTIER TOWN

The furrow in Zirca Kowalczyk's brow grew increasingly deeper as she sat at her kitchen table, drinking her coffee and listening to her daughter Phoebe's tale of woe. Many years ago, Zirca was able to take a thin body and a pretty face for granted the way Phoebe did, but a life of premature widowhood, grueling work and pinching pennies had taken its toll on her face. And a diet consisting mainly of cheap carbohydrates had taken its toll on her body. She tried not to fret, as she waited for Phoebe to finish speaking.

"Well, I warned you not to lie to Shane about his father being dead, because as I always told you, lies have short legs. And if I recall correctly, I ALSO told you years ago to keep your door locked. But you know how you are. You never listen to me."

Tears welled up in Phoebe's eyes.

"Well, I'm listening now. What should I do?" Phoebe blurted out.

"Pick up Shane later and both of you just stay over here."

Phoebe shook her head.

"I can bring Shane over, but I won't be able to stay. It would give Willie the run of the place. I'm afraid he'll start snooping around, if he's not doing it already. I shudder at the thought of having left him alone at all. I also want to cash in my Christmas Club. Then I'm going over to the empty lot where Frontier Town used to be. I want to see what I can get for some jewelry Willie gave me."

Zirca looked surprised.

"Willie gave you something?"

Phoebe nodded.

"Yeah, but it's too witchy looking for my taste. Anyway the guy who trades over there is kind of sleazy, so I don't want to go alone. Can you come with me?"

CHAPTER TEN

FANCY FEAST

Hours later, just as sunset cast a dismal yellow pall over Moriah, Phoebe parked her car, braced herself for the icy gale that lashed her face, as well as for whatever storm Willie had planned for her inside the apartment. She walked back to her trunk, unlocked it and took out two bags of groceries. When she let herself in, she found Willie sprawled across the couch. He was too busy watching television to get up and help her, but he somehow managed to take the time to press the mute button and sit up. He was wearing a pair of Phoebe's flannel pajamas and heavy white cotton socks. Since he was tall and muscular and she was small boned and petite, he looked ridiculous. His janitor's uniform and socks were in a dirty heap on the floor next to him. He shot her a nasty look.

"Where's my kid?"

When Phoebe said Shane was with her mother, Willie sneered.

"Well, what if she makes him sick?"

She sneered back at him, shook her head and lied. She told him Zirca had Sciatica.

He pointed at himself.

"I was so cold I had to borrow this stuff. I feel frostbitten, if you must know."

She sighed.

But it didn't stop you from turning MY living room into your own little command center. Did it? Phoebe thought, but she said nothing. She merely turned around and started to carry the groceries into the kitchen.

"I'll just BET you forgot the beer," he called out.

"It's still out in the trunk," she said, a little peevishly.

"Well, go get it! That should have been the FIRST thing you brought in!"

She sighed, hurried back out to the car and returned with the six pack. She separated one of the cans from its plastic holder, popped the top open and placed it on the coaster, on the coffee table in front of the couch.

"Chill them other cans and while you're in there, rustle up some grub for God's sake. I'm starving," he said.

He pointed at the cat.

"Oh yeah. I meant to ask you. What's this thing's name?"

"Yoda," she said.

He called "Yoda", in a gentle voice, elongating the

vowels. Then he made cat whisperer noises. Yoda responded by approaching him, but she stayed out of his reach. He continued making the cat whisperer noises, gently crooning Yoda's name until Yoda finally relented and got close to him. When she rubbed her cheek against his leg, he reached out to pet her and she licked his hand. Then he grabbed her by the scruff of the neck in such a way she could neither scratch him nor escape from his grasp. She squirmed, meowed in indignation and writhed while Phoebe watched in panic mode. Her hand flew over her mouth and she held her breath. Still holding the cat, Willie shot Phoebe a malevolent look. Then he stood, walked over to the aquarium and nodded his head at the heavy, two inch thick, plate of glass that covered it.

"Either you slide that there glass off of this fish tank right now or I'll just drop kick this mutt out the window," he commanded, in a menacing voice.

Like a zombie, Phoebe slowly walked over to the aquarium. She carefully lifted the glass and cautiously laid it flat on the floor.

"OK Kitty Cat, tonight's your night," Willie said, as he dangled Yoda over the aquarium.

At first, being forced to hover over the water made Yoda frantic. She wriggled until she noticed the fish swimming right below the surface. Watching them seemed to calm her down. Her eyes grew big, her tail twitched and finally, when Shane's most prized fish, his Red Star Fire Tiger Barb, dipped and swayed past her, she darted at it. With her teeth just barely grazing the top of the water, she seized the fish by its illustrious tail. From there she sucked it into her mouth and gulped it down in one fell swoop. Phoebe looked on in horror, while Willie laughed and laughed.

"That was Shane's favorite fish!" She cried out.

"Well, on the money YOU make, he should be adopting mongrels from the pound instead of buying all these exotic animals."

"And since when do you set the priorities around here?"

Just as another fish swam past, Yoda darted for it. Willie chuckled and tossed Yoda onto to the floor like a sack of potatoes.

"You know, now that you made Yoda aware of those fish, it could be the beginnings of a catastrophe," she continued.

He chuckled and glared at her all at the same time. Then he lifted the pane of glass and slid it back into place.

"Now you listen up, while I take the time to answer your question. From now on, I and I alone set the priorities around here. And that policy went into effect about two minutes ago when I showed you just one of the many things I'm capable of."

Phoebe could hardly believe her ears.

He placed his hands on his hips and nodded.

"That's right. Every time I tell you to do something

and you fail to get right on it without delay or you tell me to shut up or wait or you roll them damn eyes of yours or you even somehow manage to piss me off in any way, Shane loses another fish. And once all them fish are gone, guess what? Shane loses that alley cat," Willie went on.

"Stop calling her names! She's not a mutt or an alley cat!"

"Well she's gonna end up like one if you don't learn how to shut your trap and do as I say," he said.

He walked back to the couch and flung himself onto it.

"So stop dilly dallying and rattle them pots and pans," he added.

He pointed to the heap of clothes on the floor.

"And after you get my dinner started, I'll need you to wash this here uniform and socks. Then hang them out to dry, so I'll have something else to walk around in besides this silly shit," he said, pointing at himself.

"Now beat it," he added.

He made waving motions to shoo her out of the room. Then he restored the sound on the TV. Phoebe shook her head and started to take the remaining five cans of beer into the kitchen.

God, what a day, she said to herself.

Just as the sound came on, a news bulletin broke about a young female attorney who was missing in New York City. One of the attorney's Legal Aid clients by the name of Leland LeRoux and a friend of

Mr. LeRoux's, by the name of William Hudson were missing as well. All three were last seen engaged in an altercation in front of a black vehicle on Christie Street in lower Manhattan. The vehicle was registered to the attorney and it too was missing.

Phoebe turned around and strained to hear as much of the story as possible, just as Leland's and Willie's latest mug shots flashed across the television. Then they zoomed in on Pattie's picture. Phoebe was frozen in shock when she noticed the attorney was wearing the same moon pendant and ring she had just hocked in Elizabethtown. Phoebe may have been an uneducated, small town girl, but at the same time she was no slouch. The butterflies in her stomach convinced her that something really bad had happened and that Willie either caused it or at the very least, was part of it. Just then it dawned on her. He was using her home as a hideout. The screen changed to a live reporter who was standing in front of Leland LeRoux's doorway on Christie Street.

"This is David Huntley, reporting live from Lower Manhattan."

The wheels in Willie's head were spinning too. He glanced at Phoebe to catch her reaction, but because she was pressed up tightly against the wall, he couldn't see her. He mistakenly assumed she was already in the kitchen and he breathed a sigh of relief.

If Phoebe gets wind of this and runs her big mouth to that busy body mother of hers, Mommie Dearest will end up ratting me out to the authorities. Looks like I'm gonna have to do something before the shit hits the fan. But what though? He thought.

Over in North Hudson, the man who had bought Phoebe's jewelry also happened to see the newscast. He didn't want to get involved, but he realized he had to contact the police. He sighed and picked up the phone.

CHAPTER ELEVEN

SNAPPED

Meanwhile, downstate, in a mobile home park on the banks of the beautiful Hudson River in Verplanck, most of the double wide trailer homes were neat and well kept and they demonstrated a pride of ownership. Many were tastefully decorated with "mums" and other fall flowers as well as pumpkins and other autumn decor. Some were very pretty. One even had stained glass windows. A few even had some early Christmas decorations in place. However, there were a few that were simply "run down." One ramshackle trailer was in such bad shape, it looked as if it hadn't been cared about or even thought about in years. A beat out old truck was in the driveway. And off to the side, the rusty remains of a boat had been standing on blocks for several years. Its owners could not have cared less about it nor about their million dollar view of the Palisades across the river. They were too busy fighting.

The wife, a fearsome behemoth, stood inside the middle of the living room and towered over her scrawny husband, Ned. In her buffalo stance, with her hands on her hips, she towered over him and scowled in disgust, as he stood holding a can of Budweiser and cowering before her in his stained undershirt, torn dungarees and worn out, construction boots. As she bobbed her head, her short little ringlets of dirty blonde and grey hair shook. He attempted a weak smile in the hopes of shutting her up and putting an end to all her questions. When it didn't work, he felt despondent. So he relied on his last resort, a little liquid courage. He emptied the can down his throat and waited for the miracle. Apparently that final guzzle not only contained all the nerve it took to spout off at her, but also the wisdom to know exactly what to say. He held the empty can two inches away from her face, crushed it and threw it on the floor. Then he looked up at her, burped and answered her question.

"Well, since yer forcin' me to speak my mind, I'll just come out with it. There's nothin' perdyer than a eighteen year ole piece o' ass. An' what's also great about my charming little Honey Bunny is that she ain't obese like you!"

When she broke into tears, he knew he'd hit the jackpot. He beamed and guffawed.

"How could you even say something that cruel to me, you no good piece of shit? Let me tell you something Ned Hollander. Don't you dare go around callin' me no beast! Because I ain't no beast! You gotta stop tormentin' me like this. Besides, I don't wanna hear nothing more outta you at this point! And your Honey Bunny must be a DUMB bunny if she's eighteen years old and she's still ridin' the school bus, for God's sake," she bellowed in indignation.

Ned grinned and nodded.

"So what if she's dumb? Anyways, now that it's out in the open and everything, I might as well fill you in on ALL the details. She's my reward at the end of a long hard day. When I finally get to drop off that second to the last student, SHE becomes my last drop off. That's right. It's just me and her all alone on that little yella school bus."

She put her hands up to her ears and shook her head vehemently. As she did, her dirty ringlets jiggled. He ripped her hands away from her ears, chortled and just kept on talking.

"Then I drive her over to our special hidin' place, where I turn off the bus. We mosey on down to the back seat, which spans the entire width of the bus. It still ain't as wide as your ass, though. Anyways, that's when the fun begins. Then later of course it all turns sour. You know. When I'm forced to come home and face you. Me and her joke about it. We call it the witching hour."

She stood there glaring at him, with her hands still on her hips. She watched in wonderment as he staggered over to the refrigerator, struggled to open it and finally succeeded. He reached in for a new can of beer, popped it open and threw his head back. He took what seemed to her like an endless chug a lug. He shook his head, held the back of his wrist up to his mouth and wiped it clean. He smiled and admired his precious beer can for a few seconds, then he suddenly pushed past her and staggered back into the living room. Shaking with indignation, she decided she'd had enough. She followed him, pushed him back and waddled past him on her flat feet. He pointed at them.

"Them's Flintstone feet," he said, laughing at his own wit.

And just as she got past him, he kicked her in her backside with as much force as he could muster and laughed for so long he actually gurgled. The metal toe guards on his construction boots hurt. She let out a moan, stopped dead in her tracks and rubbed the spot where she received the blow. That's when she snapped. It was no longer herself she wished to destroy.

"Why you, son of a bitch," she muttered under her breath.

As if on automatic pilot, she trekked into the bedroom. headed for his closet and rummaged around in it. When she found the prize shot gun he kept in the back, "just in case of an intruder", she grabbed it and wrenched it out of its place. Holding onto it for dear life with her left hand, she used her right hand to forage around in Ned's dresser drawers, hoping to discover where he kept his buckshot. By the time she realized she was never going to find it, she was in a rage. She stormed back out to the living area to find Ned already lying on the couch dozing. As she approached him, she accidentally knocked over the newly opened beer can that he had placed on the floor next to him. She ignored the spill and pressed the gun against his temple. His eyes sprung open, but they twinkled with mirth, because he knew the shotgun wasn't loaded. He had run out of buckshot and never bothered to replace it. Her expression turned terrible as she spun the firearm around in her hands. She raised it as high over her head as she could stretch. The loose flab on what he teasingly referred to as her "bat wings" swayed back and forth wildly.

"Don't!"

She punctuated the word by cracking the full weight of the handle onto the bridge of his nose with all her might. Blood shot out. His arms flailed as he tried to sit up and grab the gun away from her, but the combination of her size, her position over him and the fact she was in a state of frenzy was the "Trifecta" that gave her the strength to finally do what she had been wishing she could do for the last forty four years; win a fight with Ned. There was a look of terror in his eyes.

"YOU," she grunted out the word at the exact second when she smashed the gun down on his face for the second time.

That blow sent him back down into his original prone position. Kicking with both legs and flailing with both arms, he once again tried to hoist himself up.

"HURT," she muttered, as she bludgeoned him again.

This time he didn't have the strength to even try to sit up. The fear evaporated from his face. His arms dropped to his sides and there was a rattle in his throat. But that didn't stop her.

"ME!" Another strike, but this time there was no reaction from him.

"NO," she said quietly and without passion, as she dealt him the final blow.

"MORE," she said, exhaling a sigh, along with the word.

Then she dropped the gun onto the floor. Drenched in sweat, she stood over him, looked down at the mess that was once Ned's face and seriously wondered whether she was even the one who had actually done such a thing. In spite of her dull shock and bewilderment, she pulled herself together, lumbered over to the telephone and dialed 911.

"Emergency. How can I assist you?"

"Hello?"

"Yes, hello. How can I help you?"

"Well, the good news is that the pain is now gone. The bad news is that I'm not sorry, because I just couldn't take it no more."

"Do you need an ambulance?"

"No. I just need cops and a funeral director."

"What is the nature of your emergency?"

"What are you talking about? There ain't no more emergency. It's all over with now," she said.

She hung up, walked over to the front door and unlocked it. Then she opened it, leaving it slightly ajar, while she ambled back to the couch and squeezed herself onto it.

About thirty minutes later, a pair of plain clothed investigators from the New York State Police's Bureau of Criminal Investigation arrived on the scene in a sleek, new, black, unmarked Crown Victoria. The older investigator was stout, middle aged and dressed in an old blue suit. His partner was young, handsome and dressed in a newer and better blue suit. He also wore a snazzier tie. The older investigator turned off the ignition. As they both stepped out of the car, the older investigator took a look at the late rising moon over the trailer park and the younger man waved his right arm in a circle.

"I thought they were gonna do away with all this shit and I wish to God they would. After all, why should these stupid potato like people get to feast their eyes on a gazillion dollar vista like this?"

The older man frowned.

"Like what?"

The younger man pointed.

"Like them nice Palisades over there."

"The view's not so dramatic anymore. A lot of the leaves have fallen."

"I know, but look at all them red, orange and yellow leaves. They're still there. And the cliffs and the beautiful fir trees aren't going anywhere. Not to mention the view of the river. The fact is, it's wasted on these people. Somehow the mere idea of it galls me," the younger one said.

"What idea? That beggars can't be viewers? Come on. Poor folks deserve views too. I mean, just look at that orange moon. That's God's work. No one should get to charge for that," the older one said.

A grimy looking police cruiser, containing two uniformed State Troopers, quietly pulled in behind them. Unlike the investigators, the troopers left their cruiser on idle when they got out to join the investigators. They all walked up the dirt path that led to the trailer. The older investigator cocked his sidearm and the other three followed suit. Then he knocked. When he realized the door was open, they all walked in.

They found her on the couch, sobbing quietly and cuddling up to Ned. Both she and Ned were covered in blood. The older investigator tapped her on her shoulder. When she turned around to look up at him, he introduced himself as Investigator Townley. He and his partner, Investigator Nottingham, helped heave her onto her feet. Investigator Townley recited her Miranda rights and hand cuffed her. When he nodded at Troopers Dettweiler and Twomey, they sprang into action. They flanked her, grabbed hold of her and frog marched her out to their cruiser. Just as they peeled away, a storm broke out and raindrops beat down on the windshield.

- 59 -

CHAPTER TWELVE

PLEASE LOCK ME AWAY

Trooper Dettweiler locked his very large prisoner in a bleak, chilly, holding cell that smelled like stale vomit. Then he and Trooper Twomey went in search of Trooper Conklin, a female trooper who could strip search her. When they couldn't find Trooper Conklin, they returned to the cell with an evidence bag. Trooper Dettweiler politely asked the prisoner to remove her size 3X blood stained clothes, so he could take an inventory of them. When she told him to go fuck himself, he lost his temper. As far as he was concerned, he was already annoyed as a result of having been called in to work every day over the four day Thanksgiving weekend. So, he was in no mood to be on the receiving end of any verbal abuse from some husband killer. He put on a pair of rubber gloves, grabbed hold of her blood stained clothes and wrangled her out of them. Then he gingerly stuffed them into the evidence bag. Ninety seconds later, the behemoth was standing on the cement floor of the cell, barefoot, naked and shivering, while the two troopers gawked and pointed at her. They couldn't help but laugh at her shape, although the irony was, Trooper Dettweiler wasn't exactly slender. While the two troopers were still laughing and guffawing, Trooper Conklin finally arrived. She was accompanied by her male partner, Trooper Pearlman. His face looked as young as a ten year old's. She apologized for not being there and went on to explain how she had to take a quick dinner break to go home and make sure her kids hadn't killed one another. She and the other three troopers formed a circle around the naked prisoner, while Trooper Dettweiler pointed at the prisoner and brought them up to date on the arrest. He continually referred to her as a "mad cow," which made Troopers Twomey and Pearlman chuckle. Trooper Conklin stood there frowning, but once Trooper Pearlman realized the remark caused the other troopers to laugh, he chimed in and cat-called at the prisoner with a series of elongated mooing sounds. And the more he mooed at her, the more distraught she became, until she finally burst into tears. She was in a full-blown melt down by the time Investigators Townley and Nottingham opened the door and stood in the doorway scowling. The four troopers snapped to attention. When Investigator Townley glared at all of them, they looked down at the tops of their Brogans. Investigator Townley shook his head at them in disgust and ushered them all out. The door clanged shut, leaving the prisoner alone.

The bench was far too cold for her to sit on in her naked condition, so she stood, huddled near the wall, weeping, wailing and feeling generally sorry for herself. About an hour later, a different trooper led an addict and a shoplifter into the cell. Even though it was cold outside, the addict wore a sleeveless, cotton summer dress, with nothing over it. Both she and the shoplifter took one look at the naked behemoth and made a double take. The addict even wondered whether she was tripping. She pointed at the behemoth with one of her scrawny arms. Like the other arm, it was covered in tattoos in an effort to hide her many needle marks. The shop lifter giggled nervously, but after a few minutes, the novelty wore off and they both settled down and fell asleep.

Six hours later, the watch commander from the day shift finally ordered a female officer to at least go into the holding cell and throw a blanket over their large prisoner. Then he called his wife and asked her to bring one of her mother's size 3X house dresses to the barracks. By the time that happened, the prisoner's nose was running and she had already begun to sneeze. Little did she know, once she was dressed, her interrogation would begin. And it would last for nine hours.

CHAPTER THIRTEEN

INHERITANCE

It was early Sunday morning. As a result of the time change and Jordan's jet lag, Jordan was exhausted when he finally arrived at his solicitor's office. He didn't look it though. He walked in, impeccably dressed and groomed. His solicitor, Warren Lindsay looked up from his paper work, slid his reading glasses down to the tip of his nose and peered over them at Jordan. He couldn't imagine what might have caused Jordan to be a day late.

After all, what could possibly be more important than the death of one's own father? He thought.

"Good morning. First of all, let me express my condolences. I'm very sorry for your loss. However, I was actually expecting you some time yesterday. Anyway, now that you're finally here, please DO take a seat," Warren Lindsay said, hoping he had effectively concealed his disapproval.

"Thank you for your condolences. Anyway, I'm afraid our call got dropped before you could fill me in on exactly what happened," he said, as he took a seat.

Warren Lindsay shook his head.

"Well, we still don't know everything, but from what I can gather, your father and his wife were killed in the Atlantic fog, when your father was piloting his six seater airplane on a flight to the continent. Apparently the aircraft made a series of turns and then suddenly plunged out of the sky. It appears to be engine failure, but sadly that hasn't officially been established as of yet."

Jordan scratched his head as he watched the solicitor slide his readers back up his nose and pick up the Will.

"As I told you right before our call got dropped, your father left you in excess of three hundred and seventy six million pounds."

CHAPTER FOURTEEN

YOU ARE GOOD

Meanwhile, back across the pond, in a four bedroom Colonial style house in tony Harrison, New York, a mere thirty miles away from where Ned Hollander met his unfortunate demise, Darlene Storm, a sweet blonde housewife in her mid-thirties, was in the process of clearing the dining room table. Her family was smiling, because they had just finished the homemade Sunday brunch she had prepared for them.

"Gee Darlene, you really outdid yourself. These were just about the best blueberry pancakes I've ever tasted," her husband, Mike said.

Darlene beamed and pointed at the blueberry bush outside the kitchen window.

"Remember last summer when you all teased me, because I spent so many hours picking and preserving every blueberry in sight?" Darlene asked.

"Yes!" The family answered, practically in unison.

"Well now, aren't you glad I did it?"

"We sure are. You're the best mother," Mikey, her eleven year old son, said.

"Aw, thank you. Remember, this afternoon after church I promised to go to the soup kitchen to feed the homeless," Darlene said.

"Again? You were just there on Thanksgiving. And that was only three days ago," her eight year old daughter Tiffany whined.

"Well, that was a special situation. Remember, the hungry are hungry every day. When I get back, I promise we can all do something fun together," Darlene said.

"You mean like rollerblading?" Mikey asked.

"That's up to your father."

Mike smiled and gave the thumbs up sign.

"Why not? I can stand to burn off some of the lard I gained after the incessant binge fest I've been on this entire weekend. In any case, as of right now I'm starting my diet. So, from now on, it's Discipline City all the way," he said.

He lifted his shirt and patted his bare stomach.

"Well, what makes you think you need to lose any weight? As far as I'm concerned, you're perfect. Besides, this is a crazy time of year for anyone to try to lose weight."

"Oh. By the way, did you remember to pick up that artificial sweetener for me?" He said, deflecting her remark.

She shook her head.

"No way. You know how much I hate to even think about bringing that poison into this house."

"Well, I need it to keep from losing my hard earned muscle tone."

"So I guess that means you're going to buy it anyway."

He grinned and nodded.

"Well then, since you're going to the store, could you do me a favor and pick up some windshield wiper fluid and antifreeze for the car?" She added.

"Sure."

They chatted while she loaded the breakfast dishes into the dishwasher. Later in the afternoon, when they returned home from roller blading, Darlene made hot open turkey sandwiches with a side order of piping hot potato pancakes, broccoli and left over Cranberry Waldorf sauce. Mike put the antifreeze and windshield wiper fluid into his and Darlene's cars and then placed the gigantic bottles containing the leftover fluids high on a shelf in the garage. He changed into his sweat suit and went out for a long jog around the neighborhood. When he returned, Darlene told him dinner would be served in a minute.

"Well, I'm making myself THIS instead," he said.

When he poured two ounces of concentrated caffeine powder into the blender, added a scoopful of creatine supplement and two packets of the artificial sweetener he bought, Darlene gasped.

"How much of that caffeine powder are you putting in there?"

"Less than what's in a cup of coffee or tea," he answered.

"Well,"—she started to say, but he drowned her out by turning the blender on "high."

After thirty seconds, he stopped, poured the mixture into a glass and took it into the family room, so he could drink it while catching up on the news. By the time the rest of the family finished eating dinner, he was fast asleep on the couch. Later that evening, Darlene tried to wake him.

"What time is it?"

The degree of grogginess in his voice worried Darlene. She looked at the clock on the TV's cable box.

"A little after nine."

"Really? Well maybe I should just go straight to bed," he said.

He got up, managed to make it up to the bedroom and flopped onto the bedspread without even changing out of his sweat suit.

CHAPTER FIFTEEN

MANIC MONDAY

The next morning, Mike Storm lumbered out of bed. When Darlene asked him what he wanted for breakfast, he told her he wasn't hungry and headed straight into the shower. Then he proceeded to get dressed and leave for work. By midmorning, he was vomiting so much, his boss arranged for a taxi to bring him home. When he staggered through the front door, he was pale and sweaty. He couldn't walk any farther than the bottom of the staircase in the center hall entrance. He leaned on the post and hunched over it like an inverted letter "L". Darlene was upstairs changing the sheets on the last of the beds when she heard him panting and wheezing. She ran down the stairs. The minute she laid eyes on him, her face froze in horror.

"Oh my God! You look awful! What's wrong?"

He tried to stand up and eke out a response, but all he could manage to do was bend over the railing, gasp for breath and feebly wave her away. His face was pinched in agony. She ran for the phone and called 911. When the ambulance arrived eleven minutes later, Mike was extremely belligerent. By the time he arrived at Downstate Hospital's Emergency Room, he was combative. He seemed to have gotten some of his strength back, because he was able to take a swing at the paramedic who unstrapped him from his gurney. Dr. Rogers, the Emergency Room Doctor, ordered an injection of Ativan to calm him down. When Kitty, the emergency room nurse, approached Mike to administer the shot, he slapped the syringe out of her hand and knocked it to the floor.

"Fuck off," he screamed.

It took four paramedics to hold his arms and legs down, while Kitty prepared another syringe. A few minutes after she administered the injection, he calmed down. Then Dr. Rogers went out into the hall and told Darlene she could see him.

"Where am I?" Mike asked her.

Before Darlene could answer him, he closed his eyes and slipped into a coma. Dr. Rogers admitted him to the ICU.

CHAPTER SIXTEEN

LAWYERS AND LIES

Phoebe Hudson punched the time clock at the canoe factory promptly at two forty five, just as she did every day. She raced out to her car and drove it in the sleet as fast as safety would allow. She needed to get to Shane's school in time to pick him up.

"Listen, I want you to stay at Grandma's," she said, once Shane was settled and buckled into his seat.

He looked at her with a worried expression.

"Not that I don't love being with Grandma or anything, but it seems like you're leaving me there a lot lately."

She nodded.

"I know and I'm sorry. It's just that I'm just going to the doctor to get my annual routine checkup and I think you should wait for me at Grandma's. That's all," she said, in as cheery a voice as she could fake.

Phony as hell, she said to herself.

She didn't like being dishonest, but she felt compelled to go to any lengths to protect Shane from the truth about Willie. She dropped him off at her mother's "house", a broken down, unattached trailer she rented on the corner of one of the farmer's properties on Coyote Lane. She rolled down the window and watched him step gingerly over the holes in the broken porch. She could smell her mother's only source of heat, the little wood burning, potbellied stove that dominated the middle of the trailer. Once Shane was inside, she rolled up the window and turned to leave. By that time, the sun was low in the sky, the temperature was dropping and the sleet was turning into snow. There was no way she could drive as fast as she wanted to. She slipped and slid all the way to her lawyer's office. When she finally got there, she was late, so the secretary rushed her straight back to see him. When he offered her a seat, she was too agitated to take it. Instead, she paced back and forth in front of his desk like a caged lion, as she explained to him how Willie had returned and had taken over her apartment. Then she informed him of the bizarre episode involving the cat and the aquarium. She punctuated her horror story with the newscast she'd overheard involving Willie and some "female attorney gone wrong" down in New York City. She also told him that, from what she could gather, Willie had given her that same lawyer's jewelry.

His face froze in shock.

"Well, did you at least bring it with you?"

She shook her head.

"No. I sold it. After all, times are tough and

Christmas is coming. Anyway, I'd love to get Willie out of my apartment as soon as possible. The problem is, I'm too scared to do it on my own. What can you do to help me?"

He stroked his chin, pondered for a minute and then googled Willie's name. The search led him to a YouTube link of the same newscast Phoebe saw on Saturday. They watched it together. At the end, it provided a contact number for the District Attorney's office downstate in Westchester County. The lawyer picked up the phone and called it. After pushing several buttons on the menu and having the call routed and rerouted a number of times, a live, albeit laconic, female finally picked up the call. She listened halfheartedly to everything he said and rolled her eyes when he told her he was from a small town upstate, past Lake George. Deciding he couldn't be of very much importance, she hastily scribbled the message and ended the call as fast as she could. When the call was over, the lawyer stood.

"I'll call you the minute I hear anything," he said.

Phoebe nodded and requested he call her mother instead, so Willie wouldn't find out.

"No problem," he said, as he walked her to the door.

She picked Shane up at her mother's house and when Shane went out to the car, she pretended she had forgotten something. She ran back to her mother's house and told her what had transpired at the lawyer's office.

"You haven't told this many lies since your teenage days when you lied to me so you could sneak out behind my back with Willie," Zirca said.

Phoebe chuckled bitterly.

"I know, right?"

When Phoebe and Shane got home, Willie was sitting upright on the couch waiting for them. Phoebe cooked dinner and tried to act as nonchalant as possible.

CHAPTER SEVENTEEN

GOOD BYE RUBY TUESDAY

The next morning, Phoebe got out of bed and put on her bath robe. On her way into the kitchen to make coffee, she glanced at the couch in the living room and noticed it was empty. The bedding was in a ball on the living room floor. She checked the bathroom. Willie wasn't in there. She ran into Shane's room. Shane was still in bed, sound asleep. She breathed a sigh of relief, tiptoed to the window and looked outside. She noticed her car wasn't in the space where she had parked it the night before. She silently closed Shane's door. On impulse, she returned to her bedroom to look for her handbag and car keys. They were gone. She picked up the phone and called Zirca.

About forty five minutes later, Shane woke to the sound of his mother and grandmother talking to a man in the kitchen. Shane was pretty sure the man wasn't Willie, because his mother and Willie never really held conversations. They were more like two cave people, who said as little as possible to one another and communicated with each other in what seemed to him to be little more than a series of grunts. So whatever was going on in the kitchen struck him as odd. He rubbed his eyes and listened carefully. Yoda wasn't curled up in her usual spot next to him, so he reached for her to pull her over to him. When he realized she wasn't even on the bed at all, questions flooded his brain. Questions about the whereabouts of his cat, questions about what was going on in the kitchen and what time it was. Finally, he sat up, got out of bed and threw his bathrobe on. Then he stumbled groggily into the kitchen, where he found Phoebe, Zirca and a police officer sitting around the kitchen table drinking coffee. The police officer was frowning. He had a notepad and was busily writing down everything Phoebe said. When he asked Phoebe whose name appeared on the car registration, she told him the car was registered to her. When he squinted and asked her whether Willie's name was ALSO on the registration, she felt herself getting annoyed. She shook her head and told him HER name was the only one on the registration. When he asked to see it, she countered by asking him exactly how he thought she was supposed to accomplish THAT.

The officer continued to frown at her. Shane glanced at the clock. It was 8:45, the time when school began. When he asked his mother why she hadn't bothered to wake him in time, she responded by suggesting he get dressed so Zirca could take him out for breakfast. Before he could say another word, the officer asked Phoebe if she remembered her license plate number. Shane interrupted.

"Listen, I don't even know why you're here, but since you ARE here, can you please let me file a missing person's report on my cat?"

He sounded frantic. And when no one answered him, he frowned.

Phoebe turned to him and scowled. He looked dejected, as he left to return to his bedroom. When he got there, he slammed the door. A few minutes later, he came back into the kitchen, fully dressed. He left to look in every room for the cat and then he finally returned to the kitchen again. When he said he still hadn't been able to find the cat, Zirca got up. Together she and Shane searched the entire apartment. They looked under beds and chairs and in all Yoda's favorite hiding places. Every few seconds they called out her name, but they never got a response. Zirca even opened a can of cat food, in the hopes of enticing Yoda out of hiding. When that didn't work, Shane broke into tears.

Officer Kelton closed his note pad, stood and said a few comforting words to Shane. Then he turned to walk out. Zirca helped Shane into his coat. Then she gently but firmly grabbed him by both shoulders and hustled him out the door. As they walked into the cold morning air, they passed two of Phoebe's nosiest neighbors, Beryl and Gina.

Beryl's moth eaten camel hair jacket was two sizes too small for her and it did nothing to hide her fat. Gina was older but thinner than Beryl and amazingly enough, she looked like a clone of the Scarecrow from the Wizard of Oz. Coming of age in war torn Naples, Italy, she gave up her job as a serving wench and dish washer and latched onto the first American soldier who paid attention to her. She seduced and then married him. Little did she realize she would wind up living out her days in Moriah, New York.

As soon as Beryl and Gina saw Zirca and Shane, they immediately clammed up and stopped speculating about why the police were called to Phoebe's apartment.

"I mean this is bad. Right? He was gone for so long. He never sent any money. And now he comes back here from out of nowhere? And the cops get called?" Gina said, as soon as everyone was out of earshot.

She had been in Moriah for so long, her Italian accent was barely noticeable.

Beryl nodded.

"I remember how devastated the poor thing was when he first left. But what I don't understand is why he even bothered to come back. What's even weirder is that she let him back. I mean, doesn't she know a snake can change its skin every single year, but it's still the same snake?"

Gina nodded.

Officer Kelton cruised around the block on the

offhand chance he would find Willie, Yoda or Phoebe's car, but he didn't do it for too long. He knew the more time he spent scouring the neighborhood, the more ground Willie could cover on the lam and he didn't want the trail to grow cold.

Once Phoebe was alone, she searched the apartment in a last ditch effort to find Yoda. When she looked in the closet and realized the cat carrier was gone, she knew Yoda was gone too. With her heart beating a mile a minute, she sighed, gave up her search and called her supervisor. She listened to her supervisor berate her for being late for work. When she hung up, she called her lawyer and brought him up to date on the latest development.

"Well, it sounds like he probably left again. I guess he's done with you, at least until the next time he needs a place to flop. For openers, you've got to start exerting a little control over your life, unless you want this to keep happening. So, the very first thing you need to do is get your locks changed. Get a locksmith over there today, if possible. For all we know, he could have already scrounged up an extra key or copied your own key by now. And once you get the locks changed, the next thing to do is keep your doors locked. At all times. And last but not least, your next step would be never to let him back in again. No matter what," he said.

Phoebe thanked him and hung up. She wanted to indulge in the luxury of a meltdown, but she knew she had to stay strong. So, she sighed again, kept a stiff upper lip and called a taxi. While she waited for it, she splashed some cold water on her face. She quickly brushed her teeth and threw on a pair of black knit pants. She grabbed the first pullover she found in her drawer and put it on. Then she raked a brush through her dark blonde hair and dabbed a dash of blush on her cheeks and lips. She decided to forego her usual heavy mascara. In the event she couldn't avoid crying, the last thing she needed was a river of thick, black tears rolling down her face. Finally, she grabbed her coat and went outside to stand in front of the building. Beryl and Gina were still out there gossiping about her. When they saw her, they greeted her perfunctorily and clammed up again. A few seconds later, the taxi arrived. Phoebe got in and told the driver to take her to Mad Dog's Ice Creamery.

Once they got to the restaurant, the driver idled and waited while Phoebe raced past the crowded booths and harried waitresses to look for her mother. When she finally found her, she asked for some money to pay her cab fare. She had to speak in a raised voice in order to be heard over the sound of the clattering dishes, radio and conversations all around them. Zirca dug around in her purse. When she found her wallet, she handed it over to Phoebe.

"Did you find Yoda yet? And are you taking a cab because the car broke down again? And how come Grandma has to pay for everything?" Shane asked.

Instead of answering him, Phoebe ran out, paid the driver and tipped him. When she returned, she handed Zirca's wallet back to her. By that time, Zirca and Shane were just about finished with their breakfasts. Phoebe didn't bother to order anything. She was too upset to even think about choking down food. Zirca paid the bill, then she and Phoebe took Shane to school. They drove down Viking Lane, parked the car in the fire lane of the elementary school section of the Moriah Central School and walked him all the way to his classroom. When the teacher came out into the hall to talk to them, Phoebe explained that a family emergency had caused Shane to miss half a morning's worth of school. On the way out, she and Zirca stopped in to see the principal. She stressed that under no circumstances was Shane to be released to anyone's custody other than hers or Zirca's. After that, Zirca drove Phoebe over to the Police Station. Right before they got there, Phoebe could no longer stave off her meltdown. As soon as she burst into tears, Zirca rubbed her back with one hand and steered with the other.

"I can't believe that bastard left town, taking my car, my money and Shane's poor little cat with him," Phoebe said.

Zirca sighed.

"Well, I only wish I'd have had a chance to give him a piece of my mind before he left," she said.

Phoebe nodded.

"Believe me, I hear you. By the way, I have to get to the pet store and pray they have a tiger star red tail fish, so I can buy it before Shane goes to feed the fish and notices his prize fish is gone," she said.

"Why? Don't tell me Willie took THAT too," Zirca exclaimed.

Phoebe shook her head.

"Trust me. You don't want to know," Phoebe said.

CHAPTER EIGHTEEN

IF I DIE YOUNG

Just after eleven o'clock on Tuesday morning, Mike Storm died without ever having come out of his coma. Baffled, Dr. Rogers ordered an autopsy. Then he went to Pattie's floor. When he walked into her room, he headed straight for the sink in her bathroom, washed his hands and asked her how she felt.

Pattie cleared her throat.

"I feel better, but not good," she said, in a voice that was still raspy.

He dried his hands, retrieved the thermometer from his pocket and stuck it in Pattie's ear. While he was waiting for her temperature to register, he looked into her eyes. Her pupils had receded in size and her eyes were restored to their original turquoise color. He removed the thermometer and looked at it.

"Well, your temperature is still normal. It hasn't spiked. And it's been twenty four hours."

Just as she started to answer him, the right side of her jaw cracked. She winced and touched it.

"Ouch! Did you hear that?"

He nodded, tenderly touched her jaw and then peered closely at her.

"Yes. Not only do you appear to have TMJ, it looks like you've got the beginnings of impetigo too!"

He grabbed a mirror, handed it to her and pointed at her face. Angry little patches of red and silver scales had just begun to break out across the area above her mouth. One of the scales was in the process of opening. It was oozing pus. She'd seen scales like those before. On Leland LeRoux's face. She gasped, turned away in horror and cleared her throat.

"It's highly contagious, but at least it's fully treatable. It doesn't lie dormant in nerve endings like cold sores do, so once we eradicate it, it won't come back, unless of course you get infected all over again. But, until it goes away, you can't get it wet. That means you'll have to be extra careful in the shower and when washing your face. Now I need to ask you, whether you got up close and personal with someone who had it," Dr. Rogers said.

She sighed and stared at him with great intensity, but she didn't answer him. Her pupils began to dilate again.

"Well, I suppose it's possible you don't know who it is because they were incubating it when you made contact. Therefore, you wouldn't have been able to tell."

"Well, it's not as if I sleep around or anything, if that's what you're implying," she said peevishly.

He shook his head.

"Of course not. You don't have to sleep with some body to get impetigo. In any case, I'm going to have to soak this fledgling scab right now, before I remove it altogether," Dr. Rogers continued.

After he finished, he handed Pattie the mirror, so she could watch, as he demonstrated the correct way to apply the antibiotic salve.

"Listen, whatever you do, don't scratch it or try to remove any scabbing yourself, no matter how great the temptation. Because that would only delay your healing. That's why I don't want you to get it wet. Don't wear any face make up. Or foundation or whatever they call it. Also, I'll write out a prescription for a broad spectrum oral antibiotic along with the salve. The antibiotic will not only help with the impetigo, but also with any residual infection in your lungs. Now, no matter what else happens, finish the prescribed dosage of both the prescription and the salve until they are both gone. Even if YOU think the situation has cleared up, you MUST finish both. Otherwise you'll end up fighting a superbug with a lot of unwanted complications, such as cellulitis —which is an infection of the deeper layers of the skin and underlying tissue OR scarlet fever — a rare bacterial infection that causes a fine pink rash across your entire body, post-streptococcal glomerulonephritis, an infection of the small blood vessels in the kidneys or a myriad of other nasty maladies even more difficult to pronounce and cure. Come back if you have another flareup. Come to think of it, even if everything goes well, once the pills and the salve are gone you should nevertheless have a follow up appointment. Anyway, the nurse told me you've been requesting a shower. Now that your temperature's been normal for over twenty four hours, I can authorize that. You can even wash your hair, if you like. I'll write up your discharge papers, so after your shower you'll be free to leave. I'd prefer it if someone could come and pick you up. I don't think you should go home alone."

Pattie thought that was a lot of information to process. Nonetheless, she nodded and cleared her throat, while he wrote out the prescriptions, along with a set of discharge papers. He pulled a business card out of his wallet, turned it over and wrote his private cell phone number on the back. He placed it on the night stand, along with all the other papers.

"I WILL come back and follow up with you," she said.

He nodded and gave her the thumbs up sign.

"By the way, once you've been on the antibiotic for seventy two hours you shouldn't be contagious anymore," he said.

She thanked him, they said good byes and he left. Afterwards, she took her shower and dried her hair. And as she was getting dressed, she managed to convince herself that Jordan had "ghosted out on her" once and for all. She wondered whether he had even gone to Scotland in the first place or whether that was just a lie he concocted in order to avoid being with her. She bit her lower lip and tried to decide whether it was better to call Lou or Ryan to come pick her up. Just as she decided on Ryan, the telephone on the night stand rang. Startled, she jumped and cleared her throat.

"Hello?"

It was Jordan, letting her know his plane had just landed at JFK Airport.

She breathed a sigh of relief.

"Oh thank God. I'm so happy to hear from you. Anyway, how did you know I was still in the hospital?"

He explained he didn't, but figured it was the best place to start looking for her. As it turned out, he called the main number and since she was still a patient there, the switchboard operator put him straight through to her room.

"It's such perfect timing, because they're actually ready to discharge me."

"I'll rent a car and come for you. I guess I should be there in about an hour."

Pattie finished getting dressed and packed her belongings. She reclined on the bed and dozed until Jordan raced into the room an hour later. When he held his arms out to embrace her, she cleared her throat, pushed him away and looked into his eyes. He frowned.

"Why are you pushing me away?".

She cleared her throat.

"Well, even though I'm no longer contagious with pneumonia, I've got a new problem. I've come down with a horrible case of impetigo. It's very disturbing. Anyway, you could catch it until I've been on antibiotics for three days," she said.

He stepped back and looked at her. Her skin was its usual color of pale moonlight, but a small area around her mouth was covered in salve. He felt badly for her so he complimented her on how pretty her clean, blown out hair looked and he lightly ran his fingers through it. She smiled at him and rang to notify the nursing station that she had a ride home. A few minutes later a nurse's aide rolled a wheel chair into the room. She helped Pattie into it and wheeled her to the elevator. Jordan walked alongside, carrying Pattie's personal effects. When the elevator came, they got in and rode down to the lobby. The aide wheeled Pattie out to the main entrance and waited with her while Jordan brought the car around. He let it idle, so it would be warm inside when Pattie got in. He ran around to the passenger's side and opened the door for her. The aide helped Pattie out of the wheelchair. Once Pattie was safely inside the car, Jordan closed the door, walked around and got in on the driver's side, Pattie rolled her window down, thanked the aide and said goodbye. Then Jordan pulled away. When he suggested they go for breakfast, Pattie nodded.

"Thank you for thinking of that. And I also want to thank you for rescuing me. Not just today, but on Thanksgiving night as well. If you hadn't, I might have died. But here's the thing. I can't figure out how either one of us ever get to be where we were that night. As a matter of fact, would you mind telling me WHERE we were?"

He looked at her quizzically.

"Well, I used one of the guest passes Kevin Gordon had given to me at that Golf Club up in Hudson Highlands and went up there to spend Thanksgiving by myself. While I was up there, I received word that my father had died. As a result, I had to check out and return to the city. But because it was so foggy, I got lost and couldn't find the entrance to the Highway. I stopped into a church to see whether someone could help me out. A pastor was there and he gave me directions. I followed them and just as I was ready to approach the entrance ramp, I saw a wet girl wandering around. She turned out to be you. That answers how I got there, but I have no idea how you wound up there."

He turned the car into the crowded parking lot of a nearby Greek Diner, and circled around until he found a space. Then he led her inside, where the smell of good food and fresh hot coffee made her stomach growl.

CHAPTER NINETEEN

TAKE THIS JOB AND SHOVE IT

Phoebe's supervisor was scowling as she rushed over to Phoebe's work station. She leaned over Phoebe and whispered in her ear.

"Gee, I hope you didn't do nothing illegal, because the State Police are on the phone, asking for you. I put them on hold, so you'd better drop whatever you're working on and find out what they want."

Phoebe's palms broke into a sweat. Her heart skipped a beat. She stood and followed her supervisor down the hall.

"Remember, the Christmas rush is starting. So, if you don't make your quota, you'll be the first one they let go when things slow down after the New Year. And just so you know, those decisions come from higher up. They're out of my hands," the supervisor continued.

God, I hate this place, Phoebe said to herself.

When they reached the supervisor's office, Phoebe picked up the phone.

I'm Trooper Seaver from the State Police. And because your husband's disappearance is now of statewide concern, I'll be handling the case from now on," he said.

"EX HUSBAND!" Phoebe said.

The supervisor stood behind Phoebe, hovering and straining to hear every word of the conversation.

"Yeah, well, anyway, at least I have some good news for you. Your car has been found in good condition at the Amtrak Station in Saratoga Springs. I'll need you to identify it, so I'll meet you as soon as you can get over there. Also, it was on the report that you owned a cat."

"Owned?" Phoebe asked.

"Poor choice of words. We have reason to believe there's a cat inside the car."

Phoebe's heart beat even faster.

"Is she OK?" Phoebe asked.

"I can't say. Anyhow, I'll be at the station waiting for you," he answered.

Phoebe thanked him, hung up and called her mother. When she told her supervisor she would be leaving as soon as her mother arrived to pick her up, the supervisor frowned, shook her head and wondered whether Phoebe had even heard one word of her earlier warning.

Ninety minutes later, after having seriously exceeded the speed limit, Zirca pulled into the Saratoga Springs

Amtrak Station's parking lot and brought her car to a screeching halt. Phoebe got out and ran over to her own car. Trooper Seaver lumbered out of his police cruiser, identified himself and joined her. Phoebe looked through the window and used her spare key to unlock the door. The first thing both she and Trooper Seaver noticed, was the powerful stench of cat urine. It was so strong they both took a step back. Yoda was huddled on the front passenger's seat, inside her carrier, shivering. When the Trooper put his gloves on, he opened the carrier and tried to reach inside. Yoda hissed at him and let out a low growl. Phoebe gave the trooper a dirty look, pushed past him and peered into the carrier. As soon as Yoda saw Phoebe, she let out a loud meow. It was less threatening than her growl and nothing more than a formal a protest about the ordeal she'd just been put through. Phoebe stuck her hand into the carrier and petted Yoda. Once Yoda was calm, Phoebe locked the carrier back up again and picked up her hand bag. Her license, health insurance card and ATM card were still inside her wallet, but the three hundred seventy five dollars in cash, which she had gotten from selling Pattie's jewelry and the five hundred twenty five dollars she had gotten by cashing in her Christmas Club account were gone. As a result, she had no money to change her lock, buy Shane's computer game, replace his Red tailed Tiger Fish or even pay her lawyer's bill. She started to cry.

Trooper Seaver saw a crumpled set of papers on the floor. He reached in, picked them up and uncrumpled them. They turned out to be Phoebe's Divorce papers. He tossed them onto the seat.

"By the way, did you see my car keys anywhere in there?" Phoebe asked.

He shook his head.

"Great. He must have taken them with him. Thank God I have this spare set. Anyway, I hope there's a carwash around here, because I don't know how long I'll be able to stand that cat smell," she said, as she walked around to the driver's side of the car.

She opened the door, but before she could get in, Trooper Seaver blocked her. He shook his head and gently pulled her away from the car. Phoebe looked at him in confusion and blinked, as he explained that the only thing he could return to her was her cat.

"Well, I need my car to get to work. And since I just lost my life savings, I'm not in a position to conjure up another car any time soon."

Trooper Seaver nodded at her and pretended to look sympathetic. The truth was he never believed for a second the likes of Phoebe could ever even have a life savings. He suspected she was making that up. Suddenly, a tow truck showed up to haul Phoebe's car to the impound center. Frustrated, Phoebe picked up Yoda's carrier, brought it over to her mother's car and carefully placed it down on the back seat.

"She's probably really cold and scared, not to

mention hungry and thirsty. And it never even occurred to me bring any food or water," she told her mother.

She got into the passenger's seat, closed the door and thanked her mother for everything she'd been doing since Willie arrived. While they were in the parking lot, the sun had rapidly set, which was typical for that area during that time of year. So she asked her mother to turn up the heat. Zirca nodded, cranked the heat and sped into the whistling wind.

CHAPTER TWENTY

INVESTIGATIONS

The following morning, on December 3rd, at about ten o'clock, Investigators Townley and Nottingham sat at the State Police Barracks in Westchester, drinking coffee and mulling over a new case, "Leland LeRoux". They were looking for anyone they could find in connection with the case. Since Willie Hudson was "in the wind" they decided to contact Pattie. It didn't take them long to track down Chet's telephone number. When the old, red, dial telephone rang, Edie put down the pitcher of margarita mix she was pouring into her goblet and sighed. It was to be her second one of the day. She looked like a fat little dumpling as she shuffled across her old linoleum floor in her frumpy off white sweat suit. The more she listened to Investigator Townley, the more she grimaced. When he finally finished talking, she covered the receiver with her hand.

"Chet, this is either the worst phony phone call we've ever gotten or that crazy kid of ours has been going around killing off her clients," she brayed, in her loud, coarse voice.

Chet shook his head, sniffed and heaved himself off of the couch. Edie's lower lip jutted out as she waited for Chet to limp into the kitchen. When he finally made it, she handed him the receiver.

"Who is this and what do you want?" Chet growled.

Edie reached for her pack of cigarettes, coaxed one out and lit it up with her cheap plastic lighter. Then she sucked on it as if it were a life support system. After that first puff, she relaxed a little, let the cigarette dangle from her lips and stared down at her scruffy slippers. In the meantime Chet paid close attention to every word Investigator Townley uttered. When he hung up, he called Lou.

"I need to talk to Pattie, right now. Right this very minute," he said.

Lou told him Pattie was with her boyfriend Jordan and waited while Chet hobbled around in search of a scrap of paper and a pen. He returned to the phone, sniffed and wrote down Jordan's number. When they hung up, he dialed it. When Jordan answered, he identified himself, greeted Jordan and asked to speak to Pattie. Jordan handed the telephone to Pattie, who was sprawled out on the couch, recuperating. Chet put an end to her languid mood when he informed her that the State Police wanted her for routine questioning up at their barracks in Westchester.

"Where in the hell is this place? Massachusetts?

Anyway, why should the State Police want to be bothered with me? As cops they ought to know I can't tell them anything that would violate attorney client privilege."

Chet sniffed.

"Yeah? Well, they're not investigating one of your clients. They're investigating YOU!"

Pattie's heart skipped a beat. She cleared her throat. When she didn't respond, Chet continued to speak.

"That's right. They're claiming YOU'RE the suspect. Anyway, where are you now?"

"You just called me on Jordan's phone. I'm with him."

"I know, Einstein. But what I meant to ask is what's his address?"

She told Chet Jordan's address.

"I'll be over there in half an hour to pick you up," he said.

By the time he hung up, the kitchen was a haze of smoke.

Pattie turned to Jordan and explained the situation. He patted her hand, kissed her on the cheek and told her not to worry. She smiled and returned the kiss. Then she picked up his phone, placed an emergency call to the best criminal lawyer she knew, Reginald Reese and told his secretary, Ellie, she needed to talk to Reginald right away. Even though Pattie explained it was a personal emergency, Ellie informed her that

Reginald was in court. She took down Jordan's number and told Pattie she would give Reginald the message the minute she heard from him. When they hung up, Pattie called Ryan and left him a frantic message asking him to track Reginald down at the court house and have him call her right away.

CHAPTER TWENTY-ONE

GOING POSTAL

When Chet picked Pattie up in front of Jordan's apartment building, Edie was sitting next to him in the front passenger's seat of their rusty, faded red, '93 Ford Festiva. She rolled down the window, blew out a puff of smoke and cupped her hand around her eyes to squint at Pattie. Pattie had parted her hair in the middle and had arranged it in an artful series of waves and curls. Edie didn't notice them. She was too busy sizing up Pattie's bruised and swollen jaw.

Squinting back at Edie, Pattie quietly informed her and Chet that Jordan would be driving out of the garage in a minute and that he would be taking her to the post office before they left the city. Chet frowned and told her how counterproductive he thought that was. Pattie didn't answer him. She simply cleared her throat, while Edie took a long drag on her cigarette.

When Jordan drove his rental car out of the garage, Pattie walked over to it and got into the passenger's seat. Jordan pulled up behind Chet and followed his car to the massive building that occupied the entire block between Eighth and Ninth Avenues and Thirty Third and Thirty Fourth Streets. Pattie lumbered up the huge stair case, walked past the massive colonnades and went inside. She submitted a change of address form, so her mail would be forwarded to Jordan in case anything went wrong. When she returned to the street, she and Jordan followed Chet's car up to the State Police Barracks in Westchester. By the time they arrived there, Pattie was a nervous wreck.

Jordan walked around to the passenger's side to help Pattie out of the car. Her ankles felt wobbly, so she leaned on him, while he walked her up to the main entrance. When they were all inside, Chet announced to the Desk Sergeant that Pattie Anwald was there to see Investigators Townley and Nottingham. The Desk Sergeant nodded and called them. When they showed up a few minutes later and introduced themselves, Chet flashed his badge at them. Investigator Townley looked at it, nodded and smiled at Chet, but then he turned to Pattie and explained that the protocol was to question her alone, unless she felt the need to have an attorney present.

Pattie cleared her throat and told them her attorney would no doubt be joining them later on, but that she didn't mind speaking to them in the meantime. As she said this, she secretly hoped Reginald would show up soon. Jordan kissed her on the cheek and gave her a quick hug. Then the two investigators whisked her through the door to the back of the barracks. Chet clutched his chest and shook his head. Edie shot Jordan a dirty look, as if somehow he were to blame for everything, including the condition of Pattie's face.

The interrogation room was poorly lit and chilly. Pattie immediately felt uncomfortable. Investigator Townley led her to a table and patted on a hard metal stool with no back. Once Pattie sat on it, the two investigators seated themselves in comfortable, padded chairs with backs and arms. Investigator Townley picked up Pattie's file and opened it. She was surprised at how easily she maintained her self-control, as she sat there waiting for him to stop reading. Several minutes later, he snapped the file shut and slid it over to his partner. When he asked Pattie whether she had ever been arrested before, she cleared her throat, shook her head and told him no. When he inquired about the fire outside her door the previous summer, she squinted and cleared her throat again.

"What about it? I didn't set it, if that's what you want to know. It was OUTSIDE my door and I was INSIDE."

Neither of the Investigators answered her. Investigator Townley merely shrugged and shook his head.

"Listen, we KNOW all that, but we also think you know who did. And you were probably REALLY ticked off at them too. And when you get right down to it, why wouldn't you be? Listen, it's ok to tell us if you felt compelled to get even with them. Believe me, COUNSELOR, we'll understand," Investigator Townley went on.

Pattie felt confused. She frowned.

"Look, you keep talking but you're just not making any sense. I don't know what the hell you're driving at," she said.

Investigator Nottingham looked at her with an expression that did little to conceal his disdain for her. He nodded and raised his index finger, but before he could speak, Investigator Townley interrupted him.

"I'm just saying it's only human nature that you'd want to snuff out a low life like Leland LeRoux, especially since he torched your door and kidnapped your client, Justin Edwards."

Pattie gasped. All her self-control vanished. This was the first time anyone had mentioned Leland LeRoux in connection with either the arson in her hallway or Justin Edwards' kidnapping. And hearing about it caused her to tremble.

Investigator Nottingham sat there, continuing to nod and smirk at her in a condescending way, hoping to catch a micro expression or some other evidence of her guilt.

"Yeah and you finally got your chance and went through with it on Thanksgiving Night. Isn't that what happened, COUNSELOR? And you might have even had some help doing it. But you couldn't just walk away leaving a living witness. Even if they did help you. So you had to snuff out that person too.

And judging from the condition of your face, I'd say it must have been a hell of a fight. Now, if you didn't do it in cold blood, because your mind temporarily snapped or you did it in self-defense, maybe we can still help you. Maybe we can even work something out. But of course, you'd have to tell us everything," Investigator Townley continued.

Pattie's fear and her inability to remember what happened on Thanksgiving, upset and intimidated her. She cleared her throat.

"So how many people are you saying died? And who are they? Leland LeRoux and who else? And how did they die? Where did they die? And where are their bodies now?" Pattie fired off a number of questions.

"You tell us," Investigator Townley said.

"Look, unless you actually have probable cause to charge me with something, this little chat is over," she said, with a false show of bravado.

She stood. When she turned and walked toward the door, Investigator Townley nodded at Investigator Nottingham. Then he bolted out of his seat and followed her. And just as she reached for the doorknob, he whipped out his handcuffs and pinned her arms behind her back. She trembled, as the cold metal dug into her skin.

"We have all the probable cause we need," Investigator Townley said.

"Listen, I've never hurt anybody in my life. I am

not a killer! And I'll tell you something else. This isn't over," she cried out.

She couldn't believe she was hearing Investigator Townley charge her with Murder in the First Degree. Then, when he recited her Miranda rights, the entire scenario felt to her as if it were happening to someone else. She began to shake so violently, she needed to sit. But at that point she couldn't, because she was too far away from the chairs or the stool. Suddenly a gush of urine seeped out of her. She looked down to find it had created a dark spot on the crotch of her light gray leggings. And she blushed.

Still smirking, Investigator Nottingham glanced at her soggy crotch, but said nothing. Investigator Townley stood beside her. Investigator Nottingham lumbered to his feet and flanked her on her other side. Together they frog marched her into a room at the end of the hallway. They uncuffed her, took her mug shots and fingerprinted her. When they were done, they handcuffed her again and perp walked her up to the front of the building and into the public area, right past Jordan and her parents. She was ready to faint, so the two investigators practically had to drag her along.

Jordan's, Chet's and Edie's mouths all hung open as they followed the trio out into the parking lot. They stood there, watching Pattie's knees buckle when Investigator Townley pushed her head down, stuffed her into the back of the sleek, jet black Crown Victoria and slammed the door. Chet sniffed, Edie shook her head and Jordan kept his eyes on the cruiser until it vanished from sight.

None of them knew how to shake off the shock. Finally, Jordan reached into his pocket and pulled out a plastic lighter that read "As Long As You Have Your Wealth". When he held it out to Edie, she snatched it and stashed it in her purse. They all got into their cars and Jordan followed Chet back to the city. When Jordan's cell phone rang, he picked up the call, even though it was illegal for him to do so while driving. It was Ryan. He filled Ryan in on what had happened and said he didn't understand why Reginald hadn't called back yet. Ryan told Jordan to pick him up in front of the courthouse just after five o'clock and suggested from there, they would go to Reginald's office together.

HELL

CHAPTER TWENTY-TWO

ALONE AGAIN (NATURALLY)

Even though the Crown Victoria was fairly new, for some reason it smelled like a locker room. The back seat was narrower and harder than the back seats of ordinary cars. And even though Pattie had a thin frame, with her hands cuffed behind her back, the seat was too narrow for her to remain upright. She had no way of supporting herself whenever it careened around the many hills and curves of Northern Westchester. As a result, she got bounced and tossed around like a sack of potatoes. She trembled and shook with terror, her upper lip quivered and cold beads of perspiration formed on her palms and forehead. Since she had no way of wiping her brow, the sweat ran into her eyes and burned them.

The huge, maximum security prison compound was inconspicuously tucked away in the otherwise expensive hills of Westchester County. In fact, the ride involved so many peaks, dips and curves, Pattie wound up fighting off nausea. Finally, after twenty minutes, Investigator Townley drove up the steep hill that led to the prison. As he approached the high walled entrance, Pattie peered out of the window and shuddered. Five rows of razor wire topped an eighteen foot high fence that sat atop a thirty foot embankment. The embankment, which was on a forty five degree angle, surrounded and enclosed the soulless, eleven story Gothic Horror, which had been built in 1901. Guard towers and enormous strobe lights had been installed intermittently throughout the fencing. Every window in the drab lifeless main building had been hermetically sealed and fitted with steel grey bars. Their purpose was to ensure that none of the inmates could ever successfully escape. Investigator Townley slowed down, pulled up to the gate and waved at the guard. The guard put down his cigarette, waved back and pushed the button to lift the gate from its lock down position. Investigator Townley drove through. The trip came to an end when he parked the Crown Victoria as close to the prisoner's entrance as he could. He opened the back door, where he found Pattie crouched in a ball on the floor. He grabbed her arm and yanked her to her feet. Her ankles were unsteady and her teeth began to chatter.

Investigator Nottingham exited on the passenger's side. He walked around the rear of the cruiser, flanked Pattie's other side and grabbed her arm. She stumbled and staggered, as the two investigators hustled her across the plaza. Just then, a white SUV with hazard lights blazing, passed them. The driver parked the SUV in front of the door and turned off the motor. Three guards opened the rear passenger side door and pulled three handcuffed inmates out. They were returning them to the prison after an afternoon of sexual intercourse at the nearest flophouse. The heavy prison door slid open; the sextet entered and then the door clanged shut. When it re-opened, Pattie inhaled her last breath of freedom and sucked it down as deeply as she could. Then Investigators Townley and Nottingham marched her inside. The door clanged shut behind them, in what would be the first of many unnerving crashes. Investigator Nottingham chuckled under his breath when he saw Pattie jump in surprise.

Before she had an opportunity to recover, she was hit with her next assault. The horrible stench in the air battered her nostrils. It was stale and stagnant and it smelled like a powerful combination of onions, vermin, urine, feces, vomit, fish, dust, sweaty living bodies and decaying dead ones. In fact, it was so strong, she nearly fainted. And for as long as she remained in that place, it never left her. She shivered, as she made the transition from a criminal lawyer who kept people out of penal institutions, to a criminal defendant who was now an inmate in one, Prisoner 2003 G 0205 to be exact.

Investigator Townley turned Pattie over to a

hideous looking correctional officer, who stood, nodded at the two investigators and then glared at Pattie with a look of sheer hatred. He clasped his hand around the back of her fragile neck, muscled her through a clanging door, whose sound was so loud it made her jump again and then he steered her down a cold, windowless hallway that contained even more clanging doors. Eventually he turned her over to a big, beefy correctional officer with a buzz cut.

The beefy correctional officer commandeered her through a labyrinth of dingy corridors and mazes, with even more buzzers and clanging doors. Eventually he delivered her to another correctional officer, who repeated the same procedure. As far as each officer was concerned, Pattie was no different from any other prisoner who had come through the razor wire. And the feeling was mutual. Each of the correctional officers began to merge in Pattie's mind as one monstrous guard.

At the end of the last corridor, the male officer turned Pattie over to a husky female correctional officer, whose short, eighties style perm made her look as if she had stuck her finger in an electrical socket. She escorted Pattie through a heavy sliding door and shoved her into a room that was controlled by another female officer. The female officer in charge stared at the stain on Pattie's crotch and snickered. Then, she ordered the removal of Pattie's handcuffs. Finally, in the gravelly voice she reserved exclusively for prisoners, she ordered Pattie to step forward and strip. Pattie cleared her throat, looked around helplessly and stood still, as if paralyzed. The officer in charge quickly grew impatient. She tapped her toe, waited with her hands on her hips and finally told Pattie to either start stripping or she would do it for her.

Pattie blushed, gulped back the tears that filled her eyes and cleared her throat. With shaky hands, she slowly began to remove her clothes. The female officer with the perm snatched each item from her, announced what it was and then gave it to a third female officer to shove into a big white envelope. It had Pattie's name, prisoner number and the date written on it with a red Sharpie. When Pattie was completely naked, the officer holding the envelope threw her a wink, sealed the envelope and handed it to the officer in charge.

The frizzy haired officer snapped on a pair of latex gloves. One by one she barked out a series of commands. First, she ordered Pattie to pick up her hair. When Pattie complied, she ordered Pattie to lift her breasts. The commands continued, followed by compliance, as Pattie was subjected to the same crude rite of initiation every other inmate was forced to endure. She ordered Pattie to open her mouth and stick out her tongue. Then, she beamed her flashlight into Pattie's mouth and inspected her teeth, gums, throat and tongue. After that, she aimed the flashlight straight into Pattie's eyes, then into and behind her ears. Finally, she turned the flashlight off and hung it on her belt loop. She placed her hands on Pattie's shoulders and pressed with all her might, which forced Pattie all the way down into a deep, crouching knee bend. And she suddenly removed her hands from Pattie's shoulders and motioned for Pattie to stand up again. Pattie wobbled and waved her arms as she struggled. When she finally made it back to a standing position, the frizzy haired officer ordered her to bend over, stick her head between her knees and use both hands to pull her vagina apart as far as it would go.

"Oh yeah. And cough," she added.

When Pattie obeyed the commands, the officer poked her latex covered index finger up Pattie's vagina. Pattie grunted. Then the officer ordered her to remain in that position, spread the cheeks of her buttocks as wide as she possibly could and cough again. When she suddenly rammed her finger into Pattie's rectum, Pattie felt as if she were being burned alive and she shrieked.

By the time the officer jerked her finger back out of Pattie's rectum, Pattie's nerves were completely shot. After poking and prodding Pattie in every orifice of her frail, quivering body, she ordered Pattie to lift her left foot. Pattie did so, even though she had trouble balancing. After ordering Pattie to put her left foot down and raise her right foot, she led Pattie to a shower. She shoved her in and pressed a big, red button. A nasty looking, mustard yellow, delousing powder suddenly spewed forth from a rusty, brown hose pipe. It covered Pattie's head and body. When the water came on, the officer left Pattie to shower alone. Pattie had trouble breathing, because of the fumes. Fighting her urge to wheeze, she continued with her shower until the water automatically shut itself off six minutes later. Pattie was wet and shivering when the frizzy haired officer reappeared two seconds later with a stiff, rough, hand towel.

"She's clean," she called out to the officer in charge, as she lobbed the towel at Pattie.

And clean she was. In fact, she was actually stripped bare of everything, including her hope, her dignity, her courtesy and her humanity. The officer in charge checked the appropriate box on Pattie's intake sheet, then the frizzy haired officer led Pattie to a room where she and another officer took Pattie's fingerprints. Finally, they took mugshots of Pattie's face and naked body. In the event Pattie ever managed to escape, her scars, tattoos and distinguishing marks would be matched against the photographs, making it easier for the authorities to identify her. At the end of the process, the frizzy haired officer handed Pattie a flimsy white paper jumpsuit and ordered her to change into it. Once Pattie did, the two officers walked her through a series of mazes. Pattie was barefoot, so the floors felt cold on her feet. And with every step she took, the jumpsuit ripped. By the time her journey ended at an appallingly filthy, six by nine foot cell on a diagnostic unit, called "The Observatory," she looked as if she were dressed in a set of vertical paper blinds. The officers dumped her into the cell and slammed the door, without ever having uttered a word to her.

She looked around. The wastepaper basket was filled to overflowing with used tissues, bloody tampons and filthy sanitary pads. The steel toilet had no seat. The hard, standard, wrought iron twenty six inch wide prison bunk that had been bolted to the wall, was furnished with a three inch thick, green vinyl mat which had no covering. Across from it, a desk and two chairs were bolted to the floor. The ceiling, walls and even the door were made of thick, tempered, safety glass and the door had a steel flap that someone could pass items through. The setup gave anyone who walked by, the opportunity to observe everything Pattie did, as if she were a zoo beast.

Pattie felt a complete despair unlike anything she had ever known before. It seemed to her as if she were the star in some horror movie, where any minute, the ceiling might lower, the floor might rise and the walls might close in on her. She gingerly sat on the bunk with her feet tucked under her. Once she was as small as she could possibly make herself, she rocked back and forth and tried to keep from shivering.

CHAPTER TWENTY-THREE

MURDER WAS THE CASE

Shortly after five o'clock, just as twilight turned the blue sky to light lavender, Ryan ran down the steps of the courthouse. He spotted Jordan waving at him, got into the passenger's side of the rental car and gave him directions to a garage near Reginald Reese's office in Midtown's high rent district.

Reginald's secretary Ellie, welcomed them, explained that Reginald still hadn't returned from court and told them she hoped he would arrive momentarily. She invited them to sit in the large, well-appointed waiting room and brought them coffee. The minute Reginald walked through the door, Ryan sprang to his feet, rushed over to him and introduced him to Jordan. Reginald handed his leather, charcoal colored briefcase to Ellie, removed his grey tweed overcoat and hung it in the closet. Then he led Jordan and Ryan down the hallway, past a collection of oil paintings by Dutch masters and over genuine Persian rugs whose padding was so thick, it absorbed the sound of their footsteps. Once they were inside

Reginald's enormous, mahogany paneled inner office, Reginald sat in the comfortable leather chair behind his oversized mahogany desk and invited them to sit in the leather guest chairs across from him. Then he listened in astonishment as Jordan explained Pattie's situation.

"Whatever your fee is, I'll have it wired into your account, first thing tomorrow morning," Jordan said.

Reginald handed him his business card and a deposit slip indicating this bank account and routing numbers. He also let Jordan know in no uncertain terms, that even though Jordan was paying his fee, Pattie was his client. And therefore Reginald's only loyalty was to her. Afterwards, Ryan went on to inform Reginald of the two other situations in Pattie's life that he believed formed the basis of civil suits. The first was the eviction notice Pattie's landlord served on her on Thanksgiving Eve, even though she was a tenant in good standing. And the second involved Pattie's boss Brad Curatolo at the Legal Aid Office. He had decided to fire Pattie on Thanksgiving Eve, while gaslighting everyone at the courthouse into believing she'd quit.

CHAPTER TWENTY-FOUR

IN THE DEPTHS OF DESPAIR

About forty five minutes after the door to the "Observatory" clanged shut, a doctor with a tired, world weary expression let himself in. He held the obligatory clipboard in one hand and a phlebotomist's kit in the other. Pattie cleared her throat and looked up at him. A racking shiver passed through her body.

"Hello, I'm Dr. Winston Sibley."

Pattie burst into tears.

"Thank God you're here. I only got out of the hospital two days ago, after being there for four days with a series of maladies, including impetigo, pneumonia, a bite, a bruised head and face and a broken tail bone. In addition I have TMJ," she blurted, in a voice so hoarse it was scarcely above a whisper.

Dr. Sibley nodded, seated himself at the desk and made an entry on his clipboard. He reached into his pocket and pulled out a little packet of tissues. She took one, thanked him and wiped her eyes.

"Well, actually, I'm not here to treat you. I'm only here to take your information and some blood and ask you some questions. Did you just say a dog bit you?"

Pattie shook her head, as she explained it was a human bite. He nodded as if he didn't believe her and went on to ask her whether she was an attorney. She nodded, sniffed and shivered all at the same time.

"Are you hearing any voices?"

Pattie shook her head.

"No."

"Are you entertaining any thoughts of hurting either yourself or anyone else?"

She shook her head again.

"I'm too sick to do anything, much less hurt myself or anyone else," she said, blowing her nose into the tissue.

"Have you ever had any affiliation with a gang?"

"Of course not."

He nodded and handed her a dog-eared manual of prison rules and a badge made from one of the mug-shots they had taken of her earlier.

"If you lose either one of these, it will cost you five dollars. Now, the harsh reality is that for some strange reason, 'Fate' or whatever else you'd prefer to call it, has seen fit to place and detain you here, in what I will admit, is a Godawful place. More often than not you will encounter some really dreadful characters. And at this point we don't know long you'll be here.

Tomorrow morning you'll appear in court for a bail hearing. And if your lawyer doesn't win it, you'll be right back here come night fall. No doubt they'll house you on a tier with people who have charges similar to yours. And that is where you will remain, until you're acquitted. On the other hand, if God forbid they find you guilty then you'll stay here until you complete your sentence. And if you're condemned to death or to life imprisonment without parole, that day will never come. In any case, as long as you're here, you'll find yourself with too much time on your hands and life will be difficult, at best."

Even though he had a tendency to be long winded, something about his choice of words and the honesty with which he delivered them struck a chord with her. She threw the tissue into the overflowing waste paper basket and watched, as it rolled off onto the floor. The doctor removed a rubber tourniquet from his phlebotomy kit, wound it around her arm and told her to make a fist. She nodded and complied.

He told her to brace herself for a little prick, as he expertly tapped the inside of her arm. When he found a vein he liked, he rubbed it with alcohol and stuck it. She winced.

"You know, the sooner you realize none of the other prisoners or staff members in here will ever give you so much as an ounce of sympathy for your problems, the better off you'll be. No one really gives a damn whether you're sick, how much you hate it here, how much better the food on the outside is or the fact that your bunk is hard and it hurts your back or that the mat on it is too thin or that you're too hot or too cold or that you can't sleep," he said as he waited for her blood to slowly fill the first vial.

"I know you said no one will care about my problems, so I don't even know why I'm mentioning this, but I need to get in touch with my lawyer, to make sure he represents me at my arraignment tomorrow. I guess he was in court when I called him earlier, because he never called me back," she said.

Dr. Sibley capped the first vial and started the second one. When he had three full vials, he labelled them all with Pattie's name, prisoner number and the date. Then, he handed her a plastic cup and turned his back while she stood over the toilet and urinated into it. When she handed the cup to him, he covered it and labeled it. And without responding to the last thing she said nor even saying good bye, he packed up his kit and left.

When he said they didn't care, I guess he really meant it, she said to herself.

About twenty minutes later, the flap on the door opened and someone slid a threadbare cotton thermal blanket through it. Pattie retrieved it and brought it over to her bunk. About five minutes after that, a Styrofoam tray came through. On it was a tiny Styrofoam bowl of elbow macaroni, covered with a commercial spaghetti sauce that had been diluted with a ratio of about one part sauce to nineteen parts tap water. Two morsels of what Pattie could only think of as some kind of "mystery meat" floated on top of it. The entire mess smelled like dog food. Although the portion was so small, it couldn't even satisfy Pattie's bird like appetite, there was no way she could bring herself to eat it. First of all, she didn't have the stamina to keep the elbow macaroni from sliding off the plastic spoon and second of all, she couldn't get past the smell. So she gave up.

She pushed the tray away, flopped back onto her bunk and pulled the blanket over her head. Eventually the lights went out. She was exhausted, so she tried to doze off in the pitch black silence. But since she was far too keyed up to sleep, she lay there wide awake with her eyes closed, while desolation engulfed her. She came to the inescapable conclusion that she was the victim of a hideous catastrophe and there was nothing she nor anyone else could do about it. As she lay on the bunk, in the dark, she tried to figure out what exactly had happened to her and how whatever it was, could have carried her to the brink of a future she could neither predict nor control. And although she allowed her mind to wander in many different directions, she was nevertheless unable to come up with any answers. Instead, fearful thoughts tormented her. She longed for Jordan to wrap her in his arms and tell her everything would be all right. She began to cry. Her crying intensified until she could no longer control herself. She lay there sobbing until she was all cried out. And that's when she decided, from that point forward, as long as she remained in prison, she would never shed another tear and that at all times, she would act with as much courage as she could marshal.

CHAPTER TWENTY-FIVE

ICE CREAM TRUCK

Pattie somehow managed to survive her sleepless night in the prison observatory. At four the next morning a bright light came on overhead. A second later, without even a knock to announce his presence, a burly, militant looking correctional officer with a surly attitude slam banged the door against the glass wall and barged in. Pattie bolted upright, squinted and blinked in discomfort at the glare. She rubbed her eyes several times and watched, as the officer lobbed a pair of work boots onto the floor at the foot of her bunk.

"Listen up. At the beginning of each day, you will be issued a clean uniform, just like this one," he said, as he tossed a clean pair of gray sweat pants and a maroon tee shirt onto the edge of her bunk.

"Each uniform has been worn by countless other inmates before you. Once they're collected at the end of each day, they'll get laundered and recycled to another inmate the next day. You keep the boots. The boots and the uniform are to be worn every day from lights on until lights out. So, since it's lights on as of right NOW—get dressed," he said, in a raspy voice.

His bored tone indicated he must have made this speech at least a hundred times. She stared at him until he finally left, slamming the door behind him. She removed whatever remained of the wretched paper jump suit, threw it on top of the garbage heap and hurriedly changed into the uniform. She was grateful to at least to be dressed in something made of cloth, but she found the boots uncomfortable. They were solid, rigid leather, a half a size too small for her and even though she hadn't yet begun to walk in them, they were already chafing her heels. And since they did not come with a pair of socks, there was nothing to buffer her feet against the inevitable blisters that she knew would soon be forming. She sat on the bunk. A few minutes later the officer returned. He stood in the doorway and pointed to the dingy hallway just outside the door. A group of about sixteen other inmates were standing in line. Some were very rough looking and they were all dressed in the same boots and uniform she wore. She walked out into the hallway and started to head for the front of the line. The officer pointed to the back of the line.

"The line forms to the rear," he barked.

She immediately turned around and moved toward the end of the line. He gave the command and the prisoners slowly filed down to the cafeteria. They were all served the same breakfast, a mushy, grey gruel. To Pattie, it seemed even more hideous than the inedible mess from the night before. After breakfast, the prisoners were all ordered to place their hands behind their backs in order to get handcuffed. When it was Pattie's turn, the handcuffs dug into her skin in the exact place as the day before. And since she hadn't been treated for the original abrasions, it was painful. After the prisoners were all handcuffed, they were shackled with leg irons and chained to one another. Once the correctional officers were convinced that the procession was secure, they steered the prisoners past row upon row of locked, dismal, numbered, cages that housed prisoners who cat called to them. The chains and leg irons were so heavy, Pattie felt as if she were dragging lead pipes around. Each step felt more torturous than the last. Her entire body hurt from her original injuries, as well as from the new pain in her legs, heels and wrists. The sounds of doors opening and clanging shut and buzzers wore down what little was left of her nervous system. Once the women got outside, they had no coats or jackets to protect them from the cold gusts of wind that whipped around their bare arms and faces. Pattie looked up at the clear, blue sky and the strong sunlight as if it belonged to a completely different universe from the one she had inhabited for the last eighteen hours.

"All aboard the ice cream truck" an officer bellowed through his bullhorn, as another officer led the prisoners across the asphalt to the grimy, windowless van that was waiting to transport them to the White Plains Courthouse.

They probably call it that because it's white, Pattie thought to herself.

The correctional officers, who normally didn't permit running when their charges were unfettered, suddenly barked at the inmates to "move it" and "step livelier."

"I'm already moving as fast as I can" one inmate cried out in frustration. She had a scar over her left eye.

A young, female officer in training interpreted the comment as "insolence", so she decided to try out her new pepper spray. She pumped a generous dose into the defenseless prisoner's eyes. She even chuckled to herself as she watched her hapless victim cry, struggle and cough without benefit of her hands to help her. Now that the woman was unable to see, she had an even harder time climbing up the steps of the poorly heated bus. As Pattie took her place in one of the cold metal seats, she noticed that all the correctional officers, except the driver, were armed with a rifle. One officer waved his rifle around in one hand, while he held his trusty bullhorn in the other. Once the last prisoner was finally loaded onto the van, the driver closed the door and lurched into first gear. Unable to even wipe her eyes or blow her nose, the inmate who had been pepper sprayed continued to snivel and pant for the duration of the ride and Pattie silently commiserated with her.

CHAPTER TWENTY-SIX

WHEN I GET MY NAME IN LIGHTS

Westchester District Attorney, Katrina Nero, was an ambitious go getter. An attractive brunette who was barely over five foot two, her reputation embodied the statement, "dynamite comes in small packages". And she never missed an opportunity to demonstrate that. Although she usually delegated arraignments to one of her many underlings, since Pattie's case involved allegations "of a lawyer gone wrong," it generated a great deal of notoriety. And because Katrina could never resist seeing her name in lights, she decided to step out of character and handle Pattie's prosecution herself, right down to the arraignment.

She was dressed to the nines, in a severely cut, unornamented black silk suit, in order to impress upon the Judge, Reginald and most especially the media, that "this is a bad day for the Legal System when a lawyer turns rogue." She instructed the court officers that upon Reginald's arrival, they were to escort him to her office immediately.

Reginald Reese was no slouch either when it came to capturing publicity. Dressed to kill in a navy blue Armani suit, he breezed into Katrina's office, where he found her lying in wait for him behind her massive desk. His intuition told him the best way to put her on the defensive was by playing it cool. So, he flashed his most charming smile and introduced himself.

Although Katrina felt nervous, she did her best to deflect from it. She stood and offered him her hand. After their handshake, she gestured to a chair on the other side of her desk. When they were both seated, Reginald wasted no time in addressing the situation.

"Shame on you, my dear Attorney Nero, for wrongfully pinning these allegations on my poor, innocent client. She's an attorney herself you know, with an impeccable track record. Plus, she's got a heart of gold. The one you SHOULD be going after is the real killer, Willie Hudson."

Katrina closed her eyes, tossed her head back and shook her glorious mane. Then she put her hand up like a stop sign.

"Listen Reginald, your client probably did both of them in," she quipped.

Reginald shook his head.

"You're not fooling me. The only reason you're using the unfortunate Attorney Anwald as a patsy, is because she's easier for you to catch than Willie

Hudson. You don't even know where he is at this point. Do you?"

When she didn't answer him, he continued on his rant.

"Well, whether or not you ever find him, that's your problem, but I'll be damned before I ever allow my client to do his time for him."

Katrina removed two pictures of Pattie from the file in front of her and spread them out on her desk. One was the Gothic picture with the witchy moon pendant and red lips that was spread all over the media and the other was one of the pictures Kitty took of her shortly after she arrived at the emergency room in a bedraggled condition. Reginald pointed at the hospital picture. Before he could even ask how she managed to get hold of it, a middle aged man knocked on the door and walked into the office. He introduced himself as Jasper Islington, the Presiding Judge on the case. Reginald stood and the two of them shook hands.

"Hi, I'm Reginald Reese, defense counsel for Pattie Anwald."

"I've heard a lot of good things about you. Anyway, are you two making any headway in terms of ironing anything out?"

Reginald shook his head

"Actually, the People fail to see just how big a blunder they're making, by trying to pin the rap for their seriously flawed case on the alleged victim's harmless lawyer. First of all, they have no witnesses. More importantly, they don't even have a body. Quite frankly, I can't fathom why they're even taking the trouble to prosecute her. She's the wrong defendant," Reginald said.

"Well, this should all prove to be very interesting. In any event, I'll see you both in the courtroom," Judge Islington said.

He left before Reginald could utter another word.

CHAPTER TWENTY-SEVEN

LAWYERS, GUNS, AND MONEY

The prison van pulled into the garage that was located next to the lockup in the sub-basement of the Courthouse. It was none too soon for Pattie. She felt nauseous from the diesel exhaust she inhaled for the duration of the trip. The officers brought the chain of prisoners through the gate, counted them and eventually herded them into dreary, chilly, dimly lit holding cells, where, with the exception of the time they were in the courtroom, they would spend the day. Shortly after the van arrived, Reginald went downstairs to confer with Pattie. By that time, she was so cold, so intimidated and in so much pain, she could barely stop shaking. Reginald reached out to comfort her, but it was more of a gesture than anything, since they were separated by a thick pane of plexiglass. They both picked up the phone and she cleared her throat.

"Oh, thank God you're here! What a disaster this is. After all the arraignments I've done, I never thought I would wind up as a defendant in one. Do you think those two crazy cops only locked me up to scare me and teach me a lesson? You know. Because, I'm a woman with too big a mouth? Or do you think they really intend to keep me here?"

He shook his head.

"Listen to me. I seriously doubt they're playing with you in order to teach you any lessons. The police report claims you killed Leland LeRoux. And as outrageous as the allegation may be, Katrina Nero, the DA, is not only standing by it, she's all tricked out and ready to prove it. I've already met with both Ryan and Jordan Armstrong on your behalf. They came in to see me. I'll do my best to get you acquitted, but as you know, I can never guarantee the outcome of any case."

She nodded.

"I understand. Believe me, I've given that same 'I can't guarantee the outcome' speech to my own clients a thousand times."

Reginald nodded.

"I'm sure you have. Now, if I can arrange for bail, I believe Jordan will pay it, no matter how high it is."

Pattie looked surprised.

"Really?"

Reginald nodded.

"Yes. And by the way, he's also paying my fee on your behalf. In addition, Ryan filled me in on the situations involving both your landlord and that idiot

Brad at the Legal Aid Office. I know those issues aren't a top priority for you right now, but I'll be handling them for you as well, unless you tell me you don't want me to."

She nodded and breathed a sigh of relief.

"I definitely want you to."

"OK. And I'm sure it goes without saying that I'll never bind you to anything, unless you agree to it," he added.

She nodded.

"It's also crucial that you refrain from discussing this case with anyone else but me. You never know who you're really talking to. Overly zealous prosecutors have been known to occasionally PLANT undercover investigators in a suspect's cell, in order to elicit as much information as they can to use against them at trial. I'm not saying that this WILL happen to you, but only that it has happened."

With that, he slid a pen and a set of agreements through the slit at the bottom of the window. She nodded, read them and signed them. Then she slid them all back to him.

"By the way, as your attorney, I will be the ONLY visitor whose visits and phone calls don't get recorded, so once again, I'm urging you to be mindful of what you say at all times."

She nodded again. Then an officer knocked on the door, handcuffed her and transported her up to the courtroom.

CHAPTER TWENTY-EIGHT

THE ARRAIGNMENT

Pattie shivered as she entered the brightly lit, over-packed courtroom. Her teeth were still chattering and her feet hurt from being cramped by her tight boots, with no socks to buffer them. She stood next to Reginald and tried desperately to concentrate on what was happening. In spite of her pain and terror, she turned around and looked through the sea of faces until she managed to catch a glimpse of Jordan and her parents. Lou and Ryan were standing next to them. They both looked sharp in their uniforms. Having them see her the way she was, embarrassed her. As she turned to face forward again, she caught sight of Katrina Nero glaring at her.

"Pattie Anwald how do you plead to the charge of Murder in the First Degree?" Judge Islington asked.

Pattie cleared her throat and pled not guilty. Before Katrina could even open her mouth, Reginald took the reins.

"Your Honor, other than a strong opinion, uttered by an obsessive and relentless prosecutor, whose very motive in bringing these charges so prematurely may have more to do with a pending primary and election next year, than"—

"Objection!" Katrina yelled.

"Sustained," the Judge said.

"The people have nothing to substantiate these flimsy allegations, much less prove them beyond a reasonable doubt. Armed with her own speculation, a tiny file that contains a police report filled with conjecture and poppycock and without even a murder weapon or body, the People are setting Attorney Anwald up to take the fall for a murder she in fact had nothing whatsoever to do with. And why? Because it's more convenient for them to scapegoat Ms. Anwald, than it is to invest the time and resources to locate the whereabouts of the real perpetrator. Or even a real victim. And the fact that such a thing could happen in America is frightening. Quite frankly I'm appalled. That's why I'm filing this Motion to Dismiss," Reginald said, in a voice filled with righteous indignation.

"Motion Denied. There's no way I'm dismissing a capital case," Judge Islington said.

Reginald was undaunted.

"As for bail, Your Honor, Attorney Anwald's family and friends all believe in her innocence. And as you can see, they are present in court to support her today," Reginald said, as he turned and stretched his arm in the direction of Chet, Edie, Lou and Ryan.

"It goes without saying, but I'll say it anyway,

Attorney Anwald has no prior offenses and has never been arrested before this," he added.

Judge Islington held up his hand as if to say "stop." He interrupted Reginald and remanded Pattie to prison. When he banged down the gavel, Pattie sighed, cleared her throat and whispered in Reginald's ear. The lockup officer jerked Pattie away, just as the clerk called the next case. Shortly after she was returned to the lockup, another officer removed her handcuffs and fed her lunch, which consisted of a dry bologna sandwich accompanied by four ounces of watery, lukewarm evaporated milk. Meanwhile, outside on the courthouse stairs Katrina Nero bragged to the media.

"The behavior on the part of this cold blooded lawyer gone rogue is so scandalous, I actually managed to win both motions in court today without even opening my mouth. She's as guilty as sin and I intend to prove it!"

In the late afternoon, after every prisoner on Pattie's van had their case heard, the officers called it a day. They handcuffed the prisoners, secured them in their leg irons and belly chained them to each other for their ride back to the prison.

CHAPTER TWENTY-NINE

FOLSOM PRISON BLUES

The brakes on the prison van groaned as it came to a screeching halt. The door slapped open, but the motor kept idling, as the correctional officers led the chain of women inside the prisoner's entrance to the compound. After one of the officers took attendance from the names on a clipboard, he separated Pattie from the others and gave her to another officer, who steered her through a rank smelling hallway. When the door to a dirty, chilly, dimly lit 'holding cell' opened, the officer pushed her down onto the bunk, uncuffed her and left. She jumped when the heavy steel door clanged shut.

It took her several seconds before she could regain her composure. Once she did, she looked around. The toilet was a shiny, bright red color. There was no enclosure around it to ensure privacy, nor even a toilet seat and what was worse, it was backed up. However, the most bizarre thing about it, was the huge fright clown's face that someone had taken the trouble to paint on the wall behind it. The toilet itself was the clown's mouth. The sign above it read, "Do Not Throw Any Sanitary Napkins or Paper Towels in Me," which was interesting, since neither sanitary napkins, paper towels, nor for that matter, even toilet paper were anywhere to be found.

Pattie was terrified. She felt nauseous from the smell. Her flesh crawled and her heart would not stop thumping. In addition, her feet hurt due to the blisters that had sprung up on her heels and toes from all the walking she had done in her ill-fitting boots. She sat on the bunk for well over an hour, until a big, scowling, correctional officer opened the door. He was built like a bull, with broad shoulders and a barrel chest. And he had a crewcut. His uniform showcased his muscular body. His nametag read "Garth." Something about him troubled Pattie and she was too afraid of him to make eye contact, so she didn't notice him sneering at her as if she were a cockroach. He grabbed her arm.

"On your feet," he said, as he pulled her off of the bunk.

Then he pinned her arms behind her back and handcuffed her as tightly as he could.

"Listen up. You've been assigned to MY tier, the one I supervise. The girls there have all been following your case on the news, which makes you a celebrity right now. I don't want no commotion on account of you. So, as long as you NEVER undermine me, question my authority or for that matter, cause me any trouble at all, either on purpose or by accident, we'll get along just fine. Learn how to play by my rules. Now get moving," he said in a voice that was a dead ringer for Broderick Crawford's.

He dragged her out the door and led her down the hall, through a series of mazes. When Pattie almost felt as if she'd reached the ends of the earth, Garth punched a code into a security system and a heavy steel door slid open. He pushed her through it. When it clanged shut behind them, she shivered. Twenty or so inmates had formed a circle around two other inmates, who appeared to be engaged in a quarrel. Dressed identically to Pattie, they came in all colors, shapes, sizes and ages. From what Pattie could see, every one of them appeared unwholesome and generally rough around the edges. They were all tinged with an ashen gray pallor, as if they never got enough sunlight or air. And their faces were harsh, mean looking and wizened with tension. Just then Pattie had a thought. She wondered how long it would take her to wind up looking exactly like they did. And it made her feel sad.

One of the women involved in the altercation appeared to be tougher than the others. She was an unattractive behemoth with a short crop of tiny gray and dirty blonde ringlets. They made her head look like a peanut perched on top of a buoy. She stood in a buffalo stance, with her hands on her hips like a Queen Bee. She wore no bra, so her massive breasts hung down in her maroon tee shirt. She scowled, eyeball to eyeball at her opponent, a leathery looking, yet wiry old senior citizen. A young girl with shoulder length, straight brown hair and red rimmed, anguish filled eyes looked up at the obese prisoner with admiration. A young female correctional officer with a thick, bull neck, whose French braids hugged her scalp and whose nametag read "Sistine", stood by, neither saying anything to escalate nor de-escalate the exchange. She wore her uniform pants tucked inside her boots, Nazi style.

The behemoth turned toward Pattie and gave her the once over. Then she repositioned herself with her back to Pattie, in order to keep Pattie from joining the circle. The young brunette also turned toward Pattie and stared her down until it looked as if her eyes would burn a hole right through Pattie's soul. Pattie supposed the girl was some kind of drug fiend. And those two interactions were the only welcome Pattie ever received.

The elderly inmate shook her fist.

"Listen Dutch, don't you say 'excuse me' to ME! Oh no! YOU excuse ME! I don't excuse you. After all, you may try to act like ziss bully, but za troos ist you're chust anuzza inmate locked up like za rest of uns! You haven't even been here very long. Besides, you haff no clout here. All you got ist your blubber, you vale," she yelled, in a heavy German accent.

Just as Dutch lifted her fist to shake it in retaliation,

Garth uncuffed Pattie and announced it was chow time. The women quickly broke up the circle and formed a single line. Sistine walked up to Pattie, got within an inch of her face and stared at her with an expression so hateful, she almost looked like a gargoyle. She pointed to the end of the line.

"While you're waiting, AT THE END OF THE LINE WHERE YOU BELONG, I might as well tell you that breakfast is between four and five every morning. Lunch is around eleven and dinner is around six pm. There are no in between meal snacks here, even for undernourished skeletons who look like they're 'starving to death'," she bellowed.

Then she turned on her heel and walked away to join Garth. Together she and Garth looked everyone over. When Garth was satisfied with how orderly the line was, he marched everyone down to the cafeteria, where that night's "dinner" was almost as unappetizing as the previous night's concoction. It consisted of a plain hot dog on a piece of beige, unbuttered bread. Someone had plopped a dollop of canned baked beans next to it, without even having bothered to heat them up. A helping of lukewarm fried onions flanked the hot dog on the other side. Pattie thought the bread was the least disgusting item on her Styrofoam tray, so she decided to save it for last and treat it like her dessert.

But Dutch had other plans. Her suspicious eyes followed Pattie's every move until she finally approached Pattie's table. She loomed over Pattie with a gleam in her eye. Pattie's heart raced and her palms clammed up. Pattie was tiny and frail compared to everyone there, especially "Dutch" and she had a million butterflies in her stomach. No one had ever intimidated her this much before; not her mother, nor those two God awful investigators. Not even judges, Garth, Willie Hudson or Leland LeRoux had ever made her feel as scared as she was at that moment. Although she was on high alert, she tried not to betray her emotions. Instead, she sat up as straight as she could, turned to Dutch and looked her in the eye. Then she cleared her throat. Everyone was riveted.

Dutch didn't say a word. There were matters on her mind far more pressing than discourse. She got as close to Pattie as she could, pounded the table next to Pattie's tray and swooped down. Before Pattie even had time to realize what was happening, Dutch snatched the bread out from under her hot dog. Everyone laughed, except for Pattie, who gasped and jumped. Dutch tilted her head back and literally force fed herself the bread. As she pushed it into her mouth and down her throat, her eyes rolled back like a shark's. Four seconds later the bread was gone. Dutch's dirty ringlets shook in accompaniment, as she snapped her head back into place. She smirked at Pattie like the proverbial cat that had swallowed the canary. Then she suddenly pivoted around and waddled towards the young brunette's tray.

Feeling slightly safer once Dutch was gone, Pattie

managed to bite into her hot dog. After grimacing at its water logged taste and rubbery texture, she abandoned it and tried to choke down her onions.

The brunette had a hangdog expression. When Dutch hovered over her tray and snatched her bread, she never made any fuss at all. Finally, after picking through the brunette's tray, Dutch returned to her own untouched tray. No one had dared to even breathe on it during her absence. She wolfed down her own bread in two bites and ate the rest of her dinner in peace. When she was done, she glanced over at Pattie. Then she lumbered back onto her feet and returned to see what remained on Pattie's tray.

Everyone stopped eating and watched, as Dutch's eyes zeroed in on Pattie's onions. Pattie cradled her arm around her tray as if to guard it, but that didn't prevent Dutch from snatching Pattie's milk container. She downed the lukewarm milk and drained the container with two enormous gulps. Then, she crushed it and gingerly lobbed it down onto Pattie's plate.

"LESSON NUMBER ONE about the way life REALLY works here in this shit can: Everyone pretty much lets me just take whatever I want off their tray without bellyaching too much about it. LESSON NUMBER TWO—as you probably also figured out, judging by tonight's dinner, we rarely get any fresh vegetables or fruit to eat. But the good news is, every once in a while we get a bit of fresh meat, so naturally that becomes the flavor du jour."

Fritzi, the elderly German lady nodded in agreement. Dutch glanced at Fritzi and nodded back at her. Then she looked at Pattie.

"Anyhow, LESSON NUMBER THREE—in here, your friends, your enemies and your lovers are all one and the same."

Fritzi nodded.

"Vell, zatt's pretty much za same sing on za outside too."

Dutch once again glanced at Fritzi, nodded at her and then turned her attention back to Pattie.

"And last but not least, LESSON NUMBER FOUR. I may look fat to you, but don't let that stop you from remembering that I'm the most popular bitch in this place. You wanna know why I'm so popular? Because, ever since the day I ended up snapping on my dried up old scab of a husband Ned, I ALWAYS seen to it that EVERY PIECE OF FRESH meat on this tier, starts out as MY bitch, especially you younger broads. Because nobody's gonna do to me what that old whoremaster done to me. And that's why it's not just the stuff on the food trays I get first dibs at," Dutch said.

Dutch smiled. And when everyone saw Dutch smiling, they all smiled right along with her. The only people who weren't smiling were the brunette, Sistine, Garth, who bellowed for everyone to clean up and get on line and Pattie, who couldn't stop shaking.

CHAPTER THIRTY

BABY SHARK

Dutch was a woman on a mission and her mission wasn't just about stealing Pattie's food. Once all the prisoners were back on the tier, she walked up to Pattie, looked her straight in the eye and shook her fist in Pattie's face. Pattie did her best not to flinch, but she did end up frowning and clearing her throat. Everyone else slowly formed a circle around them.

"I seen on TV that you're in here for murder in the first degree. Is it true?" Dutch asked.

Pattie nodded.

"Well, that's what I'm charged with."

Dutch whistled and clapped her hands together. Fritzi's eyes lit up.

"Wow. That's pretty cold blooded. You really hit the big time. And even though I been charged with the same thing, that don't make you equal to me. Because as far as I'm concerned, you're nothing. It's not even worth my while to snap you in two," Dutch said.

Fritzi looked at Pattie.

"Anyvay, not to chanche za subcheckt but I'll bet you can't guess vye I'm in here!"

Pattie gave it some thought. She figured it might not be such a bad idea to put her mind to some use, because there didn't seem to be any other intellectual outlets for her.

"Some white collar kind of a crime?"

Fritzi shook her head excitedly and chuckled.

"No. Za troos ist zay haff me in here for schmashing some schnott nost sixteen year olt kitt in za face who voz trespassing against mein property! So venn I tolt him to bead it, he told me to go unt fack mein selbst! He voss bigger zan me unt he vanted to fack me app but he's za von vot got facked up inschtett venn he hit za grount from mein punstch. Zay vonted me to cop a plea, but I don't fall on mein sword for nobody! Besites, if any of zees courts or chatches hatt any insight zemselfs, vitch zay apparently don't, zay coot see zat zensitive people like you unt me haff no business being here in za first place!"

Dutch and the dark haired girl frowned at each other. Then Dutch snorted.

"Excuse me? I don't have no business being here either! Who do you think you are, one uppin' people, you Nazi son of a bitch?" Dutch snarled.

"Yeah and guess what? I don't belong in here either," the dark haired girl said.

In a hurry to defuse the situation, Pattie changed the subject.

"So what WAS your job on the outside?" She asked Fritzi.

"I'm an artist. Und Gott how I miss it! I coot schtill create some great art verk, even in here, if I could only afford za zoopplies," she said.

Dutch looked at Pattie and squinted.

"Speaking of occupations, they said on TV you're an attorney. And if that's true, you must be a special kind of stupid to sink so low as to wind up here as one of us. Sheesh, they must let anybody become a lawyer nowadays, because my own Legal Aide mook is just about as stupid as you are. And on top of it, he really don't give a shit about me OR my case either. Looks like I'll be needing you to do some research for me and ride shotgun on whatever he is and isn't doing, because I just don't trust him."

Pattie instinctively knew by Dutch's tone of voice and body language, Dutch was making a demand, rather than a request. Even though Pattie realized she was a hostage, she also knew she couldn't just give her services away. So she decided to make a deal. It certainly wasn't the most stellar transaction of her lifetime, but it was the best bargain she could strike under her current set of circumstances.

"Well, if you and the others develop a 'hands off policy' when it comes to me, starting right now, I think we could probably work something out. And by the way, when I say hands off, I MEAN keep your paws off of me in EVERY sense of the word. Including my food. And that goes for all of you," she said, scanning the circle.

"Ya, except I don't take orders from Dutch," Fritzi said.

When Pattie looked worriedly over at Fritzi, Dutch snickered.

"Listen, if you're my ally and I say to leave you alone, none of the others will dare go near you, including Fritzi," she said.

The dark haired girl looked disgusted. She suddenly asked Garth whether she could take a shower. She also mentioned she needed to shave her legs and underarms. Garth walked over to a padlocked supply cabinet. He pointed at a clipboard and the pen that was attached to it by a chain. She signed her name, along with the time. Garth solemnly handed her a small, coarse, terry cloth towel, a little hotel sized bar of soap and a precious disposable razor. Then he reminded her she had to return the razor to him within the next half hour.

After she left, Garth turned on the TV and tuned into the football game. He had money riding on the outcome, so he felt impelled to keep track of the score. Everyone sat on or around the concrete bench in front of the television and settled in. Pattie gazed at the game and pretended to watch it, but in fact, she actually paid no attention to it at all. Instead, she tuned it out and pondered everything she had gone through since Thanksgiving. After a few minutes, the dark haired girl bounded back onto the floor, wielding the razor. Glaring at Pattie with a look of pure hatred, she ran up to Pattie and got within an inch of her face.

"Everybody knows I'M Dutch's bitch, you fucking whore" she screamed, as she took a swipe at Pattie's left eye.

Pattie snapped to attention. She used the skills she had learned in judo to throw her head backwards and get the girl off balance. Before she could stab Pattie in the eye, Garth's instincts kicked in. Leaping to his feet, he went from zero to ten, ran behind the girl and wrapped his gargantuan arms around her. Then he squeezed her as if he were doing the Heimlich maneuver. He maintained the pressure until she lost her breath. At that point, she had no choice but to drop the razor. When she did, he kicked it out of the way and released the pressure on her. Sistine rushed over to the razor, picked it up and stuck it in her shirt pocket, so that none of the inmates would have a chance to grab it. Pattie was so unnerved, she sat there hyperventilating, as she watched Garth ram the girl into the wall. The girl's breathing was labored from having been squeezed so hard. She groaned, doubled over in pain and put her hands on her thighs. She panted for a few minutes. Then she burst into tears.

"What am I supposed to do? She pissed me off! Who the hell does she think she is, muscling her way in here trying to steal Dutch out from under me?" She managed to gasp out the words.

"You got it backwards, Colette. She said she DON'T want Dutch touching her," Garth said.

When Colette finally caught her breath and stood upright, Garth closed both his hands into two tight fists and pummeled her face with all his might. Once his adrenaline kicked in, he couldn't stop. Colette knew resisting him or fighting back would only make matters worse for her, so she ended up cowering and grunting, while he turned her into a human punching bag.

The sliding door to the corridor opened. It was Larabee, the gentlest officer on the tier and quite possibly in the entire prison. She was returning from her dinner break. When she saw the fight, she gasped. Although the facility only housed women, upon becoming inmates, if they wanted to survive, they were forced to leave whatever femininity they possessed, outside the prison compound. And most of the female correctional officers did that voluntarily. However, Larabee was an exception. The last bastion of gentility and caring to be found, she looked out of place with her movie star looks, long blonde hair and Barbie doll shape. Her instincts to curb the situation kicked in, so she ran over to Garth, in a failed attempt to distract him from continuing his assault on Colette. At that point, Colette's nose was bleeding all over the floor. Garth pulled the razor from Sistine's pocket, snapped it in half and stuck both halves in his own pocket. He motioned for Sistine to handcuff Colette and take her down to Segregation.

When Pattie got back to her cell, she threw up her dinner.

CHAPTER THIRTY-ONE

SUSPENDED IN GAFFA

The following morning, when Lou reported for work, Lieutenant Purdy, his commander at the Detective Division, called him straight back to his office. When Lou got there, Lieutenant Purdy's face was red. He was frowning as he waved a copy of the morning's newspaper and shoved it under Lou's nose. The front page featured the stock photo the media had been using of Pattie wearing her crescent moon pendant and looking very Gothic. Lou grimaced the second he saw it.

"What do you want me to do? After all, I really can't help it if I'm related to an asshole, you know. There's at least one in every family. What's that old saying? You can pick your friends but you can't pick your relatives?" Lou said.

"Well, whoever wrote the article in this rag is singing a different tune. According to them, you were all dressed up in your uniform, doing just about everything you could to be a supportive brother to her at her arraignment. So, don't even TRY to deny it.

Sorry, but unfortunately you're gonna have to hand me your badge and gun. From there you can run, not walk, over to Ralph Carmen, the shop steward. See if he can help you get a hearing underway, because as of right now you're suspended."

Lou unfastened his gun from his holster and carefully placed it on the Lieutenant's desk. Then he did the same thing with his badge.

CHAPTER THIRTY-TWO

DUCHESS OF GLOAT

Anne Carey, Pattie's nemesis in the arraignment court, squealed with delight when she read the morning's headlines. She literally pinched her scrawny arm to make sure she wasn't dreaming. Since her boss, District Attorney Connor Dane, continually bragged that the door to his office was always open, she was hoping to rub his nose in the story. She read it on the elevator and as soon as the door opened, she closed the paper, ran down the hall and barged into his office. When she got there she waved the front page in his face.

"Connor, Connor, look! We've got a little excitement in our midst! Have you seen THIS attention grabber?" She asked.

She was completely out of breath from running and her face was pinched up with malice. She looked down at his desk. Connor's newspaper was already spread across his desk and from the looks of things, he HAD already read it.

"Sure. I mean who hasn't? Like you said, it's an

attention grabber. Anyway, even though she's never been 'my cup of tea,' so to speak, that doesn't mean I think she did it," he said.

Annie waved her hand in dismissal and decided to take the paper straight to someone who would appreciate the story, Norton Bakerman, the court officer who ran the metal detector at the public entrance to the courthouse.

CHAPTER THIRTY-THREE

RAID

By Saturday, even though Pattie had only spent three days in her strange new environment, she felt worn down to the point of exhaustion. No wonder they called it a "stretch". The hours weighed on her shoulders like a yoke, as she settled into the dull succession of endless days and sleepless nights. She began to realize that prison life was mainly about marking time during a long, unpleasant existence that consisted of aimless restrictions. The cellblock was cold and she often felt as if the walls were closing in on her. She couldn't decide who was more odd; the guards with the "authority trips" they felt their jobs entitled them to or the prisoners, many of whom were often violent, intrusive bullies. The guards arbitrarily and capriciously pushed the prisoners around like pawns in a surrealistic chess game. There was no island of peace nor solitude for anyone, except perhaps Garth, who occasionally exercised the privilege of closing the door to his tiny office. But no one else had any way of retreating from the ceaseless pressure or the constant gongs and buzzers.

By early afternoon the temperature had risen to sixty five degrees. As a result, Garth decided to give the prisoners a break from the monotony by letting them out into the exercise yard for an hour of fresh air, open sky and sunlight. Even though Pattie had never felt warm since her stint in the reservoir, she actually welcomed the fresh breeze that blew through her hair and caressed her neck. She hoped that Mother Nature would continue to cooperate for as long as possible, because she knew this hour of outdoor recreation was as close to a sanctuary as she could hope to find.

"You better take advantage of it while it lasts, because once it turns cold again, we ain't going nowheres for a long time. After all, we don't got no coats or nothing," Dutch said.

"Vell Dutch, at least you've got your padding to keep you varm," Fritzi said.

Pattie tried to tune them out. She gazed into space, at nothing in particular and wondered whether she would wind up living the rest of her life behind bars. Just the thought of it actually caused her to shudder. She sighed and pondered on how she would survive. Thinking about it depressed her. She knew she needed to figure out a way to lift her mood rather than add to the many miseries that weighed it down, so she forced herself to face the fact that even though she had spent her entire life in New York City, she had never really been removed from the natural world. Flowers, trees and nature had always surrounded her, ever since she could remember. And she had taken it all for granted. Even when she stepped outside her rundown apartment, all she ever had to do was lift her eyes and look out at the horizon beyond the crushing realism of the South Street Sea Port and the sludge of the East River. And although her mother could never be characterized as a "people person," she was certainly good with plants. Something was always in bloom in her mother's garden. Whenever one plant's glory subsided, another's sprang to life. She thought about the sea foam roses and the flowering pear tree in her parents' back yard. They looked different throughout each season. And even on a December day such as this, there was still holly to be found there. Her mind wandered to the potted flowering tea rose Jordan had given her on their first date. It was the only living thing she could ever truly call her own. She closed her eyes, tried to remember exactly what it looked like and hoped that somehow it wasn't dead. She opened her eyes, looked up at the blinding sunlight and silently thanked that yellow fireball, for simply being there to greet her and warm her chilly bones that afternoon.

Just then, a correctional officer escorted a new inmate through the gate and led her to Garth. Roughly Pattie's age, she was more cute than pretty and her big blue eyes were wide open, as if she couldn't believe where she was. Pattie could understand why, since she struck Pattie as the type of person who, like Fritzi, didn't "belong" in prison. Her shoulder length blonde hair had dried into frizzy strings, no doubt after her delousing shower. The officer uncuffed her, ordered her to mingle with the others and when she was out of earshot, he whispered something in Garth's ear. He and Garth both turned to the building and the officer pointed at it. Garth nodded, gave him the "OK" sign and the officer left.

As the newcomer got closer to Pattie, a pickup truck drove onto the compound. It was accompanied by a terrible stench that wafted toward the exercise yard. Pattie gasped and immediately pinched her nose as it stopped, turned and backed up to the rear door of the main kitchen. The odor was so strong the new girl bent over and stuck her head between her knees. A few seconds later, when she attempted to stand up straight again, she lost her balance and began to topple over. Almost as a reflex more than anything else, Pattie reached out to help keep her from collapsing. When Garth spotted her, he blew the chrome whistle around his neck and pointed at her.

"No physical contact," he barked.

"My God! What is that horrible smell? Did one of the toilets back up or something?" The new girl asked.

Dutch chuckled.

"Every so often a pig farmer comes here to buy our surplus food. He uses it to slop his hogs," she said.

Pattie started to walk upwind. The new girl followed her and Fritzi tagged along with them.

"By the way, my name is Miranda."

Pattie nodded.

"I'm Pattie."

"So, I may as vell ask you right now unt get it out of za vay, who dit you kill?" Fritzi asked.

Miranda shook her head.

"I didn't kill anybody or even commit any other crime either. I guess I'm what you'd call a victim of the system. And I don't even have a clue as to how the system even works," Miranda said.

"That's 'cause it don't work," Dutch said.

"Vell, all you neet to know is zat votever else happens, chusst don't let zem break you," Fritzi said.

"I really don't know. I once heard that at some point, everybody breaks," Miranda said.

Feeling suddenly threatened, but not understanding why, Pattie merely frowned, nodded and cleared her throat. And then, it hit her. Miranda was the spy Reginald warned her about. A breeze blew down hard from the northeast. The balmy temperature plummeted without warning. Fritzi rubbed her wiry old arms, as if to ward off the unexpected chill.

"Gee, with the weather changing this rapidly, I hope I don't wind up getting sick," Miranda said.

Pattie nodded.

"I'm beyond worrying about getting sick. I'm working on trying not to die," she said.

"Za Government plays mitt za wezzer you know," Fritzi said.

Garth picked up his bullhorn.

"OK, youse jailbirds, get into a single line for reentry. On the double," he ordered, in his gravelly voice.

"What purpose does it serve for that lout to hurry us like this? It's not as if any of us have anywhere else to be," Miranda said, as they lined up.

Fritzi nodded.

"I ackree. Ve're all chusst schtuck here in ziss dissmall place."

Garth glared at Miranda and Fritzi. He picked up his bull horn again.

"Hop to it and SHUT UP!" He bellowed.

Tiny snowflakes began to fall. Pattie cupped her hand around her eyes and looked up at the sky.

"Holy Cow! Where did all the sudden flurries come from?" She asked, on her way to the line.

She stuck her tongue out and caught a snowflake on it. Garth saw her and gave her a dirty look.

"Knock it off," he barked.

Pattie sighed, stuck her tongue back in her head and got on line.

"Now move it! All a youse," Garth roared, as if he were a drover herding a team of mules across the prairie.

CHAPTER THIRTY-FOUR

ROCK THE BOAT

Pattie's two teenaged clients, Bonnie and Justin, were both blond. Although they could have passed for brother and sister, they weren't related at all. They lived at Beau Rivage, together with another of Pattie's clients Thomas Amissah and others. Thomas was bi racial. He wore his hair in dreadlocks, the tips of which had been dipped in sepia.

Saturday was unseasonably warm. Being typical teenagers, Bonnie, Justin and Thomas wanted to take advantage of the good weather and hang out in the fresh air. They decided to sneak out without their jackets or overcoats. In fact, they left Beau Rivage wearing light, spring weight clothing. Bonnie wore a white button down long sleeve blouse with a black mini skirt, black tights and black Mary Jane style sneakers. Justin wore a pair of black jeans with white Adidas. And Thomas wore baggy jeans that were strategically ripped at the knees, along with an oversized navy blue hoodie, blue on white Puma sneakers and a navy blue Yankee baseball cap he had planted on his head backwards and which he had tilted to one side. Plus he wore heavy gold chains and white designer sun glasses.

They all decided to eat lunch at a diner. When they got there, the hostess led them to a booth by a window. They plunked themselves down onto the seat like bundles of falling packages. The hostess handed them menus, lowered the blinds to keep the sun's glare out of their eyes and informed them their waitress would be with them momentarily. When the waitress arrived, Bonnie and Thomas ordered cheeseburgers. Thomas specified that his should be extra rare. Justin ordered an open hot turkey sandwich, complete with gravy, stuffing, mashed potatoes and cranberry sauce.

About an hour later, they finished their meals and pooled their money to pay the bill. Then they ran out, "forgetting" to leave a tip. When they got outside, the weather was still nice, so they decided to jump the turnstile, hop on the downtown subway and spend some time in Greenwich Village. When they got off at the Sheridan Square Station, they were heady with the feeling of freedom and adventure. They laughed and cracked jokes as they sauntered down Christopher Street. When they happened to walk past a New Age Shop, a number of glass pipes on display in the window caught Thomas' eye. He smiled slyly at his two companions and pointed. They chuckled because they knew he wanted to go inside and buy one.

Once inside, the trio browsed around the aisles and display cases that were chock full of smudge sticks, cauldrons, Tarot cards, oracle cards, Ouija Boards, crystals, incense, essential oils, metaphysical books, CD's, DVDs, jewelry and ritual tools. Thomas went to the aisle where the glass pipes were. He studied them all and picked out the one he liked best. When he lined up at the cash register to pay for the item, Justin and Bonnie lined up behind him.

By the time the trio got back outside again, something drastic had happened to the weather. The temperature had plummeted and a light coating of powdery snow had covered the sidewalk, quickly transforming New York's mellow fall shades of russet, tan and brown to a stark wintry white. The three underdressed teenagers looked shocked as they huddled in the doorway to keep warm and plan their next move. Justin peered out at the thick huge flakes that poured out of the stormy sky and turned back to Bonnie. Something about the way she smelled reminded him of the Satanic coven his parents ran. Triggered, he turned to her, shook his head in disbelief and tried to wave the smell away with his hand.

"What's the problem?" Bonnie asked, as she stood there shivering.

"You stink!"

She looked hurt.

"You mean my personality or the way I smell?"

Thomas grinned.

"Probably both," he chimed in.

Justin frowned and shook his head.

"I'm talking about your taste in toilet water. I really can't stand it."

Thomas chuckled.

"Toilet water?"

"What are you talking about? All I did was spray myself with something in the store called Oil of Musk. I think it's lovely and I can't believe you don't like it."

"Well, I don't like it at all. First of all, it smells like you just took a bath in it. And second of all, it's making me sick."

Thomas stepped out of the shelter of the doorway and stomped around on the snowy sidewalk. He turned around and checked to see what his footprints looked like. Then he spotted a dull, beige '96 Toyota Camry that was double parked. Its engine was running, but the driver was nowhere to be seen. When he pointed at it, Bonnie stepped out onto the sidewalk. She walked up to it, peered inside the window and tried the door handle. It was unlocked. She pulled the door open, turned to her companions and grinned. Thomas nodded, but Justin just shook his head and waved his hand in dismissal.

"Sorry, but I've got to get out of here," he said.

As he braved the storm and walked toward the subway station, Thomas ran around to the driver's side and gestured for Bonnie to get in on the passenger's side.

"Let's see if we can drive and catch up to him," he said.

He opened the door, slid into the seat and waited, as Bonnie got in. She slammed the door and watched Thomas play around with the dials. When he figured out which one controlled the heat, he cranked it up as high as it would go. He looked around until he finally found the windshield wiper control. He turned it on, then he turned to Bonnie. He grinned as he placed his hand on the gear shift. He ever so slightly shifted from "P" to "R". Because the pavement was dry when the owner had double parked the car, he hadn't bothered to engage the hand brake. But with the sudden accumulation of snow, the road was slippery and there was no traction. The owner of the car came out of the liquor store across the street, just in time to see his car rolling backward.

"HEY! That's my car," he yelled.

When Thomas heard him, he slammed on the brake, but instead of stopping, the car slid on the snow and spun out of control. Another driver coming down Christopher Street, honked his horn and slammed on his brake, but he couldn't avoid smashing into Thomas. A third driver behind the other driver, slammed on his brake and rear ended him, causing a three car accident. Within seconds, traffic came to a standstill. Drivers honked and cursed and pedestrians stopped to stare.

Thomas wanted to shift the car back into park, so

he and Bonnie could flee the scene, but because the commotion made him nervous, he shifted the wrong way, into neutral. The car swerved again and slid into a parked car.

"Hey! You're not supposed to move that car until the police come," a bystander yelled.

At that point, the owner of the Camry was frantic. He stood the two wine bottles he had been carrying, on the snow covered sidewalk. Then he whipped out his cell phone and dialed 911. Abandoning the bottles, he carefully crossed the street to try to get to his car. When Bonnie saw him coming, she reached over, threw the gear shift into park and opened her door. When she got out, Thomas grabbed his bag, inched his way down the seat and followed her out of the passenger's side door. Laughing while Bonnie fretted, Thomas ran in a westerly direction down Christopher Street and Bonnie was right behind him. Just as they rounded the corner onto Waverly Place, they encountered a speeding police cruiser, complete with full flashing lights and a screeching siren. The officer driving it was responding to the 911 call. He spotted Thomas and Bonnie, slowed the cruiser and came to a stop. Knowing they matched the description of the perpetrators, he got out, opened his door and chased them on foot. He was filled with frustration at the slippery sidewalk and the four legs that eluded his capture, but when Thomas dropped his bag and bent to pick it up, the officer finally had the chance to catch up with him. He reached out, grabbed hold of Thomas' hood and pulled on it until Thomas began to choke. Bonnie didn't stop. She kept moving as fast as she could on the slippery, new fallen snow, until she was out of sight.

The officer jerked Thomas' arms behind his back, placed him in hand cuffs and opened the bag. He looked into it, closed it up again and charged Thomas with Grand Larceny Auto, Evading Arrest, Leaving the Scene of an Accident, Driving Without a License and Possession of Drug Paraphernalia. He read Thomas his rights, dragged him around the corner and slammed him up against the cruiser. Then he asked Thomas the name of the girl he was with. Thomas shrugged, chuckled and claimed it was just some skank he had picked up on Christopher Street. The officer secured Thomas in the back of the cruiser, called for backup and drove to the scene of the accident. Once he got there, he took names and statements. Several people confirmed that Thomas was the young man who had been behind the wheel of the car at the time of the accident. Once the officer took the last statement, he got back into his cruiser and transported Thomas to Central Booking.

CHAPTER THIRTY-FIVE

LOCKDOWN

Shortly after Garth led the prisoners in from the yard, alarm bells sounded. Seconds later, bright lights flashed, buzzers squawked and sirens wailed, making the entire tier appear as if World War Three had broken out. An officer bounded through the door. His name tag read "QUENTIN." His gleaming black skull was as shiny as an eight ball. There was not a single, solitary hair on it. He had a little gold hoop in his left ear and a soul patch. Pattie had never seen him before, but his tie, white button down shirt, along with the gold stripes on his sleeve and the gold bars on his collar revealed that he possessed some degree of authority.

"All right, Garth! Tell them she-devils to face the wall and march toward it," Quentin commanded.

"You heard the man! Let's go," Garth roared and the women all rushed to comply.

Quentin lifted his bull horn.

"Fold your hands on top of your heads and keep your eyes to the floor," he blasted.

About thirty seconds later, eight pairs of steel toed work boots stormed onto the cement floor, battering it and deafening everyone. Covered from head to toe in black riot gear, a Swat Team, consisting of six female and two male officers swarmed in, looking like giant Ninja Turtles. They held steel batons. The two male officers each gripped a thick chain leash that snarling, wild eyed German shepherds pulled against. The "canine officers'," lips curled under, exposing their sharp, pointy teeth. They looked and sounded as if they were just "jonesing" to take a bite out of any inmate who offered them the slightest provocation. The Swat Team circled the prisoners, singled them out one at a time and repositioned them to stand exactly five feet apart from one another. Then they used their batons to spread the prisoners' legs exactly two feet apart, so they could give each one a thorough frisking.

Sistine, who was thinking of training for the Swat Team, guarded the doorway that led to the prisoners' dank, dingy cells. Since the process of isolating each prisoner and frisking them took so long, she got bored. As a result, she tried to perform tricks with her own baton like she did back in her days as a high school twirler. She was hoping to catch Quentin's eye and impress him, but when she miscalculated one of her stunts, the baton fell out of her hand and clanged against the metal door. And since Pattie had no way of knowing what caused the sound, she panicked and flinched in terror. Her heart raced so violently she thought she was having a heart attack.

Once the last of the prisoners was repositioned and frisked, one of the male swat team members led the first prisoner into the bathroom where a female member was waiting to strip search her. They went down the line and repeated the process with each prisoner. By the time it was Pattie's turn, she was shaking, her teeth were chattering and her skinny arms were aching from being pinned on top of her head for so long.

The first female officer in the bathroom wrenched Pattie's uniform and boots from her and threw them onto the floor. The second one picked them up and carried them into an empty cell, where a third member inspected them. Pattie was then subjected to a ritual similar to the examination she received the first day she was admitted to the prison.

When her nightmare was finally over, one of the female officers beckoned to her, tossed a fresh uniform at her and returned her boots to her. Then she pointed at the door.

"OK, now scram," she said, as if Pattie were a stray alley cat.

While this inspection was being carried out, the two male team members and their dogs shook down every individual cell in search of contraband in the form of drugs, weapons, a stolen razor blade or anything else they could find. They did their best to leave each cell in as much of a shambles as they could. Three hours later the ordeal came to an end.

"Hey, this was an amazing way to spend an afternoon. I can't wait until they let us do it again," Pattie heard a female Swat Team member say to one of her cohorts, as they stormed out.

"Well, I didn't even get to strip search anyone. All I did was wind up carrying dirty clothes back and forth," her comrade complained.

Immediately after the door clanged shut behind the last of the exiting SWAT team members, Garth ordered all the prisoners back to their cells for cleanup.

"Yo, Peanut and Dipstick! Youse two lamebrains are gonna be cell mates from now on. Counselor's orders," he barked.

Alarm bells went off in Pattie's brain. Her mind began to race.

Oh my God! Reginald's warning is coming true. Miranda is a spy for the prosecution. That's why they're making her my cell mate! I'd better be on my guard. Literally, she thought.

"The nick names they gave us are so belittling," Miranda whispered to Pattie.

Pattie chose not to respond.

"I'll help them move and get organized," Larabee told Garth.

"Fine. Get 'em outta here," Garth ordered.

When Dutch approached Garth and begged to be

let off from having to clean her cell, Garth pointed to the bench and ordered her to sit there. He picked up the remote control and brought it back to his office, leaving her alone with nothing to do. About a half an hour later, the women began to slowly trickle back onto the floor. When the last one appeared, Garth returned with the remote control and turned the TV on. Relieved their trauma was finally over, the women settled back into their normal routine.

Shortly thereafter, an officer from Segregation brought Colette back to the tier. Her nose was bandaged. She had two black eyes, one of which was still swollen shut and the rest of her face was so bruised and discolored from the pummeling Garth had given her, she looked like a potato. And even though she had only been gone for one day, she appeared gaunt. She was squinting, because the change in light was hurting the one eye she could still open. She wanted to rub it or at least shield it, but she couldn't, because her hands were shackled.

Garth came out of his office. When the officer accompanying Colette removed her handcuffs, Colette attempted to walk over to the bench to join the other women, but Garth stopped her.

"Yo Stankface! Where do you think YOU'RE going?"

Still squinting, Colette pointed at the bench where Dutch was sitting.

"To be with Dutch, I guess."

Garth shook his head vehemently and pointed to the doorway that led back to the cells.

"Uh uh. Your cell looks like a fucking pig pen. Both YOUR side of it and Dutch's, so get yourself in there and clean up the whole thing now," he barked.

Colette looked at Dutch questioningly.

"Hey Dutch, why do I have to clean up after you? Why don't you get White Bread to do your dirty work for you?" Colette yelled.

Before Dutch could reply, Garth interrupted.

"Never mind HER. I told YOU to do it, so shut up and get in there. NOW!"

Dutch pointed at Miranda and snapped her fingers.

"Hey! Dipstick! Get in there and help her out," she said.

But once again Garth shook his head, pointed to the bench and snapped his fingers.

"Dipstick, take a seat and let Stankface clean up after herself," he growled.

When Larabee returned from Pattie and Miranda's cell, she tried to lessen the tension by asking Garth whether she could hook up the telephone for the prisoners. Her soft voice and feminine demeanor always had a way of softening him, so he agreed.

"Why not?" He said.

He went to the supply closet, unlocked it and handed the landline telephone to Larabee. Larabee smiled at him, thanked him and walked the telephone over to the phone jack in the wall. Before she even had the chance to announce it was telephone time, a line formed. Due to Dutch's size, she moved slowly and was therefore the last one to make it to the line. But since she cut everyone off, she took her place at the front.

Fritzi was annoyed.

"Hey you! You do ziss all za time! Vye? Vye do you haff to cut people off in za line venn you don't even haff nobody on za outside who vonts to talk to you?"

"I know you don't like phone time, Dutch, but that doesn't mean you have to ruin it for those who do. After all, it's been a rough day for all of us," Larabee said.

"Whaddarya talking about? I ain't done nothing," Dutch bellowed.

Sistine, sensing there might be trouble, came over, in case Larabee needed backup. She turned to Pattie and Miranda.

"The way it works is you place a collect call to a landline. And each collect call costs the party who answers approximately eighteen dollars. And the Prison automatically cuts off all calls after four minutes. So if the party you're calling don't have a land line and eighteen bucks to waste talking to you, then sit down and let the process flow smoothly for the others," she said.

Pattie and Miranda looked at each other, then turned back to Sistine.

"Wow. Why so expensive?" Miranda asked.

"Because the prison tacked a 'cost of incarceration surcharge' onto each and every phone call," Sistine answered.

Miranda nodded.

"Oh."

She and Pattie returned to the bench. Dutch followed them and plopped her girth right in between them.

"Say Peanut, I thought you had this steady boyfriend. What's the matter? Don't he want to talk to you no more?" Dutch jeered.

Pattie was still numb from the earlier lockdown, so her response was an insipid stare. When phone time was over, Garth returned the telephone to the closet, locked it away and looked at his watch. He picked up the remote control and changed the channel to a football game that was just starting. One by one the prisoners sat, turned their attention to the game and relaxed. When Colette came over to the bench, Dutch decided she would rather be with Colette than Miranda, so she knocked Miranda to the floor.

CHAPTER THIRTY-SIX

ROOMATES

Pattie and Miranda's new cell looked just as cramped and gloomy as every other cell in the prison. Six feet wide by nine feet long, with no window, a sink and toilet that were made of stainless steel and no toilet seat. A translucent plastic shower curtain slid back and forth along a track in front of it, but the sides remained uncovered. As a result, it didn't offer much privacy. Pattie and Miranda looked at it and then at each other.

"Listen, I'll just turn my back when you go," Pattie said.

Miranda nodded.

"Thanks and I'll do the same for you."

Garth ordered all of the prisoners back to their cells and called for "Lights Out", so Larabee bid them a good night. They thanked her. After she was gone, Pattie sat on her bunk, untied her bootlaces and stretched her feet and Miranda followed suit.

"I'm actually grateful it's 'Light's Out'. It will put an end to this really long day."

"Oh man, these boots have been killing me for the last eighteen hours," Miranda said.

Pattie nodded.

"I have the same problem."

"Do you like to play chess?" Miranda asked.

"I used to, but I haven't played it in years," Pattie said.

But I'd like to play it with you so we could match wits. Just to find out how a spy thinks, Pattie thought to herself.

"Well, I guess we should try to slumber. Good night," Miranda whispered, her voice trailing off.

Pattie sighed and turned onto her side. The only buffer she had between herself and the metal bunk was her standard issue three inch thick mat. She curled herself up on it and pressed her hands between her knees to warm them. Eventually she drifted off into whatever snatches of fitful sleep she could grab. Every time either she or Miranda moved, their bunk shook, squeaked and clanged against the wall. Each time it happened, it woke them both up and whichever of them caused the noise apologized to the other and promised to try to snooze more quietly.

CHAPTER THIRTY-SEVEN

THE BLIZZARD

What had originally started out as the innocent lone snow flake that melted on Pattie's tongue, suddenly morphed into a serious, powerful and relentless "Nor'easter". It had been snowing all afternoon and well into the night. And even at eleven o'clock, it was still in the process of blanketing an impressive snowfall onto the entire State of New York. In fact the blizzard had turned so severe, the Warden ordered, that as of midnight, all personnel at home were to remain at home and all personnel on the compound were to remain at hand and continue working. Even though they would all be compensated with overtime pay, when Garth heard the announcement, he scowled.

"SHIT! It's been a really painful day and I was just getting ready to leave," he complained to Larabee.

"Perhaps it's for the best if we don't have to drive in this mess though," Larabee answered.

"Maybe. I don't know. God how I hate winter."

Larabee nodded.

"Me too", she said.

What Larabee failed to mention was that her situation was sadder, because unlike Garth or Sistine, she actually had a spouse at home who genuinely loved her and who was waiting for her with open arms.

CHAPTER THIRTY-EIGHT

REMEMBER PEARL HARBOR

The following morning, on Pearl Harbor Day, all five toes on Pattie's right calf muscle contracted into a Charlie Horse and woke her up. She tried to pull herself up to a sitting position, but the second she moved, the sharp, shooting pain spread down her leg, wrapped around her instep and eventually encompassed her entire foot. From there it pulsated back up to her calf muscle. The agony was so unbearable she wanted to hit the celling. In an effort to avoid screaming, she gripped her narrow three inch mat with one hand, stuffed her blanket into her mouth with the other and bit down hard. When the spasm finally unlocked, she did her best to get back to sleep.

Saturday night drifted into Sunday morning. Although nothing much ever escaped the prison walls, somehow the dampness outside had managed to seep in. It felt more dank than ever. And since the taxpayers didn't enjoy paying for balmy temperatures in penal institutions, the temperature was chilly as well. The combination of the frigid air, coupled with being outside the day before with no coat and Dr. Sibley's failure to follow through with Pattie's antibiotics, all posed a challenge to Pattie's weakened immune system. So when Garth came barreling through to announce "Light's On" and hand out the uniforms, Pattie woke up shivering. Her nose was filled with so much mucus, it dripped out of her nostrils and down the back of her throat, all at the same time. She started to cough, but fought her way up to a sitting position in the hopes of stopping it. By the time she succeeded, her throat felt like someone had pepper sprayed it. She lumbered out of bed, stood and tried to shake off the residual pain from her Charley Horse. When that didn't work, she hobbled across the room, tore a small amount of toilet paper from their scantily rationed supply and blew her nose. She threw the toilet paper into the toilet and flushed. Miranda opened her eyes.

"I think I need to go to the infirmary," Pattie croaked.

Miranda nodded.

"From the sounds of things, you may be right."

Pattie sneezed.

Before Miranda could say "God Bless You," Garth reappeared.

"Hurry up, get dressed and stop your bellyaching, unless youse two wanna miss chow," he growled.

Then he disappeared. It was clear he was in a

bad mood. Pattie and Miranda changed into their uniforms and boots. Miranda finished first, but she waited for Pattie. By the time they sat down to breakfast, Pattie's throat was so sore she could barely swallow. As a result, she gave her breakfast to Dutch in exchange for Dutch's coffee. Dutch had no problem accepting Pattie's breakfast, but since she didn't want to part with her coffee, she winked at Miranda and snatched the Styrofoam coffee cup from Miranda's tray.

"Don't worry. I'll let you cop a free feel later, in exchange for this," she told Miranda.

Miranda gasped. As Dutch passed the cup to Pattie, she accidentally spilled some of it onto Pattie's hand, burning her in the process. In spite of that, the extra coffee helped keep Pattie's throat moist and warm, which was about as much comfort as Pattie could reasonably expect under the circumstances.

CHAPTER THIRTY-NINE

WINTER WONDERLAND

Anne Carey woke up feeling grateful that it was Sunday and she didn't have to race out of bed to get ready for work. She stretched luxuriously, stood and walked to the bathroom. She raked a comb through her garish, carrot colored, pixie haircut, went out to the living room and walked over to the window. She opened her blinds. Deep snowbanks covered the entire landscape. The sun's reflection on their violet blue shadows created a glare, which caused Annie to squint. As she looked out, buckets and buckets of snow continued to fall at breakneck speed. She shook her head, whistled and listened to the howling wind. She clamped down on the nail of her left middle finger and gnawed at it as if she were a beaver working to fell a tree. But before she could completely loosen it, her phone rang. She bounded across the room and yanked it out of its charger. It was her father.

"Hey Annie Girl, how are you making out down there in the big, bad city? It's a real mess up here in Lowville and the roads are all iced in."

"It's like that EVERY day up there in winter. Isn't it? Anyway, we've had a blizzard that's lasted for nearly twenty four hours down here," she answered.

"I hope you're not planning to go out in it."

"I'm not," she said, in a high pitched, falsely cheerful voice.

"I think you can afford to miss church for a day," he added.

At least, she thought.

"So, just hunker down," her father said.

What she was hoping for, was the arrival of Norton Bakerman, her own personal "Candy man". He had promised he'd bring her some coke and as far as she was concerned, storm or no storm, life was just sweeter with some razzle dazzle to perk up her nose. And if Norton was stupid enough to try to brave the elements to bring some coke to her, she was smart enough not to try to stop him.

After spending the night in a holding cell at Central Booking, which was located in the basement of the Tombs prison, the "authorities" finally allowed Thomas Amissah to call the Legal Aid Hotline in search of his lawyer, Pattie Anwald. But instead of reaching Pattie, the answering service patched him through to Millard, a young, pudgy attorney who had been home alone. Millard decided to spend the night drinking his way through the blizzard, even though he knew he was technically "on call" that weekend.

Eventually he drank so much, he fell asleep. When his phone rang on Sunday morning, he groped for his glasses. They were so thick that once he put them on, his eyes were as tiny as two peas. He picked up the call and tried to act alert.

"Who are you? Pattie Anwald's been my attorney for years," Thomas boasted, as if he were some kind of Hollywood mogul who kept a fleet of lawyers on retainer.

Millard waited for him to shut up and then began speaking.

"Well, Pattie Anwald is in prison herself."

Thomas was too stunned to even respond.

"Oh, yeah. Didn't you know? It's been all over the news. She murdered one of her clients. I guess you should be somewhat grateful it wasn't you. Anyway, I'm her replacement," Millard continued, doing his best to conceal his glee.

Jordan opened the silk draperies and French doors that led to his terrace. He stepped outside and braced himself, as an Arctic blast of wind assaulted his face. He looked out in amazement at the way the neon lights on Broadway blinked through the Winter Wonderland. He never remembered having seen tumbling white cataracts like these in all his life, even while skiing down the slopes of the Swiss Alps. Extreme winters are what caused him to look for a teaching post in Florida, instead of Canada. But here he was in New York. And judging by the conditions outside, it could have just as easily been The Klondike. He missed Pattie and as much as he had hoped to visit her, under the circumstances there was no way he could take a chance driving to the prison. He hoped the mess would be gone by his birthday, which was only three days away. If so, he would see her then. He also wished he had a way of calling her to at least let her know he was thinking about her.

Lou opened the door to his pied a Terre, which was located at the bottom of the Anwald family Brownstone. He peered out at the record snowfall which had already accumulated on the ground and couldn't believe there was even more still barreling down from the sky. He sighed. His plain Jane girlfriend Cheryl followed him, smoothed down the stray hairs on her short, tousled haircut and stared out at the city with him.

"I feel like we live in one of those glass snow bubbles," she said.

Lou shook his head in disgust and closed the door. For once, he felt grateful that he was under suspension, because otherwise, just like a mailman, neither, rain, snow, sleet or hail would have kept him from having to work that day.

Willie Hudson gazed out the window of his tiny flea bag motel room in Hell's Kitchen. He shook his head and thanked his lucky stars he had found shelter before the big storm hit. Although he would not have wanted to sleep out on the streets during a blizzard like this, it nevertheless galled him that his part time janitorial services weren't enough to pay for his room, so he hocked his USMC ring and decided to look for work once the storm was over.

Well, at least they don't work me too hard, he said, as he flopped down on the old bed.

He winced when it groaned under his weight. Then he reached for the remote and turned on the circa 1984 TV set. And when news of Pattie's arraignment flashed across the screen, he chuckled to himself in triumph.

Ryan stared out his bedroom window at the white-out. The bare tree limbs were holding at least eight inches of snow. He was disappointed, because he had planned to visit Pattie that afternoon. He turned away and tried to look at the bright side. At least all the noise of the city would be muffled for a day or two and he could try to catch up on some much needed sleep.

CHAPTER FORTY

SNOW DAY

The record snowfall tapered off on Sunday night and finally stopped on Monday morning, right before noon. At that point, conditions throughout the entire State were akin to an Alaskan tundra. Just about everyone in New York had been straight-jacketed under Mother Nature's paralyzing grip, but they somehow managed to rise to the occasion and dig themselves out. As a result, most of them spent a terrible Monday hastily shoveling, plowing and salting the roads. And as they did, they cursed Mother Nature for bringing them the apocalyptic whiteout. A few were even able to eke out some family fun by making angels in the snow, building snow men and finding hills to ride on their sleds. By nightfall, most everyone was back in the house, trying to thaw out, by sipping homemade chicken soup or hot chocolate with marshmallows.

The exception to this was Anne Carey. When Norton Bakerman called to tell her there was no way he could make it over to her apartment, she spent the weekend feeling depressed. Trapped inside her apartment, with nothing but the TV for recreation, she buried herself in one romantic chick flick after another. The movies not only kept her company, they caused her to ruminate about the ever elusive Jordan Armstrong.

How wonderful it would be, if he were HER boyfriend. That way the two of them would be snowed in holding hands and watching these movies together.

Why, oh why, won't he give ME a chance? She thought.

There simply had to be a way to help him get over his fondness for that vapid, insipid, Pattie Anwald. Bolstered by the plots of the love stories she watched, along with the ever present reminder that Pattie was under lock and key and therefore unavailable, she came up with what she hoped would be a workable scheme.

CHAPTER FORTY-ONE

BACK ON TRACK

By Tuesday morning, December 9th, The Empire State was back on track. Most New Yorkers were resilient enough to return to their ordinary routines. Even schools and colleges were open and businesses started their work day on time. Mother Nature, not having taken kindly to being cursed at and criticized, paid everyone back by raising the temperatures. This melted the snow, which created deep, gray puddles of cold, dirty slush that was too thick to drink and too thin to plow. Then at night, the slush froze over again and created black ice.

There's an exception to every rule and Anne Carey was it. She was one native New Yorker who wasn't quite ready to return to the monotony of her normal responsibilities. She woke up, stuffed a huge cotton ball into each of her tiny nostrils and phoned Connor Dane. When he picked up the call, she forced herself to cough.

"Hi, it's me, Annie. I'm really sick and I can't come

into work," she said, when her fake coughing fit subsided.

Apparently the cotton balls worked. She sounded terrible. Connor sighed.

"OK. I'll mark you down for a sick day," he growled.

"Oh come on Connor, now, don't be maaaaaaaaaaaaaaaaaad. I can't even breathe for God's sake," she squeaked.

Remembering she was supposed to be sick, she forced herself to cough again. Disgusted, Connor hung up on her.

Annie pulled the cotton from her nose, stomped her little feet and laughed at her own wit. Then she bundled herself up in a pair of silk long johns that were a carryover from her life upstate in Lowville. She topped them off with an expensive pair of ski pants that looked out of place in New York City. Then she added a fashionable velvet pullover, whose red color clashed with her hair. She stuffed each foot into a plastic storage bag, wound the bags tightly and packed her feet into her white weasel snow boots. She enveloped her diminutive body in her vintage ermine coat, placed her matching ermine cap on top of her head and covered her watery red rimmed eyes with her oversized, white, cat shaped designer sunglasses. She rammed her raw, stubby fingers into her cashmere lined, winter white kidskin gloves. Finally ready to brace the elements, she opened the door, stepped outside and inhaled a ray of hope.

I'd better make hay while the sun shines, she said to herself.

Then on the exhale she frowned and caught herself.

I'd also better cool it with the corny sayings. I'm sure an intellectual like Jordan Armstrong would never go for a girl who engages in such stupidity, she told herself sourly.

Then she brightened back up again.

On the other hand, if he likes that nitwit Pattie Anwald, he can't be all that smart, she said.

She locked her door and walked carefully on the slippery sidewalk. Her destination was the nearest card store. She did her best not to fall or mess up her boots. Once inside the store, she carefully perused the merchandise until she finally settled on a high quality ivory colored blank card that was trimmed with gold scrolls. She bought it, along with an expensive calligraphy pen and ink set. On the way home, she stopped at a gourmet coffee shop, bought herself a Peppermint Latte and walked home. She unpacked herself from her layers, stuffed her boots with the newspaper story about Pattie and planted them near the heat register to dry. She opened the Latte, licked the cream off the top and took a sip. It was still warm. She poured it into a mug that said "SUPER LAWYER", microwaved it until it was hot again and brought it over to her desk. She sat and googled Jordan Armstrong. When his work information and home address popped up, she smiled, read and took another sip. She typed the draft of a letter to him, sipped again and agonized over how she would go about editing it. Then she sipped some more. Eventually she finished both the draft and the Latte and walked the empty mug over to her sink. She washed her hands, carefully unwrapped the card and opened the calligraphy set. She made a few practice swirls until she had the exact right look for her penmanship. Then she took a deep breath, said a quick prayer to Saint Dwynwen, the Patron Saint of lovers and labored over the card.

CHAPTER FORTY-TWO

SELLOUT

Even though the storm gave Millard an extra snow day to recover from his hangover, he still wasn't ready to return to work. However, he knew he had to bite the sour apple and get dressed. He wore a double knit navy blue sports jacket, which was the perfect color for showing off his dandruff. He paired it with shiny grey pants and topped it off with a pair of galoshes over his shoes. He threw on his over coat and went straight to the bowels of the courthouse. He read the police report on the Amissah case while he waited for Thomas to be brought in from Central Booking. Then they met and argued over the situation. When he heartily encouraged Thomas to plead guilty as a Youthful Offender, Thomas stared at him in disbelief. Thomas' hands shook and his voice quivered, as he accused Millard of trying to take the easy way out on his case. When that didn't work, Thomas accused the cop of being a liar.

"Listen, several witnesses SAW you driving that car and they also saw you leaving the scene of the accident. Plus, the officer didn't appreciate having to chase you on foot."

"Well, I didn't appreciate him catching me either, but that's life. Anyway, am I wrong to think that maybe it doesn't count as theft if I really didn't INTEND to steal the car? I always remembered my real lawyer, Pattie Anwald, talking about 'intentions' a lot. Plus, I never gave him any right to go into my bag. So how did he even know I had what he referred to as 'drug paraphernalia?' " You're gonna have to get THAT suppressed.

Millard shook his head.

"I'll talk to the ADA to see if I can get him to agree that your slate will be wiped clean on your eighteenth birthday. Provided, of course, you don't mess up again. Just be smart and take the deal, kid," Millard said.

"But I'm already on Probation from the Family court."

Millard sighed.

CHAPTER FORTY-THREE

PROSECUTING YOKO

Reginald Reese also had a matter on the Criminal Docket that morning. He went to discuss it with Annie and was surprised to discover Toby Barnett was handling the arraignments that day. Toby waved him into his office.

"I'm here on the Ono case," Reginald said.

He chuckled when he saw Toby's eyes light up at the thought of prosecuting Yoko Ono.

"It's not who you think it is. They're not even related."

Toby looked disappointed.

"By the way, I was glad to hear you're representing Pattie Anwald. She's a Guardian Ad Litem in one of my cases involving a twelve year old victim named Justin. I can't believe she did what they charged her with. I won't believe it. In all my dealings with her I found her to be passionate about HELPING her clients, not killing them."

Reginald smiled.

"Exactly. I tried to tell that to Katrina Nero, but

she didn't want to hear it. In all likelihood the perp was Willie Hudson."

From there, they segued into the "Ono" matter.

When Reginald left, Millard went into Toby's office to confer with him on Thomas' case. Toby had no problem with Thomas entering a guilty plea and going on probation, but he told Millard he was sick of seeing Thomas in court and promised he wouldn't deal with Thomas kindly on any future matters.

CHAPTER FORTY-FOUR

SHOWDOWN

There was still some time before the arraignments, so Reginald took the liberty of strolling into the Legal Aid office, to pay Brad Curatolo a visit. He stood in Brad's doorway and watched Brad sitting behind his cluttered desk, looking for something. Brad didn't notice Reginald at first. When he finally found what he was looking for, he looked up and blinked at Reginald a few times with his watery blue eyes. When he didn't say anything. Reginald broke the ice.

"How are you doing, Brad?"

"Hi. What brings you here?"

"Pattie Anwald."

Brad shook his head and chuckled bitterly.

"I know. Right?"

Reginald shook his head back at him.

"No. You see, I represent her, Brad. Anyway, there happen to be a lot of lies circulating around her these days, the biggest of which, is that she killed Leland LeRoux. But make no mistake. The truth is she's innocent. She never killed anyone in her life and the charges against her WILL BE cleared. And that's because I've made it my life's mission to ensure that happens. And in addition, as you and I are both aware, another big lie that's being disseminated about her is that she quit working for you. And we both know the truth about that too. In spite of the fact she always did well by your clients, you deliberately concealed all that. Furthermore, you insulted her, gaslighted her and even staged an ugly showdown with her. All that culminated in you firing her without even allowing her to avail herself of any Union representation, which, as I'm sure you know, violated her civil rights. And why? For no other reason than you had it in for her, because you were obsessed with the fact that she's a female. You wanted a male on your staff and now you've got one. So maybe everyone doesn't know the whole story of what happened between you and her. Yet. But they will by the time I'm done. Because I'll make damn sure every LAST bit of what you did to her comes out into the open. Anyway Brad, I hope you can brace yourself for the shit storm I'll be sending your way. When I sue your ass, she'll be right back working for you. Or maybe who knows? Maybe you'll end up working for her. And we all also know that's the last thing you want. If I were you I'd stop slandering her. NOW."

Brad frowned at him, but said nothing, so Reginald turned around and made his way to the arraignment courtroom. Once Reginald was out of earshot,

Brad stood, marched over to his door, closed it and began pacing back and forth in front of his desk.

CHAPTER FORTY-FIVE

THE COURT ROOM

When Reginald walked into the courtroom, he and Ryan nodded and waved to each other. Judge Fanshaw appeared in the doorway and knocked. Ryan took his place and opened court. Then Toby Barnett took over from there, He called the Ono case first. Reginald and Mr. Ono strode up to the Defense Counsel's Table. Mr. Ono entered a plea of not guilty and Reginald argued for him to be released on his own recognizance. Toby did not object. Reginald and Mr. Ono left and Toby called the next case. Toby spent the morning calling every case where the defendants were represented by private attorneys. When the last of those cases was finally disposed of, he called the Legal Aid cases, starting with Amissah. Thomas was led into the courtroom by a lockup officer. His hands were cuffed behind his back. April Higgins from Beau Rivage, stepped forward and took her place between Millard and Thomas. Judge Fanshaw squinted at Thomas as if he had just swallowed a glass of sour milk and sighed.

"Wait a minute! I know this Defendant. Is he back again?"

"We all know him, Your Honor and I think I can speak for us all when I say how sick and tired we are of seeing his face. Nevertheless, in spite of his many past court appearances, he's only had one conviction. And that was over at the Family Court. In any case, Mr. Amissah's attorney and I have come to an agreement on this matter. The Defendant will plead guilty as a youthful offender to Joyriding and drop the ancillary charges. The People will also drop the Violation of Probation charges and roll Mr. Amissah's Family Court disposition into today's disposition. Your Honor, I personally intend to ensure that today will be Mr. Amissah's last free bite," Toby said.

Judge Fanshaw's face was red.

"It had better be. Listen to me, Mr. Amissah. Do yourself a favor and shape up, because I'm warning you now. The next time you get arrested, you can plan on going away for a long, long time," Judge Fanshaw bellowed.

Toby recited the guilty plea into the record and Thomas pled to taking a car for a joy ride. After listening to Thomas' allocution, Judge Fanshaw accepted the plea agreement. And after a brief visit with his newly assigned probation officer and a subsequent lecture from April, Thomas Amissah was back on the street.

Ryan shook his head. Being in the arraignment

court without Pattie, seeing Reginald and watching Millard represent one of Pattie's favorite clients, strengthened his determination to visit Pattie that night, no matter what the weather conditions were.

CHAPTER FORTY-SIX

THE VISIT

Ryan borrowed his father's pickup truck and used the four wheel drive to slowly and carefully make his way up to the prison. Since the slush on the streets froze over once the sun had set, most people had the good sense to stay home. As a result, Ryan pretty much had the roads to himself. As soon as he left the parkway, he discovered that conditions on the local streets were bad. He was disappointed at that and also at how poorly lit the suburbs were. Being a city boy, well-lit roads and highways were something he had always taken for granted. All during the drive, he kept praying he wouldn't encounter black ice and spin out of control.

Eventually he reached the high walled entrance to the prison compound. Amazed he got there in one piece, he pulled up to the main gate and obeyed the sign that ordered him to stop and check in with the guard. When he said he was there to visit a prisoner, the guard pointed toward the visitor's parking lot and the main entrance to the prison. Then he gestured for Ryan to drive through.

When Ryan got out of his truck, he noticed the parking lot was slippery. He watched his step and was especially careful when he climbed the icy stairs that led to the main entrance. Once inside, the first person he encountered was a correctional officer whose job was to "man" the entrance. Even though Ryan was wearing a uniform that broadcast his job with the Judicial System, when he explained why he was there, the correctional officer was barely civil to him. He looked up Pattie's name, then he ordered Ryan to empty his pockets and walk through a metal detector. When Ryan set off the metal detector, the officer scanned him with a wand. When he finally completed the scan, he handed Ryan a visitor's pass and ordered him to huddle in a dingy, yellow, closet sized waiting room with no heat and no seats.

By the time a total of fifteen visitors had assembled, Ryan was freezing. Another officer arrived and made each visitor count off one through fifteen, as if they themselves were the prisoners. Then the officer led them to a freight elevator. When they got off, they were herded like a flock of sheep past ten or so corridors with buzzers, clanging doors and rows upon rows of inmates. It was the epitome of collectivism, since the entire group could only progress as fast as its slowest member. Eventually, they reached the dingy, dim visitor's center, where they were instructed to form a line behind a wall of smudged, dirty Plexiglass. After they waited there for a few minutes, the prisoners shuffled into the room and trudged up to the other side of the Plexiglass.

"You've got ten minutes," the officer bellowed through a bullhorn.

As soon as Ryan spotted Pattie, the sight of her shocked him. The first thing that upset him was her weight. Although she had always been petite and thin, that night, she was so gaunt and haggard, she was only a mere shell of her former self. He shuddered at her pallor. She had always been pale, but that night she looked downright ashen, almost like a ghost. And because she was exhausted and very nearly emaciated, her eyes looked huge and hollowed out, with terrible, dark purple circles underneath them. She wasn't even pretty at that point. After her delousing, her hair had become dull looking and brittle. And because she had no comb, brush, shampoo or conditioner, it was matted and it hung lifelessly in knots. In Ryan's opinion Pattie looked worse than when she was in the hospital. Her posture was so slope shouldered she looked almost concave. Her entire demeanor screamed "DEFEAT," as if she had somehow given up on life and life had somehow given up on her. Her body language was that of a person who was learning how to project the impression of being invisible, so as not to stand out or offend anyone.

She stared at Ryan and tried to figure out a way to

stop shaking, so she could at least manage to wave and muster up a smile. Even though Ryan was still in shock, he did his best to smile back at her and act natural. She pointed at the phone. That's when he noticed her nail polish was chipped and her nails were broken off. He suspected it must have bothered her, but at the same time he also knew they were the least of her problems. When they picked up their receivers, she cleared her throat and pulled herself together.

"Hi. You're my first visitor. To merely say thank you for coming feels so shallow and hollow compared to how grateful I really feel seeing you here."

She spoke in a flat monotone and her voice sounded somewhat hoarse. Ryan apologized for not getting up there to see her over the weekend. When he explained it was due to a blizzard, she nodded.

"I actually heard how bad that blizzard was, but it's hard for me to identify with it, since I've completely lost touch with the outside world at this point," she said.

"Well, enough about the blizzard. I hate what has happened to you and I want to know how you're doing."

"In short, I'm a mess. To say this is not a nice place would be comic understatement. Being here is horrible, sort of like being in the bowels of Hell. Let me tell you something. Everything here either bothers, frustrates, sickens or terrifies me. We're deprived of proper nutrition and decent air. The health care is substandard and due process is irrelevant. Even though we're all supposed to be presumed innocent until proven guilty, the staff in here treats every single one of us as if we've already been convicted and sentenced. And none of us deserve to be talked down to as if we're valueless, no matter what we may or may not have done. Anyway, the hardest thing for me to handle, is being separated from Jordan. It hurts my heart. Literally. I know there's a saying that things could always be worse, but for the life of me, I can't imagine how. And I hope I never find out."

Then she went on to explain the way the prison telephone system worked. When she told him the price of a four minute phone call, he whistled.

"Wow, that sucks. Anyway, if you had a pen and paper I would give you the number of my parents' landline right now, so you could call me collect. I don't care about the cost," he added.

She thanked him and when she told him she not only didn't have a pen, a pad, nor even a pair of socks or underwear, he winced and promised to get her prisoner number from Reginald. Then he promised to mail her his parents' landline number, so she could call him collect. Finally, he promised to include a money order so she would also be able to buy some creature comforts.

"I'll get In touch with Jordan and let him know how things work, but hopefully, you'll be out of here before the phone company even installs a landline for him. Never forget. Reginald, Jordan and I all believe in you. And no matter what happens, we'll always have your back. In addition, I pray for you daily. And I promise never to stop."

Somehow that made her feel stronger. She smiled again. When the officer announced the end of the session, they each hung up and placed their palms on the grimy Plexiglass, as if they were touching each other. She mustered one last smile, before she turned away. Then Ryan and the fourteen other visitors were herded through the same rigamarole they endured only ten minutes earlier. At that point, the next group of fifteen visitors, who were huddling in the holding pen, got their turn.

Once Ryan was outside, he cautiously navigated the steps, minced across the icy parking lot and got back into the truck. He turned on the engine, cranked up the heat as high as it would go and rubbed his hands together. As the truck warmed up, he prayed, in order to shake his distress at the thought of Pattie wasting away in that prison.

"Dear God, Please help Pattie. Hasn't she already been through enough of an ordeal, without having to be imprisoned too?"

His cell phone rang. He glanced at the caller ID. It was Nancy Speck, Chief Clerk of the Family Court. Her voice came through loud and clear on his bluetooth, as she asked him whether he had any updates on Pattie. He told her he was in the visitor's section of the prison parking lot after having just visited her.

"At this point, she is the most shattered person I've ever seen in my life. I get the feeling she's not even really functioning."

"Oh my God. Well, that's because she doesn't belong there, cooped up with those criminals like that."

He nodded in agreement, even though Nancy couldn't see him.

CHAPTER FORTY-SEVEN

SICK OF IT

Run down from the previous weekend's long hours, Garth was tired. His immune system was lowered and by Wednesday, December 10th, he wound up catching the sore throat and laryngitis that was running rampant throughout the prison. It was Colette's day to go to court and he tightened her hand cuffs until she winced in pain.

"Ow, you asshole! Are you so stupid that you don't even know you're hurting me again? Or are you just a sadist?" Colette cried out, deciding to take full advantage of Garth's temporary laryngitis.

He frog marched her to the outside door. When it opened, the arctic air blasted them both in the face. He literally shoved her into the arms of one of the transport officers, who was all bundled up against the cold as he waited for the underdressed prisoners to come out. Garth scurried back inside, just as the door clanged shut behind him.

In the meantime, upstairs, Pattie woke up shaking with chills and a fever. The excess mucus in her sinuses, nose and throat had settled in her lungs overnight, causing her to wheeze. Her lips and finger nails had a bluish tinge. When she coughed, her throat was so sore, she felt like she was choking on pieces of ground glass. And her upper lip was tingling. She touched it. And because they had no mirror in the cell, she ran over to Miranda, pointed to it and asked Miranda what was going on. Miranda peered at it closely.

"Hey, you sound worse than ever. And whatever that is, it looks ugly. It's kind of like a cold sore but not really."

Pattie gasped and backed away from her.

"I certainly don't want you to catch it. It might be impetigo," she croaked out the words in her hoarse voice.

Sistine appeared in the doorway and tossed their uniforms at them.

"OK. Let's go!" She barked.

"Where's Garth?" Miranda asked.

"Not that it's any of your business, or anything, but he just went home sick," Sistine answered.

Pattie was gleeful about it, but unlike Colette, she was smart enough to conceal her feelings. It was a relief to her not to have to hear him bark out his orders in his gravelly voice or worse yet, blast them through his bullhorn.

CHAPTER FORTY-EIGHT

IT'S WHO YOU KNOW

As soon as Judge Bender arrived at the Family Court that morning, Nancy Speck followed him into his Wedgwood blue and white chambers. A weak ray of sunlight shone through the window and splashed across his massive mahogany desk. As he hung up his coat, Nancy relayed Ryan's update about Pattie. He listened, frowned and eased himself into his plush leather chair. Then he shook his head and picked up his phone. Reginald saw Judge Bender's name pop up on his caller ID, so he picked up the call and confirmed to the Judge that indeed he was representing Pattie. When Judge Bender asked him who the presiding judge was, he told him.

"Well that's great. I went to law school with Jasper. I don't know whether it will make any difference or not, but when we hang up I'll give him a call," Judge Bender said.

After they hung up, Judge Bender called Judge Islington. They chatted for a few minutes and then Judge Bender cut to the chase. He told her that Pattie did an exemplary job working with him as a Juvenile lawyer in the Family Court for well over a year and that he had a great deal of respect for her.

"As a matter of fact, I already told her defense counsel, I'll come in as a character witness for her, if it goes to trial. In the meantime, is there anything I can say to you to convince you to let her out on her own recognizance?" Judge Bender said.

Judge Islington processed the information, but made no promises. After they said their good byes, Judge Islington dropped in on Katrina Nero. He found her in her office, poring over Pattie's file. The second he appeared in her doorway, she looked up.

"Hi. What's going on?"

"Good morning Katrina. I thought I'd let you know that whether Pattie Anwald realizes it or not, she's a girl with friends in high places."

He proceeded to tell her about his call with Judge Bender. When he was finished, Katrina chuckled.

"Well, she may not know she's got these allies with such stature, but I sure do. Yesterday I got the same kind of a call from a prosecutor named Toby Barnett. He informed me that HE'S going to be a character witness for her too. Then he went on to extoll her virtues and sing her praises."

"Based on all this impressive information about her, maybe I should let her out on bail pending trial, if she wears an electronic ankle bracelet."

Katrina smiled at him.

"Are you kidding? This is a homicide case. And I might even be filing charges against her for killing Willie Hudson too, unless he turns up pronto."

CHAPTER FORTY-NINE

THE FEVER

After the prisoners returned from the cafeteria, Pattie went back to her cell. She was slowly growing accustomed to how slowly it took for each dull day to creep by with its hit or miss quality and quantity of the pallid meals that left her with a perpetual knot of hunger gnawing at her stomach, the chilly rooms and the icy steel toilet with no toilet seat or privacy, the constant stickiness from only a weekly shower and not enough time to rinse the soap off of her and the general discomfort. About an hour later, though, her counselor sent for her. Larabee escorted her to her counselor's office, uncuffed Pattie and left.

"Hi Pattie, I'm Noelle Bowman and I've been assigned as your counselor, How are you doing?"

Pattie sat there shivering.

"I'm physically ill, not to mention mentally depressed. I have a headache and this is the third day in a row I woke up with my throat on fire. The only thing that makes it halfway bearable is when I drink something hot. Plus I have an ear ache and I'm also having a flare up of impetigo, because my treatment for it got interrupted the day they locked me up in here. If you don't believe me, just take a look at the skin around my upper lip. In any case, I think I need to go to the infirmary," Pattie croaked the words through her parched throat.

Noelle frowned, touched Pattie's forehead and looked at her face. Then she nodded.

"I think you're right," she said.

She turned around, reached for the untouched twenty ounce cup of coffee that was waiting for her on the credenza behind her and opened one of her desk drawers. She reached into a plastic package of Styrofoam cups and retrieved one.

"Why don't I just split my coffee with you? I can even give you the lion's share of it. I haven't touched it yet. Hopefully it's still warm. It's got cream and sugar. Is that the way you like it?" Noelle asked.

She smiled, poured a small amount into the Styrofoam cup and handed the big cup to Pattie. Pattie hesitated.

"Here. Take it. It's all right," Noelle said.

Pattie took it and thanked her, while Noelle took a sip from the little Styrofoam cup.

"The first thing that jumped out at me when I read your file, is your education. I have an idea about how you can maximize your time while you're here. And even though you may feel overqualified for what I'm about to recommend, I think you should sign up for it. Maris Midtown University is offering an onsite MBA program. It starts the last week in January."

Pattie nodded.

"Thank you. It sounds like a really great opportunity and I would love to do something productive like that to keep my mind occupied. However, the truth is, I'm hoping to be out of here by then."

Noelle nodded.

"Well, if you sign up for the course and you get released, you haven't lost out on anything. It's not like we would keep you, just to force you to finish the course."

Pattie thought about that statement, sipped the coffee and nodded.

"Well then, I guess I'll follow your recommendation. Thank you for the opportunity. And oh. By the way. Before I forget, I also want to thank you for fixing it so Miranda Dibble would be my cell mate."

Noelle frowned.

"I'm sorry, Pattie, but I don't even know who Miranda Dibble is. And I can also assure you, I never arranged for anyone to be your cell mate. I don't even get involved in that process."

Pattie's paranoia kicked into high gear, but she said nothing.

"In any case, I will arrange your next cell mate. It's going to be whoever else is currently in the infirmary, because that's where I'm sending you," Noelle added.

CHAPTER FIFTY

SOMEBODY GET ME A DOCTOR

"I hope you feel better soon," Larabee said, when she handed custody of Pattie over to the licensed practical nurse who ran the infirmary. Although the nurse was only about thirty years old, the cynical look in her eyes revealed that she had seen more in her few short years on this earth than the average eighty year old. After Larabee left, the nurse shook her index finger in Pattie's face.

"You'd better not be a malingerer, because if there's one thing I can't stand it's a malingerer. I'm only saying this, because you wouldn't believe what people try to get away with in here. Anyway, step up onto the table and tell me what you're claiming is wrong with you," the nurse said, as she patted an examination table.

Pattie climbed up. A young inmate with a swollen, disjointed eye socket lay on the table next to her. She watched through her "good eye" as the nurse retrieved a thermometer and stuck it in Pattie's mouth.

"That thing was just up my ass," the inmate said.

Pattie gagged and spit the thermometer into her hands. The inmate giggled.

"That's a lie and you know it," the nurse snapped, as she picked up the thermometer, reset it and shoved it back into Pattie's mouth.

"Well, you'd better watch out for the Nurse's Aides. They'll slash your throat just so they can steal your identity. And THAT ISN'T a lie," the inmate said.

Pattie ignored her as she took in the feeling of the infirmary. It had a strong medicinal odor, but she was so congested she barely noticed it. When the thermometer beeped, the nurse removed it and looked at it.

"You've got a fever of one hundred four. We can't let it get any higher. There's no point in running the risk of you becoming delirious or damaging your brain," she said.

She looked in both of Pattie's ears and wrinkled her brow.

"By the way, are you prone to ear infections? Because it looks like you've got one now."

Pattie knit her brow.

"Really? Because it's mainly my throat that hurts."

The nurse didn't answer her. She looked in Pattie's throat, finished the examination and made notations in Pattie's chart. In the meantime, the other patient sat there with her arms folded across her chest.

"Hey! I'm in pain over here and you're attending

to HER? I have to say, the soul called medical care in this place is worse than what veterinarians give to people's pets."

"Yeah well, maybe that's because you're just a mutt. And who knows? Maybe the taxpayers are simply sick and tired of paying for your SO CALLED care. Besides, if you don't like our hospitality, just remember, no one invited you to commit the crime that brought you to our doorstep."

The nurse's cell phone rang. She picked up the call, walked away and hung up. Then she returned to the examining tables.

"That was Dr. Sibley. He'll be here soon to see both of you," she said.

About a half an hour later, Dr. Sibley arrived. He treated the girl with the broken orbital bone and made arrangements for two correctional officers to transport her to Downstate Hospital. Then he addressed the relapse of Pattie's pneumonia, her tail bone issues, her sore throat and her ear infection. He confirmed her impetigo was returning and he ordered her to remain in the infirmary and receive treatment.

CHAPTER FIFTY-ONE

A LITTLE GOOD NEWS

Lou lolled around in bed. Since he was still under suspension and there was nowhere else he had to be, he simply decided to remain under the covers for as long as possible. However, when his cell phone rang he hoisted himself up onto his elbow and reached for it. When the Caller ID revealed Lieutenant Purdy was on the line, he answered the call right away.

"Now before you get all carried away with an attitude of gratitude, let me give you the bad news first. I hope you liked wrapping yourself up in that uniform to go to court for your sister's arraignment, because that's going to be your work attire for a long time to come. Anyway, the good news is you're back to work and the bad news is that they're demoting you. So, get into your uniform, head over to my office and pick up your gun and badge. From there you can report to the Watch Commander for patrol duty at the Fifth Precinct. And be thankful they didn't kick your ass over to Staten Island," Lieutenant Purdy said.

He didn't wait for a response from Lou. He just hung up.

"Thanks a fucking lot," Lou muttered.

He ambled out of bed and packed himself into his uniform. A few minutes later, he slammed the door to his pied a Terre with such force, Edie actually heard it in her kitchen. She jumped, ran down the hall and made it to the front door just in time to watch him peel away in his purple bronco.

He picked up his gun and badge from Lieutenant Purdy and walked past the dispatch center on his way to see the Watch Commander. Cheryl was on duty, so when she happened to see him in uniform, she made a double take.

"Oh yeah. I'm right back at square one. It's so demeaning," he said, when she questioned him about it.

"Well, look at it this way. At least you'll be drawing a pay check again and at least we're working together like we used to. Anyway, would it cheer you up if I stayed in the city and made you a great dinner tonight?" She asked.

He nodded, gave her the thumbs up sign and continued to walk toward the Watch Commander's office. A few minutes later he stormed back out and returned to Cheryl.

"I just found out I'm working the four to twelve shift. I hope you can find a way to keep that great dinner warm until after midnight," he said, before he stomped out the door.

CHAPTER FIFTY TWO

BAD BIRTHDAY SONG

It was Jordan's birthday. He was in a solemn mood. All he wanted to do was spend time with Pattie, so immediately after his last class, he googled the directions to the prison, retrieved the rental car he was still holding onto and began his trip. When he finally walked through the clanging doors, the first person he encountered was the same correctional officer Ryan had seen the night before. He looked up Pattie's name and then looked back at Jordan.

"She's in the infirmary."

Jordan frowned and inquired as to whether she was sick.

"I don't know. I'm not her doctor. Come back another time."

"You mean I can't see her?"

The correctional officer crossed his arms.

"I thought I just told you. She's in the infirmary, Sir. NEXT," he called out, beckoning to the man behind Jordan.

"But wait a minute. When she was in the hospital I was able to see her."

"Well, that's because a hospital ain't a prison infirmary. Get it?" The officer measured out his words in even tones, as if Jordan were a moron.

"But she's innocent."

"So who isn't? This entire joint is FILLED with nothing but innocent people."

A supervisor materialized from out of nowhere. Before he could even ask what the problem was, the officer pointed at Jordan.

"This guy has the nerve to come in here, talking like he's the Duke of Earl or something and then he acts all superior to me."

The supervisor nodded and chuckled.

"Well, I look at it this way. It takes all kinds to make a world. But the truth is, no matter how good they talk or dress; if they were anybody important, they'd be spending their spare time at a country club instead of visiting criminals," he said to the officer.

The officer nodded.

"Yeah, it probably means they're criminals themselves," the officer said.

The supervisor nodded.

"Exactly. After all, it takes one to know one," he said.

Then both of them ignored Jordan and directed their attention to the man behind him.

Jordan went outside, walked across the parking

lot and got into his car. He was crestfallen and disturbed by his few minutes of exposure to those two so called "civil" servants. It upset him to think that Pattie had to endure such treatment twenty four hours a day, with no means of escaping it. He thought about calling his friend Clint, but Clint was still on his wedding trip. Not knowing what else to do, he googled the address of the Presbyterian church he had accidentally discovered on Thanksgiving Night. He followed the directions, driving through the hills and curves that ran deep into Northern Westchester County. By the time he passed Amawalk Falls, he admitted to himself that he never remembered the church having been so far out of the way. Finally, after what seemed like an eternity, he found it. He was relieved to see the lights on. He pulled into the driveway, parked and said a quick prayer, hoping the pastor could spare a few minutes to speak with him. He got out, walked up the path and noticed a sign above the door, "May Peace Prevail On Earth." When he opened the door, his prayer was answered. The pastor not only greeted him; he remembered him.

"Hello. I see you're back. Are you lost again?" He asked.

Jordan shook his head.

"No. Can you spare a few minutes for a chat?"

The pastor led Jordan to his office. They sat while Jordan poured his heart out, reciting the woeful events that had been casting a shadow over his life since Thanksgiving. The pastor listened patiently.

"Perhaps you can contact her attorney tomorrow. Hopefully he'll be able to shed some light as to why she's in the infirmary. With any luck, it will put your mind at ease, " he said, when Jordan was finished,

"That's a good idea."

They prayed for Pattie just like they did three weeks before. Then once again, the pastor sent Jordan back to New York City with a measure of peace in his heart. Jordan parked the car in his garage, retrieved his mail and rifled through it. Nestled among the circulars was an expensive looking, beautifully hand addressed envelope, with no return address. Underneath it, was an official looking envelope which had been addressed to Pattie and forwarded. He was intrigued by the card. Imagining it to be some sort of birthday card from Pattie, he opened it as soon as he got into his apartment.

"My dearest Jordan,

I don't know how you feel about me, but on the night I met you last Spring, I was smitten. And why wouldn't I be? You're the total package and just my type. I knew right then and there that you were the only man for me. Although a lot of time has gone by since then, I've never forgotten you. I dream about you and I want nothing more than to

be with you. Let's get together again. May I take you out to dinner at your convenience? Make it soon though, because I can't wait.
xoxo

Love,
Annie (Carey that is, in case you forgot).
212 555 2534"

As he read it he literally found himself recoiling from it. He blushed and shook his head.

How shocking! Good grief, how could I forget that tone deaf caricature of an Assistant District Attorney who asked me to accompany her on the piano, as she croaked out a song at Frank Bernard's birthday party? Her only talent is the ability to turn a pleasant show tune into a cruel parody and all without even knowing it, he thought.

Disgusted, he tossed the note on his desk. Bracing for even more bad news, he sighed and ripped open the other envelope.

"Dear Attorney Anwald:

Due to the serious nature of the unresolved felony charge against you, your license to practice law in the State of New York has been suspended pending further information."

CHAPTER FIFTY-THREE

RIDIN'

Lou felt as if time were standing still. The night dragged on and on and yet it was only eight o'clock. He was halfway through his shift, but it felt to him as if it were midnight. He drove across Fourteenth Street and turned the corner onto Park Avenue South. Traffic was backed up as far as he could see, but at least getting to the root of it would distract him from obsessing about his demotion. From what he could gather, the cause of the problem was a silver Mercedes 450 with Louisiana license plates. It was stalled in the middle of the intersection. Lou sighed, lumbered out of his cruiser and walked up to it. A middle aged, grey haired man, with a care worn face and teary, red rimmed eyes sat behind his steering wheel, gripping it for dear life. His head hung low. The lineup of drivers behind him honked. Some even opened their windows and cursed at him. God how Lou hated it when people acted like that, but what irritated him even more were the out of staters who drove to New York in their luxury cars and then ended up causing trouble. He called out to the man. Once he got his attention, he snapped at him for blocking traffic in such a heavily traveled thoroughfare. The man lifted his head and looked Lou straight in the eye.

"Well, it's not as if I deliberately arranged for this to happen. As a matter of fact, I was hoping you could at least help me instead of shouting at me," the man said.

His tone of voice was "flat affect."

"Call Triple A," Lou yelled, not caring that he was escalating the situation.

He couldn't help it. Something about the man's twangy accent reminded him of someone. Who was it again? Someone on TV? No. Wait a minute. That dirtbag, Leland LeRoux, the cause of all his problems.

"Well, for your information, I couldn't renew my membership with Triple A, because I lost my job and for that matter, my cell phone's been shut off too. Not to mention some retail clerk actually had the nerve to cut up my credit card with a scissors."

Lou shrugged.

Cry me a river, he said to himself.

He wondered whether the man was drunk. After all, he looked half asleep and crazy. When he asked whether the man had been drinking, the man shook his head.

"I'd LOVE to drown my sorrows right now, but I can't even afford to buy myself a drink."

When Lou inquired whether the man had any

injuries that would prevent him from being able to get out of the car, stand on one leg and then walk and turn, the man shook his head again.

"Nope."

Lou got close to the man's face and smelled his breath. There was no sign of alcohol. He looked into the man's eyes. His gaze was steady and not jerky. Lou held up three fingers.

"Head's up. How many fingers am I showing you right now?"

"Three," the man answered.

Lou nodded.

"I'm going to push this rig out of everybody's way," he said, satisfied that the man had not been drinking.

As he began to push the Mercedes off to the side of the road, three civilian motorists got out of their cars and tried to help him. However, as hard as they all pushed, they couldn't get the car to budge. When Lou angrily asked the man whether his car was still in park, the man nodded and told him it was. Lou shook his head and told him to at least shift the vehicle into neutral.

"OK. Then what do I do?"

I don't care if you jump in the river, you asshole, Lou thought.

"Just sit there!" Lou bellowed.

I've somehow got to try to keep from losing my shit, Lou told himself, as he and the others pushed.

Once the car was safely out of harm's way, Lou

thanked everyone who helped him. Then he radioed for a tow truck and told the man to wait. Shaking his head, he returned to his cruiser. And even though there was no actual emergency, he turned on his siren and flashing lights. He was in a bad mood and he just didn't feel like waiting in traffic. He raced around the corner, zipped across Fifteenth Street and watched the motorists pull over to the side of the road. It always put him in a good mood to see the expressions on people's faces when they heard his siren and thought he was planning to pull them over. He shook his head and chuckled to himself.

Funnier than hell. So priceless. And they say cops don't have a sense of humor, he thought.

A few seconds later, some more amusement presented itself in the form of three broken down prostitutes who were huddled together under a street lamp. From the looks of things they were trying to keep from shivering in their flimsy rabbit jackets. One was a blonde who looked older than her two companions. She wore a micro mini skirt. She bent her right knee and swung it back and forth to let the world know her shapely gams were part of her package. The light turned red. He turned his siren and flashing lights off and stopped there. Even though the streetwalkers saw him, they made no move to disperse. Lou lowered the window.

"Well now, what have we here? Ritzy, Glitzy and Ditzy?"

"Um hum. That's right. Hey, I'll just bet you wouldn't even know how to party no matter how hard you tried, " the blonde said.

The skinny red head next to her nodded. She may have been thin but her low cut V neck mini dress and the way she displayed her ample cleavage, indicated that engaging her services might not be without some advantages.

"Yeah. Like that song about the guy who never had a day's worth of fun in his whole life," she said.

Something about that statement struck Lou too close to home. He scowled.

"You look nasty, but even so. You know as well as we do that you can't arrest us. 'Cause you ain't seen us doin' nothin' wrong," the third one said. She was African American.

Lou chuckled just as the light turned green.

"You got that right. Catch you next time," he muttered.

He rolled the window up, turned the siren and flashing lights back on and sped off. After a few minutes, he got dispatched to a nearby apartment building and hurried to the scene. By the time he arrived, a crowd had already gathered. He waded through it and found a man dead on the ground. There were two bullet holes in his stomach. Blood, intestines and bits of other organs ran out of him. The smell assaulted Lou's nostrils. Another man stood over him, holding a smoking gun. Lou gingerly took the gun, hand cuffed the man and read him his rights.

"She shouldn't have done it, man. She cheated on me. With him," he said, jerking his head in the direction of the dead man.

Lou hand cuffed the man and read him his rights.

"OK, you're coming with me," he said, as he frog marched him to the cruiser and secured him in the back. Then he bagged the gun and called for backup. While he waited, he returned to the dead man and crouched down. A few minutes later, two detectives arrived on the scene, along with two additional officers in uniform. Lou literally felt his face burning with jealousy.

If it hadn't been for Pattie and that damn Leland LeRoux, I'd be the one asking the questions instead of having to crawl around on the ground, sniffing blood and gore, while searching for spent shell casings.

He was still on the ground when the ambulance arrived. Its horns wailed and its red lights twirled. Finally it came to a stop and two paramedics got out. They placed the victim on a stretcher, covered his face and slid his corpse into the back of the ambulance. After they drove off, Lou found the shell casings and returned to the precinct with the prisoner. He logged in the gun and the shell casings, along with the statement the defendant made. Then he returned to the street to finish his shift.

When he finally walked into his pied a Terre at

twelve thirty, Cheryl was in the kitchen, wearing a pink frilly apron and draining rotini pasta through a colander. She turned to him and greeted him with a big smile and a cheery voice. She tried not to react to his smelling like stale blood and cop sweat. He grunted, took off his coat and went into the bathroom to wash up. When he returned to the table a few minutes later, she served up two sausages. She poured just enough sauce over the pasta to cover it. Then she doled out a generous portion of the pasta, poured more sauce over it and placed a helping of cauliflower next to it. She grabbed the Parmesan cheese, carried everything over to the table and lovingly placed it in front of him. The second he glanced at it, he gagged. He couldn't help it. It looked just like the victim's innards. His stomach convulsed in spasms of nausea. He bolted from the table, charged back down the hall and ran into the bathroom. Cheryl ran after him. Just as she caught up with him, he slammed the door in her face. She stood and waited, while he vomited on the other side of the door. A minute later, he flushed the toilet, gargled with mouthwash and rinsed his face and wrists with cold water. When he opened the door, his eyes looked glassy and his face was ghostly white. He shook his head, brushed past her and walked down the hall toward the bedroom. As soon as he reached his bed, he flopped onto it, face down.

"This whole stupid city is nothing but a magnet for assholes anymore and the disgusting things I'm forced to deal with on this job are killing my soul," he said.

His words were muffled, because he spoke them into his pillow.

CHAPTER FIFTY-FOUR

I FALL TO PIECES

On the early morning of Thursday December 11th, Pattie was asleep. She had been hooked up to a non-stop IV drip that pumped antibiotics into her veins all through the night. At four in the morning the nurse came to wake her.

"An officer is here to take you to the cafeteria for breakfast. It looks as though you've got court this morning," she whispered as she placed a fresh uniform at the foot of Pattie's bed.

Pattie was confused. She sat up, rubbed her eyes and blinked. She didn't remember having to be in court that day. When the nurse unhooked her from her drip, she staggered out of bed, changed into her uniform and laced herself into her boots. The nurse opened the door to let her out, so she could take her place at the end of the chow line in the hall.

Meanwhile, about an hour later, Garth made his rounds on Pattie's usual tier, calling for "lights on".

"OK, hurry up and get dressed," he barked, as he handed out the uniforms.

Even though Dutch walked more slowly than anyone, by the time the women got to the cafeteria, she felt too hungry to keep her place at the end of the line. She pushed her way to the front, where Fritzi was holding a Styrofoam tray and waiting for her gruel. And just as the worker reached out to serve her, Dutch pushed Fritzi out of the way and snatched the tray. This caused Fritzi's hot cup of black coffee to splash onto Fritzi's hand. Fritzi hollered in pain and snatched the tray back.

"Oh no you don't! No vay you get to cut ME off. You're alvays cutting people off, you facking glatton," Fritzi yelled so loudly, that everyone within earshot heard her.

Everything came to a standstill. Dutch's mouth forced itself into a straight line, making her face look like a fifth President on Mount Rushmore. She once again ripped the tray away from Fritzi and upended its entire contents over Fritzi's head.

Covered with the remains of the hot coffee, plus a serving of powdered scrambled eggs and gruel, Fritzi flew into a rage. She closed her fist, swung her arm back as far as she could and with as much force as she could muster, she gave Dutch a roundhouse punch in the jaw. Even though she was old, she was feisty and strong and the blow sent Dutch reeling backwards. There was a cracking sound as Dutch's head smashed into the unpainted cinder block wall. Dutch was in so much pain, she literally saw stars. When she recovered, she was in a rage.

"Why you," she said.

Larabee moved to get between them and break up the fight before it escalated, but Garth pulled her back.

"I know you want to help, but getting in between two angry prisoners is the Number One way WE get killed," he said.

Dutch put all three hundred two pounds of her might behind herself and jabbed Fritzi with a powerful right hook that knocked Fritzi onto to the cement floor. Fritzi struggled to get back onto her feet, so she could finish Dutch off once and for all, but try as she might, she couldn't get up. She lay there panting.

Larrabee's mouth hung open as she, Garth and Sistine stood there and watched. Sistine could barely conceal her glee. She grinned from ear to ear as she waited and wondered which of the two prisoners would eventually demolish the other. All the officers, cafeteria workers and inmates followed suit and formed a circle. At that point Garth knew he could no longer afford to stand idly by. He rushed over to Fritzi and motioned for Larabee to assist him in helping Fritzi to her feet. But Fritzi pushed them away.

"Lass mich alleine. Can't you see I'm hurt?"

"I think she really broke something, which means I'm gonna have to write up a report, which means I'm gonna get written up too, because it happened on my watch. Oh God, what a nightmare," Garth whispered.

Larabee looked at him sympathetically, patted him on the back and walked away. Then she whipped out her cell phone.

"Hello, Infirmary? I'm requesting you dispatch two orderlies and a stretcher to the cafeteria. A fist fight broke out between two inmates. They're both senior citizens but one of the them is actually in her eighties. And she's the one who is down on the floor and can't get up," she said.

Dutch hurriedly padded over to the chow line. She managed to pilfer a roll, which she hurriedly stuffed down. Eventually, two orderlies rushed in with a stretcher, but they couldn't get through the circle of people.

"Uh, we can't gain access to the patient," one of them called out.

Garth blew his whistle.

"Either youse all back off and move out of the way to make room right now or we all go back to the tier, where youse can wait till lunch time to eat," he ordered.

Once Sistine pushed everyone out of the way, the orderlies lifted Fritzi onto the stretcher. They strapped her in and carried her off. After they left, Miranda got in line right behind Dutch and the cafeteria worker returned to her work station. She poured coffee into a Styrofoam cup for Dutch. Then she handed Dutch a tray with a portion of powdered scrambled eggs and a helping of gruel. And just as Dutch turned around to take it back to her table, Garth cut her off. He snatched her tray and coffee cup, handed them to Miranda and pointed to a table.

"Take this stuff over there and beat it, Dipstick. And as for you Dutch, it looks like you're finally gonna miss a meal," he said.

Sistine laughed.

"What are you talking about? I already missed more meals in this fucking joint than I could ever care to remember. I'm really hungry and I really don't give a shit who I have to kill in order to get fed. So you'd better FEED ME!" Dutch screamed.

Without touching Dutch's pendulous breasts, Garth pushed on her sternum and sent her moving backwards. She wriggled and struggled to push back with every ounce of her body mass against Garth's brute force, but in the end, Garth pushed and pushed until he finally had her backed up against the very same wall where she had cracked her head. Once she actually touched the wall, he snapped his fingers.

"Yo Sistine. Make yourself useful and get this "Wide Load" a sturdy chair to sit on," he said.

When Sistine returned with a chair, Garth pushed Dutch down into it. Dutch was so fat, that just like with every other chair in the prison, her buttocks hung off the edge on both sides.

CHAPTER FIFTY-FIVE

BULL PEN THERAPY

When Pattie arrived at the courthouse, she learned Reginald would not be appearing that day. And the reason for that was that her case had never even been scheduled for that day's docket. One of her cell mates in the lockup looked at her slyly.

"Didn't nobody ever explain how it works?" She said to Pattie.

Pattie looked at her quizzically and shook her head.

"Somebody done signed you up for 'Bullpen Therapy', girl."

When Pattie continued to stare at her mutely, she went on.

"You ain't never heard of bull pen therapy? It's one of them harassive techniques they like to pull on us from time to time. You know. Taking us back and forth to the courthouse to sit here in the bull pen all day when we don't even have no court date. And you seem sick too, so that's even worse luck for you. And if what you got is catching, well then it's bad luck for the rest of us too, because we all breathin' your air."

CHAPTER FIFTY SIX

YET ANOTHER FALSE ACCUSATION

Darlene Storm just wasn't the same in the week and a half since her husband died. First of all, she hadn't completely processed that he was really gone. She still loved him and somehow it still felt to her as if he would be coming through the door at six o'clock. And when he didn't, in spite of her children being home, it made her nights very lonely. And then in the mornings when she woke up and he wasn't there, the cycle started all over again. She had no clue as to how she would ever be able to make it on her own and support her family, but every day she forced herself to function as well as she could, mainly for their sake. In her heart, she knew she was almost pushing herself beyond her limits. It seemed to her as if it took her forever to do even the most mundane tasks. When she finally finished loading the dishwasher, she turned it on, then glanced out her kitchen window at the heavy rain that lashed her poor blueberry bush. Just as she let out a sigh, her cell phone rang.

Her Caller ID let her know it was Dr. Rogers. Anxious to hear the results of Mike's autopsy, she picked up the call on the first ring.

"Your husband's death was caused by acute methanol poisoning," he said, a little too acidly. He hadn't even bothered to say hello.

"What's methanol?" She asked, in a sweet tone of voice.

"A very pernicious alcohol."

"How could something like that have happened? My husband was too weight conscious to ever drink. Even on holidays."

"Well, you'll have to take that up with the police," he said.

Then he hung up. Darlene didn't know what to do, other than remark to herself about the doctor's bad bedside manner. She stared at her phone for several seconds, as if somehow the answer would pop up on the screen. When it didn't, she called the police. The dispatcher forwarded her call to the Troop Commander of the State Police. He informed her that Investigators Townley and Nottingham had already been assigned to the case and that they would be reaching out to her later that day.

"Great, because I'd really like to help them with the investigation," she said.

She went into the living room, flopped down on the couch and stared into space. She sat there brooding about poor Mike, until she was interrupted by the ringing of the doorbell, shortly after one thirty.

"Who is it?" She called through the door, hoping it wasn't a salesman.

Investigator Townley stood under the portico. Sheltered from the rain, he was flanked by his partner, Investigator Nottingham. Two uniformed troopers stood behind them, exposed not only to every drop of the pouring rain, but also to the gusts of heavy wind that assaulted them.

"Open up. It's the police," Investigator Townley answered.

Wow. Now that's fast service, she thought, as she opened the door. The two investigators flashed their badges.

"Darlene Storm?" Investigator Townley said.

Darlene nodded.

"I'm Investigator Townley and this is Investigator Nottingham."

"Great. I've been hoping to hear from you. Would you like to come inside?"

Investigator Townley handed her a search warrant. He and Investigator Nottingham stepped into the foyer and dripped water all over her white marble floor.

"Sure. We wouldn't have it any other way. By the way, this is a warrant authorizing us to search the premises," he said.

She looked at the warrant in confusion while the

two uniformed officers pushed their way inside. Investigator Nottingham pointed at the garage.

"Search the premises for what?" She asked.

No one bothered to answer her question. They went about conducting their search, while the two uniformed officers hovered over her. When she followed Investigator Nottingham into the kitchen, the two uniformed officers walked alongside her. Investigator Nottingham opened the cabinet door under the sink and began rifling through it. When he didn't find what he wanted, he left the cabinet door open and began to look elsewhere. Darlene picked up her cell phone and called her mother.

"Hi, can you come over here and just in case I'm not around, please wait for the kids to get off the school bus?"

"Sure. What's going on?" Her mother asked.

"The police are here."

Investigator Townley came in from the garage, carrying a bottle of windshield wiper fluid in one hand and a bottle of antifreeze in the other.

"Bingo!" He called out to Investigator Nottingham.

Investigator Nottingham walked up to Darlene, took the phone out of her hand and hung it up.

"Darlene Storm, you are under arrest for the murder of your husband Michael Storm. Please turn around," he said, as he shoved her phone into his pocket.

Tears rolled down Darlene's face. Investigator Townley spun her around, pulled her hands behind her back and handcuffed her. Then he recited her Miranda rights.

"There must be some mistake. Don't you understand? I loved him. I still do," she sobbed.

"It's common knowledge that we often kill the thing we love the most," he answered, as he literally pushed her into the waiting arms of the two uniformed troopers, who frog marched her out to the cruiser.

CHAPTER FIFTY-SEVEN

FRUSTRATION

Once again, just like the night before, Jordan decided to drive back up to the prison in the hopes that Pattie was out of the infirmary. The heavy rainstorm that battered New York City and Westchester County all day washed most of the snow away. It finally ended around sunset, but by the time Jordan drove to the prison it was dark and there was a ring around the moon. When he finally arrived, he encountered the same officer he had met the night before. Once again, the officer checked the prison roster.

"She's not back from court yet," he said.

Jordan frowned.

"Court? I thought she was in the infirmary."

The officer shrugged.

"What do you want from my life? I'm not her social secretary. I can only tell you what's on here," he said, tapping the computer monitor a little too roughly.

Jordan left, silently cursing the officer, whom he assumed was being disambiguous.

CHAPTER FIFTY-EIGHT

I CRY

Meanwhile, in another part of the compound, Noelle was in her office with Colette for her last private counseling session of the day. When Larabee dropped Colette off and uncuffed her, Noelle noticed the bruises on Colette's face. She inquired about them, but Colette merely shrugged.

"What? Oh, you mean these? I fell. That's all," she answered, just a little too quickly.

Noelle didn't believe her, but she didn't press the issue, so the bruises remained between them, like a white elephant. When Larabee returned Colette to the tier an hour later, everyone was watching reruns of "Hogan's Heroes". Colette bounded through the door, walked in front of the television and stood there grinning.

"Guess what? I'm going to be taking free drama classes next month! AND the Director of the Hampton Court Drama Society will be my teacher! AND I'll also be taking classes toward my GED," she announced in a loud voice.

Everyone congratulated her, except Garth, who deflected from the situation by ordering everyone to line up for chow. Just as they were ready to go, Quentin stormed through the door, with his steel baton in one hand and his bullhorn in the other. He scanned everyone with his eyes. Then he blew his whistle and pointed at the wall.

"Everyone halt right where you are and line up with your backs touching the wall," he bellowed through the bullhorn.

They all sighed, but no one dared disobey the command.

"You know the drill. Hands on them heads," Garth ordered, as everyone complied.

"Due to a physical altercation which took place in the cafeteria this very morning, one of your fellow inmates wound up with a broken hip," Quentin announced.

Everyone gasped.

"The infirmary sent her to Downstate Hospital to be operated on for a hip replacement, And now I need to get to the bottom of just how it all got started," Quentin continued.

He walked up to Colette and punched her in the solar plexus. She let out a groan and doubled over in pain. Then he moved down the line and zeroed in on Dutch.

"These things happen because we're grouchy

from not getting enough to eat in this joint," Dutch lamented.

"Well, YOU sure don't look like YOU'RE missing any meals," he replied.

"Yeah, well, I am."

She removed her hands from her head in order to protect her solar plexus from what she perceived would be Quentin's inevitable blow. And the blow came. But it didn't land near her solar plexus. Instead, he punched her nose so hard, everyone heard it crack. Then giant sized drops of dark, red blood splattered out of her nostrils and onto the floor.

Quentin looked at Larabee, snapped his fingers and pointed. Larabee ran off, while Sistine whipped out her pepper spray. She aimed the nozzle straight at Dutch's eyes and looked at Quentin pleadingly, praying he would give her the go ahead. When Quentin shook his head, Sistine was disappointed. She put the pepper spray away and watched, as Quentin approached Miranda.

"Well, well, well, we all know YOU'RE too stupid to have done it," he said, as he pinched her left breast.

Larabee ran back in, wearing latex gloves and carrying a mop, a pail and a box of tissues. She set the mop and pail down. When she tried to hand the tissues to Dutch, Quentin lunged at her and slapped them out of her hand. Just as they landed on the floor, he ordered her to pick them up and get busy cleaning up the mess. And without missing a beat, he went down the line to question the next inmate. He systematically questioned everyone. And when they didn't confess or at least point the finger at the culprit, he sucker punched them.

The metal door clanged open and an officer walked in to return Pattie from her grueling court run. Quentin motioned for the officer to bring her over to him and uncuff her. Once she was standing before him, he pulled her hair, dragged her to the wall caveman style and slammed her up against it. He turned to Garth and nodded at Pattie with his head, while he kept her pinned in place.

"Oh, that's just Peanut. She was in the infirmary when all this happened, so I know she didn't see nothing," Garth said.

Quentin released her with a jerk. Then he turned around and walked back toward Dutch.

"Anyway, Moby, I knew all along it was you. By the way, you give a whole new meaning to the term, 'Princess of Whales'."

Then he pointed to the young officer.

"You. Cuff this here Royal Pain and get her on down to Segregation for processing," he said.

The young officer struggled to fit the handcuffs around Dutch's wrists. When he finally succeeded, he frog marched her off of the tier. As soon as they were gone, Quentin lifted his bullhorn.

"Ya'll have choices. You can go to dinner or the infirmary, where y'all can spend the night blah blah blahing about what just DIDN'T happen here. OR you can simply 'hold it down' and slither back to your cells for the night," he said.

His voice reverberated around the room. Sistine batted her eyes at him and suggested he let Pattie make the decision for everybody. He nodded, then turned to Pattie and stared at her. Pattie frowned, stared back at him and cleared her sore throat.

"All I know, is that I'm actually supposed to be in the infirmary right now," she answered, in a hoarse voice.

He pointed toward the doorway that led to the cells.

"Yeah, that's what they all say. Just g'wan back to your cell. And that goes for all y'all. Just get on back to your cells," he ordered.

Once everyone was back in their cell, he called for "Light's out." He ordered Sistine to go into town to pick up a large pizza, a gallon of root beer, an ice cream cake and a box of Joe, along with creamers, sugar and a quart of milk. Then he ordered Larabee to get the CD player and some CDs out of the cabinet.

About forty five minutes later, when Sistine returned with the refreshments, he reimbursed her and opened the lid on the box of pizza. He closed his eyes, sank his teeth into the tip of his slice and stretched the cheese. Garth took the next slice out of the box, then Sistine took hers. Larabee was last.

"Ain't handling them bitches fun? You wanna

know why I like it so much? Because it's kind of like shooting fish in a barrel," Quentin said.

"I don't mind supervising them all that much. It's just the paperwork that gets to me," Garth said.

Sistine stood, thrust her arms in front of her and clomped around in circles, like Godzilla storming a town.

"Look at me. Unfortunately, I'll be back from Segregation sooner than you know," she said in a deep, husky voice.

They all chuckled.

"Go Dutch, go!" Garth said.

"Very good," Sistine said.

Then she pulled the red plastic circle from the milk container, stuck it around her left eye as if it were a monocle and goose stepped around the room.

"Now who am I?" She asked, chuckling.

Everyone chuckled along with her.

"Colonel Klink?" Garth asked.

Sistine shook her head.

"Nope! I'm Fritzi! What a scream!" She answered.

CHAPTER FIFTY-NINE

PILLOW TALK

As Pattie and Miranda lay on their bunks in the dark, Pattie did her best to squeeze back her tears. When she finally got them under control, she cleared her throat.

"You know, my whole body hurts from being slammed into that wall. What the hell brought all of this on tonight?" Pattie whispered, figuring she'd let her personal spy from Hell give HER some information for a change.

"That fat obnoxious Dutch got into a fist fight with the old German lady in the cafeteria this morning," Miranda answered.

Pattie shook her head even though Miranda couldn't see her.

"This place is such a nightmare. I feel like I'll die if have to put up with too much more of it," Pattie said, hoping her derogatory remark didn't incriminate her in the eyes of Katrina Nero's mole.

"Listen, I understand what you're saying. I never expected to find myself in a place like this either. Not in my wildest dreams. I wonder when we'll ever get to eat again. Or IF we will?" Miranda whispered.

Pattie chuckled bitterly.

"Yeah. I know what you mean. You know, it might be nice to actually eat a meal without Dutch hovering around to steal it. I sometimes wish we could talk about something positive, like my boyfriend. I miss him so much, it's to the point where my heart is breaking. What makes it worse is that he hasn't called or visited me at all yet. He hasn't even sent me a card."

"Be patient. I'm sure he will."

"I wish I were as sure of that as you are. I keep thinking the longer I'm in here, the more likely it will be that he'll end up forgetting about me."

"Believe me, if you keep the faith, not only will it bring him to you sooner, it will also give you great comfort while you're waiting for it to happen. The mind is a very powerful thing, you know. So put that power to some good use by visualizing it, as if it's already occurring right now in the present moment."

"That brought the tears back to Pattie's eyes.

"Thank you for that."

"Your welcome. And send him some thoughts via mental telepathy," Miranda said.

Pattie closed her eyes and tried to recall the feeling of having Jordan's lips touch hers. And as she was beaming those thoughts to him, the aroma of the coffee and pizza wafted down the corridor and into their cell. It was so strong, it intensified Pattie's hunger pangs and interrupted her train of thought.

"Oh my God! Do you smell that coffee? Oh how I miss the Raspberry Lattes I used to drink and also my yogurt. It's funny the little things we end up missing," Pattie whispered.

"Yes. I guess we lose so much in here that we took for granted on the outside. But try not to get depressed. I can't believe I'm even saying this, since I'm having such a hard time following my own advice with this. But, I've come to the conclusion that this planet is actually Hell. And by the time any of us finally get around to realizing that fact, it's already too late to do much about it," Miranda said, her voice trailing off.

"Hey, that's fascinating. I have a feeling you're onto something. By the way, you never told me what caused you to wind up here," Pattie said.

But Miranda had already fallen asleep. Pattie once again tried to beam thoughts to Jordan. Eventually she fell sleep to the muffled sounds of the guards dancing to the music on the CD player.

They spent the night having a ball, with their pizza, music and jokes. They ended up playing poker until shift change.

CHAPTER SIXTY

WAKE UP CALL

Pattie and Jordan were back in her apartment on Peck slip. Pattie looked out the window at the grey sky. Then the raindrops began to pelt her window pane. Jordan reached out to her. When she turned around, he wrapped her in his arms and kissed her. It felt so sweet. After the kiss, he leaned over to whisper something in her ear, but the overhead lights startled her back to consciousness. Garth stood in their doorway and tossed Pattie and Miranda's uniforms onto their bunks.

"OK youse lamebrains, it's lights on. Chow time. Let's go, Peanut. You too Dipstick," he yelled.

It was December 13th and after breakfast, the prisoners returned to the tier, just as they always did. Because everyone was still stressed out from what happened the night before, the mood was somber. After breakfast, most of the women were still hungry and their stomachs were growling. The TV was off and Garth was in his office writing up the incident report involving Dutch and Fritzi's fight in the cafeteria. The door clanged open and an officer escorted a pretty, young, blonde woman onto the tier. Sistine followed them back into Garth's office. The officer handed Garth a file.

"This is your new prisoner, Darlene Storm," he said, as he uncuffed her.

Garth nodded. The thought of a new prisoner annoyed him, because it meant even more paperwork. He skimmed the file, shooed Darlene off and told her to join the others. Then he went on to finish the incident report. Shortly thereafter, another officer arrived with some mail for the tier, which Larabee proceeded to hand out. Miranda smiled when she read the notification informing her that some money had been deposited for her to use at the canteen. She asked Larabee to escort her there and Garth agreed to let them go. Later, she returned with some underwear and necessary toiletries for herself and a container of yogurt and a cup of coffee for herself and Pattie.

And even though Pattie was grateful, her inner conviction that Miranda was a spy, prevented her from trusting her. Nevertheless, she smiled and accepted the gesture with thanks. Because of her relationship with her mother, Pattie had never really gotten close to any women. Her closest friend was Ryan. When they were finished with their snacks, Miranda challenged Pattie to a game of chess. Larabee got the black and white plastic chess set out of the closet and they played. When Garth was finished with his paperwork he came out onto the tier, noticed they were playing and challenged the winner to a game. Even though they were actually evenly matched, Miranda won, so Pattie vacated the chair and Garth sat down. Within two minutes he had Miranda in a checkmate, which caused him to chuckle with delight.

CHAPTER SIXTY-ONE

RAPE ME

By Monday December 15th, Pattie woke up feeling sicker than she had felt the day Noelle sent her to the infirmary. Plus her body hurt from being slammed into the wall by Quentin. She and the other prisoners went to the cafeteria for breakfast and shortly after they returned, Dutch arrived back on the tier from Segregation. It was just in time for Group Counseling. Although she had two black eyes and a bandage on her nose, she made no reference to her injuries. Instead, she dominated the session by recounting the physical and psychological abuse she had received at the hands of Ned, the husband she had bludgeoned to death with his own shot gun in the living area of their trailer in Verplanck. She hardly even stopped to take a breath, until Pattie inadvertently interrupted her soliloquy by breaking into a severe coughing fit. She glared at Pattie.

"Take that shit outside. I'm talking and you're drowning me out," she bellowed.

Then she looked sheepishly at the therapist.

Pattie sighed, shot Dutch a hateful look and threw her hands up in the air. The therapist asked Pattie to tell a little of her own story, in an effort to defuse the situation and remove Dutch from center stage. Pattie nodded and tried to clear her aching throat.

"Yeah. It might be nice to know a couple of YOUR deep, dark secrets, Peanut."

Although Pattie spoke until the session ended, she told as little about herself as she thought she could get away with. And she revealed nothing that could ever be used against her.

When the prisoners returned to the tier, Garth walked up to Pattie and shoved three envelopes into her hands. One was from Ryan, the other was from Jordan and the third was from the prison accounting services. Just like with every other piece of correspondence to a prisoner, all three items had been opened to ensure they contained no cash or contraband. Garth stood over her shoulder as he watched her remove the contents from Jordan's envelope. It contained a picture of him and a letter. Ignoring Garth, Pattie walked over to Miranda and showed her Jordan's picture.

"Miranda, look! This is my boyfriend, Jordan!"

They both smiled at the picture. A few seconds later, Dutch joined them and peered over Pattie's shoulder.

"Lemme see what you got there. You showed something to Miranda. Now show it to me."

Pattie quickly folded the note and stuffed it into the envelope, revealing only Jordan's picture. Dutch looked at it and shrugged.

"You wanna know what I find suspicious? He sends you a picture, but he's never bothered to visit you. I wonder how long it will take before he gives up on you completely," Dutch said, secretly gloating that she wasn't the only prisoner who longed for visitors who never came.

Pattie cleared her throat and walked over to the corner so she could read Jordan's letter in peace. It was short.

"Pattie my Love,

I want you to know I deposited money for you in the prison canteen. Please let me know if you need more. The number for my landline is 212-555-2824. I have enclosed a photograph. Please remember, I love and miss you."

Since he had written the letter before either of his attempted visits, no mention was made of them. After Pattie returned the picture and the letter to the envelope, she opened the notice from accounting services. She was pleasantly surprised by the generous amount of money Jordan had deposited into her account. Ryan also made a deposit, as promised. She folded the notice and smiled. Dutch was watching her and when she saw the smile on Pattie's face, she once again lumbered across the room toward her. When Pattie saw Dutch coming her way, she walked over to the bench and sat down to watch TV. As a result, she didn't have a chance to read Ryan's letter. Dutch immediately changed direction and circled around to join her on the bench. Later, when Garth took his dinner break, Pattie asked Larabee to let her call Jordan. Larabee nodded, walked over to the supply closet and hooked up the phone.

"I noticed you received some correspondence from Accounting Services. I don't know how much money was deposited, but if I were you, I'd make sure no one finds out. Especially Dutch. It's amazing how people can find a way to spend other people's money in this place," Larabee whispered.

Pattie nodded.

"Thanks."

As soon as Larabee plugged the phone into the wall, a line formed behind Pattie. Dutch walked over, cut to the front as usual and hovered over Pattie's shoulder. Pattie tried to turn away, so she could call Jordan without Dutch breathing down her neck, but Dutch never budged an inch. Jordan's voice mail answered. Since there was no one on Jordan's end to accept the charges, the call automatically terminated. Dutch laughed at Pattie's misfortune and walked away.

"Where's that exciting new gal pal of mine and what is she up to?" Dutch bellowed at Larabee.

Larabee frowned.

"If you're referring to Darlene, she's in her cell. She'll be back out here in a minute, so why don't you wait here for her?" Larabee asked.

Dutch waived her hand in dismissal and shambled down the hall, while Colette stood there glaring. She felt humiliated that even Larabee knew Darlene had replaced her as Dutch's bitch. Pattie stood by the telephone scowling and fretting. The poisonous seed Dutch had planted in her mind began to take root. Maybe Jordan really WAS out with someone else. Scenes of him in bed with Darla or Valerie, two staff members who worked at Jordan's favorite Microbrewery, flashed through her mind and caused her mood to crash.

Dutch found Darlene alone in her cell, rinsing her face with cold water. She had no choice, since there was no hot water and she had no soap. Darlene shut the water off and dried her hands and face on her shirt. She gasped when she turned and saw Dutch looming large in the doorway, leering at her. The terror on her face fed Dutch's adrenaline. Dutch used that power surge to propel herself toward Darlene. And once she was within arm's reach, she spread her tough, leathery bear paws and pressed them against Darlene's chest, just the way Garth did to her in on the day she fought with Fritzi. She put all three hundred two pounds of her body weight behind her and pushed. Since the cell was only six feet wide, it only took three good thrusts before she had Darlene lying face up on her bunk. She heaved herself on top of Darlene. When Darlene eked out a groan, Dutch roughly clasped her left hand over Darlene's mouth and pulled Darlene's pants down with her right hand.

Colette decided to run after Dutch. Just as she broke into a trot, Garth returned from his dinner break. When he caught Colette running, he blew his whistle and pointed at her. She slowed to a walk and stopped when she reached the doorway to Darlene's cell. When Dutch heard someone approach the doorway, she turned around, saw it was Colette and gave her the finger. Then she turned back to Darlene, removed her hand from Darlene's mouth and pressed her mean, thin lips against Darlene's. Her big rough hand slid up Darlene's shirt. Darlene jerked her head away.

"Stop it! Please! What the hell are you doing?"

Dutch clamped her hand back over Darlene's mouth.

"You're a sweet lady. Why do insist on giving me such a hard time? I can make it as good for you as it is for me, you know," Dutch said, as she began to rub Darlene's crotch.

Darlene tried to push Dutch away, but it was no use. Dutch was too heavy and strong. Darlene and Colette both burst into tears at the same time. Darlene shuddered and trembled. And Colette ran back onto the tier.

Garth caught her.

"Two seconds after I catch you running, you're doing it again? This time I'm giving you a ticket," he snarled.

He put his hand on her decollatage, pushed her all the way over to the bench and shoved her down onto it. She sat there and waited while he wrote the ticket. When he handed it to her, he tried not to gloat as she fought back her tears. Then he walked over to the TV and made an announcement.

"Listen up. It's almost time for my favorite Christmas program, 'The Grinch Who Stole Christmas'."

He picked up the remote control and turned the TV on. As soon as the program started, Pattie sat down beside Miranda in the middle of the bench. About twenty minutes later, Dutch appeared. She elbowed Pattie out of the way, until she made enough room for herself between Pattie and Miranda. Then she squeezed herself onto the bench and assumed her "rightful" place in the middle. She casually flung her arm around Pattie's neck. To Pattie, it felt like a yoke, but she was too intimidated to complain about it. Then with her other arm, Dutch knocked Miranda onto the floor.

CHAPTER SIXTY-TWO

GROUP THERAPY

The following morning at four o'clock, Dutch was roused out of bed and transported to court for her Pre Trial Hearing. When Pattie realized Dutch wasn't around, she breathed a sigh of relief and appreciated the sense of peace that always accompanied one of Dutch's absences. The feeling was even more pronounced in group therapy, when Dutch wasn't there to dominate the session. It gave the others an opportunity to share their stories for a change. Even Colette spoke up.

"I learned early in life that I could trade my body in order to gain access to the drugs and alcohol I felt I needed in order to stuff down my feelings," she said.

Pattie sat there surprised at how self-aware Colette was. Colette's story was followed by other stories. After a while, Pattie came to the conclusion that, with the exception of Darlene Storm, the prisoners started out their lives as victims. After many years, they eventually switched categories and began to victimize others. Pattie also got the feeling that the husbands and boyfriends whose names cropped up, all sounded like Dutch's husband, Ned. Every one of the women could have been talking about the same man. A man who was a law unto himself and who did whatever he pleased, whenever he pleased, with whomever he pleased and all without remorse. A man who, when confronted with his wrongdoings, not only denied the allegations against him, but repeatedly accused his wife or partner of doing those very same things, even though he knew he was lying. The men they described, systematically neglected, insulted, demeaned or mistreated them until they were completely devoid of self-esteem. Occasionally, when the men realized they might have gone too far, they engaged in a series of short spurts of love bombing and rosy promises of a better future. Sadly, those promises only served to seat belt the women in place for yet another spin on the Roller Coaster. And by the time the their journey ended at the main doorway to that very prison, the women had been corkscrewed into a hole so deep, they were hard pressed to even envision a way out of it. Hearing it all made Pattie feel sorry for every single one of them, but she didn't show it, because she didn't want to be in a position where they could use her empathy against her.

When the session was over, Larabee and Sistine escorted everyone back to the tier. Once they were settled, Pattie asked Larabee to accompany her to the canteen. She wanted to take advantage of her opportunity to shop without Dutch around to interfere and make demands. Garth gave the go ahead. When they got to the canteen, Pattie noticed the cashier was a civilian employee who could have passed for Dutch's twin sister. When Pattie asked her whether they carried under wire bras in her size, the cashier shook her head.

"Nope. We only got what's in stock. We don't allow bras with wires in them, because in the past you people removed them and used them to try to poke each other's' eyes out. But judging from the looks of you, you don't need no wire. You ain't got nothing to hold up anyways," she said.

Pattie tried to ignore the insult and proceeded to stock up on tampons, sanitary napkins, toilet paper, a toothbrush, toothpaste, shampoo, conditioner, two containers of yogurt and two cups of coffee, one for herself and the other for Miranda. She also bought some art supplies for Fritzi, so Fritzi would at least be able to draw and paint, in the event she ever returned to the tier. Then she bought a long-john top to go under her uniform and a sweat shirt for future excursions outside in the exercise yard. She also bought deodorant, three flannel nightgowns, seven pairs of underpants, seven pairs of socks, seven bras, a hair brush, two pens, three lined pads of paper, stamps and a journal. She knew time would hang less heavily on her hands if she could spend some of it journaling her thoughts. When she walked past the popcorn she reached for a large bag on impulse.

"Maybe I should get Dutch SOME kind of a snack. Is there going to be another movie night soon?"

Larabee nodded.

"I believe there's one coming up on Saturday, unless it gets cancelled."

"Well, I'll get her this. Is there anything YOU would like?"

Larabee shook her head.

"Just remember what I told you. Keep YOUR money for YOUR benefit."

Pattie was delighted with her purchases. She couldn't wait to get back to her cell so she could use them. After she and Miranda enjoyed their yogurts and coffee, Pattie brushed her teeth and washed her hair. Even though she conditioned it, when she tried to comb it afterwards, it was so full of knots, it hurt her. She picked up the pens and the journal, sat on her bunk and took a deep breath. Staring into space, she wondered what she would be doing if she were free. When an answer came, she put pen to paper.

"I would like to think maybe I'd be helping someone. But then again, I wouldn't be working for Legal Aid, so I don't know exactly what I would be doing," she wrote.

Then she tried to answer other questions, such as, "what REALLY happened on Thanksgiving night"?

Her thoughts were soon interrupted by the

clanging of the door and Garth's announcement that it was time to line up for dinner.

"What will become of me if my amnesia surrounding Thanksgiving night makes me unable to assist Reginald in my defense?" She wrote.

Garth showed up in her doorway again.

"Why do I always have to give you a personalized invitation to line up for chow? This ain't no resort hotel, Peanut," he bellowed.

Pattie nodded.

"Sorry," she said, but she kept writing.

"Oh my GOD, will I wind up spending the rest of my life in this hell hole?"

She snapped the journal shut, jumped up and stuffed it under her mat. She left her cell and got on line. Just as the prisoners were ready to leave for the cafeteria, the door clanged open. Two officers were returning Dutch to the tier. When they uncuffed her, she waddled toward Colette, who was standing in the chow line right behind Pattie. Colette looked up at Dutch and let her cut right in. Dutch immediately poked Pattie. When Pattie turned around, Dutch gave her a menacing look.

"You know Peanut, me and you had a deal. Remember? Hands off you, in exchange for you doing my research and legal legwork. Turns out you welched," Dutch said.

Pattie felt threatened. She cleared her throat.

"Listen, Dutch, I'd love for you to be out of here," she said, meaning it.

That night's prison slop consisted of a morsel of strange looking mystery meat. It hung from an oddly shaped bone that was so white and shiny, Pattie wondered whether it was made out of plastic. After the meal, they returned to the tier and Pattie went to her cell. A few minutes later she reappeared with the bag of popcorn she bought for Dutch. She held it out to her, as a peace offering.

"Here's a little something for you to enjoy on our next movie night," she said.

Without even thanking Pattie, Dutch snatched the bag, ripped it open and plunged her face into it. She began to devour it, as if she were a mule gobbling from a feed bag. When Pattie gasped, Dutch stopped eating and looked up at her. Little pieces of popcorn hung from her face.

"Well, I'm hungry. Besides, I'm gonna need a hell of a lot more than THIS to keep ME fed. Don't you have nothing else you could offer me?"

Pattie cleared her throat again and shook her head.

"Frankly, I don't."

Dutch glared at her.

"You know, I could kill for a chocolate bar right now. And don't forget, I've killed for less."

"Now, Dutch!" Pattie said.

"Now, Dutch nothin'. I really do mean it. The first thing tomorra' mornin', the minute that liberry opens, you're gonna get your scrawny ass down there and start researching some legal loopholes that my REAL mouthpiece can use to spring me. And then when you're done with that, me and you are gonna stroll on over to that canteen. Because there's stuff in there I need," Dutch said.

Once again, Pattie waited for Garth to take his dinner break. When he did, she asked Larabee if she could try to call Jordan again. Just like before, Larabee agreed and set up the phone for her. Jordan picked up the call on the second ring and accepted the charges.

"Oh my God Jordan! I've been thinking about you all the time. It's so uplifting for me to finally hear your voice! And I also want to thank you for your picture and the money. The only thing I don't understand is why you haven't come to visit me. I miss you so much. I just want to see you and be with you," she blurted out.

As she was speaking, she didn't notice Dutch had ambled over to eavesdrop. Before Jordan had a chance to answer, Dutch jabbed her in her rib cage and pointed at the telephone.

"Let him know I'll be calling him when you're done," she said.

Pattie frowned.

"Why?"

Pattie asked Jordan whether it would be all right for Dutch to phone him after their call ended.

"Believe me. It would make my life easier if you would simply agree," she added.

They talked until their four minute deadline was up. Then the phone line went dead. Dutch stood there with her arms folded across her chest, tapping her toe.

"Thank God, that's over with. So come on now, Peanut. Let's get this show on the road," she said, making circular motions with her hand, as if to hurry Pattie up.

Pattie sighed and called Jordan again. Dutch stood over her shoulder, listened to her give the prison operator Jordan's number and made sure she memorized it. As soon as she heard the phone ringing on the other end, she ripped the receiver out of Pattie's hand and rudely shoved Pattie out of the way.

"How are you Jordan, honey?" Dutch said, when Jordan picked up the call.

She actually did a good job of making her voice sound syrupy sweet, in the hopes of mimicking a telephone sex operator.

"Listen, I want you to know I don't usually date based on appearances, but I seen your picture and all and I thought you were a cute guy with a nice smile. And now, after hearing your enchanting British accent, I'll just bet you're a ten in bed. I don't know, but you sound like pure lust to me. Irresistible. I really like it, Babe. Your accent and all. And I really like you. But then again, who knows? I don't want you to get too, too swell headed now. So I'll have to put you down a little. You're not perfect, you know. In fact, you're as skinny as fuck. Anyway, if I can get the hell out of here, maybe we could hook up and who knows what can happen from there? Maybe we can even take the relationship further."

Jordan chuckled, nervously.

"Well, I'm sure Pattie mentioned to you that she's my girlfriend," he said.

Suddenly, Dutch dropped all pretense of sweetness.

"Well, I don't know about that. All I know is that she bragged to everybody how much money you sent to her recently. Then she laughed and said she's only using you to get more."

"Wait a minute. Why would Pattie ever do such a thing? She's too nice a girl to ever act that way."

"She's NOT nice. You're the one who's nice. Way too nice for her. And that's why I'm giving you a heads up," Dutch said.

Her voice was so strident and her words were so chilling, they made Jordan nervous enough to start shaking.

"I can't believe I'm hearing this. Anyway Dutch, I've had a long day and I honestly believe we should end this call right now."

Dutch picked up on his adrenaline and used it to her advantage.

"Starting tomorrow, I'm gonna starve Pattie by

eating all her food. Which means, she'll be dead in eleven days. Or maybe even less. Who knows? Who even cares?" Dutch whispered, so only Jordan could hear it.

The four minutes were up. When the line went dead, Dutch burst into tears and slammed the receiver down as hard as she could. She was hoping to break it, so Pattie would never be able to use it again. Larabee saw what she did, so she rushed over and pulled the phone out of the jack. The others who were on line, waiting to make a call, sighed.

"What's going on?" Larabee asked, as she wrapped the cord around the phone.

Dutch shook her head and waved her hand in dismissal. Her ugly, dirty ringlets shook along, like demented mini Slinkies. Then she walked away without even answering Larabee's question.

In the meantime, Pattie was back in her cell, sitting on her bunk. Although she was tired, she forced herself to stay awake so she could stare at Jordan's picture and write about him. She felt it was important to do everything possible to keep his memory fresh in her mind. She thought about his smiles, his frowns and every other expression in between. And as she got lost in her thoughts, she closed her eyes and reminisced about the special day she had spent with him at the South Street Seaport the previous summer. That was the day she realized she was in love with him. It seemed like a lifetime ago and yet it was less than seven months ago. In any case, just thinking about it comforted her.

When she saw Dutch walk past her cell, she went back out onto the floor. She showed Larabee her tangles and asked Larabee to cut her hair. Larabee agreed, but warned her that she was no hairdresser. Pattie shrugged and said she didn't care. All she wanted was for Larabee to cut her hair short enough so that there would be no more knots or tangles when she tried to brush it. Larabee agreed. By the time she finished trimming Pattie's hair, it only reached the bottom of her collar bone. However, the ends were even and the result wasn't too disastrous. Pattie thanked her, went back to her cell and pulled out Jordan's picture. She stared at it until the door clanged open and Garth broke the spell.

"OK, light's out," he bellowed.

Pattie kissed Jordan's picture, slid it under her mat and lay down. A few minutes later, Miranda returned to the cell. Pattie wished her a good night, closed her eyes and thought about Ryan. She recalled a special Sunday picnic she enjoyed with him in Battery Park the previous summer. It had been a beautiful day and they had eaten his mother's home baked blue berry muffins, in full view of the Statue of Liberty. Then her thoughts returned to Jordan. Once again, she visualized his face and beamed thoughts of love, gratitude and kisses at him. She added some pink and red hearts and beamed those at him, as well.

CHAPTER SIXTY-THREE

MAKING PLANS

Jordan held Pattie and kissed her passionately, until he was interrupted by the sound of his alarm clock. He woke, stirred and turned to reach for her, but then he realized she wasn't there. Knowing it was only a dream felt like a stab in the heart. Feeling terrible, he sat up, turned the alarm off and sighed. It was December 17th and Jordan was beside himself with worry. As disturbing as his awful conversation with Dutch had been, there was still a part of him that couldn't believe she was really capable of carrying out her threat. He got out of bed and headed for the shower. As the warm water gradually woke him, he tried to figure out a way to help Pattie more. After he dried off, he slipped into his robe, decided to make a pot of tea and while he waited for the water to boil, he stared out the window. His cell phone rang. Relieved to see it was his friend Clint, he quickly picked up the call.

"Hi Clint! I'm so happy to hear from you! Please forgive my missing your wedding. I promise to make it up to you somehow, but the way things are going, I have no idea when that will be."

"Please don't even worry about it. I got your message about losing your Dad. Please accept my condolences. I can only imagine the hard time you must be going through," Clint said, in his slow paced Southern accent.

Jordan thanked him for his understanding and quickly brought him up to date on Pattie's tale of woe, including her amnesia surrounding the events that took place on Thanksgiving Night, as well as her subsequent hospitalization and incarceration. He also explained how her amnesia had the potential to jeopardize her case.

"Well, I don't know what to say, other than recommending hypnosis as a possible way to trigger her memory. Obviously it would be improper for you to conduct it, but if either you or her attorney want me to, I'll volunteer to come up there and hypnotize Pattie myself. Feel free to discuss it with him and give him my number."

"Thanks. I actually believe that could work," Jordan said.

After they hung up, Jordan called Reginald.

"Since Pattie can't remember anything that happened on Thanksgiving night, my former boss, a Psychologist and Psychology Professor at St. Agnes University in Florida has offered to hypnotize her to try to jog her memory. If you like, I can give you his number so you can speak to him directly," Jordan said.

When Jordan also explained his two thwarted attempts to visit Pattie, Reginald offered to take him up to the prison so they could visit her together. They agreed to meet the following morning at nine o'clock. Jordan gave Reginald his address and Clint's telephone number.

CHAPTER SIXTY-FOUR

THE PAPER CHASE

Pattie wound up spending all day Wednesday and all morning Thursday in the law library researching statutes and case law, in order to "save the day" for Dutch. It was difficult for her to concentrate, because she felt so sickly, but what made it worse was Dutch standing over her shoulder, watching and questioning her every move. At one point Dutch jabbed her in her rib cage. When Pattie turned to see what Dutch wanted, Dutch was in her familiar buffalo stance. Her hands were on her hips and her mouth was set in its usual, mean, thin line. Before Dutch could open her mouth, a dour faced Pattie preempted her.

"You know Dutch, before you even get started haranguing me, let me tell you something. My brain isn't exactly operating as well as it used to. My attention span is shorter and so is my RETENTION span when I read something. Anyhow, here's the thing. In order for your lawyer to get you an acquittal, he'd have to either prove you were acting in self-defense or that something snapped in you to turn you insane at the time Ned died. He should also be asking you whether Ned ever threatened you in the past, beat you up or whether you were afraid of him. Another option would be to raise reasonable doubt, by showing the jury that someone else was in the house that day and that THEY did it. Did you have any guests that day? Or even a home invader? Don't answer any of these questions with me. Remember, I'm not your lawyer, so nothing you tell me is confidential under the law. Besides, according to my own lawyer, the walls around here have ears," Pattie whispered.

Dutch laughed derisively.

"In addition to being stupid, my lawyer don't care enough about me to help me," she said, through clenched teeth, in a stage whisper that was loud enough for the librarian at the desk to hear.

Pattie sighed and the librarian covered her lips with her index finger.

"Shhhh," the librarian ordered.

Dutch snapped her head around and glared at the librarian. Then she held her hand up like a stop sign.

"Listen lady, you don't get to stop me. If anything I'LL be the one who puts a stop to you and your bullshit. And right now," she said.

Then she grabbed a chair, dragged it loudly over the asbestos floor and plopped into it. Pattie cleared her throat.

"Just remember. Since I'm not your lawyer, I'm not privy to ALL the information in your case, but based on the things you mentioned to me, it would seem as if a temporary insanity defense would be the best way to go. That's just my nonprofessional opinion as an outsider. Of course, if such a trial strategy were to fail, you would be facing the death penalty, just as I am right now."

"Do you think it would fail?"

Pattie looked into Dutch's face. For the first time, she noticed how old and tired Dutch looked. Her eyes were as shiny as if they were made out of glass. And her hands were shaking. Pattie had never seen Dutch look so vulnerable before. She cleared her throat before she spoke.

"Well, that kind of thing is always up to the jury. It might make things easier if you just pled guilty in exchange for not getting the death penalty. And let the judge sentence you to prison."

Dutch sighed.

"Well, Peanut, I was wondering how long it would take before you started sounding exactly like my real lawyer."

"I'm just trying to spare your life. That's all. No matter which tack your lawyer takes, he should be pleading to the judge to spare your life."

"Get this, Peanut. There is something I do want to tell you. And I don't think it will jeopardize my case to talk about it. If anything, I'm hoping you'll think it will help," Dutch said.

She told Pattie the details of how she was stripped,

then taunted and tormented during her arrest. Pattie listened intently, weighed the information and wondered how much of it was true. However, as soon as Dutch uttered the names "Townley" and "Nottingham," Pattie's ears perked up. After Dutch finished her story, Pattie decided she had no choice but to believe it. She frowned and shook her head.

"You know, Peanut, I can't even remember the number of times in the past I went on a diet and waited for it to work. Even though I knew I'd never exactly be thin, still in all, I hoped I could be at least halfway decent looking. I only did it so Ned would stop cheating on me. He always said how I let myself go and there were other mean things he said about my weight. Anyway, finally one diet worked for me. I nearly had to starve myself. And it took forever. But you know what? The minute I stopped starving myself all the weight piled back on me. And fast too. And with a few extra pounds for good measure. And I certainly didn't have to wait for that to happen. That's the one thing in life I didn't have to wait for. For all the weight to pile back on me. Do you know how many times I waited around for Ned to come home? And how often I waited to just feel "good enough" for him, because I knew I was so fat? I can't tell you how long I waited for him to stop whoring around. He usually did "it" with skinny bitches too. Do you know how many years I waited for him to spend some time with his fat, ugly, giant of a wife? To actually WANT to spend some time with me? Or to give me a hug? Or even just pay attention to me? Or even to lie to me and pretend I was pretty? Because I know I never was pretty and I never will be. Even when that diet kicked in and made me thin, I was passable, but the truth is I was still far from being pretty. And do you know how many years I've waited for the fat jokes to stop? And the wise cracks at my expense, just because I weigh more than thin people think I should? Even in here I'm always waiting for something. For my lawyer to help me. Or for you to help me. Or for the next meal. Or for a visitor. Oh God Peanut, it seems I never really lived my life. All I ever did was wait for stuff. Believe me when I tell you, I'm so sick and tired of waiting. It seems like I've spent my whole life just waiting," Dutch lamented.

Before Pattie even had a chance to respond, Larabee and Sistine appeared in the doorway and walked up to them.

"Pattie, you have two visitors and one of them is your lawyer. So we have to get going," Larabee said.

Pattie breathed a sigh of relief. She guessed that the visitor with Reginald was Ryan. Dutch put her hands behind her back and Sistine cuffed her. They all waited while Pattie saved her work on the computer and logged off. When she was done, Larabee handcuffed her and they all walked back to the tier in silence. Larabee dropped Sistine and Dutch off. And before the door slid closed, Dutch nodded.

"I'll be WAITING for you," she said to Pattie.

The minute Sistine uncuffed Dutch, Dutch went to search for Darlene, while Larabee escorted Pattie to the visitor's center.

CHAPTER SIXTY-FIVE

PLEASE RELEASE ME

The second Pattie laid eyes on Jordan and Reginald, she waved and tried to eke out a smile. It was weak and halfhearted, since it only reached her mouth. Because Reginald was her attorney, the visit did not have to take place behind Plexiglass. She trudged up to the four foot wide grey metal table and sat across from Jordan and Reginald. They were so close to her, she had a sudden urge to just reach out and touch Jordan's arm, but the sign on the wall expressly forbade physical contact.

As happy as Jordan was to finally see Pattie, he was astounded by her terrible condition. For that matter so was Reginald. She looked exactly the same as the night Ryan had visited her, except her hair was clean and brushed, but short. Furthermore, it was a dull color. And the expression in her eyes was equally as dull. However, the most disturbing thing was the return of Pattie's impetigo. The crusty rash that had taken a foothold around her lips was starting to spread to other parts of her face. And although both men did their best to conceal their alarm, she could glean from their expressions just how awful she must have appeared to them.

Jordan tried to smile. She cleared her throat, thanked them for coming to see her and then informed them that they and Ryan had been her only visitors.

"I'm not trying to defend anyone else, because I don't know their particular circumstances. However, I can tell you I tried to visit you twice and got turned away," Jordan said.

Pattie looked at him in shock.

"You did?"

He nodded.

"Yes. The first time, they told me you were in the infirmary. Then I returned the following night and they told me you hadn't yet returned from court. So, it's possible something like that happened to others as well," Jordan said.

When Reginald heard the word court he looked perplexed. Pattie nodded and told him even though she had only been admitted to the infirmary hours before, with a fever of one hundred four, they pulled her out of bed at four the next morning. Then they bussed her down to the courthouse for a nonexistent court date. Upon her return that night, they sent her back to her tier, rather than to the infirmary. She also mentioned having bought a journal with some of the money Jordan had sent her. She said, even though she had hoped writing would help jump start her memory, so far it hadn't. She also said the only thing she knew was that she didn't have it in her to ever kill anyone. When Jordan told her Clint suggested they hypnotize her, she asked Reginald if he thought it would help her case.

Reginald nodded.

"I do, just as long as I file a Motion in Limine," he said.

Jordan looked at him quizzically.

"Oh for God's sake, I've lapsed into legalese again. Anyway, a Motion in Limine is when we lawyers seek to have certain evidence excluded at trial. So in the unlikely event Pattie were to, God forbid, say anything damaging while she was under, I'd move to have such a statement excluded," Reginald explained.

"Anyway, I have some additional news for you, Pattie. I contacted your landlord. He made an offer to settle your housing dispute quickly, by agreeing to pay you fifty thousand dollars right now. But you'd have to relinquish the premises immediately," he added.

She nodded, thanked him and told him to accept the offer. He nodded back at her, closed her file and stood. Although, she followed his lead, Jordan remained seated, so they both returned to their seats. Then Jordan informed them of his telephone conversation with Dutch.

"What does this Dutch look like anyway?" Jordan asked.

Pattie looked down at the tips of her boots, then back up at Jordan.

"Like a pig with an eighties perm," she said.

She stood, walked toward the door and waited for the officer to come in and handcuff her. When she was gone, Jordan turned to Reginald.

"I just hope the hypnosis works. Pattie is not only down to skin and bones, she's practically at Death's Door. And ever since this Dutch character told me she was planning to starve Pattie, I've been terrified for her," Jordan said.

CHAPTER SIXTY-SIX

THE WARDEN

Reginald's first stop after leaving the visitor's center was Warden Phyllis Eppes' office. Warden Eppes listened, as Reginald presented Clint's idea. She pondered what he said and shook her head.

"What I don't understand is why you can't just give her a lie detector test."

What part of "she can't remember anything", don't you get? Reginald thought.

But instead of being sarcastic, he politely explained how a polygraph test wasn't appropriate in cases where the person had amnesia around an event.

"By the way, as things stand now, don't be surprised if I file an Order to Show Cause against you in the near future," Reginald added.

Warden Eppes frowned.

"Excuse me?"

Reginald nodded.

"Yes. That's right. I have no choice. You see, one of your staff members saw fit to drag my client out of the infirmary, where she was receiving a legitimate and prescribed course of medical treatment for pneumonia, impetigo and a number of other serious, not to mention contagious ailments. On top of it, whoever pulled this stunt also arranged for my client to take a trip to the courthouse and spend the day in their lock up. You know. For a little 'bull pen therapy' as they call it, since her case wasn't even on the docket that day," Reginald continued.

The warden's frown deepened and she bit her lip.

"And instead of returning Attorney Anwald to the infirmary to finish out her therapy, whoever made these arrangements transferred her back to her original tier. And that's where she's been ever since. As we all know, starting treatment and stopping it halfway through is the way ordinary infections morph into these enhanced untreatable God knows whats. Besides, it violates her rights under the Eighth, Ninth and Fourteenth Amendments. I'd like to add that she had only been out of the hospital for one day and taking prescribed outpatient medications the day she turned herself into the State Troopers who brought her here," Reginald continued.

"I remember the bogus court date was December 11th, because it was the day after my birthday. I want you to know, as a taxpayer, I really don't approve of the way she's been treated since she arrived here," Jordan added.

Then he went on to tell the warden about his interaction with the guard at the main entrance on the two nights he visited Pattie and then about the threat Dutch made to starve Pattie. The Warden stood and scurried behind her desk.

"Do you know Dutch's real name?" She asked.

Both Jordan and Reginald shook their heads.

"It's not a problem, since I can ask one of the officers on the tier. You see, since all our outgoing telephone calls get recorded, I'll also be able to hear everything she said to you."

Reginald stood, thanked her and picked up his briefcase. Then everyone said their goodbyes. When he and Jordan got outside, the overhead sun hung yellow in the clear blue sky. The two men crossed the parking lot and walked over to Reginald's brand new monster sized red Mercedes Benz SUV. He unlocked it. Once they were both inside, he turned the seat warmers on and asked Jordan whether he knew Lou Anwald's telephone number. Jordan picked up his cell phone, found Lou's number and called it. Then he handed the phone to Reginald.

"Hello, this is Reginald Reese, your sister's attorney. I'm sitting here with your sister's boyfriend, Jordan. I borrowed his phone so I could call you. Anyway, we're just about to leave the Prison Parking lot, after just having visited Pattie. Let me cut right to the chase here. She's truly in bad shape and she really needs everyone's support right now. It's my understanding that so far, none of her family members have even bothered to visit her yet and for the life of me, I can't understand why."

"Well, my parents and I had planned to drive up last weekend, but because of that fucking blizzard we had to postpone it," Lou said.

For a second, Reginald wondered whether he was listening to Katrina Nero.

CHAPTER SIXTY-SEVEN

LIKE A BOSS

By the time Pattie returned to the cell black, Dutch was as angry as a rattlesnake. She waited impatiently for the correctional officer to uncuff Pattie. The second Pattie was loose, Dutch heaved herself off the bench, waddled over to her and blocked her path. She stood in her familiar buffalo stance, with her arms folded across her chest. Her mouth was set into its famous horizontal stripe. When Pattie tried to get around her, she pinched Pattie's upper arm as hard as she could. Garth blew his whistle and rushed over.

"You know there's no physical contact between prisoners," he bellowed.

Dutch laughed derisively. The phone rang in Garth's office, so he hurriedly left to answer it. Taking advantage of Garth's absence, Dutch asked Larabee to escort her and Pattie back to the library. She looked crestfallen when Larabee told her she'd have to run it past Garth. When Larabee went back to Garth's office, he was still on the telephone. He was holding the receiver in one hand and mopping the sweat from his brow with the other. He put his handkerchief down, picked up Pattie's file and perused it.

"While it's true, Warden Eppes, that Pea—I mean Pattie Anwald, WAS treated in the infirmary, I personally have no idea as to how or why she was removed from there or sent to court or even why she was returned here instead of back to the infirmary to finish her treatment. Yes Warden, we do have an inmate on our tier called 'Dutch'. Her real name? It's Beverly Hollander," he said.

When he hung up, he ordered Larabee to place Pattie back in handcuffs and escort her to the infirmary.

CHAPTER SIXTY-EIGHT

D. A. BLUES

When Katrina Nero heard Reginald Reese was in her waiting room, her curiosity got the better of her. She dropped what she was doing and went out to greet him. He introduced her to Jordan and she escorted the two men back to her private office. When Reginald finished presenting Clint's idea, Katrina shook her head.

"Come on Reginald. I mean, isn't that a little too ooga booga?"

Reginald was used to Katrina's brusque mannerisms and verbiage, but Jordan wasn't. He sat there trying to conceal his shock. Instead of answering her, Reginald simply added an additional request. He asked Katrina to stipulate, that in the event the results of the hypnosis proved harmful to Pattie's defense, The People wouldn't use them against her.

"Oh, Reginald, I never understand how you're always so able to sit there and come up with all these tall orders where I always wind up having to serve YOUR needs. Especially after your comments about how obsessive and relentless I can be. I still haven't recovered from those insults," she snapped.

"Even though I'm sorry I said that, I still don't remember ever requesting any tall orders before today, Katrina. Since we all know how slowly the wheels of Justice can turn, for once I'd like to speed things up and do this as soon as we can get the expert here. That way if the results of the hypnosis exculpate my client, I would have a shot at getting her out of jail for Christmas."

"I'm going to need time to line up my own expert for possible rebuttal purposes."

Reginald nodded.

"Well, let's just try to get EVERYONE lined up for this coming Monday, so we can ALL have a Merry Christmas. Including Pattie," Reginald said, skirting around Katrina's request for more time.

They shook hands and the meeting came to an end.

No wonder everyone hates lawyers, Jordan thought.

CHAPTER SIXTY-NINE

CALL ME

The afternoon went by slowly and in the evening, when the prisoners returned from the cafeteria, Garth left to take his dinner break. As soon as he was out of sight, Dutch approached Larabee and suggested Larabee let her use the phone to call Jordan. She claimed she wanted to let him know that Pattie was in the infirmary.

Something about it didn't ring true to Larabee, but in spite it, she walked over to the closet, unlocked it and retrieved the phone.

"Well, if the guy is as much of a bastard as you say he is, he might not accept the charges," she said.

Just as she began to unwind the cord, Dutch snatched the phone out of her hand.

"Hey!" Larabee yelled.

Dutch ignored Larrabee's protest, walked the telephone over to the jack and plugged it in. Then she hurriedly placed the call and lied, telling the operator she was Pattie. Jordan just happened to walk through the door when he heard the landline ring. Thinking it was Pattie, he ran to pick up the call. As soon as he accepted the charges, he regretted it, since Dutch greeted him with her sweet, telephone sex operator's voice.

"Listen 'Dutch', or whatever your real name is, I honestly don't wish you any ill will, but on the other hand I don't want you phoning me ever again. And you might as well know I went to the Warden's Office this very afternoon and met her in person. I reported your attempt to extort money from me, as well as your threat to starve Pattie. And by the way. The warden had no trouble believing me. Also, they happen to record all outgoing calls, including this one. So let's just end this right now. Shall we?" Jordan said, in a tone of voice so calm, it belied his actual apprehension.

Then he hung up. This triggered Dutch to once again slam the phone down hard, in the hopes of breaking it. She never even bothered to tell him that Pattie was in the infirmary.

CHAPTER SEVENTY

MOVIN' OUT

On the morning of Saturday December 20[th,] Lou parked his purple Bronco on the slippery cobblestones around the corner from Pattie's small, wretched, studio apartment on Peck Slip. Ryan and Jordan were with him. Their aim was to sort through, classify and pack Pattie's few shabby belongings as quickly as possible. When they stepped out of the Bronco, they practically gagged at the smell of the diesel fuel the oversized, noisy fish trucks had belched and the unmistakable stink of raw seafood that mixed with it. The day was so dreary, it almost looked like nighttime. As the three of them carried some plastic bags and cardboard boxes through the misty drizzle, the wind from the charcoal colored East River whistled, shrieked and pushed against the outer door of the building. As a result, it was almost impossible for Lou to pull it open. He shook his head and cursed under his breath.

Jordan and Ryan stood behind him. When he finally forced the door open, they followed him into the dismal vestibule that stunk like a combination of Lysol and cabbage. It was lit by dim bulbs that cast very little light. Lou climbed the rickety wooden staircase with Jordan and Ryan behind him. When they got to the third floor landing, Jordan stepped forward, pulled out Pattie's key and unlocked the door. The apartment smelled musty from not having been occupied in almost a month. Ryan pulled the string on the fluorescent light above the cheap, scratched, folding bridge table that served as Pattie's desk and dinette set. The light flickered several times before it turned all the way on. Once it did, it revealed not only the gloominess of the apartment, but some unexpected chaos, as well. Every single item had been upended, overturned and strewn all over the apartment. All three of them gasped.

"I can't understand why she'd even want to keep ANY of this shit. But don't go by me, because I could never understand her attraction to this low class hovel in the first place. What boggles my mind even more, is the landlord thinking he can convert it into condos. Just how does he think he's going to accomplish that? Besides, who'd be nuts enough to buy one?" Lou asked.

Ryan glanced at Lou and Jordan. He deliberately refrained from telling them how he and Pattie had tried to make her pathetic apartment homier, by spackling and painting the walls and ceiling. He also didn't mention how he and Pattie had picked out a bed cover with matching curtains, which he had hung over the only window in the apartment. In addition, he never mentioned having been the one who installed the smoke detector that saved Pattie's life on the night of the fire or having been the one who set up the electronic rodent repellents that helped to ward off the army of rats that overran the building.

Lou walked over to the bridge table, stood it upright and picked up a piece of paper that was lying on the floor next to it. It was a Warrant authorizing the State Police to search the premises for a 'switchblade, knife or machete.'

But more important than what he said, was what he didn't say. On Thanksgiving, when he arrested Leland LeRoux, he was supposed to have logged in the switchblade he had confiscated from him. Instead, he went home for Thanksgiving dinner and brought the switchblade with him. He fully intended to log it in that evening after dinner, but before he could do so, it had disappeared. He had always suspected Pattie of having taken it and now that the State Police were looking for it in connection with their murder case against her, it confirmed his suspicions. As he pondered, he sincerely hoped the State Police hadn't found it. His career and pension could be on the line, not to mention Pattie's very life.

Jordan walked past him and picked up a journal that was on the floor. He opened it to Pattie's last entry, dated Thanksgiving morning.

"For years now, I have felt like a lone sparrow, cast upon a housetop, meditating in the dead of winter, looking down at the world, while at the same time looking up at heaven."

He felt a lump in his throat.

"Well, we'd better start packing," Lou said.

Jordan snapped the journal shut and placed it in one of the plastic bags. The next thing he spotted was the Tea Rose Plant he had given to Pattie on their first date. It was lying lopsided on the counter, no doubt swept into that position during the execution of the Search Warrant. He carefully picked it up, inspected the soil and realized it was practically dehydrated. Surprised and grateful it was even still alive, he placed it under the tap to water it and stood it upright on the counter. Then he helped Ryan and Lou clear out the apartment.

When they were almost finished, Lou went downstairs to bring the Bronco in front of the entrance. Then, one by one, he, Ryan and Jordan carried the boxes and bags downstairs. On their last trip, a young woman with a porcine face stepped out of the shadows. She was dressed in maroon colored leggings and a tight, pink cotton pullover, both of which showed off her exquisite hour glass shape and beautiful legs. She also wore maroon colored, satin slippers with kitten heels and marabou trim. Her sleek, straight hair hung to her shoulders. Her face was made up and she had false eye lashes. She nodded at Lou, batted her eyes a few times and smiled at him. Even though the entire effect made Lou think of "Miss Piggy," his facial expression softened for once. He even managed to smile back at her. She took a long drag on her Gauloise, exhaled and said hello.

"I remember you from the day of the fire. Isn't 3A your sister's apartment?" She asked in her thick Czech accent.

Lou nodded.

"It sticks out in my mind, because you had an argument with the neighbor in 3B. Gladys," she added.

Lou nodded again and chuckled.

"That's right," he said.

The girl chuckled along with him.

"Well you don't have to worry about arguing with her again. She wound up moving into one of those high rise apartment buildings for seniors sixty two and over. Pretty much everybody is out of the building except me. I only met your sister twice and both times it was under very bad circumstances. I'm Tereza by the way. Listen, if you give me a second, I'll go back to my apartment and get my card. Maybe you can ask your sister to call me. I'd like to keep in touch with her."

Lou nodded, but instead of waiting for Tereza to return, he followed her into her apartment. Jordan and Ryan listened to the exchange, looked at each other and shrugged. Then Ryan pulled down the curtains, folded them, along with the bedspread and removed the rodent repellents from the plugs in the wall. After he packed everything in the plastic bags, Jordan turned off the light and locked Pattie's door for the last time. He and Ryan carried Pattie's belongings down to the Bronco. A few minutes later, Lou joined them and drove them to a storage unit that Jordan had rented earlier that morning.

CHAPTER SEVENTY-ONE

DO THE RIGHT THING

Right after dinner, the nurse called Garth and requested he send a member of his staff to the infirmary to retrieve Pattie and escort her back to the tier.

"Don't YOU have somebody who could do it?" Garth asked.

"Actually, we don't. It's holiday time and we're practically down to a skeleton crew as it is," she said.

Garth shrugged, hung up and sent Larabee.

"I think Garth has a movie scheduled tonight, so if you stop by the canteen now, it would prevent Dutch from tagging along and pestering you later," Larabee told Pattie.

Pattie smiled and nodded.

"Good, because I missed dinner while I was in the infirmary."

While they were at the canteen, Pattie bought Dutch a giant sized chocolate bar, a huge package of cherry licorice and a bag of popcorn, along with a bag of popcorn for herself, each of the inmates and one each for Larabee, Sistine and Garth. Then she bought two cups of coffee and two containers of yogurt; one for herself and the other for Miranda. When she and Larabee returned to the tier, Dutch's eyes lit up. She approached Pattie and without even welcoming her back or asking her how she was, she pointed and asked which snacks were hers. When Pattie answered, she snatched them out of Pattie's hand, without even bothering to say thank you.

Larabee took the three bags of popcorn back to Garth's office and left Pattie to distribute the remaining snacks to the prisoners. In addition to his popcorn, Larabee handed Garth a set of orders which had been personally signed by both Dr. Sibley and Warden Eppes. Until further notice, Pattie was to be escorted to the infirmary every morning after breakfast and then again every evening after dinner, so she could receive her proper dosages of antibiotics and salve treatment.

Garth sighed, filed the notice in Pattie's folder and turned off the lights in his office. Then he picked up the remote control and the popcorn and walked up to the television set. Larabee and Sistine took their popcorn and followed him. He informed everyone that the Christmas movie he had chosen was, "Jack Frost."

Dutch sat at her usual place in the middle of the bench. She patted the space to her left and indicated that Pattie should sit there. Then she beckoned for Colette to sit on her right side. When Pattie took her place, Dutch offered her a token piece of her chocolate bar. She watched like a hawk, as Pattie broke off the tiniest portion she could manage. Dutch lobbed her enormous arm onto Pattie's shoulders. It hung so heavily, Pattie felt like screaming, but she didn't say a word.

Dutch started off by gripping her licorice in both hands. Then she tore the plastic wrapper with her teeth and spit it onto the floor. Garth, who had taken a seat in the last row with Sistine and Larabee, blew his whistle and pointed at it. Dutch jabbed Colette in the ribs and Colette stood, picked up the plastic and walked it over to the nearest waste paper basket. In the meantime, instead of pulling off one strand of licorice the way most people do, Dutch took a huge bite out of the corner of the entire bundle. She wadded it around in her mouth for a second, then bolted it down. A second later, she sunk her teeth in again, took another big bite, mauled it and gulped it down. She gnawed one enormous mouthful after the other, until the licorice was gone. Then she repeated the process with the chocolate bar. Finally, she used her right arm to scoop up and shovel handfuls of buttered popcorn down her throat until the bag was empty.

When the movie ended, Garth called for "lights out". The tier was quiet until shift change. Garth was busy in his office going over the log with the next shift's supervisor. Larabee left. Sistine put her coat on, turned out the lights and pulled a thick red laundry marker out of her pocket. Knowing Pattie hadn't had much negative excitement since the day she had signed her up for Bull Pen therapy, she quietly tiptoed over to the bench in the darkened room, where Pattie had been watching the movie with Dutch. She scrawled, "DUTCH IS A MOOCHER—A LIAR AND A HOAR." And then she clocked out and went home.

CHAPTER SEVENTY-TWO

CLEAN UP WOMAN

The next morning, right after the women returned from breakfast, Larabee handcuffed Pattie, in order to escort her to the infirmary. Garth was in his office, engaged in yet another telephone call with the Warden. Colette walked over to the bench, in the hopes that Garth would come out of his office and turn on some Sunday morning cartoons. Just as she sat, she read the inflammatory words.

"Oh my God Dutch! You're not going to believe what Peanut did," she yelled.

At the mention of the word "Peanut", Pattie's heart skipped a beat. She gasped and tried to turn around, but the pain in her wrists from the pressure of the handcuffs stabbed her.

Dutch sighed.

"NOW WHAT?" She bellowed, as she ambled over.

What now is right, Pattie thought as she and Larabee walked over to the bench. Sistine was waiting on standby with her ticket book in hand. She opened it and walked over to the bench. Once Dutch read the inflammatory words, she pointed at them, placed her hands on her hips and glared at Pattie. Pattie scanned the Graffiti, squinted and then glared back at Dutch.

"Listen Peanut, I really don't care how you do it, but you'd better find a way to scrub off every last bit of this bullshit or you will find a shiv in your scrawny little rib cage," Dutch said so softly, that Pattie was the only one who heard it. Before Pattie had a chance to protest, Sistine ripped the already completed ticket from her ticket book and served it on Pattie.

CHAPTER SEVENTY-THREE

CHINA TOWN

Late that afternoon, Jordan went down to his garage, got into his rental car and drove through thunder and lightning to LaGuardia Airport. Sheets of rain crashed onto his windshield. Even though he had the windshield wiper working at top speed, it couldn't remove the rainfall in time to help his visibility. When he finally arrived at the airport, he parked the car in the short term parking garage. He opened his trunk and pulled out a leather aviator's jacket with a fleece lining. Convinced that the traffic made him late, he rushed across the parking lot to the terminal. When he got there, he read the arrival and departure notices. That's when he learned the weather had caused a delay in Clint's arrival. He waited and watched through the gigantic window, until he saw Clint's plane land on the shiny wet runway.

At least it's not snow, he told himself, shuddering at the memory of the recent blizzard.

He listened to people chattering and yelling in what

must have been at least seventy different languages, while he waited for Clint to come through the gate. And when he spotted Clint, he hurried toward him. Clint was in his mid-forties. He had a kind face, hazel eyes and medium brown hair that was just starting to turn gray at the temples. He wasn't as tall as Jordan and he was slightly stocky. He was carrying a maroon garment bag. Even though he thought he had dressed for winter, his Florida clothes afforded him no protection against New York's rugged December temperatures.

"Hi Clint. Thanks for coming. I can lead you right over to the baggage claim."

Clint smiled and held up his garment bag.

"Believe it or not, this carry on is all I brought," he said.

Jordan handed him the jacket.

"I'll bet you don't have one of these in there though," he said.

Clint smiled.

"You mean Sin City is that cold?" Clint asked.

Jordan nodded and chuckled.

"It will warm up in April."

Clint put his garment bag down while Jordan helped him into the jacket. They ran across the parking lot. Mercifully, the rain had subsided to the point where only a few stray drops splattered onto them. By the time they got back to the car, night had fallen. As Jordan drove toward Manhattan, Clint looked around and smiled at the sea of lights, the Christmas decorations and the sky scrapers that loomed in the distance like large mountains to form the famous New York City Skyline.

"I must say, it's an impressive sight. But I can't believe the prices on these tolls and the amount of traffic," he remarked, when they crossed the bridge into Manhattan.

Jordan smiled and nodded, but kept his eyes on the road. When they reached China Town, it took him a while to find a parking space. When he finally did, they walked up the street to a local eatery that was famous for its Dim Sum. After they finished dinner, they returned to Jordan's apartment. Clint looked around admiringly and then Jordan opened the draperies and French doors in order to showcase his terrace. Clint walked out, stood there and shivered in the frosty air. He delighted in the panoramic view and soaked in the hum of the city's sounds.

"Hey, where's the Waldorf Astoria?" He asked, as the wind whipped and howled around him

Jordan smiled, pointed in a Northeasterly direction and ushered him back inside.

CHAPTER SEVENTY-FOUR

RUSTY CAGE

Garth announced "Light's Out" and everyone returned to their cells. It had been an excruciatingly long day for Pattie. She was exhausted and grateful that it had finally come to an end. When she and Miranda returned to their cell, she looked under her mat to get a measure of comfort from Jordan's photograph, but the envelope was gone. She lifted her mat to check whether it had gotten stuck to the bottom of it and frowned when she didn't find it. A few seconds later the lights went out. Pattie lay on her mat feeling very sorry for herself.

Another weekend with no visitors and now Jordan's picture is gone too, she thought as she cried herself to sleep.

CHAPTER SEVENTY-FIVE

HYPNOTIC

On December 22nd, after having spent the night on Jordan's couch, Clint woke to the smell of sausages, eggs, toast, home fries and strong coffee. He got up, neatly folded his bedding and followed the scent. He found Jordan in the kitchen, putting the finishing touches on their hearty breakfast. As they ate, Clint chatted about the campus where they once worked together. Afterwards, they got dressed and took the elevator down to Jordan's immaculate, elegantly furnished lobby and waited for Reginald. Even though it was midmorning, the sky looked as dark as night. New York City was experiencing yet another rainstorm. A few minutes later, Reginald drove up to the front of the building. When Jordan and Clint saw him, they ran in between the cold raindrops and got into Reginald's Mercedes. As Reginald drove northward to the prison, the air temperature dropped. Eventually the rain turned to sleet and by the time they reached the prison parking lot, it was snowing.

When they got out of the car, Clint stopped, looked up at the sky and held his hand out.

"Oh my. I have to say. This is the first snow I've ever actually seen in my life," he said.

When the correctional officer at the entrance realized they were on The Warden's Special Guest List, he handled them with kid gloves and called for a staff member to personally escort them up to her office. Jordan said nothing, but he resented the disparity in the way he had been treated by that exact same officer when he attempted to see Pattie just a week and a half before.

The warden had set up her office to accommodate the hypnotism. She even placed a light thermal blanket and a pillow on her fluffy white couch so Pattie would have a comfortable place to recline. When Reginald, Jordan and Clint arrived, she was showing a court stenographer the best place to set up. Katrina Nero and her rebuttal expert were already there. The only one missing was Pattie.

A few minutes later, Garth brought Pattie in. Not knowing what was happening, she felt scared. She thought she was being brought before the warden, because of the false allegation about having vandalized the bench on the tier, so she stopped dead in her tracks before crossing the threshold. When she saw Reginald, she asked to speak to him in private. Garth followed along to make sure they weren't planning a prison break, but he stayed far enough away, so they could speak confidentially.

Pattie cleared her throat and nervously asked Reginald what was going on.

"Didn't they tell you? You're being hypnotized today."

She shook her head, as she informed him that no one told her anything.

"In any case, don't worry. Everything will turn out fine," he said.

While Pattie and Jordan were out in the hallway, Katrina and her rebuttal expert approached Clint.

"I'm wondering just how confident you are that this whole thing will even work," Katrina said.

Before Clint could respond, Pattie and Reginald returned. Reginald introduced Pattie to everyone and then he reminded her that the stenographer would be taking down everything, everyone said. Clint patted the couch. Pattie sat on it, removed her boots and reclined. She covered herself and sank into the softness.

"Good morning everyone. For the record, I'm Reginald Reese, Defense Counsel in the matter of The People of the State of New York v. Pattie Anwald. The parties to this case are hereby stipulating that Attorney Anwald has suffered traumatic brain amnesia surrounding the events and experiences that transpired this past Thanksgiving."

He went on to recite every other stipulation into

the record. When he finished, Katrina agreed with the stipulations. Then, Clint followed up by stating his credentials and explaining the procedure. Finally, he turned to Pattie.

"OK now, Pattie, I'd like you to listen carefully to everything I say to you."

He removed an antique gold watch from his jacket pocket, just like they did in the movies. It was attached to a gold chain. He dangled it in front of Pattie and let it swing back and forth like a pendulum.

"I'd like you to simply gaze at this watch and keep your eyes fixed on it as it moves back and forth in front of you. And if your eyelids happen to get heavy or if you feel drowsy, it's perfectly fine for you to just give in to the feeling and let your eyes close," he said slowly, as the watch swung back and forth.

Pattie's eyelids began to flutter. Then they drooped. When they were completely closed, Clint put the watch back in his pocket.

"Now Pattie, I'd like you to begin counting backwards, starting with the number ten."

Pattie started to count and dropped off at the number five.

"Pattie, if you can hear me, let me know," he said.

She nodded.

"Good. Now continue breathing and when I lift your right hand, you will go into an even deeper sleep, but you will still be able to hear everything I say."

He raised Pattie's right hand. It flopped down at her side like a wet dish rag.

"Now, I'm going to begin asking you some questions and I want you to answer them as truthfully, as factually and as precisely as you can, no matter what, even if what you say could have a negative impact on you or someone else. Do you understand?"

She nodded again.

"Good. What is your full name?"

"Pattie Anwald."

"What did you have for breakfast this morning?"

"The same slop they give us every morning. Gruel. And the most horrible coffee you could ever imagine. But at least it's hot and it soothes my aching throat," she said, without passion or malice.

Everybody but Garth looked at the warden, who blushed and shifted uncomfortably in her seat.

"Pattie, are you relaxed right now?" Clint asked.

She smiled and nodded.

"Quite frankly, this is the first time I've actually felt comfortable since the day I arrived here. And I have a feeling this office, with its art work and plants, is the only nice room in the entire compound."

Once again, everybody but Garth made a sidelong glance at Warden Eppes.

"Pattie, what happened last night?" Clint asked.

"Well, after an entire day of scrubbing every piece of furniture on the tier, I finally got to sit down with everyone to watch the tail end of a movie."

"Why on earth did you spend your Sunday scrubbing all the furniture on the tier?"

"Because I was falsely accused of vandalizing the bench where we sit to watch TV and no one believed me when I said I didn't do it."

"I see. So, going back in time to this past Thanksgiving, tell me what happened on Thanksgiving night."

She shook her head.

"Can you remember?"

She shook her head again.

"No."

"All right then, Pattie. Moving backward in time from Thanksgiving night, tell me the last thing you DO remember happening that day."

"Oh my God, what a mess! What right did you have to answer my phone and throw it?" Pattie yelled.

"Pattie, who are you talking to?"

"My brother Lou."

"Why did he throw your phone?"

"Because my client, Leland LeRoux called me to tell me he'd been arrested and for some reason Lou really hates this particular client! Oh my God, Lou's stomping on my phone and smashing it to pieces! That's it. I'm out of here."

"Where is 'here'?"

"My parents' house."

"Where are you going?"

"I don't usually help clients arrange for bail. It's

not my job. But I can't stay here. Believe me, going and helping Leland LeRoux with his bail is as good an excuse as any for leaving."

Her hand flew to her temple.

"Why are you holding your head like that?"

"Because my mother just grabbed the wooden eagle that fell from the mirror Lou broke and banged me in the head with it," she said.

She continued to rub her temple.

"That did it. Two can play the same game. I'll just take Lou's switchblade. I can hide it under my car seat."

"Ask her what happened to that switchblade? When was the last time Pattie ever saw it?" Katrina Nero wrote on her notepad and slid it over to Clint.

"Moving forward into the day, what happened after you arranged for Leland LeRoux's bail?"

She shook her head back and forth violently and her breath became labored.

"What's going on, Pattie?"

She cleared her throat.

"Leland's on top of me and he has me pinned down on the seat of my car. Ow! Ow! He's hurting me! Oh my God! He's ripping my dress and he's actually try-ing to rape me. Help me," she screamed.

Her voice was panicky. She writhed and struggled.

"Pattie, it is important for you to remember at all times, that these are only memories and memories cannot hurt you."

"Well, he just bit my shoulder with his scaly mouth and now he's trying to kiss me," she gasped out the words.

She squirmed, crooked her right arm and made a fist.

"I wish I could escape, but I can't. He took my car keys. Now that I've got him in a headlock, getting hold of that switchblade is my only chance of surviving," she added, as she relived the ordeal she suffered on Thanksgiving.

She groped around on the floor underneath the couch, with her left hand. Then she held it up in triumph. Her eyes were still closed and she finally stopped squirming.

"There! I've got it. He's scared. Thank GOD he's coming to his senses and getting out of the car. I still have to figure out a way to get those keys back without losing control of the switchblade, though."

"Pattie, did you cut Leland with that switchblade?"

She shook her head.

"Did you cut him with anything else?"

She shook her head again.

"No."

"Where are you?"

"I'm still in the car."

"Well, where is the car parked?"

"Oh. On Leland's Street, in front of his apartment."

She wrung her hands around manically and moaned.

"I'm out of the car now, but Willie Hudson just came around the corner. He's wearing a diamond in his ear, just like. Just like. I can't remember, but it seems very familiar to me. Anyway, he's demanding I give him the switchblade. Ow! He just punched me in the face. Oh my God! I'm on the ground. The switchblade is next to me. I just tried to grab it, but Willie scooped it up before I could get to it. He keeps cursing at Leland and now he's demanding Leland give him my car keys,"

"Are you saying Willie has the switchblade?"

She nodded.

"I wish I could have grabbed it in time."

Katrina took her pad back, wrote another question and passed the note pad back to Clint. He read it and nodded.

"Pattie, where is Leland now?"

"Willie just threw me into the hatchback like I'm just a sack of potatoes or something. I think he thinks I'm dead. Now he's chasing Leland. Oh my God! Willie is hacking Leland to bits with the switchblade and Leland is bleeding to death. Willie just stuffed him into the front of the car. My God, the smell is worse than anything you could ever imagine! It's even worse than Leland's breath. Oh my God, they're ruining both my car and my life."

"Let's fast forward a little bit. Where is Willie now?"

She nodded and her teeth started chattering.

"He's in the car driving."

"Let's fast forward to where Willie reaches his destination."

She held her nose with her left hand and her right arm flailed.

"I just landed in water. It's so icy it stings and it's hurting me so much. I'm sinking fast and I don't know how to swim! Ouch! I just hit rock bottom. Wherever this water is, the bottom must be made out of cement. It's very hard. Anyway my car just landed next to me. I guess I'm lucky it didn't land on top of me."

She shivered and jerked her head to the left.

"Leland's head just floated past me and eels are fighting to peck at his eyes," she screamed.

Katrina Nero and Warden Eppes gasped. Their hands flew over their mouths. The second they uncovered their faces, they looked at each other in horror. Pattie put her hands above her head and exhaled with force.

"I don't think I can hold my breath anymore."

"It's OK, Pattie. You're not going to drown. Remember, it's just a memory.

Now tell me where Willie is."

She shook her head and made dog paddling motions with her arms and legs.

"I'm back on the surface of the water. If I can somehow get myself over to the edge and grab onto it, I could probably hoist myself out of here. I get the feeling where ever this place is, it's not New York

City. As I get nearer to the edge I'm beginning to realize whatever this body of water is, it's located in some kind of an empty parking lot."

"You didn't answer me, Pattie. Where is Willie? Is he with you now?"

She shivered and shook her head. Her teeth were chattering.

"I can't tell you where Willie is, because I don't know. The only thing I do know is that I'm soaking wet, freezing cold and all alone. As icy as the water felt, it was warmer than this air is right now. I'm in so much pain. I'm scared. I see a gate and I'm just going to have to start walking toward it and see where it leads."

"Where did Willie go?"

"I guess he must have disappeared after he dumped Leland, my car and me in the water, but I have no idea where."

"Well, where is the switchblade?"

She shook her head.

"I don't know where that is either. I guess Willie kept it and took it with him."

"What is happening now?"

She nodded.

"I'm walking through the gate of the parking lot and out onto a street. A car is coming toward me. What if it's Willie coming back to finish me off? Oh God, the car is slowing down. Now it's stopping. Wait a minute. It's ok. It's Jordan. He just got out of the car and now he's walking toward me."

"Did Jordan hurt Willie, Leland or you?"

She shook her head.

"OK Pattie, as I count from one to ten, you'll gradually find yourself returning to consciousness. When I reach the number ten, you will feel warm, healthy and pain free, as well as emotionally stable. You will retain the accurate memory of everything that happened on Thanksgiving Day and Night and in addition, you will recall it easily and without trauma when requested. Do you understand?"

Pattie nodded.

Clint slowly counted from one to ten. At the count of ten Pattie opened her eyes, stretched and sat up. The warden handed her a paper cup filled with water. Pattie thanked her. When she finished it, the warden took the cup away, threw it in the wastepaper basket and nodded at Garth. Garth stood and escorted Pattie out of the office. When she reached the doorway, she turned and said good bye to everyone.

Katrina put her note pad away. She invited everyone in the room to lunch and they all accepted. They formed a caravan and after a treacherous drive through Westchester's snow covered hills, they all arrived safely at one of the County's finest, most beautiful five star restaurants. They each feasted on a sumptuous lunch and at the end, Katrina paid the enormous tab, courtesy of the taxpayers. Meanwhile,

Pattie was back in the prison cafeteria, defending her peanut butter and grape jelly sandwich against Dutch's advances, with the murder charge still hanging over her head.

CHAPTER SEVENTY-SIX

RESCUE ME

At four o'clock on the morning of December 23rd, as soon as the lights went on, Garth appeared in the doorway to Pattie and Miranda's cell. Pattie squinted, because the light hurt her eyes. Garth tossed Miranda's uniform onto her bunk and handed Pattie the envelope containing the clothes she wore on the day Investigators Townley and Nottingham brought her to the prison.

"Here. Put these on. You're going to need them for court," he said.

Pattie frowned, wiped her eyes and wondered whether Garth was setting her up for a day of "Bullpen Therapy". In any case, she got out of her bunk as soon as Garth left. She and Miranda turned their backs on each other so they could both get dressed with a modicum of privacy. A few minutes later Larabee appeared in the doorway, asked Pattie to turn around and handcuffed her, but she did not put leg irons on her.

"Garth asked me to escort you downstairs," she said.

As Larabee walked Pattie past everyone on the tier, Dutch pointed at her.

"Hey! Where is SHE going? How come she's getting to eat first? And why isn't she in a uniform? Peanut you better help me with my case today! After all, a deal is a deal!" Dutch bellowed.

Without taking Pattie to the cafeteria, Larabee brought her downstairs, handed her over to one of the transport officers and said good bye. She and Pattie were on opposite sides of the prison door when it clanged shut. Pattie looked up at the early morning sky. It looked dismal. No sooner did she inhale a breath of fresh morning air, when the Pig Farmer drove his truck around the corner. Seconds later, the stench invaded her nostrils, forcing her to gag. The muffler on his truck backfired, just as the transport officer opened the rear door to the cruiser that would bring her to court. The sound made her jump and she stopped dead in her tracks.

"Let's go!" The transport officer barked as he nudged her into the cruiser.

LIMBO

CHAPTER SEVENTY-SEVEN

FREE BIRD

The transport officer pulled up to the prisoner's entrance at the courthouse and left Pattie in the hands of a lockup officer. The lockup officer thought it was weird that this prisoner was arriving alone and by car, rather than by way of the van, but in accordance with the orders on Pattie's Habeus papers, he took her straight past the lockup and brought her directly up to the courtroom. It could not have been any later than five thirty in the morning, but when Pattie walked through the doorway, court was already in session. The officer deposited her in a seat next to Reginald at the counsel table and stood behind her.

"In accordance with an agreement reached between the People of the State of New York and the Defendant's Attorney in the matter of People v. Pattie Anwald, I am ordering Ms. Anwald's release from incarceration, effective immediately," Judge Islington said.

Pattie's red rimmed eyes lit up in disbelief as Judge Islington banged the gavel. One second later, the court officer behind Pattie unshackled her. She looked up at Reginald, but before she could even thank him, he interrupted her.

"Pattie Dear, stop by my office as soon as you can. I'll give you your checks and discuss your charges then," he whispered.

She nodded.

"But I haven't had a thing to eat since five o'clock last night," she said.

Reginald looked shocked.

"That's incredible. I'd take you for breakfast myself, but I have an early morning client. So, why don't you just go enjoy a nice breakfast and THEN come see me?"

She smiled and nodded.

"Thanks for everything. See you later."

While Pattie was talking to Reginald, Jordan was trying to plow through the crowded courtroom to get to her. He called her name and reached for her, the way an ocean reaches out to touch the shore, but just as she turned to stretch her arms toward him, the court officer got between them.

"Please. Just meet us at the Clerk's office on the first floor and wait there until they process her paperwork. Then you can be with her all you want," he said to Jordan, in a testy tone of voice.

He turned around, escorted Pattie through the same door she entered and then down to the Clerk's Office. It took about twenty minutes for the clerk to finalize Pattie's release papers. When she was through, the court officer left. Pattie rushed over to Jordan as fast as her legs could carry her. He swept her into his arms and pulled her toward him, in full view of everybody in the Clerk's Office. And with an ease neither of them had expected, she melted into his embrace. His touch, his kiss, his hands and his voice were all familiar and sweet. Tears of release and joy rolled down her cheeks as they hugged for what seemed like an eternity.

Jordan could literally feel her bones when he held her, but he didn't say anything. When he let go of her, he took hold of her hands, raised them up as if in victory and looked at her. Then he gently released her left hand. Still holding her right hand, he led her out of the courthouse and into the daylight. He stood and watched while she practically gulped her first breath of freedom in several weeks. She looked up at him with a tentative expression. He felt uncomfortable seeing how pale she looked. She reminded him of a marble statue. And the deep circles under her hollowed out eyes also bothered him, however, he was relieved that at least the crust on her face had disappeared and her hair was brushed neatly. Two Cardinals flew in, ushered by a Southwest breeze. They chirped and sailed by. Jordan and Pattie smiled gently at each other. Then he led her to the garage and opened the door to his rental car. Before she got in, he pressed his lips against hers. They kissed deeply and breathlessly. Afterwards, he helped her into the car and closed the door.

The first thing she did was brace herself. Then she snapped the visor down, gazed at her reflection in the mirror and gasped. She shuddered at the sight of the haunted face that gaped back at her so intensely. There was nothing else for her to do at that point except frown, sigh and snap the visor back into place. When Jordan opened the driver's side door and got in, she gave him a peck on the cheek.

"Reginald told me to be at the courthouse at five thirty this morning. That's all I know. I guess we'll find out more when we get to his office."

"He told me he has to meet with a client first. So, as anxious as I am to meet with him, do you think it's possible for us to go somewhere and eat first? You wouldn't believe how hungry I am," she said.

CHAPTER SEVENTY-EIGHT

BREAKFAST

When the hostess at the diner led Pattie and Jordan to their booth, the smell of coffee in the air felt like heaven to Pattie. A few minutes after they were seated, their waitress came to deliver the menus. She was wearing a Santa Clause hat complete with a Jingle Bell. Pattie ordered a cup of coffee. The bright morning sun was already climbing the sky but it was still low enough to shine through the clear glass picture window and place a glare on their menus. When the waitress delivered the coffee, Pattie ordered a he-man breakfast that was fit for a lumberjack. When it arrived, she wolfed down every bite. At the end, she tore her English muffin in half, used it to sop up every last bit of her egg yolk and ordered more coffee. That was the biggest meal she had ever eaten in her life. Afterwards, Jordan paid the bill and as he drove to Reginald's office, Pattie sat quietly and soaked in the sights.

CHAPTER SEVENTY-NINE

WE'RE GOING HOME

Pattie and Jordan walked arm in arm, as Ellie led them back to see Reginald. The minute he saw them, he stood, smiled and greeted them. Then he gestured for them to take a seat.

"Well, you're sprung! But remember, just because you're out, it doesn't mean the charges went away. They're still pending. But your hypnotic session with Clint convinced Katrina you're innocent. So she claims her game plan is to dredge the reservoir in order to leave no stone unturned and then she'll dismiss the charges. Naturally I'd like that to happen as soon as possible. Wouldn't it be great if someone could just find Willie and get him to confess?" Reginald said.

He slid a card across his desk. Pattie picked it up, read it and knit her brow.

"As a condition of your release, Katrina insists you call the number on this card from the same land line every single day, WITHOUT FAIL, until the case is disposed of. Listen, it's better than having to wear an electronic bracelet."

He smiled and slid one of his Trustee checks across the desk at her. She looked at it and noticed it was for the sum of Fifty Thousand dollars.

"From your landlord with love. And with strings attached, of course. You have to sign a stipulation agreeing never to return to the apartment. Also you're to sign this release, holding him harmless from any and all future claims. And he'd like the key back."

While Jordan removed Pattie's key from his key-ring, Reginald slid two identical copies of the General Release and the Stipulation across his desk. Pattie read them and signed them. Then Reginald pushed another check across the desk toward her. She picked it up and looked at it. It was a personal check in the amount of five thousand dollars and signed by "Brad Curatolo." Reginald chuckled as he watched her scrutinize it. She looked up at him and smiled.

"Amazing," she said.

"If you want I could hold him up for more. Although he claims it's all he has," Reginald said.

When Pattie shook her head, Reginald slid two identical copies of a General Release across his desk. She read them, signed them and slid them back toward him.

"Anyhow, what I think is more important than the check, is the fact that he agreed not to fight you when you apply for unemployment and Cobra Benefits.

And said he'll even give you a glowing recommendation when you start looking for work," Reginald continued.

"Thank you again. For everything," she said.

They wished each other a Merry Christmas. When the meeting was concluded, Jordan put his arm around Pattie's waist, escorted her out to the car and opened the door for her.

"Well Love, you know I think you're a marvelous girl. You're beautiful inside and out and I hope you're smart enough to have figured out by now that I've been madly in love with you for quite some time. My love for you is unconditional. I need you and I think you need me. And, last but not least, I adore you. I think we're, dare I use the word soul mates? I can't even begin to describe how lonely I was without you all these weeks. I promise to do my best never to fight with you again. So, would you please just give US a chance by coming to stay with me?" He asked, point blank.

She looked deeply into his eyes and pondered all he said. Finally she nodded, smiled and cleared her throat.

"The only answer I can give you is that I love you and I missed you too. You can't imagine how often I dreamt of my everyday life with you while I was— away."

He blushed and smiled back at her.

"Actually I can, because I dreamt of you as well."

"Jordan, I have nowhere else to be. I didn't make plans to go anywhere, because when I woke up this morning, I didn't even know I was going to be released. But I don't want to give you the impression that's the only reason I'm coming to stay with you. While it's true that I'm technically homeless, I'd be crazy not to accept your offer, even if I lived at the Taj Mahal, it's been a blessing just knowing you. Oh. And another thing. I promise to try to never fight with you either," she said.

He reached for her hand and squeezed it warmly. They kissed again briefly, then he helped her into the car and closed the door. Twenty minutes later they were at her bank. She filled out a deposit slip and walked up to the counter. Instead of taking Pattie's deposits, a new teller, whom Pattie had never seen before, gasped and shoved Pattie's checks and deposit slip back across the counter at her with a vengeance.

"My God! Aren't you that killer I saw all over the news? How do I know these checks aren't stolen?" She shrieked.

Her voice was so loud, every head in the branch turned toward her. Pattie blushed, cleared her throat and looked at Jordan. Tears formed in her eyes. Jordan frowned, pulled her away from the counter and took her to see the manager. The manager apologized profusely and handled Pattie's deposits himself. He told her Reginald's Trustee check would clear by the

26th and Brad's check would clear by Monday December 29th.

Pattie and Jordan's next stop was the storage facility where Pattie became reacquainted with her long lost possessions. She went through them, while Jordan got a cart so they could take some of them back to his apartment. Her eyes lit up when she saw her laptop. She picked it up, handed it to Jordan to place in the cart and then she spotted her journal. She picked it up, opened it to her last entry and read it to herself. Then she looked at Jordan and wondered whether he had read it too. When he didn't react, she assumed he hadn't. She gave it to him to place it in the cart. She arranged her clothes and shoes in the cart herself. She picked up her favorite doll, "Kelly" and asked Jordan for his handkerchief. When he gave it to her, she used it to wipe the dust from her Kelly's hair and velvet dress. Then she passed "her" to Jordan to arrange neatly in the cart. After that, she dashed over to her bottle of black nail polish and put it in the cart. When she caught a glimpse of her magic eight ball, she ran over to it and picked it up.

"I've been meaning to ask you what that is," he asked.

She smiled.

"It's my magic eight ball from when I was a kid. If you ask it a yes or no question it will give you a psychic answer."

Jordan shook his head, smiled and created a space

for it in the cart. Pattie also packed her cosmetic bottles, along with her shampoo and conditioner and the bottle of perfume Jordan had bought for her at the South Street Seaport the previous summer. She pawed through her remaining belongings and became increasingly more frantic. Finally she stopped.

"I'm going crazy trying to find my pendant, ring and watch."

"I remember you asking your brother about them when you were in the hospital."

She nodded.

"I know they must be someplace, but I didn't see them the day we moved you out," Jordan said, as he fought to secure the padlock on the storage unit.

The cold wind whipped around them as he wheeled the cart out to the car. He carefully stored the items in the trunk and back seat. Once they were on their way to his apartment, Pattie asked him if she could borrow his cell phone. When he nodded, she took a deep breath and dialed her parents' land line. Even though it was only mid-morning, when Edie answered the telephone her speech was already slurred. Pattie could also hear the television blaring in the background.

"So what happens now?" Edie asked.

Pattie cleared her throat.

"I'll be staying with Jordan."

"You know, I come from an era when girls had high moral standards. Today's young women are in a state of social decline and now I realize you've jumped on their band wagon. You know, living in sin with a man isn't MY idea of emancipation. Anyway, that's my roundabout way of telling you I think you should just come here," Edie brayed.

Jordan overheard Edie's diatribe. He raised his eyebrows slightly, but continued to keep his eyes on the road as he drove.

"I don't know how tell you this without being blunt, except to just say I'd rather be with Jordan. He's always been very good to me. Anyway, I'm not trying to change the subject or anything, but did you happen to see my pendant and matching ring? Or my watch?"

"Why? Did you lose them? I'll just bet HE'S got them. Don't forget, he's a thief, you know."

Pattie shook her head and hung up. Jordan looked at her sideways, but said nothing.

CHAPTER EIGHTY

THE HOMECOMING

Jordan ushered Pattie into his apartment. Pattie looked around and felt grateful to be there. It was a beautiful, loving home, a haven of refuge where only good things happened, a sanctuary that whispered promises of "the good life"; a life of comfort, ease and peace of mind. It reflected a lifestyle she had heard about, but had never actually experienced until she met Jordan. It was so different from the hardship and squalor she had become accustomed to. She thought about all the gourmet breakfasts and romantic dinners Jordan had prepared for her there.

Jordan leaned down, cupped her face in both his hands and lifted her chin. He kissed her neck, then her mouth. They gazed into each other's eyes and smiled. Afterwards, he walked over to the small Christmas tree he had set up the night before. When he plugged it in, Pattie watched the pink and white lights twinkle and glow. Then she glanced around the room. The apartment was just as she remembered it. Jordan's baby grand piano, his leather bound classic book collection, the crystal Buddha that rested serenely in its alcove and the Armstrong Coat of Arms were all in their exact places. Two things were different. One was the Christmas Tree and the other was the white Tea Rose. Since rescuing it from Pattie's apartment, Jordan had replanted it in a blue and white delft pot. Pattie smiled. She remembered the day he gave it to her and she was glad to see it was thriving. She walked over to it and looked at it lovingly. From there, she walked over to the French doors that led to the terrace.

Sensing she wanted to go out there, Jordan followed her. He opened the draperies and led her out. He watched, while she walked up to the railing. She gripped it and looked into the distance. Even though the air was cold and the trees were bare, she thanked God for letting her be right where she was and prayed that she could stay there forever. Before she even had a chance to immerse herself in the pulse of the city, her eyes welled up with tears of gratitude. She didn't want Jordan to see her crying, so she turned around and rushed back inside. Sensing he was right behind her, she quickly wiped her tears on her sleeve and walked over to the white leather couch. She planted herself in the same spot she had always occupied. Then she sprawled out and melted into it. It felt as soft as butter. She slid her shoes off and dug her aching feet into the soft, plush, carpeting. It felt so soothing, she couldn't help but revel in it, but when she looked down at her blisters, ragged toenails and calluses, she felt embarrassed, so she curled her toes under her feet and closed her eyes.

A few seconds later, Jordan sat next to her. She opened her eyes, turned to him and once again smiled. He reached out, wrapped her in his arms and pulled her toward him. They clung to each other for close to twenty minutes. Neither of them pulled away to look at or even kiss one another. It was a pure embrace from the heart, without an ounce of selfishness in it.

"By the way, I'm very sorry you wound up having to talk to Dutch on the phone," she said, when they broke their embrace.

He nodded and reached for her hand.

"Well, don't be. It wasn't your fault. By the way, right after Reginald and I visited you, we stopped at the Warden's Office so Reginald could arrange for your hypnosis session with Clint. While we were there, he threatened to sue the Warden on your behalf, because you were doing so poorly as a result of not receiving any proper medical attention."

Pattie looked surprised.

"Wow. I always knew Reginald was a good lawyer, but he really does go the extra mile."

He nodded.

"I agree. He certainly does. You're very fortunate."

She nodded.

"You know, society is so blunt about calling it 'maximum security' and yet they don't mind mixing it with the softened down term, 'correctional facility'. But since there's nothing 'correct' about it, why don't they just call it what it is? A freaking zoo. No. Wait. At least in a zoo the ASPCA comes to the animals' aid."

Jordan remembered his own unpleasant experiences there and nodded in agreement.

Pattie stood, walked over to the Christmas Tree and delicately touched one of the boughs. Then she looked at Jordan.

"Anyway, would it be all right if I took a shower? I'm dying to finally get out of these clothes and get cleaned up," she said.

He nodded, walked over to the linen closet and pulled out two fresh fluffy towels, a wash cloth and a bar of orange and papaya soap. It was beautifully wrapped in delicate tissue paper. Pattie walked over to the bag that held her belongings and dug around until she found the shampoo, conditioner and hairbrush she had brought from the storage unit. Then she and Jordan walked down the hall together. Jordan turned on the showerhead and showed her how to adjust the water temperature. When he left, she closed the door, locked it and took a deep breath. She realized it was the first time she had been alone in several weeks. She shed her clothes as if they were an old skin, rolled them into a ball and stuffed them into the trash basket. Then she braced herself and turned toward the full length mirror on the back of Jordan's door. She stared for a long time at the haggard wretch who stared back at her. Her face was wan and sallow. Her eyes were hollowed out and her bony body was drooped with fatigue. She shook her head and told herself she looked pathetic. Then she spotted a scale and stepped onto it. When it registered a scant ninety three pounds, she stepped off. When she stepped back on and it still only registered ninety three pounds, she sighed, stepped down and unwrapped the soap. She sniffed its decadent scent. Then she stepped into the shower. She made the water as hot as she could stand it and stood under its thunderous rush. She smiled as it pulsated on the crown of her head. She inhaled the steam and got busy washing her hair. Although her shampoo was lackluster at best, it was wonderful compared to the cheap products the canteen sold at exorbitant prices. When she rinsed it off and applied an overly generous amount of conditioner, she felt like the richest girl in the world. Feeling as if her skin was screaming to get clean, she let the conditioner soak into her hair, while she lathered her body from head to toe with the sumptuous soap. As she scrubbed and scrubbed, she wished she could wash away the whole experience of having been in prison.

Meanwhile, Jordan used the time to make room for Pattie's clothes in his closets and drawers. After he was done, he could still hear the water running. He'd heard of people taking long showers before, but something just didn't feel right to him. Worried, he walked down the hall, stuck his ear against the door and knocked. When she didn't answer, he tried the door handle. It was locked. He called out to her. Only after she fully rinsed her hair and body, did she finally shut off the water. That's when she heard Jordan calling her.

"Pattie? Are you all right?"

He sounded upset.

"Yes, Jordan. I'll be out in a few minutes."

He breathed a sigh of relief, returned to the kitchen and unloaded the dishwasher. In the meantime, Pattie unfolded the towels. They were six feet long. She looked at them and shuddered when she realized they were the same length as the width of the cell she had shared with Miranda. She wrung the excess moisture out of her hair, patted it and wound one of the towels around her head like a turban. Then she draped her body in the other towel and tucked the corners in. She unlocked the door and headed for the kitchen.

Jordan heard the bathroom door open and walked toward the bathroom. When they met in the hallway, he scooped her up in his arms and carried her into the bedroom. He gently placed her on his pale apricot silk bedspread, carefully unwound the towel from her head and used it to gently rub her hair dry. He went into the bathroom, retrieved her hairbrush and spent the next several minutes tenderly brushing her hair. She wallowed in the pleasant sensation of sitting on a real bed with a comfortable mattress for the first time in weeks, all while having her hair brushed.

When he was finished, he placed the hairbrush on the nightstand. That's when Pattie spotted a black and white photograph of a beautiful woman in a sterling silver frame. She frowned.

"She's very pretty," she said.

"Thank you."

"Is she someone you met while I was in prison?"

He shook his head.

"God no. It's a photograph of my late mother," he said, as he massaged her shoulders.

He couldn't help but notice her vertebrae jutting out from the stalk of her spine. It scared him. He pulled the skin up on the back of her hand to check her skin turgor. She looked at him weirdly, frowned and cleared her throat. Since her skin turgor was fine, he knew she wasn't dehydrated. Because he didn't want to alarm her, he smiled at her and shook his head.

"Sorry. Just playing around," he said.

When he pulled the bedspread down, she saw the baseball shirt he had given to her the previous summer. It was sticking out from under his pillow. She pointed at it and cleared her throat again. He blushed, chuckled and pulled it out.

"You may as well know, keeping it nearby helped me," he said.

Glad to know he had missed her, she smiled, gently took it from him and let the towel drop from around her body. She slipped into the shirt, but didn't button it. They kissed passionately and wantonly. Her damp hair grazed his neck. His eyes burned with desire. Her fingers wound themselves around his thick, wavy hair. They lost themselves in the pleasure of one another and later, Pattie felt calm and safe as she experienced the long awaited joy of snuggling up to the coziness of his body. They spent the rest of the day nestled together under the Porthault sheets, entwined in each other's arms.

CHAPTER EIGHTY-ONE

GOLDEN SLUMBERS

Although it was the deepest sleep Pattie had enjoyed in a long time, some of the problems she encountered in prison continued to haunt her. She had no way of knowing that she ground her teeth while she slept or that her legs jerked and twitched to the point where on a few occasions she accidentally kicked Jordan. By four thirty that afternoon one of her twitches was so violent, it actually woke her up. She was disoriented. It took her a few seconds to realize where she was. She heaved a sigh of relief when she remembered she wasn't in her cell. Instead she was safe and sound in Jordan's warm, cozy bed. She prayed she wasn't dreaming, as she had done so many times in prison. And when she realized it wasn't a dream, she stretched and unwound herself from Jordan's embrace. And that's when it happened. The Charley Horse kicked in. Shock waves shot down her left calf all the way down to the sole of her foot. She panted, clutched the blankets and tried not to scream. The way she arched her back from the

Charley Horse reawakened the injury in her tailbone. When the pain finally subsided, she looked over at Jordan, who had managed to sleep through the entire ordeal. His mouth was soft and his dark hair formed a serious contrast to the pillow case. She sat up, peeled herself out from under the covers and buttoned her baseball shirt. She hobbled into the bathroom. A few minutes later, she tiptoed out of the bathroom and into the living room, where she opened the draperies and the French doors. When she stepped out onto the terrace, the cold needles that soared up from the soles of her bare feet actually felt good. They somehow managed to cool down the residual ache from the Charley Horse. She waited while the sun setting behind the purple, jagged rocks of the bare Palisades brought daylight to an end. Across the river the dusky sky offered up pink clouds and the last vestiges of sunlight spilled red golden rays onto the terrace. She watched the last minute Christmas shoppers scurrying down on the ground. The faster they moved the more free they seemed and the more free they seemed, the more she felt gripped by terror.

What will become of me?

She waited until it the sky was dark and intense and then she went back inside to sleep some more.

CHAPTER EIGHTY-TWO

IT CAN'T RAIN THIS HARD FOREVER

Because Pattie was used to getting up early, by four thirty the next morning, she was already standing outside on the terrace. She watched daybreak's first inkling of misty light gradually ease its way across the thick, velvety Manhattan sky. It lifted the pitch black color to navy blue and continued to spread until it brightened the sky to the blueish light typical of an early morning. Hues of rosy dawn appeared, but were short lived. A heavy cloud bank rolled in and hung low, eclipsing the sun and turning the heavens to a lead grey color. Then, the storm clouds burst open and drenched the city with torrential rain. The people on the street quickly ducked into nearby doorways, while the wind from the river blew the downpour right onto the terrace. Pattie stayed there and began to cry. She shook and sobbed, until she unleashed every pent up, unshed tear from the past three weeks. Even though she was soaked by both the rain and her tears, the catharsis felt good.

Jordan turned, stretched and reached for her. When he realized she wasn't there, he frowned and got out of bed. He wrapped his thick, white terrycloth robe around himself and walked down the hall. In spite of his robe, when he reached the living room, he felt chilly. He noticed the door to the terrace was wide open and the draperies were blowing. He spotted Pattie. She was standing out there, weeping in the clattering rainstorm. He coughed ever so slightly to let her know he was standing in the doorway. Startled, she jumped, turned around and smiled weakly at him. Seeing the worried expression her smile could not hide, he walked out to join her. He tenderly turned her around, draped his arms over her shoulders and gazed into her eyes. He lovingly ran his fingers through her hair. In return, she tenderly stroked the contours of his face with her fingertips and caressed his lips with the tip of her index finger. They turned and looked out at the tempest together. Then he turned back to face her. Seeing how she was shivering, he slipped his arms around her waist and pulled her toward him.

"Don't worry. It can't rain this hard forever," he whispered.

He picked her up, carried her to the bathroom, slid off her wet baseball shirt and hung it over the shower door. He dried her hair and body, smiled at her and gave her his robe to wear.

"Since it's Christmas Eve, let's make a special breakfast," he said, as he slipped into a sweat suit.

He took her by the hand and led her to the kitchen. He brewed some coffee, opened the refrigerator door and pulled out smoked Nova Scotia salmon, onions, eggs and caviar, for what he promised would be "An Omelet of Distinction." He placed the items on the counter and retrieved two large potatoes, the cinnamon rolls and some butter. Pattie sipped her coffee and kept him company while he cooked. When the food was ready, they ate. Afterwards, he poured them each a second cup of coffee. They relaxed for a while until Pattie got up from the table. She fished in her bag for the card Reginald had given to her and used Jordan's landline to call the Probation Department. When she finished the call, she dialed Lou's number. Lou congratulated her on being released. Without actually admitting he was the one who broke her cell phone, he offered to take her out to shop for a replacement. And when she agreed, they made plans for him to pick her up at Jordan's apartment at one o'clock on the day after Christmas. They wished each other a "Merry Christmas", said good bye and hung up. While Pattie still had the phone in her hand, she decided to call Ryan to let him know she was out of prison.

"Thank God," Ryan said, as he breathed a sigh of relief.

He invited her and Jordan to have Christmas

dinner with him and his family at two o'clock the next day. She immediately accepted. After she hung up and told Jordan, he frowned.

"What's the matter? Why are you frowning?"

He stared at her.

"Nothing's the matter, except I just think we need to run invitations past one another before we accept them. That's all."

She met his look with equal intensity as she processed that thought. Then she nodded.

"Oh, ok. I see your point. Forgive me. I'm just not used to being a 'we' yet. I've only ever been an 'I' until recently. Do you want me to call Ryan back and get us out of it?"

He shook his head.

"Of course not. By the way, do you remember me telling you about the nice pastor at the Presbyterian Church up in Yorktown?"

She wondered where this was leading and hoped he wasn't suggesting they go there for some Christmas Service. She held her breath and nodded.

"Yes," she said tentatively.

Sensing her distress at the mention of the church, he said nothing. He cleared the table and got dressed. An hour or so later, they hit the streets. It being Christmas Eve, everything was lit up for the shoppers. Upscale store windows featured chic fairy tale lights in miniature fir trees that beckoned to the customers to come in and spend their money. Pattie and Jordan decided to split up for the day and meet at three o'clock at Volpe's, one of New York's finest gourmet delis. As soon as Pattie was on her own, she headed straight over to Tiffany's and bought Jordan a pair of twenty four karat gold cufflinks that were shaped like star fish. Then she went to Bloomingdales and bought a leather wallet for Ryan and a green velvet dress as a Christmas present to herself, from herself. At that point, she had maxed out the remaining balance on her credit card.

CHAPTER EIGHTY-THREE

BLUE PERIOD

Meanwhile at the prison, right after the prisoners returned from lunch, the nurse at the Infirmary called Garth to inform him that Fritzi had been released from the hospital. She asked him to send someone down to escort Fritzi from the Infirmary back to the tier. He decided to send Larabee. Twenty minutes later, an orderly pushed Fritzi's wheel chair onto the tier. Larabee walked alongside, carrying Fritzi's crutches and paperwork. Fritzi greeted everyone except Dutch and Colette and everyone except Dutch and Colette applauded her. Dutch and Colette merely stood there with their arms folded across their chests. They both gave Fritzi the evil eye and stalked off to their cell. The orderly helped Fritzi onto her feet and assisted her with her crutches, while Larabee handed the paper work to Garth. Fritzi hobbled back to her cell. A few minutes later, Miranda appeared in her doorway. She was holding the art supplies and sketch pads. When she explained that Pattie had bought them for her at the canteen, prior to her release, Fritzi's eyes lit up.

"Ach ziss is so nice of her. Alzo I didn't realize she got released. I'm glatt for her, even zoe I vish I coot haff sanked her personally," she said.

CHAPTER EIGHTY-FOUR

CAN'T HELP MYSELF

By the time Pattie arrived at Volpe's Deli, it was slightly past three in the afternoon and Pattie felt like she was starving. When she opened the door, she spotted Jordan sitting at a table, waiting for her. Since it was Christmas Eve, Volpe's was planning to close early. As a result, Jordan and Pattie decided to order "take out." Pattie went overboard, ordering prosciutto, Kalamata Olives, a loaf of sourdough bread, a pound of mixed nuts, a pound of gourmet coffee, light cream, thinly sliced smoked turkey, a dozen poppy seed bagels and cream cheese. Jordan added foie gras, egg, tuna, shrimp and cucumber salads along with generous portions of hand sliced smoked salmon, Cole slaw and rugelach. Having remembered how great the cinnamon rolls tasted at breakfast that morning, Pattie decided, at the last minute, to buy a dozen more. Then she suggested they buy four huge black and white cookies, four enormous Linzer Torte cookies, a box of petit fours and four brownies, along with a pound of gourmet chocolate candy and a bag of popcorn to eat while they watched television later that night. Then, before heading home, they went to the liquor store and stocked up on a dozen bottles of chilled Dom Perignon. When they got back to the apartment, they set the groceries and champagne down on the counter. Jordan kissed her on the cheek and lit the tree. Then he returned to the kitchen, to help unpack their delicacies. When they were done, he served some of them on beautiful Wedgwood dishes, which they carried over to the table. Just as they were about to sit down to eat, the doorbell rang. Pattie frowned and cleared her throat.

"I wonder who that could be," she said nervously.

When she opened the door, a young man was standing there holding a long white box.

"Pattie Anwald?"

She nodded tentatively, all the while wondering whether this was an elaborate way of serving her with some kind of legal notice.

"Merry Christmas," he said, as he handed her the box.

Still frowning, she closed the door, brought the box over to the table and opened it. Inside, were a dozen long stemmed red American Beauty roses with baby's breath and a card from Jordan. Jordan came out of the kitchen, nodding, smiling and carrying a tall Lalique vase. Pattie ran over to him and hugged him. They brought the flowers and the vase back into the kitchen, filled the vase with water and arranged the flowers. Then Jordan opened a bottle of Dom Perignon and poured it into two Baccarat champagne flutes. He raised his flute in a toast, but Pattie hesitated.

"Listen. I know how you feel about alcohol, so don't feel you HAVE to drink this if you don't want to," he said.

She smiled, picked up the flute and shrugged.

"Oh, what the hell? After everything else I've been through, I might as well. After all, what else could happen to me?"

Jordan clicked her glass with his.

"Well, in that case, cheers!" He said.

After Pattie's first sip, she giggled.

"It tickles my nose. And it's sweeter than I imagined it would be. It slides down my throat kind of nicely too. It's also warming me up, which I like, since...well, let's face it, I'm always freezing."

Jordan nodded.

"Oh yes. It's very pleasant," he said.

Pattie lifted her glass again, closed her eyes and took another sip. Then she giggled once more and drained her glass.

"I can't say I'm used to the feeling of being relaxed, but I can see how this could get me there. Hit me again," she said.

She stretched her arm out and held the glass for him to refill. He looked at her nervously, but she didn't notice. When he refilled her glass, she took an oversized sip.

Since Jordan didn't have a fireplace, she tuned into one of the local TV stations that broadcast "The Annual Christmas Eve Yule Log from Gracie Mansion". She tilted her head back, closed her eyes and let the magic of the Christmas Carols wash over her. At eight thirty, "It's a Wonderful Life" was scheduled to air, so they switched the channel in order to watch it. And right before it started, a commercial for the eleven o'clock news flashed across the screen, along with a giant sized picture of Pattie.

"Scared yet? Homicidal gal lawyer back on the loose! Details at eleven," the anchorman said.

Pattie gasped and poured herself another glass of champagne.

"Oh my God! Where the hell did they even find that picture of me?"

Then, forgetting all about the popcorn and chocolate, she drank the champagne and ate nothing, while she cuddled with Jordan and watched the movie.

CHAPTER EIGHTY-FIVE

INSPECTION TIME

Right after the prisoners returned from their Christmas Eve dinner at the cafeteria, Garth turned the TV on. They all sat around and relaxed to the sounds of the Christmas music that accompanied the Yule Log. Fritzi took out her sketch pad and pencil and began to sketch Miranda, while Dutch hovered behind her and breathed down her neck. Garth announced that because it was Christmas Eve, he was letting them stay up beyond light's out to watch, "It's a Wonderful Life." Right before the movie started, everyone settled into their usual places on the bench, except for Fritzi and Miranda. Fritzi continued to sketch Miranda's portrait, while Miranda maintained her pose. When the news bulletin about Pattie flashed across the screen, everyone's mouth hung open.

About halfway through the movie, Quentin showed up. Although he wished everyone a Merry Christmas, the bullhorn in his left hand and the steel baton in his right, certainly revealed a motive other than spreading holiday cheer. Everyone's mood dropped at the sight of him. Most of the women were well aware that Quentin felt he was entitled to take advantage of any "new meat" that happened to tickle his fancy. At that moment, the thought running through everyone's mind, except Dutch's, was, "if he's in the mood to mess with anyone, please Dear God, let it not be me." Dutch, on the other hand, thought, "well, if he wants a roll in the hay, I won't mind."

Quentin picked up the remote control, snapped off the television and lifted his bullhorn. He bellowed that it was time for everyone to line up for inspection. A few minutes later, when the women were standing with their backs against the wall, he walked in front of them and examined each of them individually, from head to toe. When he reached Dutch, he stopped in his tracks as if he had never seen her before in his life. He shook his head and winked at her. Feeling hopeful, she winked back. A second later he moved onto the next inmate. He stopped when he reached the sweet faced newcomer, Darlene Storm. He backed up a few inches, looked her over and ordered her to return to her cell. After she left, he spent a few more minutes assessing each of the women and made an occasional wise crack. When he finished his inspection, he told Garth to turn the TV back on. Then he and Garth took a stroll back to Garth's office, where he questioned Garth about Darlene. After Garth told him what little he knew, Quentin left, walked down the corridor and quietly crept into Darlene's cell. As he walked over to her bunk, he found her, face down crying into her green, vinyl mat. He sat beside her, tapped her on the shoulder and pulled her around to face him. When he opened his fly, Darlene began to hyperventilate, which made him chuckle.

"You know, I never knew 'til I met you that not all Killer Widow Spiders are black. Some could even be blonde. And with blueberry eyes no less," he whispered.

She squeezed her eyes shut until her entire face was nothing more than a tight grimace. He jabbed her in the ribs, used his forefingers and thumbs to pry her eyes open and popped his own eyes until they were as wide as a bug's. After he stared her down, he pulled off her uniform, handcuffed her and raped her. His body odor was so bad, she had all she could do to keep from gagging. He stroked her hair and put his index finger over her lips. Then he stood, zipped his fly and walked back onto the tier, as if nothing out of the ordinary had happened. He strode right up to Dutch, pulled a set of papers out of his pocket and pointed at them.

"Well Moby, the Warden herself has ordered you to do some time in Segregation. Looks like you done hit the big time when you started clutterin' up our phone lines," he said.

Then he snapped his fingers at Larabee and Sistine and jerked his head in Dutch's direction. The two of them rushed to hand cuff her. Right after Quentin left, Colette got up and stormed down the hall to Darlene's cell. Darlene was once again lying face down, shaking and sobbing into her mat. Colette raced into the cell, flounced down on Darlene's bunk and dug her nails hard into Darlene's shoulder blades. When Darlene turned around, her eyes were puffy. Colette pouted, glared at her and slapped her in the face as hard as she could.

CHAPTER EIGHTY-SIX

IT'S A WONDERFUL LIFE

When "It's a Wonderful Life" was over, Pattie yawned. Because Jordan didn't want the news to upset Pattie so close to bedtime, so he turned the television off, reached for her hand and pulled her up into a standing position. Then he picked her up and carried her down the hall to the bedroom. She fell asleep the second her head hit the pillow.

CHAPTER EIGHTY-SEVEN

SHIFT CHANGE

Once shift change was over, Quentin opened an account for Darlene in the canteen with the sum of exactly one dollar. Then he clocked out and went home to wish his fat monster of a wife a "Merry Christmas".

CHAPTER EIGHTY-EIGHT

NIGHTMARE

A few hours passed before Pattie began to flail in her sleep. She woke up covered in sweat and screaming incoherently. Alarmed, Jordan reached out to comfort her, but she continued to jerk her arms and legs so violently, he backed away. He was pretty sure she wasn't having an epileptic seizure, but he wasn't sure exactly what was happening. When she finally calmed down, he asked her whether she was all right. She looked at him with a confused expression, muttered something incoherent and went back to sleep as if nothing had happened. Jordan sat there for a few minutes, shaking his head.

CHAPTER EIGHTY-NINE

THE CHRISTMAS SONG

Christmas in the prison began just like any other day. The prisoners were shuttled down to the cafeteria for an early morning breakfast. As Darlene waited on line with the others, Quentin materialized from out of nowhere. His baton was in his right hand. By now, Darlene had come to understand what everyone had already known for quite some time. Whenever Quentin showed up, it meant trouble for at least one person and quite possibly for everybody. By the time he walked up to the chow line and singled Darlene out, she was trembling in terror. When he swung his arm around her shoulder, she did her best not to flinch. He turned to the cafeteria worker who was just about to spoon a dollop of gruel into Darlene's Styrofoam bowl and smiled at her. She smiled back.

"Good morning and Merry Christmas to you," the worker said.

"Same to you. I hope you realize by now that I like a little meat on my Cutie pies' bones. Right?" Quentin said to the worker.

The worker grinned from ear to ear.

"I sure do."

"So that means anything this little gal here wants, she gets and as much of it as she can stand. And don't let nobody take none of it away from her, neither," Quentin warned.

After the cafeteria worker nodded and gave Quentin the thumbs up sign, Quentin leaned over, gave Darlene a peck on the cheek and vanished the same way he materialized. When he was gone, both Darlene and the worker heaved a sigh of relief.

CHAPTER NINETY

ALL I WANT FOR CHRISTMAS IS YOU

After Pattie's episode, she slept fairly soundly. When Jordan woke on Christmas morning, he smiled at her and gave her a quick kiss on the cheek, but she slept right through it. She finally got out of bed and slipped into her baseball shirt at eleven o'clock. She walked down the hall and found Jordan in the kitchen making Mimosas. They kissed each other and wished each other a Merry Christmas. Then, he handed her a large crystal goblet. When he asked her whether she remembered waking up in the middle of the night, she said she didn't.

"Anyway, this is a Mimosa. I made yours very weak. You know, I can remember my first hangover just as if it happened yesterday. I threw up incessantly; my vision was blurry and my head weighed about a hundred pounds. In short, it was terrible and I guess I'm just wondering whether you might be in the same shape. In any case, I put only enough hair of the dog that bit you in it to keep you stable, but not enough to start you off on a habit of morning drinking," Jordan said.

She informed him she wasn't feeling any pain or discomfort at all. Then she took the Mimosa into the living room, He watched with concern, as she drank deeply. He knew that people who were genetically predisposed to alcoholism rarely experienced hangovers. They were often quite able to drink with impunity, which is one reason they enjoyed drinking so much. He decided not to mention it. After all, it was Christmas.

She placed the empty glass on the coffee table and walked over to the Christmas tree. When she bent over to plug in the lights, she noticed a huge white envelope with her name on it, lying under the tree. Next to it was a tiny box wrapped in white tissue paper and tied with an enormous red velvet bow. She bent down, picked up the box and held it to her ear. Just as she started to shake it, Jordan came into the living room. She turned around, ran over to the closet and retrieved his present. After she handed it to him, she picked up the white box again, shook it and unwrapped it. Inside, was an electronic car key. She frowned and looked up at him with a stunned expression. He smiled back at her and nodded.

She ran into the bedroom, hurriedly threw on a sweat suit and her black velvet Mary Janes with the red dragons embroidered on them. She returned to the living room, grabbed the car key and ran out the door. Jordan walked over to the closet, retrieved their jackets and followed her. It felt like an eternity before the elevator arrived and it felt like another eternity when it finally reached the garage. However, when the door finally slid open, she ran out, hit the panic button on the key and waited for the horn to blast its response. She followed the sound until it led her to a shiny, powder blue BMW convertible. She gasped and smiled when she noticed it bore the same license plate as her original car.

"WILSUEU2."

She clicked the key again, in order to stop the ear splitting noise. Then she unlocked the car and got in. She closed her eyes and relaxed into the white leather seat. When Jordan got in on the passenger's side, she kissed him on the cheek.

"Thank you so much," she said.

He explained to her that all she had to do was put her foot on the brake and push the ignition button. Once she did, just like magic, the engine purred to life. He showed her how to turn on the seat warmers. She honked the horn. When it worked, she laughed. She released the hand break, pulled into reverse and backed out of the space. Five minutes later they were travelling North on the West Side Drive.

About a half an hour later, they returned to the apartment, arm in arm. Jordan picked up his present, gently removed the white ribbon from the robin's egg blue Tiffany box and opened it. He looked in surprise at the cufflinks and smiled.

"Thank you!" he said.

He fixed brunch while Pattie called the Probation Department's landline. Afterwards, they prepared a tray of cookies for Ryan and put a ribbon on a bottle of Dom Perignon, to take to him. Nervous about her appearance, Pattie made a special effort to style her hair in a very sleek French twist and she artfully applied her makeup. In spite of her efforts, she was still in awful shape. She was thinner than ever. Even at the height of her so called "Goth Phase", her face never seemed quite as drawn or as haunted as it did that afternoon. She picked up Ryan's gift, while Jordan went into the kitchen and picked up the champagne and cookies. Then they left to spend Christmas with the Pilgrim family.

CHAPTER NINETY-ONE

THE NIGHT STALKER

On Christmas night, halfway between lights out and shift change, Quentin quietly arrived on the tier, without fanfare or any pretense of inspection. He nonchalantly walked down the corridor, unlocked Darlene's cell and raped her. Afterwards, he left the tier, finished his shift and clocked out. Right before he went home, he made sure to deposit another dollar in Darlene's canteen account. When he opened the front door to his house, he found his long suffering wife lying in wait for him. So he fabricated some new and improved excuse about why he was too tired to have sex with her.

CHAPTER NINETY-TWO

I'VE GOT A FEELING

That night, just like the night before, Pattie had no trouble falling asleep. But at some point during the wee hours of the morning, she cried out, without waking up. The sound of her sobs woke Jordan. Alarmed, he sat up, frowned and touched her arm gently. She opened her eyes and looked at him with a vacant stare.

"What's the matter?" She asked, absently.

They both sat up. He didn't answer her. Instead, he held her and rocked her for the next several minutes, until she fell back to sleep.

CHAPTER NINETY-THREE

BOXING DAY

Once again, Jordan woke up before Pattie. While she was still sleeping, he showered, shaved and got dressed. When he went downstairs to retrieve the mail, he gave his amiable doorman, Joe, a Christmas card with money in it from him and Pattie. By the time he returned to the apartment, Pattie was awake.

"Glad you're up," he said.

She smiled and kissed him on the cheek.

"Me too."

He handed her an envelope that had been forwarded from her old address. She opened it. Inside, was a Christmas Card from Martha and Gus. Underneath their signature, they had written their phone number and asked her to call them. Jordan peered over her shoulder and looked at her quizzically.

"Who are Martha and Gus?"

"A kind of aging hippie couple who used to be my neighbors over on Peck Slip."

She placed her daily call to the Probation Department and then called Martha and Gus. When Gus answered, they exchanged Christmas greetings. Then Gus went on to tell her that he and Martha had been evicted and were living with Martha's mother. Pattie gave him Reginald Reese's telephone number and urged him to use it. She also gave him Jordan's address and phone number and said her own cell phone number would soon be working again. They cracked a few jokes about their old neighbor Gladys, wished each other a Happy New Year and said good-bye.

Afterwards, Pattie called Reginald to wish him a belated Merry Christmas. She thanked him again for everything. Then she informed him she was staying with Jordan and could be reached there indefinitely. Finally, she mentioned a couple named Martha and Gus Claxton who might be calling him. Just as the conversation wound down, she cleared her throat and asked whether Reginald had heard any news about her case. When he told her he didn't, she sighed, thanked him again and they said their good byes.

She and Jordan sat down to a small breakfast. Then she hopped in the shower and got dressed. Just like the day before, she went to enormous lengths to enhance her appearance. An hour later, as she was finishing up, the doorbell rang. She cleared her throat, answered it and greeted Lou.

Even though Lou tried not to be obvious about it, he wound up giving Pattie the once over. And what he saw shocked and terrified him. As far as he was concerned, Pattie looked like hell. She was stick thin and her face was haggard. For once in his life, he was at a loss for words, so he simply held his arms out and hugged her. After their embrace, she shook her head.

"Why didn't you at least come and visit me when I was stuck up in that Godawful place, you lousy stinker? Anyhow, what's that old saying? You only find out who your real friends are in times of adversity."

He shook his head.

"Listen, I am your real friend. And as nuts as this may sound, the truth is every time I wanted to get up there, I was either working or a blizzard stopped me."

"Yeah. I keep hearing about that damn blizzard."

"Why didn't you think to call US?"

She shook her head.

"I don't know. I really don't know."

"Plus, I visited you in the hospital. Don't I at least get some credit for that?"

She nodded vaguely, kissed Jordan good bye and led Lou out the door. When they stepped into the elevator, she pushed the button for "G". The minute the door opened in the garage, she took hold of his hand and walked him over to her splendid BMW. She beamed and gloated, as he eyed it with a mixture of awe and envy. She decided she wouldn't mention how she came by it, nor did she divulge the settlements Reginald had obtained for her.

She clicked the locks. They both got in, relaxed into the seats and smiled at each other. Then she showed him how to use the seat warmers. Once she drove the car outside, she realized it was a nice day. Even though it was December, it wasn't cold or damp and there wasn't even a cloud in the sky. She drove over to her old neighborhood and circled around until she found a parking space near her bank. She pulled into it, shut the engine off and told Lou she would return in a minute. Lou nodded, leaned back into the seat and closed his eyes.

Once inside the bank, Pattie asked the manager whether either of her checks had cleared. A few minutes later she came out with a smile on her face and a sizable amount of cash in her wallet. Before long, she was on the FDR Drive, heading Northbound. Lou suggested they drive up to Beau Rivage later in the day to visit Justin and her other clients and Pattie agreed.

"You know, The State Police and that DA up in Westchester finally applied for an arrest warrant on Willie Hudson. And they got it. So, if he's at Beau Rivage, that means I can lock him up right on the spot. Wouldn't that make for a hell of a collar?"

Pattie smiled and nodded. When they reached Midtown, she found a parking space right in front of the phone store. Lou was very generous. He encouraged her to upgrade to a smart phone. As they were leaving, he spotted a diamond ring in the window of the jewelry store next to the phone store and pointed at it.

"What do you think of THAT?"

Pattie looked at him quizzically.

"What's going on? Are you thinking of proposing to Cheryl or something?"

He chuckled.

"No, not really. I'm just curious as to what would be a nice engagement ring."

She shrugged.

"OK, but since no two people have the exact same likes and dislikes, the answer to that is highly subjective."

He smiled.

"I hear you, but let's go inside and look anyway," he said.

Once they were inside, the jeweler showed them his selection of diamond rings. Pattie admired them all. Then she went into the back of the store to explore the Estate Sale section. When she pointed to a four karat heart shaped Edwardian Platinum pink diamond ring that was surrounded by rubies, the jeweler told her she had exquisite taste. He explained it was designed in London, back in 1910, in the Edwardian era, by a man named Archibald Knox. Then he gave her a card so she could slide her ring finger through the holes. After a few pokes, she discovered her ring size was five. Then, before she even had the chance to try the ring on, Lou suddenly became anxious to leave. Both Pattie and the jeweler were confused when, without any warning, Lou practically dragged Pattie out of the store.

Their next stop was a clothing store, where Pattie got three gift cards, one each for Justin, Thomas and Bonnie. She signed them "from Pattie, Lou and Jordan." Then she drove up the West Side Highway, where she was forced to deal with pot holes, aggressive drivers who cut her off from the right side and ambulances that darted in front of her from out of nowhere.

"The way I have to dodge and weave in order to avoid all these pot holes I'm surprised I don't get stopped for a DWI."

Lou waved his hand.

"Well, if you do, I'll talk you out of it," he answered.

"Gee thanks. What a guy," Pattie said.

When they finally arrived at West End Avenue, Pattie swerved to avoid two errant jaywalkers and searched for a parking space. They walked up the block until they reached the five story Brownstone with its terra cotta sculpture and art work. Every window on the front of the edifice was bowed and sand colored brick blocks surrounded every one of them as if they were actual shutters.

Pattie looked up at the copper roof, which had turned the same shade of green as the Statue of Liberty. Then she walked up the path to the front door, tried the brass handle and realized it was unlocked.

She walked in, led Lou down the hall to April's office and knocked.

A few seconds later April opened the door. She greeted Pattie coolly and looked at her with a jaundiced eye. The truth was, she never really liked Pattie very much. In the past Pattie had criticized the way she ran Beau Rivage. And she blamed Pattie for inconveniencing her on a more personal level as well. She had been forced to hire and train the janitor who replaced Willie Hudson. Inwardly, she suspected Pattie was somehow connected to Willie's disappearance, even though she knew she couldn't prove it. At times she even wondered whether Pattie could have actually killed Willie. At least that's what the news stories were implying.

And yet she's large and in charge, sauntering around the city. Well, I guess it pays to be a lawyer, she thought.

She also wondered what Jordan Armstrong ever saw in the likes of Pattie. And even though Lou was Pattie's brother, in April's opinion, he was a horse of a different color. She liked HIM. After all, he was the detective who rescued Justin and saved his life. She turned to him, smiled and greeted him warmly.

When Pattie asked to visit her former clients, Justin, Thomas and Bonnie, April told her Thomas was out, but she walked her and Lou back up the hallway to the Victorian style sitting room. She asked them to wait, while she went upstairs to fetch the two teenagers. A few minutes later they bounded down the stairs and ran headlong into Pattie's arms. After they finished hugging her, Justin also hugged Lou. Both teenagers looked good, especially compared to the last time Pattie had seen them. Bonnie seemed prettier and softer.

After April returned to her office, Justin told Pattie about his kidnapping. Hearing the details made Pattie feel so bad, she actually cried. She could hardly believe another of her clients, Leland LeRoux, turned out to be his kidnapper. No wonder it was so easy for people to believe she was the one who murdered Leland. Justin's kidnapping certainly gave her a motive.

As Justin spoke, Pattie noticed he wasn't wearing the diamond earring he usually wore in his ear. Come to think of it, it was the first time she could remember seeing him without it. It triggered a flashback to Thanksgiving and she put two and two together. Willie was wearing it that day when he tried to kill her. She decided not to mention it.

A few minutes later, Thomas walked in. When he saw everyone in the sitting room, he joined them. He looked down at his sneakers before addressing Pattie. Then he confronted her about being in jail when he needed her most. Pattie nodded and when she asked him whether he had been following her story on the news, he shook his head.

"No. I never watch the news. It's too boring," he said.

Pattie explained how she was wrongfully arrested for a crime she didn't commit. She was careful not to drag Willie Hudson's name into it. Then she changed the subject by distributing the gift cards to each of them. They thanked her and shortly thereafter the visit ended. By the time Pattie and Lou reached the West Side Drive, the sun was setting pink behind the Palisades and the city lay in shadows. Pattie and Lou shared a silent drive back down to Chelsea. For Pattie, so many days in a row of being out and about after having been cooped up for so long, had taken its toll on her nervous system. She parked her car in its assigned space, turned the motor off and yawned. Then she and Lou walked toward the elevator. She pushed the button for the eighth floor. When Lou reached behind her and pushed the button for the lobby, she turned to him and squinted.

"I'd come up and spend some time with you and Jordan, but I have to meet Cheryl. We'll get together again real soon, though. OK?"

The elevator door slid open. He kissed her on the cheek and gave her a quick hug.

"Enjoy your new phone," he said.

She thanked him. When she walked into Jordan's apartment, she found him in the kitchen, preparing a spread with their deli items. He washed his hands, helped her out of her coat and gave her a hug. She showed him her new phone and set it up in the charger. He went back into the kitchen and she followed him.

"Are you hungry?" He asked.

When she nodded, he opened a bottle of Dom Perignon. He took two champagne flutes and brought them to the table. Pattie walked behind him, carrying the tray of food. When she set it down, they went back into the kitchen and got plates, napkins and knives.

"You're just in time for 'White Christmas'. Since it didn't snow yesterday, I guess this movie is as close as we'll get to having one this year," he said.

She nodded, picked up her glass and sipped. They turned on the movie and ate. Halfway through, Pattie's new phone jangled with its first cry of life. She ran over to it and looked at the caller ID. When she saw it was her parents, she was actually surprised the caller ID could even pick up a number from their antiquated dial phone. She let the call roll over to voice mail and finished watching the movie. Afterwards she retrieved the message.

"Merry Christmas. We're sorry we never made it up there to see you while you were away. We just couldn't help it. Anyway, I hope they dismiss the charges against you real soon. Bye," Chet said.

After she hung up, she shook her head, glanced at her nails and looked through her belongings for her bottle of black nail polish. Just as she started to jiggle it, Jordan looked at the color in horror and shook his head.

"How would you like me to treat you to a manicure tomorrow at the nail salon of your choice?"

She smiled.

"Yes and while we're out, I should probably file for unemployment AND arrange for a follow up visit with Dr. Rogers from the hospital. I'm long overdue. Anyway, it looks like tomorrow will be a busy day."

He nodded.

"Apparently. Anyhow, aren't you going to call your father back?"

She nodded and yawned.

"It's too late and I'm too tired," she said.

He turned the lights and the television off, gently wrapped his arm around her waist and walked her down the hall. Just like the previous two nights, she fell asleep the second her head hit the pillow. However, a few hours later, she wound up sobbing in her sleep and muttering incoherently, all without waking.

CHAPTER NINETY-FOUR

EAT, DRINK AND BE MERRY

The following morning after breakfast, Pattie called Probation. Afterwards, she called her credit card company and paid off her balance. Then she dug around in her bag for her hospital discharge papers. When she reached Dr. Rogers, he told her to just come into the emergency room whenever she wanted to, because he would be on duty there until midnight.

She and Jordan got dressed, went to the rental car agency and surrendered Jordan's rental car. And from there, they went up to the hospital. They didn't wait long before Dr. Rogers called Pattie into an examining room. He gave her a physical and drew some blood, Then he prescribed an inhaler for her breathing and some additional cream in case her impetigo returned. He told her unless it did, he didn't believe any more antibiotics would be warranted. He also promised to contact her if there were any abnormalities with her blood tests. Afterwards, Pattie and Jordan ate lunch and drove around until they found a beauty salon that was able to take them on a walk in basis. Jordan got his hair washed, trimmed and styled, while Pattie got a manicure, a pedicure and a proper haircut to even out the haircut Larabee had given her. Plus she got a shampoo and blowout. When they left, she was wearing paper flip flops to protect her newly polished red toenails, so Jordan drove the BMW back to Chelsea. When they were in the elevator on their way up to the apartment, Jordan's neighbors, Miltie and Kay got in at the Lobby level.

"We're having some people over to help us ring in the New Year. If you don't already have plans for New Year's Eve, why don't the two of you join us?" Kay asked.

Jordan accepted the invitation on the spot. However, once he and Pattie were behind closed doors, Pattie stood in the foyer with her hands on her hips.

"I thought YOU were the one who made the decision that neither of us could accept an invitation on behalf of both of us, without at least discussing it first," she hissed.

Jordan blushed.

"You're right. I did say that. But in my own defense, they were standing right there. If you like, I can make excuses to them and we can do something else instead."

She shook her head.

"I'd actually like to go. That's not the point."

"Well then, what exactly IS the point?"

"The point is that I just want you to understand how these things can happen. Even to the BEST of people."

He chuckled.

"Well, from now on, neither of us will ever dare let this happen again."

She smiled when she saw him reach for a bottle of Dom Perignon. He opened it and fixed a tray of deli snacks. He poured the champagne into two flutes and held his flute up in a toast. Still smiling, she nodded, lifted her flute and watched, as Jordan sipped his champagne.

"Where have you been all my life?" She said to her own flute, as she took a huge sized gulp.

"By the way, these are the last of the delicacies from Christmas Eve," he said.

She chuckled.

"Well, since my New Year's Resolution is to eat, drink and be as merry as possible, we might as well go out tomorrow and buy some more," she said, vowing to herself to live her life to the fullest, for as long as she could, in case she ever had to return to prison.

When she picked up her flute and took another good sized swallow, her heart began to race. Just like the previous three nights, she fell asleep the instant her head hit the pillow. However, just like those other nights, she did not enjoy a quality sleep. Her arms and legs twitched and her newly styled hair was drenched with sweat. She cried so loudly in her sleep, she actually woke Jordan. And yet she slept right through it.

Jordan was alarmed, as always. He grabbed hold of her shoulders and turned her around. Then he deliberately woke her and helped her to a sitting position. Once she was awake, he reached for her hands and gently placed them in his. He looked deeply into her eyes. Her face and neck were splotchy, her cheeks were wet with tears and her eyes were bloodshot and puffy.

"What's the matter, Pattie? You MUST tell me what's wrong."

She shook her head.

"I'm scared. Several weeks have gone by and yet the charges are STILL hanging over my head."

"But at least you're not in prison."

She nodded.

"I know, but for how long? I just wish I knew once and for all whether I'm going to have to go back there. Maybe that way the nightmares would stop."

"Well, you know the old saying. 'No news is good news'."

She looked up at him quizzically and shook her head.

"Not for me. I'm starting to feel paranoid about the delay to the point where I'm wondering whether something sinister is actually happening behind my back."

He thought about that for a few seconds, shook his

head and stood. Then he left and returned a few minutes later, holding a crystal goblet filled with sparkling spring water. He handed it to her and gently stroked her hair while she sipped it. After a minute or so her eyes were dry. She looked up at him and tried to smile. Then she emptied the glass and placed it on the nightstand. When he turned out the light, they both lay down and closed their eyes. Jordan fell back to sleep right away, but it took Pattie a while longer.

CHAPTER NINETY-FIVE

PORTRAIT

It was January 3rd and Fritzi finished signing her initials to the beautiful portrait she had completed of Miranda. Garth showed up, looked at it with approval and smiled. Fritzi smiled back at him and beckoned him to take Miranda's place in the portrait chair. When Miranda stood, he blew his whistle and ordered Larabee to escort the inmates out to the exercise yard. Larabee looked at Garth quizzically.

"I thought it was too cold," she said.

He just pointed at the door and plunked himself down in the chair, like an emperor about to be immortalized on a coin.

The way his crew cut outlines the shape of his head, he looks exactly like a Neanderthal, Fritzi thought, but she smiled at him and sketched.

Once the women were outside, Miranda, who was dressed in the long johns and sweat shirt Pattie had bequeathed her, stood with the soft spoken Darlene and chatted to her about her portrait. Without Pattie to talk to, she got closer to Darlene, who was only too happy to befriend anyone who wasn't a predator. A few minutes later, Quentin showed up in the courtyard with Dutch, who had just been released from Segregation. He uncuffed Dutch and crooked his finger at Darlene. Darlene blushed.

"Excuse me," she said to Miranda.

What now, she wondered, as she walked up to Quentin.

He led her inside, past Fritzi and Garth. She was surprised when he brought her back to Garth's office, instead of to her cell. Once they were both inside, he closed the door.

"Lord knows you need an honest 'trade', so I'll be asking your counselor to sign you up for some keyboarding and steno classes that start at the end of this month. And that's good news, because it could ultimately lead to you becoming a high class secretary or something."

Before quitting her job to get married and have children, Darlene had a secretary of her own. Nevertheless her eyes lit up at the opportunity to do something to occupy herself. Quentin held his hand in a stop sign, as if to calm her down.

"Now, wait a minute though. Don't thank me just yet, because in the meantime, I signed you up to work in the laundry. As a matter of fact, they're waiting for you right now," he went on.

"You mean after rec time?"

He chuckled.

"Honey, for you, this IS after rec time. Let's go," he said.

He took the same hand cuffs he had removed from Dutch, shackled Darlene and led her through a series of mazes, until they reached the laundry. Darlene wasn't there three seconds, before its heat and humidity caused her to break into a sweat. It felt especially weird to her after having just been outside in the cold. Quentin brought her over to the supervisor and winked. The supervisor was wearing a sweat band around her forehead. She sized Darlene up.

"I'm Magda. As of right now, you'll be doing general washing and ironing, but in addition, your duties will also include personally steam cleaning and pressing all of Quentin's uniforms, along with laundering and ironing his personal off duty clothes and underwear and getting them all nice and spiffy, the way he likes them."

Quentin pointed to his feet.

"Oh yeah. I almost forgot. AND you'll also be in charge of polishing and shining all of Quentin's boots and shoes," Magda said.

Quentin, barely able to conceal his glee, grinned from ear to ear and left so Darlene and Magda could get to work.

CHAPTER NINETY-SIX

I FOUGHT THE LAW

Two days later, Garth woke Darlene at four o'clock in the morning, so she could have her breakfast and make it onto the ice cream truck in time for her court date. Since her husband died, she didn't have the funds to hire a private defense attorney and because Legal Aide originally appeared on her behalf at the arraignment, they continued to represent her. Fed up after spending her weekend in the laundry and her nights being roughed up by both Quentin AND Dutch, she told her defense counsel the whole story.

"It's unbearable and I just can't take it anymore," she whined.

She broke into a violent sobbing fit that was so severe, she could hardly breathe. Her lawyer listened to her, but in the end all he did was shake his head.

"Wow. As bad as I feel for you, I don't know what to do about it, because that's not part of my job. My only job is to defend you on the Criminal charges."

With that, he snapped her file open and reviewed

it. At the end of the day, nothing was resolved on Darlene's case and she was shuttled back to the prison. After dinner, when Garth went on his dinner break, she asked Larabee for a razor blade so she could take a shower and shave her legs. When Colette saw Larabee pull out her key and walk over to the supply closet, she took advantage of the situation. She joined them and asked Larabee for an extra tampon. Larabee handed Darlene the razor, made her sign for it and then dropped a couple of tampons in Colette's open hands.

Thirty minutes later, when Garth returned from dinner and Darlene had not returned the used razor, Larabee went back to Darlene's cell to check on her. Darlene was lying on the floor face down, next to the toilet, in a pool of blood that had oozed out of both of her wrists. The razor glistened on the floor next to her. Larabee screamed. Garth, Sistine and all the inmates came running. Garth immediately dialed the infirmary. Then he bent down and checked Darlene's pulse. Due to the glacial pace at which Dutch moved, she was the last to arrive. Even Fritzi, who was still hobbling around on crutches, got there before Dutch. By the time Dutch showed up, she was panting and out of breath. Garth gave her a dirty look. Then he ordered Sistine to usher everyone back onto the floor. He waited with Darlene until two orderlies arrived. They placed Darlene on a stretcher and rushed her off to the infirmary.

CHAPTER NINETY-SEVEN

GROUND HOG'S DAY

The month of January dragged on slowly, but those who were trapped behind prison walls felt it more severely. On January 28th, Pattie and Jordan celebrated Pattie's twenty sixth birthday. Five days later, on Ground Hog's Day, Jordan woke early. He had no choice. It was the first morning of the Spring Semester at Omnia University and he wanted to get there well before his first class started. When he got out of bed, Pattie woke up. He would have liked her to get up and eat breakfast with him, but Pattie's haggard, careworn face told him she needed her rest far more than he needed her company.

"Just take it easy and catch up on your sleep, Love. I can eat on my own this morning. After all, I've been doing it for years."

"My goodness. Now you're making me feel guilty."

He shook his head and chuckled.

"Don't be crazy. I'll be fine."

"Well, even if I do doze a while longer, I'll call Reginald later. I think enough time has gone by since he and I last spoke and quite frankly, I can't stand the suspense anymore," she said.

"Good idea,"

He took a shower, ate breakfast and by the time he returned to the bedroom, she was snoozing. Her breathing was uneven. He walked over to the bed, looked at her and wondered why, after having been out of prison for six weeks, her skin was still so pale. He leaned over her and kissed her on the cheek. She rubbed her eyes and smiled.

"Oooh, your lips are so warm. Anyhow, I'll miss you today," she said.

"I'll miss you too and I'll try to call you later. Have a nice day. In any case, I look forward to seeing you tonight," he said.

He slipped into his camel hair coat, walked over to his desk and opened his briefcase. He pulled Annie's card out from under the blotter, stashed it in his brief case and snapped the brief case shut.

CHAPTER NINETY-EIGHT

IS IT ANY WONDER

As soon as Jordan got to his office, he opened his briefcase, pulled out Annie's card and re-read it. He decided to type his response to her, in order to make it appear as impersonal as possible.

> Dear Ms. Carey,
>
> Although I was flattered by your note, I have no desire to be in any relationship other than the one I'm in with Pattie Anwald. In order not to waste your time, I won't be contacting you again. I wish you success and happiness.
>
> Sincerely, *Jordan Armstrong*

He printed it, addressed an envelope to her and put a stamp on it. He carelessly tossed Anne's card into his waste paper basket and dropped the response in the mail.

CHAPTER NINETY-NINE

DETECTIVE WORK

Two hours after Jordan left for work, Pattie woke up. She took her time getting out of bed and when she finally did, she walked over to the full length mirror and took a long, hard look at herself.

No wonder Jordan wanted me to catch up on my sleep. I look like a train wreck, she thought.

She placed her call to Probation, took a deep breath, then called Reginald. Ellie said he would be out of the office all day, but she took Pattie's number and promised to have him return the call. Pattie poured herself a cup of coffee, brought it over to the table and retrieved her laptop. She sat, sipped and waited for the laptop to power up for the first time since Thanksgiving. Once it did, she went to Google's home page and typed in the name, "Miranda Dibble". Within three quarters of a second, the name popped up. According to Google, Miranda had a New Age Yoga show on some obscure Cable channel up in White Plains. Her sponsor was "All About Yoga," and it was also located in White Plains.

Interesting the lengths Katrina Nero went to in order to create a "cover" for her spy. But after all, how hard could it be? She's in White Plains too, Pattie thought.

She googled the Yoga Studio, which led her to a website. The studio described itself as a "relaxed yoga and meditation studio". Surprised it looked so legitimate, she googled the Cable channel as well. She knew one thing. It would drive her crazy to sit alone in Jordan's apartment pining over Jordan and waiting for Reginald to call, so she decided to hit the streets and explore the situation further. She finished her coffee, shut down the laptop and took a shower. Then she spent the next hour dressing. When she was done, she pulled Jordan's leather aviator jacket out of the closet, grabbed her keys and went down to the garage. With the help of her GPS, she managed to successfully navigate the hills of White Plains. They reminded her of pictures she had seen of San Francisco. She made her way through the mazes and mayhem of the downtown streets, where most of the cars were double parked. She avoided running into a Hasidic woman who was arguing in the middle of the street with a woman dressed in a hijab and she managed to avoid being hit by a taxi driver who backed into the heavy traffic, without bothering to look. Eventually the GPS brought her to the front of "All About Yoga." She stopped and peered out the window at it. It was in a narrow store front in a row of old buildings that were built right after World War One. She turned the corner, pulled into a small parking lot behind the studio and dug around in her purse for some loose change to feed the parking meter. Once she fed the meter, she walked around to the front entrance. A chilly breeze ruffled her hair as she pulled the door open. The studio was so quiet, she wondered whether anyone was even there. She walked softly down a long hallway with periwinkle colored walls. She passed a life sized movie poster of a beautiful Indian film Diva from days gone by and a painting of Krishna playing the flute. When she reached the end of the hallway, she found herself standing on the threshold of an office with a giant "OM" painted on the back wall. The "OM" almost stretched from the ceiling to the floor. It was outlined in red paint and covered with large gold sequins. Above it, "Balance, Renewal, Joy" were designed in an identical way. A man sat at a desk with his back to it. His eyes were closed. The minute Pattie cleared her throat, he opened his eyes, looked at her and tried to ignore the fact that she was wearing a leather jacket. Then he stood, introduced himself as "Raj" and reached for a brochure.

"Thanks for the brochure, but I'm actually here to inquire about someone named Miranda Dibble. Can you tell me where I might find her?" She asked, as she accepted the brochure.

He nodded and scratched his chin.

"Yes. I can. Unfortunately, she's been in prison for the past month or so."

Pattie nodded, scratched her head and tried to figure out whether he too was part of the scam. She cleared her throat again.

"So you mean, she doesn't work for the DA?"

Raj looked shocked.

"I think the DA would be the last person Miranda would ever work for. That District Attorney did a fine job not only of ruining Miranda's career, but of ruining her whole life as well. Miranda used to host a beautiful weekly New Age alternative stress release television program on a local public access station. She had hundreds of viewers, but that's all over with now."

He looked into her eyes, scratched a note on a slip of paper and handed it to her.

"This is the address of the Station where Miranda had her show. I'm sure they can fill you in on the whole story and answer all your questions. It's really not very far from here at all."

Pattie nodded, thanked him and said good bye.

CHAPTER ONE HUNDRED

THE TRUTH SHALL SET YOU FREE

When Pattie arrived at the cable station, she parked next to an oversized red Harley Davidson "Hog" and walked into what was little more than a bare bones studio. It had unvarnished maple wood floors and very little furniture. The best that could be said about it, was that it was immaculate. She cleared her throat. A few seconds later, a burly man with greying hair and a pony tail came from out of nowhere. He greeted her with a pleasant expression. She somehow had the feeling the "Hog" belonged to him. They introduced themselves to each other and shook hands.

"Raj from the Yoga Studio told me you'd probably be coming around to discuss Miranda's connections to the District Attorney."

Pattie nodded.

"That's right."

"Yeah well, her 'connection', if you can even call it that, is that one day Miranda got a tip on a big story and when she refused to reveal her sources, the District Attorney tossed her in the clink and threw away the key."

Pattie shook her head.

"Anyway, since you're here, I'm hoping you'll make a donation to her fundraiser," Jesse said.

Pattie squinted.

"Whose fundraiser? The DA's?"

Jesse shook his head.

"Hell no. Actually, we started a campaign to 'Free Miranda.' We're trying to raise enough money to hire a lawyer to get her out of prison. Unfortunately, it's not going very well. Nevertheless, I do my best to discuss her plight with anyone who is interested, in the hopes they'll help raise money for her. Come with me. A video speaks a thousand words," he said.

He walked toward a vault, unlocked it and pulled out a DVD. He stuck it into a nearby DVD player. A few seconds later a very grainy, black and white film began to play. The date in the upper left hand corner read, December 4th, 2003, 7:00 am. First it showed the very studio where they were standing. It was empty. A few minutes later, it showed Miranda letting herself in. She looked very different from the way Pattie remembered her in prison. In fact, in spite of the poor quality of the picture, Miranda looked adorable. She was dressed in a cute coat and boots. Her large barrel curls bounced around her shoulders and her artful cat like eyeliner enhanced her pretty eyes.

She slipped out of her coat and hung it up, revealing a stylish yoga outfit with a wide sash. She removed her boots and socks, turned the lights on and placed her keys and brief case outside the camera's range. Then she rolled out a yoga mat. She lowered a scenic backdrop behind her and lit some incense. Finally, she prepared the lighting for her show. Her routine appeared seamless, as though she had done it a million times.

She heard footsteps coming down the hallway. Someone was there. She stopped in her tracks and listened. A few seconds later, a sinister looking, middle aged man wearing sunglasses, a dark overcoat and a dark fedora, appeared in the doorway of the studio. He was carrying a large, beat up looking manila envelope. He walked up to her and asked her whether she was Miranda Dibble. When she nodded, he handed her the envelope. She didn't open it. She merely squinted at it, then looked up at him.

"My daughter is one of your viewers. She watches your show all the time. She admires you and constantly tells me how holistic and honest you are. She hopes to be a journalist too, some day. She said one of your dreams has always been to host your own show on a major network. That's why I wanted to make sure I gave this story to YOU. Even though you're not the most seasoned reporter, my daughter speaks highly of your professionalism and she's confident I can trust you not to reveal my identity. I can't afford any of this to get linked back to me. Because if it does, I'll wind up wearing a pair of cement shoes," he said.

She nodded.

"You don't have to worry. I took a vow to protect my sources no matter what."

He nodded.

"Good. Anyway, this involves a seventeen million dollar drug deal that's going down right now and it's right under our noses. There's enough evidence in that envelope to lead to a significant drug bust," he went on to say.

"Let me ask you something. Did you give this information to anyone else besides me?" Miranda asked.

He shook his head.

"Well, if you wouldn't mind, I'd appreciate it if YOU would open this. Just in case there's a bomb in it. Or Anthrax or something," she said, as she handed the envelope back to him.

He looked at her with an amused expression, opened the envelope and removed the papers. By the time she finished reading them he was gone. She glanced at the clock. It was a few minutes before air-time, so she stepped out of the studio and returned a minute later without the envelope. She was wearing the local newscaster's royal blue blazer, which bore the Station's Logo. She effected a deadpan facial expression. A few seconds later when Jesse and the camera man arrived, she opened her show with the news flash.

"Three men have allegedly trafficked approximately seven hundred thirty four kilograms of cocaine into Westchester County by way of the Long Island Sound. Its street value is approximately seventeen million dollars. They are alleged to have transported the drugs to a warehouse right here in White Plains."

Suddenly the phones at the station lit up. By then Jesse and the newscaster had arrived and they were scrambling to handle the volume of calls. Miranda finished her broadcast, removed the jacket and segued into her regularly scheduled Yoga program. When it concluded, calls were still coming in, so Jesse told her to put the jacket back on and repeat the announcement, for the benefit of anyone who missed it the first time. She complied. Then the newscaster took over to start his local news show. When the recording ended, Pattie looked up at Jesse wistfully, took a deep breath and thanked him for showing her the video.

"By the way, who has the envelope now?" Pattie asked.

Jesse shrugged, shook his head and changed the subject by offering her a cup of coffee. She accepted. A few minutes later, when they were sitting together in Jesse's office, she shared her own tale of woe. When they finished their coffee, she stood. Jesse gave her his card and took down her phone number. Then she left. As she was programming her GPS to direct her back to Jordan's apartment, her cell phone rang. It was Reginald, returning her call. He told her after concluding a hearing on a civil matter in White Plains, he managed to drop in on Katrina, unannounced.

"Really?

"Yes.

"Well, I hope she told you something good, because the idea of returning to prison makes me sick. Literally. I mean it was hell on earth. Which reminds me. There's something I'd like to run past you on another day. But since I'm in White Plains too right now, what I'd really like more than anything would be to just meet you somewhere and talk about my case. I mean if that's possible," she said.

He gave her the address of a nearby diner. When they hung up, she plugged it into her GPS.

<u>**CHAPTER ONE HUNRED ONE**</u>

THE DINER SONG

As Reginald sat across from Pattie, he noticed an intensity in her that he had never seen before. He listened patiently and nodded sympathetically, as she lamented.

"I can't believe Katrina Nero hasn't dropped these charges against me already. What's going on? What does she have up her sleeve?"

"I guess she thinks since you're out of prison she put your case on the back burner. But now she wants to file a Motion to dredge the Reservoir and I agreed we wouldn't oppose it."

At the mention of the word "prison", all the diners within earshot, stopped their conversations and looked at Pattie. Reginald ignored them, but Pattie blushed. They ordered coffee and turkey club sandwiches. Reginald paid the bill and headed straight back to the city, while Pattie stopped on an impulse at a chocolate shop called "The Epicurean Delight."

CHAPTER ONE HUNDRED TWO

ARTHUR

Just as Jordan was about to lock his office for the night, the janitor wheeled his cart up to Jordan's doorway. They smiled and nodded at one another. When Jordan left, the janitor wheeled his cart into the office and picked up Jordan's waste paper basket. Just as he got ready to empty it, he spotted Annie's beautiful card and envelope. He figured they were too lovely and expensive to throw away. Suspecting they might have landed in the trash by accident, he picked them out, blew the dust off them and slid them under Jordan's blotter for safe keeping.

When Jordan arrived home, he picked up the mail. As he rode up the elevator, he wondered whether Pattie had managed to figure out a way to light the stove and cobble a meal together. Even though he was hungry and looking forward to having dinner, he had to chuckle at his own cockeyed optimism. In any case, his fantasy of a home cooked meal was dashed the minute he opened the door. The living room was dark and so was the kitchen. He heard the faint sound of the television in the bedroom, so he followed it. That's when he found Pattie sprawled across his unmade bed, wearing her baseball shirt and a pair of underpants. A two pound box of hand dipped chocolate covered cherries and a half finished bottle of Dom Perignon were on the nightstand, but no glass was in sight. Her laptop was in the bed next to her. It was turned on, but in "sleep mode", because she was engrossed in the movie, "Arthur".

Startled, she jumped, looked up at him and waved. Then she returned to her movie. Chuckling at one of Dudley Moore's wise cracks, she reached over, wrapped her fist around the neck of the champagne bottle and scarfed down a big, long swig. She reached over to the night stand again, put the bottle down and dipped into the candy.

A sullen look of disapproval spread across Jordan's face. He couldn't believe this was the way Pattie chose to spend her first day on her own. Something about it reminded him of Edie and he silently wondered whether Pattie inherited the distressing trait of alcoholism from her ne'er do well mother.

Who would have thought I'd long for the good old days of unspiked Raspberry Iced Tea and a lecture about the evils of alcohol, he said to himself.

He bent forward, rested his hands lightly on Pattie's shoulders and looked earnestly into her eyes.

"Do you ENJOY hang gliding, Pattie? Because I

don't mind telling you, I think you're drunk. But perhaps I have no one to blame but myself. After all, I'm the one who encouraged you to try some champagne in the first place. On the other hand, I never remember telling you to just go ahead and compulsively guzzle down every last drop of it. And without a glass, no less. Remember, there ARE always consequences for everything we say, do, think or ingest. I can help you, Pattie. But only if you'll let me. In the meantime, I'm in no mood to cook and if you don't know how, I guess I'll have to order some takeout," he said.

Even though he hoped his words weren't too harsh, his expression was dark and unfamiliar to her. Neither liking nor understanding what she saw, instead of responding, she simply looked back at him with a vacant stare and cleared her throat. Then she burst into gales of laughter.

Shaking his head, he walked out of the room in disgust. After he was gone, she waved her hand in dismissal and continued to watch the movie. Once he was in the living room, he called a local gourmet shop and placed an order for two people, consisting of a lobster salad, some dinner rolls, a rotisserie chicken, a fruit salad and an awfully good brie. Then he gave his address and asked that it be delivered. About forty minutes later, when the food arrived, he moved the apricot silk bedspread out of harm's way and served Pattie her "dinner in bed."

When she finished eating, she dropped the chicken

bones onto her plate. She licked the grease from her fingers and picked up her champagne bottle. With a defiant gleam in her eye, she polished off the remaining champagne. He sighed, picked up her napkin and handed it to her. She snatched it, used it to wipe her mouth and hands and then flung it on top of the bones. When she thrust the empty bottle at him, he brought it, along with everything else, back into the kitchen. A few minutes later, he returned to her with the iced tea. With a scowl on his face, he watched the remainder of the movie with her. When it ended, he turned the television off. She snatched the remote control out of his hand and turned it back on, just in time to catch the beginning of "Arthur Two".

Sickened by the entire scenario, Jordan returned to the kitchen and cleaned up. When he was done, he came back into to the bedroom and found Pattie fast asleep and snoring. The iced tea was untouched. He shut down her computer and once again turned off the television.

At three thirty in the morning, Pattie bolted upright in bed. Her heart was beating wildly, her left hand was wrapped around the headboard and her right hand was clenched into a fist.

CHAPTER ONE HUNDRED THREE

FEAR

The following morning, Pattie and Jordan woke up at the same time. Jordan propped himself up on his elbow, stared at Pattie and point blank asked her whether she even remembered anything from the night before.

"I do and I'm sorry. I swear I'm not unstable or anything. It's just that I've been feeling for weeks now as if my very life is at stake and yesterday it all got to me. My nerves were just shot. As a matter of fact they still are, but I promise you. I won't let myself turn into my mother."

He nodded, pulled her over to him and hugged her. She couldn't see the worried expression on his face.

TOMORROW NEVER KNOWS

That night Jordan came home to find Pattie sitting on the couch, looking disheveled and staring into space. She greeted him. His heart started beating rapidly and his eyes quickly scanned the living room for evidence that she had been drinking. He was relieved to find there wasn't any. He walked up to her and kissed her on the mouth. Mercifully, there was no sign of alcohol on her breath. He went into the kitchen and although there were no signs of alcohol there, there were no signs of any meal looming large in their future, either.

WATCHING THE WHEELS

It was shortly after lunchtime on February 11th. The women on the tier were sitting around the television watching a soap opera when the mail came. Garth handed Miranda an envelope from the prison accounts division. Miranda moved away from the group and took it into the corner, so she could read it in peace. When she opened it, she gasped. Pattie Anwald had deposited the sum of five hundred dollars into her account. Pattie wasn't secure enough about her own future to transfer funds from her own account. She just let that lie fallow, in case she had to return there, but she at least wanted Miranda to have some creature comforts in any event. Dutch peeled her eyes away from the TV, carefully eyed Miranda and heaved herself onto her feet. When Miranda saw Dutch lumbering toward her, she hurriedly folded the notice, slid it back into the envelope and stuffed the envelope into her boot. Seeing that annoyed Dutch. She plunged her mouth into its usual grim, straight line and her eyes took on their all too familiar mean expression. She pointed at Fritzi; then pointed at Miranda.

"You know Dipstick, if I can fuck up Fritzi's hip, just imagine what I could do to you. So, let's cut to the chase. You got all of Peanut's canteen money. Didn't you?" She bellowed.

"That's none of your business."

"Well, Valentine's Day is coming up and that IS my business. Because I'll need to buy some gifts for my two best gal pals, Colette and White Bread over there. And since nobody ever forks money over to ME in this can, it looks like you're the one who's gonna have to supply it."

Just then, Pattie's name and picture flashed onto the TV screen. A newscaster announced that Pattie Anwald and her attorney would be appearing at the Civil Division of the White Plains courthouse at two o'clock that afternoon. Then the headline broke into a commercial. Garth scratched his head and Dutch shrugged.

"Whatever she did wrong this time must be civil, but people don't usually go to jail for that kind of stuff though," Dutch said.

Miranda chuckled bitterly.

"They don't?" She said.

"Well, in any case, I guess we'll find out soon enough. All we need to do is stay tuned for the details," Garth said.

"If she doesn't come back here, it will spell bad

luck for me. She's still got a ton of research left to do on my case," Dutch said.

Just then Quentin showed up and turned off the television.

CHAPTER ONE HUNDRED SIX

TALK TO MY LAWYER

The weather in White Plains was cold and drizzly and the sky was flat and gray. But that didn't stop the throngs of environmentalists, homeowners, tax payers, protesters, bystanders, television crews and newspaper reporters from flocking to the courthouse to hear about or report on the fate of the Katonah Reservoir. Reginald pushed past the crowd, climbed the well-worn stone steps and led Pattie and Jordan inside. Once they were finally in the courtroom, Reginald walked up to the counsel table and sat between the Attorney for the County and the Attorney for the Environmental Management Council. Katrina Nero was at the Counsel Table on the opposite side of the courtroom. Pattie and Jordan waited nervously in the gallery. Pattie looked around the packed courtroom and started to sweat. As soon as the Honorable Dexter Charles appeared in the doorway, everyone stood and the court officer opened court. Then Judge Charles took his seat and everyone but Katrina took theirs.

"Good afternoon, Your Honor. Since the People brought the original Motion, even though there is nothing to add that's not already contained within the four corners of the Motion and Supporting Brief, I'd like to state for the record that Justice requires the People to accurately resolve Leland LeRoux's murder. And since we'd like to serve Justice the best way we can, we need to ensure that all guilty parties are prosecuted and all innocent parties remain free. Therefore, at this point, the only way we can accomplish that, is by dredging the reservoir. And we further request that this happen as soon as possible," Katrina bellowed. Her words were like bullets that punctured the air.

Jordan scratched his head.

"What the hell did she just say?" He whispered to Pattie.

Judge Charles glanced at him, frowned and then looked at Reginald.

"Now, Attorney Reese since you filed no papers either supporting or objecting to this Motion, is there anything you'd like to say at this time?"

Reginald stood.

"No, your Honor."

The Attorney for the County stood.

"Your Honor, The County is requesting a permanent injunction against The People's crazy course of action. As reflected in our supporting brief, The Fifth, Eleventh and Fourteenth Amendments to the

U.S. Constitution limit the power of either state or federal governments to impinge upon any exclusive use of water. Furthermore, the Ninth Amendment protects rights that aren't even enumerated in the other Amendments. Therefore we object on all these grounds," he said.

Reginald was secretly grateful the Attorney for the County took that position.

"And you Attorney Curley? You're representing the Westchester County Environmental Management Council?"

Attorney Curley stood.

"Yes, Your Honor. The Council is in full agreement with the County. As a result, we are therefore urging you to grant the County's injunction. Dredging the Reservoir is not only harmful, it's unlawful. There are a lot of fish in that reservoir that people eat and water that people drink. I believe drinking water and eating would fall right within the scope of rights set forth in the Ninth Amendment. In any case, once the water's gone, we won't have to be bothered protecting any of our other rights, because we'll all be dead," he added.

"Your Honor, we've LITERALLY got to get to the bottom of the reservoir in order to solve Leland LeRoux's murder and unfortunately, we can't make an omelet without breaking an egg," Katrina said, making sure she was the one who uttered the last word.

Judge Charles banged the gavel, stood and flew out of the courtroom without saying anything. His clerk followed him and returned a few seconds later to let everyone know the Judge would be taking the matter under advisement and rendering a decision in the near future. Katrina, who knew better than anyone how to work the press, stepped outside into the misty drizzle, eclipsing everyone else. She had the last word out on the steps, just as she had inside the courtroom.

CHAPTER ONE HUNDRED SEVEN

THE IDES OF MARCH

The wheels of justice turn very slowly, but eventually they do turn. And on February 17th, after a long President's Day Weekend, Judge Charles finally issued his ruling in favor of the People's Motion and ordered the immediate dredging of the reservoir. But the wheels of Justice weren't the only things that moved slowly. In spite of the word "immediately," the wheels of Commerce moved almost as slowly as the wheels of Justice. Bids had to be placed, to ascertain which company could perform the work at the lowest possible cost to the taxpayers. Then, once the job was awarded to the lowest bidder, safeguards were required to preserve and store the water and the fish in it, without compromising its integrity, so that it could be used once again to replenish the reservoir. Once all that was finally accomplished, a schedule for dredging was set to take place on March 15th, 2004. In the meantime, Pattie lived with the charges hanging over her head and faithfully called the Probation Department on a daily basis.

A month later, the weather on March 15th was typical for that time of year. Even though it was almost Spring, the sky was gray and the air was chilly. Many of the people who were in court on the day of the Motion were also present to witness the dredging. They stood and watched as the heavy equipment arrived on the scene. Then the trucks that would carry the tanks arrived. The tanks would preserve the water and marine life. The County Police, The Army Corp of Engineers and many private citizens who had wanted to be in the courtroom, but couldn't fit, were also there.

Pattie told Jordan she couldn't bring herself to even think about going there. Katrina Nero felt differently. She treated it as an opportunity to be seen watching the procedure like a hawk, to schmooze with "The People" like a boss and to pander to the press like a Rock star. By midday, it appeared as if the Carnival had come to town. Everyone stood and watched as the water got pumped out. By the end of the day, the only items at the bottom of the reservoir were a red baseball cap, a decapitated skull, a skeleton which had been completely picked clean by the fish and eels, some stray hair and the rusted remains of Pattie's car.

Pattie and Jordan watched the story on the evening news. When Pattie saw them pull her car out of the water, she broke down and sobbed in Jordan's arms. When the reporter remarked that the murder weapon was alleged to have been a knife or a switchblade, which no one could find, Jordan finally remembered to tell Pattie about the search warrant he, Ryan and Lou had found in her apartment. Upon hearing that, she cried even harder.

CHAPTER ONE HUNDRED EIGHT

FORENSICS

Exactly one week after the dredging, on another raw, windy day, the Chief Medical Examiner and the Chief Forensic Examiner met with Katrina Nero. She stood behind her desk as she waited for them to hand down their findings and summarize their reports. Her long, hot pink lacquered nails dug into the back of her chair so deeply, she almost punctured the leather.

"Since the cochlea was intact, we were able to work on it using new methods of DNA testing. So, with that, the bone marrow and the remaining teeth which matched LeRoux's dental records in Louisiana, we were able to ascertain that the skull and bones were indeed his. And as everyone who witnessed the dredging knows, there's no evidence of any other corpse," the medical examiner said.

Katrina nodded.

"Fascinating. So it's all playing out just as I suspected. Leland LeRoux ended up as eel fodder, but

Hudson must still be on the loose. Can you give me a cause of death?"

"Judging by the severed head and some marks we found on his ribs, the cause of death was decapitation and probably multiple stab wounds," the medical examiner said.

Katrina nodded, thanked him and turned to the forensic examiner.

"And what have you got for me?"

"Fingerprint tests on the car were somewhat vague, because it had been submerged under water for so long. However, prints on the steering wheel matched both Hudson and Pattie Anwald's prints."

"Well, it would make sense for HER prints to be there, but Hudson's prints would tend to confirm the statements she made while under hypnosis," Katrina said.

Then she turned to the Medical Examiner, once again.

"Tell me something. She's a petite, kind of a scrawny person. Could someone her size even wield a knife and sever a head like that?"

He shook his head.

"Probably not. Anyway, do we share this report with her counsel?" He asked.

Katrina nodded.

"I suppose we have no choice. After all, we can't get around the old Sixth Amendment."

The Medical Examiner chuckled.

"Oh yeah. THAT," he said.

When the two men left, Katrina sat, skimmed through the reports, stuck them in the file and racked her brain.

What am I going to do now? Once Reginald Reese gloms onto these, he'll be badgering me to dismiss the charges. On the other hand, I can't exactly let these murders appear to go unsolved. After all, it's an election year. If I only had another scapegoat lined up to take the blame. Dammit. Where the hell are you, Willie Hudson?

DROPPING THE BALL

On Monday March 28th, Katrina Nero's secretary buzzed her.

"It's Attorney Reese from down the city."

Katrina sighed and picked up the call.

"I thought we had a deal that I wouldn't object to you dredging the reservoir in return for you dismissing the charges against my client."

"Yeah, yeah, yeah. I forgot. My bad."

"Well, in the meantime, my client's life is in tatters. Plus, she's been on tenterhooks for months now. It's just not right. For God's sake let her clear her name so she can move beyond this. The time has come for you to focus on finding and prosecuting Willie Hudson. And by the way, the reason you could never locate the murder weapon is because Willie probably still has it. And last but not least, did you think it was funny or something when you decided to send me the results by way of snail mail with postage due?"

"Listen, you'll look more like a hero to her if YOU

just file the damn Motion, instead of waiting for me to do it. Don't worry. I won't oppose it," she said.

"Thank you VERY much," he said.

He hung up, buzzed Ellie and told her to type in that day's date and print the Motion to Dismiss he had prepared for Pattie weeks ago. Once she did, he read it, signed it and personally delivered it to the Clerk's Office at the White Plains Courthouse.

CHAPTER ONE HUNDRED TEN

OH HAPPY DAY

Reginald's Motion finally came up on the Docket for Wednesday May 5th at 2 pm. It was a warm, spring day and a happy one for Pattie, but as she was dressing for her court appearance, she frowned. Much of her joy evaporated, because NONE of the clothes she used to wear to court even came close to fitting her anymore. She weighed herself on Jordan's scale and gasped when she realized she had gained nineteen pounds since December.

When Reginald walked past the celery green trees and forsythia lined streets in White Plains, he took one last look at the pastel blue sky. Then he climbed the stairs and walked through the metal detector at the main entrance to the courthouse. By the time he reached the courtroom, Katrina was already there. He strode up to the counsel table, opened his briefcase and organized his paperwork. A few minutes later, Pattie, Jordan, Ryan, Lou and Chet came into the courtroom, with Edie waddling behind them. Reginald stood and walked back towards Pattie and brought her to stand next to him. When they both sat, he turned to her and smiled, but between her nervousness about the motion and the fact that she was dressed in her flannel baseball shirt and a pair of Edie's pants, with an elasticized waist, she could barely smile back at him. A few seconds later, Judge Islington appeared in the doorway. Everyone rose as the court officer opened the session. And without further ado Judge Islington took the bench.

"Seeing that no objection has been filed, The Defendant's Motion to Dismiss in the matter of People v. Anwald, is hereby granted. Since Double Jeopardy has attached, this case is dismissed with Prejudice. Congratulations Attorney Anwald! Have a nice life," Judge Islington said as he banged down the gavel and whisked himself out of the courtroom. Pattie threw her arms around Reginald and kissed him on the cheek. Tears of relief ran down her face.

"Thank you so much," she said.

Then she turned around to look for Jordan.

"Oh Jordan!" She cried out.

They raced toward one another and hugged until the court officer shooed everyone out of the courtroom. Knowing there would be newspaper and television reporters waiting on the courthouse steps, Katrina walked outside with them. One of the reporters stuck a microphone in Pattie's face.

"Would you like to say something about your case?"

Reginald stepped in between them and beamed at the camera.

"Well, maybe now that the People don't have my client to push around anymore, they can focus on finding the real perpetrator, Willie Hudson," he said.

Katrina pushed her way through the crowd to get to the press, so she could make sure she got her usual last word.

"Law enforcement officials are in the process of attempting to locate William Hudson as we speak," she said.

The camera woman eyed Lou, liked what she saw and pointed the camera at him. The reporter followed suit by sticking a microphone in his face.

"And you are?" She asked.

Reginald slid next to Lou, nodded and explained that Lou was Pattie Anwald's brother and a member of NYPD. Katrina stood by listening and eyeing Lou from head to toe. When the reporters wrapped up the questioning, everyone dispersed. When they all reached the bottom of the stairs, Lou turned to Reginald.

"I'd really like to meet with your investigator and get some information about this case," Lou said.

Reginald looked at Pattie. When she nodded, Reginald gave Lou the thumbs up sign. Afterwards, Reginald took Pattie, Jordan, Lou, Edie, Chet and Ryan to the most expensive restaurant in Westchester County, where he treated them to a five star gourmet lunch. Pattie looked around and noticed how sophisticated the restaurant was, with its antique furniture, tapestries, white table cloths, napkins, real silverware and French menus. She leaned over to Jordan.

"I'd like you to take me to places like this in the future," she whispered.

Jordan chuckled.

When the celebratory bottle of Dom Perignon came around, Ryan lifted his glass and toasted Pattie.

"Here, here" Chet said.

Then everyone drank to Pattie. She smiled and thanked everyone. The waiter came around and everyone except Edie ordered lunch. Pattie decided on a marvelous caviar for her appetizer, a bowl of onion soup and an entrée of filet mignon fit for royalty. When it arrived, she watched it sizzling in its creamy Bearnaise sauce. Her mouth watered as she stabbed the cheddar cheese topping on her twice baked potato.

Edie spent the entire time slouched in her chair. She consumed margarita after margarita, eating nothing, as she watched the others all enjoying their meal. Through some miracle, she remained on good behavior as long as they stayed within the confines of the restaurant. By the time everyone finished their meal, it was late afternoon. Jordan invited everyone back to his apartment to continue the celebration. Reginald begged off, because he had to prepare for his next day's cases, but everyone else followed Pattie and Jordan home.

Although Lou had already been to the apartment, it was the first visit for Ryan, Edie and Chet. For weeks Edie had been dying to get up there and "get a peek at the place." Pattie and Jordan parked in the garage and waited outside the front entrance for the others to find available spaces on the street. They watched the orange sun light up the spectacular new greenery of the spring foliage on the Palisades, just before it sunk out of view. Seconds later, as the sky turned to twilight, the streetlights turned on. They twinkled and lit up the dusky sky.

Jordan chatted with Joe the Doorman, who looked dapper in his navy blue uniform and gold braided trim. A few minutes later, they spotted Ryan and the Anwalds, walking up the street together. By that time, Edie's blood sugar levels had crashed from her afternoon of drinking. Her lower lip was curled under and a malicious glint was in her eye. Chet and Lou flanked her and held her up, as she reeled and lurched down the street. She staggered up to Joe the doorman and gave him a cockeyed salute. Joe smiled at her.

"Hey! Salute me back, you son of a bitch," she said.

When Pattie heard the insult and the severely slurred speech, she cringed and almost died of embarrassment. Her hand flew to her face and she cleared her throat. Seeing Pattie's discomfort made

Edie chuckle. Everyone followed Jordan and Pattie into the luxurious lobby and waited for the elevator to bring them to the eighth floor. Once they were inside the apartment, Jordan announced that he was serving afternoon tea. Edie scowled and for what was probably the first time in Pattie's life, Pattie found herself agreeing with her mother.

After tea time, Pattie and Jordan walked everyone to the door. Pattie returned to the living room, sunk down into the couch and slid her shoes off. Just as she dug her toes into the thick, plush carpeting, Jordan sat next to her. She rested her head on his shoulder. He kissed the top of her head and looked at his watch.

"It's almost time to watch ourselves on TV," he said.

He switched the television on. As if on cue, the anchorman announced Pattie's dismissal. Then the scene changed to a video of the interviews on the courthouse steps.

Pattie and Jordan weren't the only people who watched the newscast. Everyone on the tier huddled together as Garth turned the TV on. Even Fritzi looked up from her sketch pad in order to peer at the screen.

"If Peanut gets any fatter she'll look like you Dutch. You know, I voot do your portrait, but I don't sink I haff enough paper to fit you," Fritzi quipped.

Everyone, but Dutch, laughed. Dutch glared at her. Then everyone got quiet and watched the news. When they heard it was a victory for Pattie, they all cheered. Even Colette and Sisteen managed to crack a smile.

But not all the television viewers had Pattie's best interests at heart. Still smarting from the sting of Jordan's rejection letter, Anne Carey now harbored a grudge against both him AND Pattie. When she watched David Huntley describe how Pattie wept tears of joy in the courtroom seconds before running into the arms of her boyfriend, her anorexic face tightened with jealousy. And when she watched the film clip of Jordan gently escorting Pattie down the courthouse steps, she flung herself onto her couch and cried bitter tears into the pillows. As far as she was concerned, the only silver lining in this storm cloud was that Pattie Anwald was now fat.

As Willie Hudson watched the newscast, he literally felt himself getting hot under the collar. Seething with rage, he leaned forward on the edge of his bed in the roach infested motel room where he was still holed up and went into a silent tirade.

I've got to find a way to snuff out this bitch lawyer. But how? And why, oh, why did I ever let that idiot Leland convince me she was dead when she wasn't? I could have polished her off right after I did HIM in, he growled to himself.

And as for that doctor, Willie remembered him

swaggering around at Beau Rivage. He was the very same doctor Pattie Anwald had dragged up there to meet those brats she called "her clients," so he could write reports about them.

And he had memorized Reginald's name and face the day he saw him on the news. Although he couldn't afford a computer, he knew how to schmooze that ugly wretch Donna at the front desk into letting him use her laptop. He suddenly snapped off the television, stormed out the door and made his way down to the dingy, dusty lobby. A few minutes later, he was on line.

What was that doctor's name, again? Armstrong? He asked himself.

He typed "Armstrong Psychologist" into the search engine. Bingo! Then he researched Reginald.

When the news story concluded, Pattie got up, walked into the kitchen and opened the refrigerator door. She peered inside, pulled out a bottle of Dom Perignon and headed straight for the cabinet. She retrieved two crystal flutes, brought everything into the living room and placed it all on the table. Jordan looked at her and frowned.

"What are you doing to yourself Pattie? Can't you just relax, now that the murder charge is no longer hanging over your head?"

She nodded.

"Sure. And this is how I do it."

He shrugged and opened the bottle for her. They

snacked, drank and watched television. When they went to bed later that night, Pattie had no trouble getting to sleep, but she ground her teeth for several hours. Once again, in the middle of the night, she woke up covered in sweat. Pain stabbed her left calf muscle and quickly traveled down her leg until it reached the sole of her foot. She bolted upright in agony and tried not to scream.

HEAVEN

CHAPTER ONE HUNDRED ELEVEN

RESENTMENT

Early the next morning, Annie ran into Connor Dane's office waving the morning newspaper. She threw it on top of Connor's desk, flounced into the visitor's chair across from him and immediately began to pick at her cuticles. Connor's dark wavy hair hung down over his cynical brown eyes. He scrutinized Annie's malignant intensity and picked up the newspaper.

"Before you even open your mouth, I want you to know I've already read it. And as I mentioned before, I've always believed in her innocence. That's why I'm happy the case against her got tossed," he said.

Annie shook her head and frowned.

"What kind of a prosecutor ARE you, Connor, that you could ever side with the likes of her? And I guess an even better question is what kind of a Prosecutor is that Katrina Nero? Up until today I honestly thought she was one of the good guys. I don't understand either of you and what's more, I don't suppose I ever will."

Connor chuckled and tapped his right temple with his index finger.

"Most people have been able to at least muster up some happiness for Pattie, but you can't seem to allow any human kindness at all to scratch up from the dark side of your soul. And I know why. You see, I have a memory like a steel trap, so I KNOW what the malice is all about. You're still carrying a torch for her boyfriend, who likes HER and not YOU. Methinks The Lady might be jealous."

Annie shook her head, rolled her eyes and waved her hand in dismissal. Her mouth was set in a mean thin line.

"I am not! You're always twisting everything around! Anyway, you don't think she would ever dare come back to work here. Do you?"

Connor shrugged.

"Actually I don't, but even if she did, why should it be any skin off your nose?"

Annie bit down on a loose cuticle and nibbled at it with her two front teeth.

CHAPTER ONE HUNDRED TWELVE

SALUTE ME

Meanwhile across town, Jordan and Pattie woke up in each other's arms. They got out of bed and went into the kitchen together. Pattie watched while Jordan opened the refrigerator and peered into it. As he handed her the bacon, eggs, coffee, croissants, butter, cream, tomatoes, potatoes and jam, she placed them on the counter. Then he went to the cupboard and got out a can of baked beans.

In the meantime, across the street from Jordan's apartment, an already drunken Edie was a woman on a mission. Muttering under her breath and with a lit cigarette dangling out of her mouth, she craned her neck in order to judge whether it would be possible to squeeze her Ford Festiva into an illegal parking space without causing an accident. And it was no easy feat, since she was drunk and the vehicle had lost its power steering about two years before. Ashes dropped onto her left shoulder and made a sizzling sound when they burned a hole in her nylon tank top. When she somehow managed to pack the car into the space, she shut the engine off, took the last drag of her cigarette and opened the door. She staggered out, flung her cigarette butt onto the street and mashed it out with the toe of her Naugahyde black sandals. She grabbed her black Naugahyde hand bag, slammed the door and zig zagged to the other side of the street, just outside the crosswalk. She held her arms out to balance her, while trying not to be too obvious about it. When she finally arrived at the entrance of the building, she ran headlong into Joe the doorman.

Remembering her from the day before, Joe knew exactly who she was. He had been watching her every move for several minutes, all the while chuckling to himself. She tried to push her way past him, but he blocked her.

"Let me guess. You're here to see Doctor Armstrong," he said, greeting her, good naturedly.

She glared at him and shook her head.

"Why do I always have to remind you to salute me, you Son of a Bitch?"

He saluted her.

"Well, ma'am, there's your salute, but I'm afraid that's not enough to automatically gain you access to the building. By the way, you look a lot like your daughter,"

Edie went into a rage.

"Don't you mean SHE looks like ME? Anyhow, we're NOTHING alike! NOTHING," she screamed.

That must be a relief for the daughter, Joe thought, as he picked up the house phone to call Jordan.

"Dr. Armstrong, I have someone down here who wishes to pay you a visit."

After explaining to Jordan who it was, he hung up and looked straight into Edie's eyes.

"Although Dr. Armstrong and your daughter appreciate you stopping by, neither of them are in a position to receive callers this morning," he explained.

Edie squinted at him. Her arms swayed and her dyed black hair blew wildly in the breeze.

"How can she NOT be in a position to receive her own mother? What kind of position IS she in? Or don't I want to know?" Edie bellowed.

Even though Joe basically liked Jordan, he relished every second of this. It was an exciting departure from his usual dull routine. Besides, he knew it would make for some exciting "cawfee tawk" later, when he got together later with the superintendent and the janitor. He tried to keep a straight face.

"Well, Ma'am, I really don't know what to tell you, except that maybe next time you'd be better off to telephone them first. You know. Before just showing up here. I also think it wouldn't be a bad idea for you to move your car. It's in a tow away zone, you know."

"This is such a crock of shit," Edie brayed.

Other tenants who were coming and going, relished the scene almost as much as Joe did, but most of them had enough decency to pretend they didn't notice anything. Meanwhile upstairs, Pattie was in a state of shock. Once the call came in, she got up from mopping up the last bit of her egg yolk with her croissant and started pacing. Finally she stopped in her tracks and faced Jordan.

"Try not to get too wound up over this. As I've told you before, it's always a mistake to believe other people's behavior is somehow a reflection on US. The reality is that none of us can ever control anything anyone else does, whether it's good, bad or neutral," Jordan told her.

"Yeah, I know all that, but of course it's easy for you to say, since it's not YOUR mother down there! You know, I've often wondered how different my life would have been, had she only been normal. When I was growing up, she said and did so many outrageous things, just like she's doing right now. That's why I never dared invite anyone to my house. Because I never knew what condition she'd be in when I walked through the door or what kind of stunt she would pull. After never receiving any invitations from me, people then stopped inviting me, which meant I became a very lonely person. And now, all these years later, she's following me over here. It's like I can't get away from her. Is she deliberately TRYING to destroy my life?" Pattie asked quietly, just before she burst into tears.

He stood, patted her on the back and took her into his arms. She literally cried on his shoulder, while he stroked her hair in an effort to calm her down. Once she stopped crying, he broke the embrace.

"For what it's worth, your friends will always be welcome here," he said.

She smiled at him and wiped her eyes on her sleeve.

CALL OF THE WILD

About forty five minutes later, Pattie's cell phone rang. The call was coming in from the Anwald land line. Pattie sighed and let it roll over to voice mail. Two minutes later, Pattie's cell phone rang again, so Jordan reached over and picked up the call. Because Edie wasn't expecting to hear Jordan's voice, she didn't know what to say, so she said nothing and simply breathed into the receiver.

"Hello Edie. Pattie can't take your call right now. I'm sure she'll phone you back very soon," he said and hung up.

Pattie snatched her cell phone out of his hand and shut it off.

A few minutes later, Edie puffed her cigarette and watched, while Chet dialed Pattie's number. His face turned beet red and he sniffed when the call automatically rolled over to voice mail. He slammed the receiver down. Edie turned to him, exhaled her smoke in his face and stuffed her cigarette butt into her already overflowing ashtray. Then she cried, stormed down the hallway and locked herself in the bathroom.

CHAPTER ONE HUNDRED FOURTEEN

TOO GOOD NOT TO BELIEVE

On Friday May 14th, Jordan came home from work, sorted through the mail and handed Pattie a thin, plain, white, envelope. It was addressed to her from the Law Division in Albany. She looked at it, looked up at him and cleared her throat. Then she closed her eyes, held the envelope against her heart and took a deep breath. Finally, she opened her eyes and tore into it. It was short, sweet and to the point. .

"This is to inform you that your law license has been officially reinstated in full, as of May 6th, 2004."

Jordan nodded and winked at her.

"Why don't we go down to our favorite Bistro in the Village? We can make it a double celebration. Your law license and the anniversary of our first date."

She smiled and hugged him.

"That would be great!"

He kissed her. Afterwards, she picked up her phone, dialed Reginald's number and broke the news of her reinstatement to him. He congratulated her and asked her about her plans.

"I actually don't have any. I really have to sit down and process everything that's happened to me first," she answered truthfully.

"Well, a friend of mine happens to be a really great civil rights lawyer. He'd always in the market for an associate. So if you ever want me to call him, just give me the word and I'll furnish you with a glowing recommendation."

"Thanks. I'll call you when I'm ready. In the meantime, I just want you to know that I think you're an amazing lawyer," she said.

He thanked her and they hung up.

Jordan looked at her.

"You know, there's got to be an easier way to make a living than Law."

CHAPTER ONE HUNDRED FIFTEEN

SCENES FROM A BISTRO

Later that night, Pattie and Jordan sat side by side, holding hands at a dimly lit table in the same bistro in Soho where they spent their first date. Pattie wore a fetching little black mini-dress she had bought to fit her curvy, new figure. It was short, in order to show off her legs and it was also low cut and sleeveless, in order to show off her bosom and arms. The light from the votive candle in the center of the table danced across the pink linen table cloth, exactly the way it had the year before. As Pattie scanned the restaurant and smiled, the glow from the sconces on the wall created a halo effect around her face. Jordan couldn't help but smile at her. She smiled back at him and thanked him for everything. Then she told him she needed advice.

"About what?"

"Well, no matter how much I eat or drink, I never seem to get enough. It's as if nothing can ever fill up the hole in my heart. As a result of never having focused on eating or drinking before, I never bothered to figure out which wine should be paired with which meats, but since eating and drinking are now a big new part of my lifestyle, I need to know these things. For instance, right now I'm in the mood for a steak, but I've acquired the habit of drinking champagne. So, I'm sitting here wondering whether there are rules about this sort of thing. Can a person eat a steak AND have champagne? Or do they have to stick to red wine? Is rose` a possible alternative?"

Jordan continued to smile at her.

"Well, there are several reasons why I believe champagne is in order tonight. After all, we have lots to celebrate and who can do that properly without their bubbly?" He said.

He ordered champagne.

"Well, now that we've got that bubbly—" he started to say, but then he interrupted himself by suddenly plunging his hand into his pocket and pulling out a tiny white box.

He gently placed it on the table, between them. Pattie looked at it and glanced up at him. When he smiled and nodded, she slid the ribbon off the box, opened it and gasped. Inside was an antique four karat heart shaped Edwardian pink diamond ring. It was surrounded by rubies and set in a platinum band. She stared at it in shock for a few seconds, as it winked and glittered at her from its bed of white velvet.

"Pattie Anwald, I love you. And as far as I'm

concerned, nothing else matters. That's why I need to know. Will you to spend the rest of your life with me, as my wife? Will you marry me?"

Even though he posed the question in a soft voice, everyone within earshot turned to them and eavesdropped, which caused him to blush. Tears filled Pattie's eyes. Just then her phone rang. She reached inside her tote bag, pulled it out and glanced at the caller ID. It was Edie. She frowned and let the call roll over into her voicemail.

"For God's sake Lady, don't leave us all in suspense over here. Will you or won't you marry him? Inquiring minds want to know," a man at the next table called out good naturedly.

Pattie looked around at everyone. All eyes were still on her, which made her feel self-conscious. Continuing to frown, she turned back to Jordan, cleared her throat and nodded.

"Yes," she whispered.

Everyone applauded and raised their glasses in a toast to the newly engaged couple. Congratulations were bandied about, as Jordan picked the ring up and slid it onto Pattie's finger. It fit perfectly. He watched as she smiled and turned her hand in the candlelight to admire the way it glistened. When she was done, he gently took hold of her hand and kissed it. Then he and Pattie lifted their glasses, toasted each other and the people at the other tables. Afterwards, Pattie toasted the ring and Jordan toasted her reinstatement. By the time the waiter returned with a platter of chilled crudités and hummus, the champagne bottle was nearly empty. Jordan ordered another one. Then he ordered a Chateaubriand for two. They downed glass after glass of champagne, one sip at a time, all throughout the meal.

"By the way, if you're wondering how I happened to choose this particular ring, it's because I asked your brother to do some detective work for me and find out the size and style you would most like."

After Jordan paid the check, they left. As he drove back to the apartment, a full moon from high in the sky shone a whitish blue light on them. When they walked in the door, the first thing Pattie did was run to her Magic Eight Ball. She picked it up and held it to her chest. Jordan walked over to her, peered over her shoulder and watched as she closed her eyes. She shook the Magic Eight Ball and waited for an answer to float up into the little glass triangle at the top.

"WITHOUT A DOUBT," it read.

"I don't know what your question was, but my answer is 'when in doubt, just live love'," he said.

"Well, wait a minute. From anything I've ever seen so far in life, the world we live in has never supported, much less nurtured love. So, how do we 'just live love' as you suggest?" Pattie asked.

"By not settling for what other people do, think or say. And by doing our best to spread love ourselves, so WE can keep positive energy going," he said.

He walked into the kitchen to retrieve a bottle of Dom Perignon and two crystal champagne flutes. When he returned to the living room, they sat on the couch and drank. Several hours later, Pattie had a nightmare and punched the headboard in her sleep.

CHAPTER ONE HUNDRED SIXTEEN

COUNT ON ME

The following morning, as Pattie was getting dressed, the knuckles on her right hand hurt, but she had no idea why. As she stood in the bedroom rubbing them, she looked up and noticed the strong rays of sunlight streaming through the window. Jordan was already in the kitchen, brewing coffee. When he heard her moving around, he walked down the hall and stood in the bedroom doorway.

"Good morning. The coffee's made and since it's a nice warm day, why don't we drink it out on the terrace?"

Pattie smiled and nodded.

"Great idea!"

She followed him into the living room, opened the draperies and French doors and walked out onto the terrace. She sat and let the heat from the sun warmed tiles soak into her bare feet. The soft spring breeze caressed her neck. She smiled at the way the sun lit up the windows of the buildings across the street. He was still in the living room, searching for a pen and a canary yellow legal pad.

"How cozy it feels it to be out here," she called to him.

A few seconds later, he joined her.

"I'm glad you like it. Quite frankly, so do I. Anyway, if we get started today, I'm confident we can pull a lovely wedding ceremony together by August. There's nothing more beautiful than a summer wedding, in my opinion. And I would really like it if that nice pastor in Yorktown were to officiate."

She didn't answer him. Instead, she just sat there staring at him and biting her lower lip. He frowned.

"Pattie, I notice something comes over you every time I mention that pastor. Do you have something against him?"

She shook her head.

"Why would I? It's not as if I've ever met him. My problem is actually with the church itself."

"Why? What's wrong with it?"

"Its location. I just don't want to be anywhere near the reservoir OR that prison and the church is up there, smack dab in that very neck of the woods. Plus, I don't understand how anyone can stand driving around on all those narrow, windy roads up there. Doesn't it make you car sick?"

He shook his head and looked at her quizzically.

"I agree there are a lot of curves, but no. I can't say they bother me at all.

she is real before rushing forward, splashing across the stream, and grabbing Nicole in his arms.

Artemus Pennywell | Beyond Space and Time

Aboard the Advisers' spacecraft, a robot attendant ushers Pennywell to a cozy seat replicating his favorite Scandinavian rocker. A second multi-armed wonder places a tumbler of Lagavulin on an extended table within hand's reach. Pennywell's gaze lands on the inviting amber liquid, "How nice. They thought of everything."

Settling back in the chair, Artemus reaches into his suit jacket and removes Charles Pike's original notebook, tapping the hole in its leatherbound cover. Flipping through the pages, he mumbles, "The very idea that I would let this precious notebook out of my sight …."

Patting his shirt pocket, he sighs, "Damn. Where is my pen?"

An exquisite fountain pen manifests on the table beside his drink. Unscrewing the cap from the heavy barrel, inlaid with intricate gold and gems detailing scenes from *Paradiso*, the third part of Dante Alighieri's *Divine Comedy*, Pennywell appreciates the symbolism with an ironic smile. With the priceless writing instrument pressed between his long bony fingers, the former CEO flips past Charlie Pike's maps, charts, Fibonacci spirals, and diagrams of Fordlandia with its Brazil Nut tree circled in red. Perusing familiar renderings of secret cartel airfields, hidden river passages, and the prehistoric rift where the lost ship waited to be found, he stops at a page delineating the shipwreck's precise coordinates. Above the detailed map of the Amazon, he writes a final entry in shimmering, blue-inked longhand:

The blue spark is activated.
May God have mercy on my soul.

yourself, Andrew. I don't want to return a century from now and find you fucked things up."

The hatch seals shut, and the Advisers' spacecraft ascends through a misty layer and shoots skyward toward the Heavens. Andrew watches it go and mutters, "Goodbye, my friend."

With Pennywell's dramatic departure part of the PTB historical record, Richard King enlists a multi-armed robot to extricate the world killer missile from the streambed and place it in the cargo ship's hold.

While waiting for Richard to complete his work, Penny and Nina help Rachel onto a makeshift hospital bed inside the craft. Concerned for his wife and unborn baby, Hannah, Owen busies himself, scooping up the ragged, dirty bags and gear and stowing it in lockers on the ship.

Helping douse the fire and police the campsite, Flynn turns and finds Andrew gazing up at the lost ship, "So this is what all of the fuss was over?"

Exhibiting uncharacteristic humanlike frustration with his departed former boss, Andrew produces an irony-laced chuckle, "Something tells me Artemus knew where this was the whole time."

Flynn frowns, "Jesus, mate, I hope that was not the case." Never close to Andrew through his years with the PTB, Flynn decides to needle his new boss, "So, Mr. CEO, now, is it?"

Andrew turns to his agent and smiles, "Yes, it appears so."

Flynn nods, "Uh huh. Did they teach you how to fly that piece of shit PTB cargo ship in CEO school?"

Andrew turns to his agent with a confused look, "No. I can fly a chopper, but … Oh, you must be curious who is behind the rudder." With a quick and easy laugh, he turns toward the cargo ship and motions toward the dark-tinted windscreen at someone seated in the cockpit.

Flynn's eyes lock onto a familiar young woman leaning outside the ship's portal with an effervescent smile in a fetching light blue PTB flight suit, "Hello, Flynn."

Not believing his eyes, Flynn squints through the mist to ensure

"Well they bother ME. Anyway, I swear I'm not trying to be difficult here and I hope you can understand where I'm coming from."

He nodded.

"Let's put it this way. I'm trying. Anyhow, if the Reverend could possibly officiate at some other venue, would that sit better with you?"

She nodded and cleared her throat.

"Yes, but there's something else. I'd like to invite a friend I met in prison to the wedding. Her name is Miranda."

He grimaced.

"Well, I'll contact Dutch and arrange for her to organize a prison break."

Shocked at his sarcasm, she shook her head, looked him in the eye and cleared her throat again.

"Actually, that's NOT what I had in mind. I was thinking more along the lines of hiring Reginald to bring a motion to get her out of there."

"I don't understand what the point would be. After all, what could you possibly have in common with some female thug you met while in prison? Other than the prison experience itself?"

"Believe it or not, she's a poor innocent victim, who is being held there unjustly."

"That's what you always said about most of your clients."

"Trust me Jordan, there's a lot you don't know about the way our system works. That's why I'm choosing to overlook your negative attitudes and misconceptions. But at the same time, I'm asking you to open your mind and consider that not everybody in prison is a thug. Second of all, not everybody in prison is guilty. Case in point? ME. And, the world being the way it is, people at some point will no doubt formulate and jump to the same conclusions about me, like you just did with Miranda. Are you ready for THAT? Because that's probably what will happen and believe me, it won't feel pleasant."

Then she proceeded to tell him Miranda's entire tale of woe, right down to how she originally thought Miranda was a spy for Katrina Nero. Jordan nodded and breathed a sigh of relief when he realized Miranda wasn't a criminal, but was "only" there on a civil contempt matter.

"All right then, lesson learned," he said.

She ran over to him, threw her arms around him and thanked him. Then she informed him that if Reginald were to succeed in getting Miranda out of jail, she wanted Miranda to be one of her bridesmaids. That caused Jordan to brace himself for a horrible Gothic style wedding, with convicts as bridesmaids in red and black gowns and a red velvet wedding cake that spewed black lava. She broke his revery by informing him that she didn't want a videographer. She harbored visions of her own, about Edie embarking on a drunken rampage and some videographer recording the entire tirade for posterity.

He nodded.

"Fine, but we DO have to hire a photographer," he said.

As she nodded in agreement, he handed the pad and pen to her. Then he picked up his phone and called the church. When the call rolled over into voice mail, he left a message. Afterwards, he went inside and took a shower. Pattie sat there, bit on the pen and gazed into the distance. When Jordan got out of the shower, he dressed and went downstairs to retrieve the mail. Pattie used that time to take her shower. When she got out of the shower, he handed her an envelope that had been forwarded to her. She opened it, gasped and began to shake. He peered over her shoulder, looked at it and whistled. She looked up into his eyes. Then she went on to explain that even though she had been making every effort to pay the monthly minimum on her college and law school student loans, it never seemed to matter. The balance still kept creeping up because of the interest. She told him she had resigned herself to the fact a long time ago, that she would never be able to pay off this debt in her lifetime, but she promised to keep on trying.

"Now you know my reason for being so hesitant in accepting your proposal. I didn't want to be responsible for ruining your credit. Why should we both become deadbeats? After all, once we get married, my debts will automatically become yours. I can't imagine you'd like THAT very much. And I wouldn't blame you. I never want to be in a position where I would do anything to make you resent me."

He shook his head and waved his hand twice in dismissal.

"Pattie, there's something important I need to tell you. Something I believe you have a right to know about me, especially once we're married. There's a reason I keep telling you to hang onto your money and let me pay for everything, including the wedding."

Pattie looked at him and shook her head.

"Well, I've always felt kind of guilty that you're paying for the wedding. After all, that responsibility usually falls on the father of the bride. And if he can't or won't, I should probably do it. After all I have money now."

He smiled at her and shook his head.

"Not to worry. I told you I'll take care of everything. Including your student loans."

She shook her head again and frowned.

"No. I can't ask you to take on my student loans. That wouldn't be fair."

"Yes it would, Love and here's why. You see, when my father died, he left me three hundred seventy six million pounds."

She gasped and shook her head, as her mouth hung open. Finally, she cleared her throat.

"Wow. I only ever knew one other rich person. It was during my first semester of college. I shared the dorm with the daughter of a Detroit automobile manufacturer. But then she went on drugs and dropped out. After that, we fell out of touch," she said.

Before he could respond, his cell phone rang. He picked up the call, greeted the Reverend Thomson and explained his reason for calling. Then he gave the Reverend his address, thanked him and said good bye. When he hung up he smiled.

"The Reverend Thomson will be here for tea next Saturday, at three o'clock. Anyway, let's just go out and enjoy the day. And while we're tooling around, let's buy a folder where we can keep all the ideas, receipts and brochures pertaining to our wedding."

She nodded and stood.

"By the way, I meant to ask you something. Did you ever return your mother's call from last night?"

She shook her head.

"Well, why don't you call her now? And while you're talking to her, ask her when it would be a good time for us to stop over there."

Pattie walked over to her tote bag, fumbled in it until she found her phone and then she called Edie.

"What's wrong, Miss High and Mighty?" Edie brayed.

Because Edie had been drunk the night before, she had no recollection of ever having called Pattie. Pattie shook her head and said she and Jordan would be stopping by later in the afternoon. Before Edie could even respond, Pattie hung up. Jordan gave her a sideways glance. She blushed and snapped the phone into the charger. When she walked out of the room, Jordan picked up her student loan invoice, stuck it in his briefcase and decided he would call Monday morning to get an exact payoff figure. Then he would pay the debt in full.

CHAPTER ONE HUNDRED SEVENTEEN

MOTHER IN LAW

Later that afternoon, Pattie drove to West Twelfth Street. The chestnut tree in front of the Anwald brownstone was in full bloom, so she didn't park under it. Instead, she found a space nearby. She locked the car, took a deep breath and braced herself. Then she and Jordan walked toward the house. As they got closer, they noticed how the geraniums in the flower boxes underneath the diamond shaped lead paned windows gave the house a festive air.

The fox terrier who lived next door spotted Pattie and Jordan. He immediately bounded up to the wrought iron fence that separated his property from the Anwald's and went into a litany of barking. Jordan chuckled and stooped to pet him. The terrier responded by wagging his tail. Pattie ignored the dog, continued walking up the path and climbed the stairs. Before she even had the chance to knock on the old black lacquered oak door, Edie swung it open and stood there, cradling her ever present jumbo sized margarita goblet in one hand and her ubiqui-tous cigarette in the other. Pattie beamed and shoved her ring under Edie's nose. It refracted bright bursts of sunlight and color as she moved her hand. Edie squinted, scrutinized it and licked a wad of salt from around the rim of her glass. Then she took an extra-long drag on her cigarette and gave Pattie the once over.

"Let me guess. Judging by your size, your jailhouse pallor and your newly acquired engagement ring, I'd have to say you're pregnant."

Pattie felt crushed. She had really wanted Edie to like her ring. She tensed up, shook her head and cleared her throat.

Edie was gratified that her remark removed the smile from Pattie's face. The jolt of adrenaline from her small victory pushed the alcohol and nicotine through her body faster. She deliberately exhaled her cigarette smoke in Pattie's direction. Pattie coughed and did her best to wave it away.

Chet finally made it to the door. As soon as he smelled Edie's cigarette smoke, he sniffed. Jordan finished petting the terrier and leapt up the stairs two at a time. Once everyone was inside, Chet closed the door and led everyone down the hall. As they walked past the dining room, Pattie noticed the empty space over the sideboard where the antique mirror designed by John Mueller had hung for nearly two centuries. Thanks to her hypnosis, Pattie was able to remember that both the mirror and her cell phone were sacrificed on the altar of Lou's rage.

Once Chet, Edie, Jordan and Pattie were all in the living room, Chet turned the Yankee game off. He noticed Pattie's ring, reached for her hand and examined it. Then he smiled and told Jordan if he was coming to seek Pattie's hand in marriage, he approved. Jordan smiled and thanked him for having made it so easy.

Edie arched her eyebrows and took a long, deep drag on her cigarette.

"Have you figured out which Judge will officiate? Because once you do, we can synchronize the ceremony to coincide with a sentencing. You know. Like the judge ordering some poor schnook to twenty five to life in prison and then order the two of you to spend twenty five to life with each other," Edie said.

She cackled at her own wit, took a long drag on her cigarette and once again exhaled her second hand smoke in Pattie's direction. Chet sniffed and shook his head.

"Edie's not herself today. Nevertheless, it might be nice if you held the wedding here," he said.

"Well, I'm sure Jordan will be the one doing all the planning and thinking from now on. For the wedding. For the honeymoon. And probably for everything. Forever," Edie said,

All of a sudden, Pattie felt hot. She glanced down at her décolletage and realized it was dappled with splotches, just the way it had been on Thanksgiving. Rather than wait for her body to start shaking, she took the hives as her cue to leave, so she stood. Jordan looked at her, followed her lead and stood as well.

"Well, whatever and however you decide, the only thing I ask is that you let me know the details as soon as you can. That way I can try to get the announcement into the newspaper," Chet added.

Just then, the outer door slammed. A few seconds later, Lou and Cheryl bounded into the living room.

"Ah, how nice. It's not very often I get to have both my children under the same roof anymore," Chet said.

When Pattie showed Lou and Cheryl her ring, Lou whistled, winked at Jordan and gave Pattie a hug. Cheryl could not find it in her heart to rejoice with Pattie. Longing to be engaged, she eyed the ring jealously, wondered why Pattie got all the good breaks in life and at the same time secretly wished Lou would get a ring like that for her. As Edie vehemently stubbed out her cigarette, Jordan apologized to Lou and Cheryl for having to leave so soon after their arrival. He and Pattie walked out into the hall. Chet walked them all the way out to the door, but because of his limp, he had to hustle in order to keep up with them. When Pattie opened the door, Chet got between them and the doorway.

"Don't be strangers now," he said, as he opened the door.

Pattie nodded. She put her hand on his arm, smiled and led Jordan out. Chet continued to stand in the doorway. He watched, as Pattie and Jordan got into Pattie's BMW. Just as Pattie was about to push the ignition button, Jordan put his hand on her arm and stopped her.

"I have something to say, before we drive off," he said.

Pattie frowned, dropped her arm and turned to look at him. Then she cleared her throat.

"Are you calling off the engagement or something?"

He frowned at her.

"Of course not. Anyway, I know what I'm about to say is going to sound a bit weird, especially after what your mother just said, but here goes. Without much choice in the matter, you wound up being removed from a city you never wanted to leave and it was under the worst of circumstances. After all, you nearly drowned and after that you ended up in prison. But, what if we were to leave town for three weeks and go to Scotland for our wedding trip under the best of circumstances? Would you agree to that? Would you even be up for it or would you be too afraid to fly?"

She looked him in the eye.

"Well, you're right about one thing. I did leave this city under the worst of circumstances. So, chances are, whatever happens, it can't possibly be as bad as the hell I've already been through. As a result, whatever you decide will be fine and I'll agree to it."

Chet continued to stand in the doorway. As he watched the two of them, he wondered what they were talking about. When Pattie finally started the engine and drove away, he shook his head, sniffed and quietly closed the door. All of a sudden he felt old and very, very lonely. He limped back down the hall and returned to the living room.

"You just can't resist torturing that kid, can you, Edie? And don't think I don't know why. You're jealous," he lamented, as he eased himself back into his usual place on the couch.

The malicious glint was back in Edie's eyes, but she waved her hand in dismissal.

"Oh, pipe the fuck down. I am not," Edie brayed.

Chet sniffed.

"Yes you are. And I don't understand why. Can't you just be happy for her?"

Instead of answering Chet, she turned her full attention to Lou.

"Say Louie, this is the second time I've had to ask you to pull a rap sheet on that guy," she bellowed.

CHAPTER ONE HUNDRED EIGHTEEN

BUSY MAN

Although it was only May 17th, it felt more like the middle of July. The air hung sticky and still, but it didn't bother Lou in the slightest. In fact, he liked it. And since he had the day off, he made a date to meet with Reginald Reese's investigator, Fred. Fred was a retired Detective with NYPD, so he and Lou had an instant rapport. They discussed "The Matter of Leland LeRoux" over breakfast at a coffee shop near Madison Square Garden. When the meal was over, Fred slid Pattie's file across the table.

"Listen, if you ever need anything else or even if you just want to bounce some ideas off me, feel free to give me a call. Reginald keeps me pretty busy, but I'll always try to do whatever I can to help you in my down time," he said.

Lou nodded, thanked him and gave him the thumbs up sign. He paid the tab and tipped the waitress. Armed with the file, he headed for his purple Bronco. On a whim, he called the investigator in the

Westchester DA's Office who was assigned to the case. They spoke for a few minutes. Finally, Lou said he would like to set up a meeting. The Investigator put him on hold and after a short time, he got back on the line.

"Would you be able to meet me today?"

"Sure," Lou said.

Lou arrived at the Westchester District Attorney's office within an hour and the investigator escorted him into one of their many conference rooms. A few minutes later, Katrina Nero showed up, clutching a folder in the crook of her left arm. Both men stood. She studied Lou for several seconds before she introduced herself. When she offered her hand. Lou noticed she wore no wedding band and her nail extensions were oval shaped and hot pink. As he briefly shook her hand, he realized her palm was surprisingly cool and dry to the touch. When she rolled out the closest chair and sat in it, both Lou and her investigator took that as their cue to follow suit. When they were all seated, she asked Lou what brought him to White Plains.

"Well, I'd like nothing more than to find Willie Hudson, lock him up and throw away the key. And I'd like it to happen as soon as possible. I believe if we work together we could probably make that happen," he said.

She patted the file.

"Well, before I can disseminate anything to you, I'll need you to break out some ID," she said.

She stretched her arm, looked lovingly at her nails and curled her fingers into a "gimme" motion. Once Lou produced his NYPD badge and driver's license, she snatched them, scrutinized them and shoved them back at him. When she snapped her folder open, the first thing she noticed was a phone message that had been hand written in purple ink. It was floating around loose on top of the file. It contained big loopy letters. The "I's", had heart shapes instead of dots. Katrina scowled and picked it up. Her face turned beet red and her dark brown eyes flashed. She slowly shook her head and read it verbatim.

"Willie Hudson's ex-wife's divorce lawyer up in Moriah, New York called to say that Willie Hudson is up there now. Blah blah blah. Boring. (Gasbag) 1-518-555-4400. Signed Lillia, November."

When she turned to her investigator, her eyes were like two pinpoints of light that burned holes right through him. Continuing to glare at him, she shoved the message down the table in his direction.

"Just who in hell's bathroom is this Lillia?"

He shook his head.

"I honestly don't know. A temp maybe?"

"Listen to me, you senseless imbecile. THIS VERY IMPORTANT MESSAGE doesn't even contain the name of the caller or the actual date he called. And what's with all this blah blah blah at the end of it?

And the word Gasbag?" Her voice sounded tough enough to grind glass.

The investigator frowned, picked up the message and read it. Disgusted, Katrina reached over and snatched it away from him. Then she turned to Lou.

"I wanna know exactly how something like this could happen," she said.

Lou looked down at the table, not really knowing what to say. Still gripping the message, Katrina picked up the phone and pounded out the attorney's number. When the secretary in Moriah let her boss know who was on the line, he was only too glad to drop what he was doing and accept the long awaited return call.

After Katrina apologized for not getting back to him any sooner, he told her how rude the girl in her office was. She apologized again for Lillia's general incompetence, then immediately deflected from it by questioning him about Willie's present whereabouts. He said he no longer had any idea, because Willie had left for parts unknown within days after he had placed that call. Finally, they exchanged personal cell phone numbers and promised to call each other the minute either of them heard anything. About anything.

When the lawyer hung up, he told his secretary he couldn't get over the fact it took those city slickers downstate six months to return a phone call. His secretary shook her head.

"I wonder whatever happened to the concept of a New York City minute," she said.

Katrina stabbed the message with the binder clip and made sure it was filed properly with the rest of the papers. Then she offered Lou a cup of coffee.

"Sure. Straight black. Nothing in it at all. Thanks," he said.

She smiled at Lou, turned to the investigator and frowned.

"Well? You heard him. Go get the two black coffees," she ordered.

The investigator nodded, stood and left. As soon as he did, she laced into Lou with a barrage of questions pertaining to his experience and skill as an investigator.

"Well, I was promoted to detective last Labor Day, but when Pattie got arrested, I was busted back down to a uniform. As if I had anything to do with it. I guess it made them feel better to penalize me just because I was Pattie's brother."

Katrina nodded.

"It's not that I can't relate to what you're telling me, because I can. But it still doesn't excuse the fact that you haven't had much more than two or three months of investigative experience. That's not a lot. And as you know, this is a high profile case. So, be honest here. Do you truly believe you can bring ANYTHING of value to the table or are you just here because you want to pin the killing on someone other than your sister?"

Lou nodded.

"Well, for openers, the least and I do mean the very least I could do would be to handle a vital phone message without merely shoving it into a file. And I would also look at what else is in that file without letting six months' worth of time elapse. Let's face it. Even though the temp who took the call was obviously an idiot, I mean, anyone with a half a brain would have realized the message was important. If only they had bothered to open the file, But they didn't', which boggles my mind. And yes. It's true I have somewhat of a personal stake in this. Even though my sister and I hardly ever agree on anything, Willie Hudson ruined not only the career she worked so hard for, but actually her whole life. And I really do take that personally. But it's not only for my sister. MY stake in this is that I got demoted over it," he said.

Katrina nodded, smiled and slid her file down to Lou. When she reached for Lou's file, he hesitated.

"Double jeopardy. Remember?" Katrina said.

With that, Lou released his file to her. They skimmed through each other's notes, until the investigator returned with the coffee. He placed three cups on the table, but before his buttocks even made contact with his seat, Katrina held her hand up like a stop sign.

"You're going to have to leave. I can't even look at

you right now. This last caper with the message was just more bullshit than I can handle," she said.

Then she asked him to take his coffee back to his office, find out who Lillia was and ascertain the exact dates she worked in their office. The investigator knew he had no choice but to pick up his cup and go. Once he did, Katrina and Lou sipped their coffee and continued to examine each other's files. When they finished, they discussed the case and took notes. After an hour Katrina looked at him and smiled.

"You know, if you were to work as an investigator on my team, you'd be back doing detective work, instead of working as a street cop. And I might even be able to bump you up a pay grade. So, having said that, would you like to hop on board?"

Lou chuckled.

"I thought you'd never ask."

CHAPTER ONE HUNDRED NINETEEN

TEA PARTY

The week sped by. On the morning of Saturday May 22nd, Pattie and Jordan woke entwined in each other's arms. They got out of bed, ate a quick breakfast and spent the early part of the day cleaning. Afterwards they baked, scurried and put the finishing touches on the tea party they organized for The Reverend Richard J. Thomson. Pattie watched Jordan cut the crusts from the extremely thin slices of white bread that formed the basis of the lavish assortment of dainty egg salad, ham salad and chicken salad sandwich squares. And she helped him trim the salmon, dill and cream cheese sandwiches in the same manner. Jordan put bean sprouts on some of the sandwiches. Once they made the last of the sandwiches, they carefully wrapped them, placed them in the refrigerator and tidied the kitchen. Pattie also helped Jordan set up the tea with his best delicate, porcelain Wedgwood tea set. Seeing it reminded her of the initial tea she drank in his office on the cold, rainy night

they met. When they were done, they showered and dressed in casual, but conservative attire.

At precisely three o'clock, the doorbell rang. Jordan smiled at Pattie, answered the door and greeted The Reverend Thomson, who was holding a King James Version of the Bible in his hand. Jordan ushered him into the living room and introduced him to Pattie. Pattie and the Reverend shook hands.

"It's a pleasure to see you again Jordan and to finally meet you today, Pattie. I've heard lot about you," he said.

Pattie and the Reverend sat on opposite ends of Jordan's soft white leather couch, while Jordan disappeared into the kitchen.

"I had a very pleasant ride down here from Yorktown. I suspect the fact that it's Spring helped to make the trip so enjoyable," the Reverend said, trying to start a conversation.

Pattie didn't know what to say, so she simply nodded, smiled and cleared her throat. A few minutes later, much to the Reverend's relief, Jordan wheeled the tea cart into the living room. On it was a pot of Earl Grey tea. It filled the room with the uplifting aroma of bergamot. Next to it was an extra pot of boiling water, a silver pitcher of milk, a small Wedgwood bowl containing lemon slices, a tiny fork, a silver sugar bowl, tongs, the Wedgwood tea cups, plates, napkins and the platter of sandwiches.

"Whenever an individual finds and falls in love

with that special person who best complements them, I guess the people of today would call it 'their soul mate'. Well, I have to say, whatever you call it, the relationship is truly a gift from God," the Reverend said, as Jordan carefully handed Pattie a cup and saucer.

Pattie and Jordan both nodded, while Jordan poured Pattie's tea. When the cup was almost full, Pattie hoped her nervousness wouldn't cause her to drop it.

"But you know, at the same time, I also have to say that marriage is truly a serious matter. Because when two separate individuals become united as a couple, they consummate the marriage and hopefully go on from there to establish a household and a family," the Reverend continued, as he carefully took hold of the cup and saucer Jordan handed to him.

Jordan nodded and poured his own cup. The Reverend put his cup and saucer down, picked up a napkin and spread it on his lap. Then he chose a plate and sampled one of the egg salad squares.

"So, am I correct in presuming the two of you would like to get married in the church?" The Reverend asked, hoping that a yes or no question would at least elicit some kind of a response from them.

He waited for at least one of them to say something, but they never did. They merely looked at each other. Finally, Pattie frowned. Then Jordan turned to the Reverend and shook his head.

"Of course I'm sure there are hundreds of wonderful secular venues right here in New York City. Unfortunately I don't know of any," the Reverend went on.

When the couple looked crestfallen, the Reverend continued.

"On the other hand, I do happen to know of a gorgeous site in Rye, called 'L'Abbaye', I've officiated at weddings there," he said.

Jordan smiled, nodded and stood. He walked over to his desk, retrieved his canary yellow pad and pen and wrote the name 'L'Abbaye'.

"I think we'd like to explore this venue. And as soon as we finalize our plan, we'll contact you so we can zero in on a date," Jordan said, as he returned to the couch.

The Reverend, grateful that at long last one of them said something, took hold of his cup and saucer, held them in midair and posed another question.

"May I ask you both your religious backgrounds?"

"Well, I grew up Presbyterian," Jordan said.

The Reverend smiled and nodded.

"I surmised as much. And what about you Pattie?"

Pattie cleared her throat and shrugged. Although it wasn't much of a response, at least it was something.

"But you do believe in God. Is that correct?"

As she nodded, Jordan stood, cleared the first course and returned from the kitchen with the second course. It consisted of a tray of raisin scones and date nut bread with clotted cream, butter, seedless raspberry jam and marmalade. As Jordan refreshed everyone's tea, the Reverend picked up a scone, sliced it in half and buttered it. After they finished the second course, Jordan cleared the path for the third course, returned with more hot water and a dessert spread that consisted of frosted devil's food cake squares, oatmeal raisin cookies, lemon cookies, orange cookies, vanilla sugar cookies and a poppy seed cake with a lemon drizzle. When they finished their tea, Reverend Thomson handed the Bible to Jordan.

"Well, I've enjoyed getting to know you both. I have a really good feeling about the two of you and I am honored that you asked me to officiate. Please accept this Bible as my gift," he said.

They all stood. Jordan and Pattie thanked the Reverend for coming and for the gift of the Bible and walked the Reverend to the door.

Odd pair, the Reverend thought, as he walked down the hallway toward the elevator.

When he was gone, Pattie and Jordan brought everything back into the kitchen. Once the food was put away, Jordan smiled, pointed at the tea set and silverware and handed Pattie a dish towel. He turned on the faucet.

"These are too good to go into the dishwasher," he said, so he washed and she dried.

YOU CAN RUN BUT YOU JUST CAN'T HIDE

Meanwhile, further downtown, Edie was having a gathering of her own. She, Chet, Lou and Cheryl all sat around her dining room table. The tension was so thick, anyone could have cut it with a knife. Cheryl had a look of hopeful surprise on her face, which Edie tried to douse with her infamous mean glint.

"What do you mean you have an announcement to make about your work? I thought the announcement would be that you were finally popping the question to me," Cheryl said.

"Let's hope they're reinstating you with the detective Squad, at long last," Chet said.

Lou shook his head. Edie drained her margarita glass. Her lip curled under as she lit a cigarette.

"Well then, what the hell is it for God's sake? Why all this cloak and dagger bullshit?" She brayed.

When Lou broke the news that he was leaving NYPD to work for the Westchester DA's office, Chet sniffed and popped a handful of peanuts into his mouth, while Edie just sat there stunned. Cheryl reacted by standing, running down the hall and out the door to Christopher Street, where she caught the first Path Train home to Jersey City.

CHAPTER ONE HUNDRED TWENTY-ONE

SO CLOSE BUT YET SO FAR

As late afternoon deepened into twilight, Cheryl's mother sat in the place she felt most comfortable, the red Naugahyde chair at the head of her grey, faux, marbleized Formica kitchen table. The building she lived in was a four story walk up on the Riverfront in Jersey City. Being one of the oldest buildings in Hudson County, its architecture was beautiful, but it had seen better days. The original neighborhood was built to house the elite, however, as years went by and newer, more modern housing became available, the gentry moved out and working class families moved in. And as Cheryl's mother stared out the window and tamped her pack of cigarettes, even she knew it was rundown enough to be considered barely more than a tenement. It was so old, no matter how often she dusted, more dust kept settling. The best thing she could say about it, was that she had a dazzling view of the New York City Skyline. She scratched her head. Her yellowing gray hair was pinned against her dirty scalp with tiny bobby pins. And as she sat there in the same nightgown and faded pink chenille bathrobe she'd been wearing for the last day and a half, she tore open the exposed silver foil, inverted the pack and gently coaxed one of the cigarettes out. As she lit it up and inhaled, she wondered why that wonderful first puff was always the best. A few seconds later, the sky line across the river came to life. She sat there and let the grandiose lights of the Big Apple reel her in and tantalize her, just as they done for as far back as she could remember. Manhattan may have only been four miles away as the crow flew, but to her it felt like an entirely different world. And knowing that had been the bane of her existence. As she sat there ruminating, she became so lost in thought, she didn't even realize she was twirling the lone stray hair on her chin. She finally turned away, glanced around at her dusty apartment and sighed.

When the front door slammed, she literally jumped out of her chair. It took her a few seconds to recover and by the time she did, Cheryl had already stormed into the kitchen. She wrapped her gnarled, nicotine stained fingers around the top of the chair next to her and pulled it out for Cheryl. She coaxed an unfiltered cigarette out of her pack, stuck it between her lips and lit it up, just as Cheryl slid into the chair. She usually enjoyed the mini vacation a cigarette and a beer provided, since they were her only pastime, but that particular cigarette was more therapeutic than recreational, because the expression on Cheryl's face worried her.

"I can already tell, by that puss you got going on, that one of them did you wrong. Which one was it this time? Him or his mother?"

"Him. Get this. He's quitting the police force to take some kookamunga job at the Westchester DA's office."

Her mother scowled, slowly shook her head as she processed the news and then finally burst into tears.

"Why are YOU the one crying?" Cheryl asked.

"Because I have this sinking feeling I'm never going to make it across that river."

"I guess it just never occurred to him that he's screwing up all our lives," Cheryl said.

Her mother stuck her cigarette in one of the grooves on her salmon colored plastic ashtray, nodded in agreement and wiped her tears. Then she took a good long drink from her beer can.

CHAPTER ONE HUNDRED TWENTY-TWO

GO REST HIGH ON THAT MOUNTAIN

It was Saturday morning on Memorial Day weekend, the unofficial beginning of the summer season. It was a powerful time, because it had the ability to put an end to everyone's memories of the long dreary winter that preceded it. Weatherwise, the weekend was off to a great start, with a clear blue sky and balmy temperatures.

Jordan helped Pattie into the passenger's seat of her car. He closed her door and got in on the driver's side. Pattie entered "L'Abbaye's" address into her GPS, while Jordan started the engine. He drove out of the garage and turned North onto the West Side Drive. Because most New Yorkers were desperately engaged in a mass exodus, in any direction that could possibly lead them out of the city, Pattie and Jordan sat in traffic for a long time. Eventually they made it onto the New England Thruway. Normally, the trip would have taken about forty minutes, but that day it took well over an hour.

When Jordan drove off the exit ramp in Westchester, he and Pattie suddenly became silent. The lovely scenery provided by Mother Nature and the riot of late spring colors that dotted the suburban landscape grabbed all their attention. After a short time, Pattie caught sight of L'Abbaye in the distance. It was hard to miss, since its breathtaking Gothic Style Abbey and fantastic spiral tower were perched like a crown jewel at the top of one hundred thirty nine acres of wide open spaces and gently sloping hills. Just seeing it drew Pattie into a near trance of excitement. Even Jordan was impressed.

"My God! If that's the place, it reminds me a little of St. Andrew's Golf Course back home. Doesn't it give you a churchy kind of a feeling?" He asked.

Pattie smiled and nodded vaguely, as Jordan drove up the hill. And when the GPS finally announced their arrival. Jordan turned, drove through the rococo wrought iron archway and into the long driveway. It was wider and more well maintained than many public roadways. The blue crushed stones crackled beneath the tires, as he made his ascent to the Abbey's main entrance. Just as he shifted into "park," a uniformed valet smiled, approached the car and opened Pattie's door. He welcomed her and helped her out. She thanked him, looked around and gasped at the ordered loveliness of the landscape. She admired the broad avenues that were filled with ancient purple and white lilac trees, all of which were in bloom. They contrasted with the smooth, huge expanse of the sprawling, yet perfectly manicured lawn that spread out like an emerald green evening gown. It held a promise of "peace." She looked up at the turrets atop the building and the towering tips of the fir trees that were so tall they looked as if they were scratching the sky. Then she breathed in the fresh clean air that teased her with its faint lilac scent. Finally, she looked down at the magnificent view of the deep blue Long Island Sound, whose waves shimmered and hissed in the distance below.

Once the valet greeted Jordan, opened his door and drove off to park the car, Pattie and Jordan walked around the grounds hand in hand. They passed a pristine, park like setting that was interspersed with stone curved and wrought iron benches. It led to a serene lake that housed a family of two adult swans and their six baby cygnets. Pattie smiled in delight as she walked over to the banks and watched them glide and swim. Jordan pointed out a dock and an old fashioned mill that was actually working. And then she saw an arrow shaped sign that read "Wedding Garden". She grabbed Jordan's arm and followed the path. Eventually they found themselves in a lovely park like setting right behind the Abbey. It over-looked a large, magnificently tiled swimming pool with cobalt colored water and a fountain. Feeling

enchanted, she ran into the middle of the garden, stood there and spread her arms. She grinned from ear to ear and twirled around, hugging herself and giggling. Suddenly all her misgivings about getting married vanished and were replaced with a desperation to celebrate her special day right there, in that splendid place.

Jordan smiled at her, took her hand and led her back down the path that led to the main entrance of the Neo Gothic style abbey. Once they walked through the massive walnut double doors that led inside, they noticed the main lobby was deliciously cool and no less luxurious than the outside. Its marble floor, matching pillars, beautiful Persian rugs, fine statues and oil paintings were simply gorgeous. A genteel, elegant hostess greeted them. When Jordan told her he wished to speak to someone about a wedding, she led them down a corridor that featured a set of genuine medieval tapestries. Finally, they reached the office of the bridal concierge.

The concierge stood, smiled warmly and shook their hands. Then she invited them to take a seat in the comfortable, overstuffed chairs across from her desk. When Jordan explained they wanted to get married in August, she looked at her calendar.

"Would July 31st work for you? Or is that too soon?"

Pattie and Jordan looked at each other, grinned and nodded.

"That would be great," they answered in unison.

The concierge went on to describe the various nuptial and reception packages L'Abbaye offered. When she explained that one of their packages included an evening, candlelight ceremony outside in the Wedding Garden, Pattie squealed with delight.

"We'll be happy to arrange that for you. And if Mother Nature decides to become uncooperative at the last minute, don't worry. We'll simply end up erecting strong overhead awnings. But since July is usually a pretty hot, dry month, that probably won't happen. Does eight pm sound good?"

Pattie and Jordan looked at each other again and smiled. Jordan called the Reverend Thomson. And when Pattie heard he was available to officiate that evening, she clapped her hands together. Jordan used his credit card to make a sizable down payment. Then, armed with a stunning catering and cake menu to take home and study, along with recommendations for flower arrangements, choices of music and the concierge's business card, he and Pattie left. Once they were both inside the car, Pattie said she wanted to call Ryan and invite him for coffee. Jordan smiled and nodded at her.

CHAPTER ONE HUNDRED TWENTY-THREE

I CHOOSE YOU

Pattie and Jordan walked into their apartment carrying a double chocolate cake from the "Epicurean Delight" in White Plains. They no sooner cut the cord on the box, when the doorbell rang. Pattie answered it and broke into a smile at the sight of Ryan standing there in his waiter's uniform. He was both happy and relieved to see how good she looked. He smiled back at her. They hugged and she led him into the living room. When she held up her ring to show it off, he smiled again.

"Wow! What a surprise! It looks like best wishes are in order."

They both sat, while Jordan wheeled the tea cart into the living room. This time, instead of tea, Jordan served coffee. Ryan drank his black, as always. Pattie and Jordan put cream in theirs and they all had a slice of cake. Pattie told Ryan their wedding plans.

"Of course invitations will go out, but in the meantime, I have a question to ask you."

"Shoot."

"Would you be my Man of Honor? I guess that's what they would most likely call it," Pattie said.

Jordan looked shocked, but Ryan didn't seem to notice. He nodded and smiled.

"I'd be delighted."

Pattie smiled back at him.

"Thank you."

"My pleasure. By the way, I have a couple of announcements of my own. Believe it or not, after eight long years of full time employment in the Court-house, weekend employment as a waiter and grueling undergrad classes, I'm finally getting my Bachelor's Degree!"

"Congratulations," Pattie said.

"My parents are planning to throw a big party at Cosmo's, right after the Graduation ceremony. It's the last Saturday in June. My mother will be sending out the invitations in a day or two! I hope you both can make it."

"Well, it looks like invitations and RSVPs will be flying up and down the West Side, so be on the look-out for our wedding invitations. Anyway, we wouldn't miss your party for the world! Would we Jordan?" Pattie said, accepting the invitation on the spot for both of them.

Ryan smiled.

"My other big announcement is that I got accepted to the Yale School of Drama's Master's Program. I can't believe it. This will be the first time since High School that I'll be a full time student. I'll continue working at the courthouse and Elvis' Restaurant until about two weeks before classes start. Then I'll give myself a short vacation right before I have to vamoose."

"Wow. Congratulations again! I sure will miss you," Pattie said.

He smiled and shook his head.

"No you won't. You won't have time to. I'll be back before you know it. Besides, I'm not going that far. After all, on a good day, New Haven is only an hour and a half away."

They finished their coffee and cake and Ryan caught Pattie up on the courthouse gossip. An hour later, the visit ended on a happy note and with a hug, so Ryan could arrive on time at Elvis' restaurant. By then it was twilight. When Ryan left, Jordan closed the door, turned the lights on in the living room and glared at Pattie.

"I want you to know how much I hate this ludicrous, downright disturbing notion of Ryan serving as your 'Man of Honor'. It's a ridiculous title which you pulled out of a hat, because such a thing doesn't even exist. And probably for a damned good reason. So, as far as I'm concerned, you should never have asked him to serve in that capacity. I don't know what's crazier, that or emptying the prison to furnish members of your bridal party."

Pattie was so shocked, she gasped.

"Oh now that's just downright nasty. First of all, I thought we settled the Miranda issue on good terms. And now you're bringing it up again? And as far as Ryan goes, it's like Déjà vu all over again, with you and me arguing over him. And why? You know, just because you're insanely jealous, it doesn't mean you have the right to tell me who I can have as the person of Honor at my own wedding. Quite frankly, I can't believe, after the way you and Ryan pulled together during the darkest time of my life, that you could actually still feel threatened by him," she yelled.

"Yes, well, that's only one of the issues. I also thought YOU were the one who insisted on the brilliant idea of you and I at least discussing invitations with each other before accepting them," he said.

She bolted from the couch and ran down the hall in tears.

CHAPTER ONE HUNDRED TWENTY-FOUR

FIGHT THE POWER

On May 27th, carrying a set of papers in one hand and a briefcase in the other, Reginald Reese swooped into Katrina Nero's office without even bothering to knock. Katrina, who was wearing a red silk power suit, had her nose buried in a file, so when Reginald banged his briefcase on top of her desk, she jumped. When she looked up and peered over her readers at him, he flashed a grin worthy of a Cheshire cat and she grinned back at him. He took that as an invitation to fling himself into the chair across from her desk. Her smile faded when she glanced at the Writ he handed to her.

"Oh God! Don't tell me you're representing that damned Miranda Dabbler AND you've managed to finagle whatever this is onto this morning's docket," she said, as she tossed the papers onto her desk.

He nodded.

"Yeah, well I am. Come on now, Katrina. It really is high time you stopped being a monster and just let her out of her cage. This has been going on for six months now, you know."

She shook her head.

"Sorry, Sir Galahad, but she's too ridiculous to merit journalistic protection."

And with that, she stood and walked out of her office, leaving Reginald to sit there and shake his head. Finally he stood, went down to the lobby to wait for Pattie and the expert witness. They arrived, accompanied by Raj from the Yoga Studio and Jesse from the Cable Station, who held the DVD in one hand and the Subpoena Deuces Tecum Reginald had served on him in the other. Once they all made it through the metal detector, Reginald greeted them and thanked them for being there. The group moved over to the wall and chatted for a few minutes until a court officer announced that the van from the women's correctional center was pulling into the garage. Hearing that sent chills down Pattie's spine. Impatient to speak to Miranda, Reginald asked everyone to go up to the courtroom and wait for him, while he went down to the lockup.

HABEUS CORPUS

About twenty minutes later, Reginald walked into the courtroom and strode up to the counsel table. Katrina was already waiting for him on the opposite side of the room. A few seconds later, Judge Dexter Charles entered the courtroom. Everyone stood as the court officer opened the session. When Judge Charles sat, so did everyone else, except for Reginald. When the clerk announced the case, an officer from the lock up escorted Miranda into the courtroom. Her face was ashen, her shoulders were slumped and her head was bowed. All eyes followed her, as she made her way from the side door, to take her place beside Reginald. The contrast from her appearance on the DVD was marked. She was at least thirty pounds thinner and she looked tired and pallid. Pattie wanted to cry. It depressed her to see Miranda practically down to skin and bones, being dragged around in handcuffs and with her hair a mess. Reginald explained to the Judge how Miranda distributed a legitimate news story over her Cable TV program on December 4th and then he began his argument.

"Together, the First Amendment and the New York State Shield Law safeguard media personnel like Ms. Dibble from having to reveal their confidential news sources. In spite of the protection these laws afford journalists, on the evening of the telecast, the People singlehandedly decided to flush Ms. Dibble's rights down the toilet. When ordered to reveal her sources, Ms. Dibble refused and wound up spending the night in a maximum security wing of the women's prison, a place where she clearly doesn't belong. One night turned into one hundred seventy two nights, because she has been there ever since."

Judge Charles frowned.

"Did you say, 'maximum security wing'?"

Miranda and Reginald both nodded.

"As unbelievable as that sounds, Your Honor, yes. And she was there as recently as this very morning," Reginald replied.

Katrina stood.

"The People are making a Sua Sponte Oral Motion to Dismiss. May I remind Your Honor, that 'We the People' have an obligation to fight for the citizens of this County against deadly and dangerous narcotics trafficking. And the way we do it, is by painstakingly identifying, disrupting, dismantling and prosecuting high-level drug dealers and members of their enterprises. Miss Dabbler's defiance, by obstructing us in these endeavors, was already ruled as Contempt of Court by Judge Ryerson back in December. And because nothing has changed since that ruling, I'm asserting Res Judicata," Katrina said.

The Judge shook his head.

"Well, a number of things have changed since that time. Nearly six months have gone by, for one thing. And it is also my understanding that the drugs were seized and the defendants were apprehended, based on the information in the envelope Miss Dibble turned over to your Investigators. And I'm now sitting on the bench. The People's Motion to Dismiss is denied."

Katrina sighed loudly and folded her arms across her chest. Both Reginald and the Judge shot her a dirty look.

"I'm going to need a TV and a DVD player at some point during this hearing, although I can begin by calling Ms. Dibble as my first witness," Reginald said.

The Judge nodded at one of the court officers, who immediately left the courtroom. Then Reginald whispered to Miranda and pointed to the front of the courtroom. The lockup officer escorted her up to the stand. The clerk swore her in and Reginald asked her to describe how her day began on December 4th."

"Well, as I was preparing to go on the air at the Westchester Cable TV studio, a man wearing a black overcoat with a matching Fedora hat, came in and handed me an envelope with important documents containing information about what appeared to be a seventeen million dollar narcotics transaction that was taking place right here in White Plains. And as he gave me the information, he made me promise never to reveal his identity or his source. I agreed and broadcast the story. All went well, I guess, until the end of the day when I walked into the lobby of my apartment building at home. That's when I encountered two Investigators from the County Police who were lying in wait for me. They swirled around and surrounded me. Then they served me with something called a Motion to Compel and demanded that I not only surrender the envelope and documents to them, but also the name of the person who gave them to me. I gave them the documents which identified the three alleged traffickers, along with the address of the warehouse where the drugs were. Then the investigators began to pressure me. They demanded I give them the name of the man who handed me the envelope. I refused and told them I wasn't required to reveal that information, because I was legally entitled to assert the First Amendment and the NY Shield law. I also told them I would rather die than reveal my sources. And one of them, I think his name was Townley, said 'you just might have to.' Then he handcuffed me and threw me in prison for the night. Then, first thing the next morning I found myself here in this courthouse. A judge ordered me to either reveal my source or face the consequences. The next morning I came to court and they sent me back to prison, where I've been ever since."

"Thank you. Your Honor I have nothing further of this witness," Reginald said, as he walked back to the counsel table.

Katrina stood, walked right up to Miranda and positioned herself directly in front of her. She pulled her diminutive height up as tall as she could. Then she glared at Miranda.

"Now, isn't it true that your so called cable TV show was nothing more than some obscure, New Age, Hippy Dippy blip, blip, blip about Yoga and other such useless topics, Miss Dabbler?" Katrina said, in an aggressive tone of voice.

Miranda lifted her head and looked Katrina directly in the eye.

"Well, to answer your question, even though you keep getting my name wrong, my show is about Yoga and other New Age topics. And their usefulness is in the eye of the beholder and not for you to value or devalue," Miranda said, in a tired voice.

Katrina placed her left hand on her hip, tapped the side of her skull three times with her right index finger and shook her head.

"Apparently, I can't get through to you, but I'm going to try. Do you even realize that if you would only yield to The People's simple request and submit the name of your source, you could walk out of here right this very minute?"

"Since I promised not to reveal his identity, I never bothered to ask him his name and he never told me what it was. Therefore, I don't even know it," Miranda continued.

The Judge frowned again.

"Let me get this straight, Ms. Dibble. Are you saying, you don't actually KNOW the name or identity of the man who handed you the envelope?" he interjected.

Miranda nodded and said yes.

"No further questions," Katrina said, as she stormed back to the counsel table.

Reginald looked at the judge and indicated he had no questions for Miranda on redirect examination. The Judge nodded and ordered her to step down. As soon as she stood, the lockup officer sprang to her side and walked her back to the counsel table. A few seconds later, the other court officer returned with a television cart, which he wheeled into the courtroom. Reginald walked back to Jesse, took the DVD from him and handed it to the court officer. He asked the court officer to position the television so that everyone, especially the Judge, could see it. The court officer complied and inserted the DVD into the DVD player and just as he picked up the remote control, Katrina stood.

"Your Honor, I have no way of knowing where this DVD came from or who could have doctored it.

There's no chain of custody. Therefore, I am requesting it not be allowed into evidence."

"Your Honor, the man who has had sole custody of the DVD ever since the day it was recorded, is right here with us in court. His name is Jesse Yarborough," Reginald said.

The Judge pointed at Jesse and waved his right arm as if he were calling down a contestant on "The Price is Right." Jesse turned as white as a ghost. His face was a question mark as he pointed to himself. When the Judge nodded, Jesse stood and took the stand. After the clerk swore him in, Reginald pointed at the television.

"Now, as to this DVD, can you please tell the court who recorded it?" Reginald asked.

Jesse nervously explained how he programmed the equipment to record everything, every morning. He went on to say his habit was, after every twenty four hour interval, to remove the DVD, store it in a vault at the studio and replace it with a new one.

Reginald nodded.

"I see. And just who has access to this vault?"

"Well it's locked and I'm the only one who has the key."

"Does anyone else ever do this job?"

"I suppose if I get sick or if I ever go on vacation, someone else may have to, but so far that hasn't happened."

"Have you ever given this DVD to anyone to hold?"

Jesse shook his head.

"Not until you took it from me just now and gave it to that bailiff over there."

"This court hereby finds that this DVD is a crucial and genuine piece of evidence, therefore, it stays in," the judge said.

Then he nodded to the court officer, who pushed the play button. Everyone watched the same DVD Pattie watched at the Cable Studio a few months earlier. When it came to an end, Reginald resumed his questioning.

"Mr. Yarborough, after having just seen this DVD, has it been altered in any way since the time you recorded it?" Reginald asked.

Jesse shook his head.

"No."

When Reginald walked back to the Counsel Table, Katrina stood.

"I have no questions for this witness, Your Honor," she said.

"Your Honor, at this time I'd like to call Dr. Oliver Farnsworth to the stand," Reginald said.

Jesse breathed a sigh of relief and stepped down. Then Dr. Oliver Farnsworth, PhD took the stand. The Clerk swore him in and asked him to be seated. Upon being questioned, Dr. Farnsworth testified that he was the Associate Dean of the Omnia Graduate School of Journalism. As he started to relay his educational background, Katrina Nero stood, smiled at him and stipulated to his credentials. Knowing he had connections in high places with members of the press who had clout, she did not want to risk alienating him.

"As an expert, after having viewed this DVD, would you characterize Ms. Dibble as a bona fide journalist?" Reginald asked.

Dr. Farnsworth nodded.

"Absolutely. She delivered a genuine news story of such monumental importance, the District Attorney couldn't wait to get her hands on it. And as she stated herself, it not only helped The People's investigation, it was the linchpin of their case."

"Thank you, Dr. Farnsworth. Is there anything else you'd like to add?" Reginald said.

Dr. Farnsworth nodded.

"When looking at the First Amendment and the New York Shield Law, the proper question isn't WHO happens to be delivering the news, but rather what function the information is designed to serve. And if we should decide these laws don't apply to Miss Dibble, because she's not a famous enough journalist, then we have begun our descent down the slippery slope that eventually ends up in the hell of censorship."

Reginald nodded.

"No further questions, Your Honor," he said, as he returned to the counsel table.

Katrina stood.

"I have no questions of this witness, your Honor."

"Your Honor, I believe my position is clear from my brief in support of my Motion, the DVD and the testimony today, that American Justice demands Ms. Dibble be entitled to journalistic protection. And it's clear that she has been denied that," Reginald said.

The Judge nodded and looked at Katrina Nero.

"Miss Nero, since you only found out about Attorney Reese's Motion this very morning, if you need time to prepare for a hearing on any objections, I will grant you an adjournment."

She shook her head.

"No. Never mind. I have to say however, I find it fascinating that if Miss Dabbler over there is such an important journalist, why haven't ANY other journalists brought her dubious cause to the attention of the media?" Katrina said.

"In all my years on the bench I've never been able to figure out why anyone acts the way they do, but I DO know it has been demonstrated to my satisfaction, that the informant KNEW he was engaging with a reporter he trusted; someone whom he handpicked to disseminate an important news account in a candid and straightforward way, while at the same time keeping his identity confidential. The police interface with confidential informants all the time and in those instances the People don't object, so I don't see why they should object here. The instant Miss Dibble accepted that information on those terms and broadcast it as agreed, to an audience over the media, no matter how small or off the beaten path that audience might have been or what types of tastes they may have had in television fare, Miss Dibble was indeed acting in a professional capacity as a proper journalist. Therefore she is automatically allowed to obtain AND assert ABSOLUTE immunity under both the First Amendment and the New York State Shield law. Even if that weren't the case, the Court must take into consideration that Ms. Dibble also testified she did not know the man's identity Therefore it's impossible for her to be in Contempt of Court, because there is no defiance. It's patently obvious, she can't provide something she doesn't even have. As a result, I'm ordering Miss Dibble be released from prison FORTHWITH. Congratulations, Miss Dibble," Judge Charles said.

He banged down the gavel, stood and left the courtroom.

Just as with Pattie, it took about thirty minutes for Miranda's release to be processed through the Clerk's office, but when she walked out onto the steps of the courthouse, surrounded by Reginald, Pattie, Dr. Farnsworth, Raj and Jesse, Katrina was nowhere to be found. David Huntley, the newscaster, was waiting on the courthouse steps, with cameramen who were scanning the hectic scene. He walked up to Dr. Farnsworth and stuck a microphone in his face.

"Dr. Farnsworth, do you have anything you wish to say today?" He asked.

Dr. Farnsworth smiled and nodded. David Huntley had been one of his former students.

"Oh yes. Today we witnessed an important victory for Journalism. The Founding Fathers made the First Amendment the FIRST Amendment for a reason."

"Thank you," David Huntley said and then he turned to Miranda and stuck the microphone in her face.

"In the end, all any of us have is our integrity. And it was crucial for me to preserve my integrity by protecting the identify of my source. I will continue to do so, even to my grave. Knowing I was keeping my integrity is the only thing that kept me from losing my sanity while I was squirreled away so unjustly," she said.

Even though she looked bedraggled from her long siege, she spoke with the aplomb of a person who had the benefit of intensive media training. Everyone within earshot, especially the reporters, applauded her statement.

"What was it like inside the penitentiary?" David Huntley asked.

Tears came to her eyes. She waved her hand and turned away and David Huntley nodded to the camera man.

"Well, there you have it. I'm delighted to report that, thanks in no small part to this courageous young lady, Journalism has once again won out over yet another threat. The First Amendment and the New York State Shield Law are both still thriving and healthy today and I'm reporting this victory live, from right here on the steps of the White Plains courthouse."

After the cameras folded, Miranda hugged Reginald. Pattie reached out to join in the embrace. Miranda thanked them both and promised she would find a way to pay Pattie back. Pattie told her not to worry about it and held out her engagement ring, in order to change the subject. Miranda smiled.

Afterwards, Reginald treated Pattie, Miranda, Dr. Farnsworth, Raj and Jesse to one of his expensive gourmet lunches. By the time the meal was over, it was late afternoon. When they left the restaurant, the sky was a battleship gray color. Clouds hung low in the sky and the air felt wet. A few seconds after everyone made it to their cars, leaden sheets of unstoppable rain beat down on them.

CHAPTER ONE HUNDRED TWENTY-SIX

HELL'S KITCHEN

Early on Saturday June 5th, just as the morning sun painted a streak of silver high above the rolling white caps of the Hudson River, Willie Hudson slithered out of his flea bag motel room in Hell's Kitchen.

The city was relatively quiet and the air still felt fresh and dewy, because the cars, buses and trucks hadn't yet clogged it up. Willie turned the corner and slid out of the heat and humidity by darting into his usual coffee shop.

He poured himself a steaming hot cup of coffee at the self-service counter, added his half and half and snapped a lid on it. He grabbed a newspaper, ordered a cruller and paid for it all. Then he returned to his room, plopped into the dirty old armchair with a thud and slouched there. He reached into the bag for his cruller, bit into it and sipped his coffee. Then he opened the newspaper and perused it. When he bought the paper, he had no idea Pattie's wedding announcement would appear in that day's edition.

When he saw it, he became so upset he threw his cruller into the garbage can and poured his coffee down the sink drain.

CHAPTER ONE HUNDRED TWENTY-SEVEN

CREEQUE ALLEY

Meanwhile in Chelsea, Pattie sighed as she struggled to pack herself into last summer's jeans. She flung herself down on the bed, inhaled for all she was worth and yanked on the zipper. It worked, but then she had to rock in order to force herself back onto her feet. She was having a hard time breathing.

Oh my God, soon I'll need a jaws of life just to get into and out of my clothes, she thought.

She tried on one of her blouses and felt frustrated because the buttons across her chest kept bulging, so she removed it and replaced it with one of Jordan's polo shirts. She knew she couldn't survive the day with her air supply cut off, so she took advantage of the fact that Jordan's polo shirt was long enough to cover her fly. As a result, she left it untucked. She walked down the hall to Jordan's desk, rummaged around in the drawers until she found a rubber band and unbuttoned her jeans. Then she looped the rubber band around the button hole to give herself some breathing room, pulled the shirt down to cover the whole mess and exhaled a sigh of relief. The doorbell rang. As she went to answer it, she walked past Jordan. He smiled, stood and followed her. As they walked past a mirror, she stuck her tongue out at her reflection.

"Oh my God, I'm a fucking monster now."

Jordan chuckled, shook his head and kissed her tenderly on the cheek. When she opened the door, Miranda was standing there. Pattie and Miranda hugged and Miranda and Jordan shook hands.

"Hi Jordan, it's a real pleasure to finally meet you. I can never thank you and Pattie enough for ending my nightmare for me and giving me my life back. I'll always be grateful."

Pattie nodded and Jordan smiled and blushed.

"Jordan, you ended both our nightmares. I shudder to think about where either one of us would be without you," Pattie added.

"By the way, it's stifling hot outside today. I've been sweltering all morning," Miranda said.

Pattie smiled.

"Good. Maybe I can melt a few pounds away," she said.

Jordan went into the kitchen and while he was gone, Miranda handed Pattie an envelope. Pattie looked at it quizzically, looked at Miranda and when Miranda didn't say anything, she opened it. She reached in, pulled out the picture that Jordan had sent to her while she was in prison and smiled. Miranda smiled back at her.

"I snatched it out from under Dutch's mat on one of those occasions when she was suddenly whisked off to Segregation. Somehow I just knew she was the one who stole it from you. Anyway, I can see why you love him. He's very sweet, not to mention generous AND good looking," Miranda whispered.

Pattie nodded, thanked her and fetched her tote bag. She reached inside and stashed the picture inside her wallet, just as Jordan returned with two bottles of ice water for them to take on the road.

"Thank you Jordan," they both said in unison.

" Anyway Pattie, let's shop 'til we drop'!" Miranda said.

Pattie kissed Jordan goodbye. Miranda hooked her arm through Pattie's and the two of them headed down the hallway, toward the elevator.

"Remember those Gawd awful boots they made us wear? I swear they deliberately issued them a half a size too small just to torment us," Miranda said.

Pattie nodded and cleared her throat.

"My blisters have finally healed over. Oh. That was a play on words. Blisters heeled. Anyway, I guess I'll always have the calluses and the Charley Horses though. And those Charley Horses are painful."

"Well, then maybe it would make us feel better if we were to end our shopping day today with a nice manicure and pedicure. I think that's the least we deserve," Miranda said.

Pattie nodded. The elevator came. They got in and Pattie pushed "G". They rode down to the garage in silence and when the elevator door opened, she led Miranda to her car. Just as Miranda was about to get inside, her cell phone rang. She looked at the caller ID, picked up the call and walked away so she could conduct her conversation in private. In the meantime, Pattie got in, closed the door and waited for her. A few minutes later, Miranda hung up, returned to the car and got in. She was all smiles.

"David Huntley just called to say his producer wants to do a story on me. So next week, I'm going in to meet them."

"Wow! He's with a major network! And I ought to know, because he covered my news story night after night. Unfortunately, he always put me in the worst possible light every single time."

Miranda nodded.

"I'm sorry to hear that. If I were you, I'd try to forget about it. After all, you found your Mr. Right and today's the day we pick out your bridal gown and get you listed with a registry, so you can marry him in peace. Anyway, I happen to know this French couturier named Madame Rosalie. She makes the best bridal gowns from scratch. I thought we could go over and see her right now. "

Pattie started the engine. Miranda dictated

Madame Rosalie's address and Pattie logged it into her GPS. And just as she was getting ready to pull out of her space, her cell phone rang.

"Your insurance company just contacted me. They're FINALLY convinced you didn't total your car on purpose. As a result, they're now going to pay out the replacement value on your claim," Reginald's voice blared over the bluetooth.

"Talk about perfect timing! I can use that money to pay for my wedding gown, which I'm on my way to shop for, as we speak. By the way, you'll never guess who's right here to help me with this joyous task."

"Hi Reginald! It's me Miranda!"

"Hi Miranda! Pattie, did you get my RSVP?"

Pattie nodded, even though Reginald couldn't see her.

"Yes. It's so great that you're going to be there."

"I'm looking forward to being a part of it," he said.

"So am I!" Pattie said.

Everyone chuckled. Pattie thanked him again. They said their good byes and hung up.

"Let's live dangerously," Pattie told Miranda.

She put the top down on her convertible, drove out of the garage and turned the corner onto the West Side Highway.

"I have a confession to make. Even though I basically liked you, I was actually pretty scared of you the entire time we were in prison together," Miranda said.

Pattie frowned.

"Why?"

"Because they said you were in for Murder One."

Pattie chuckled.

"Well, if truth be told, you weren't he only one who was scared. I must confess I was afraid of you too. The whole time we were there I had myself convinced that you were a 'plant' sent to spy on me by Katrina Nero."

"Hah! That'll be the day. I know I'm supposed to be a spiritual person and I truly believe I am. As a result, I know I'm not supposed to hate. But the truth of the matter is I really do hate that Katrina Nero. And I don't know how I'll ever figure out a way to forgive her. Mainly because I don't want to."

Pattie nodded.

"Believe me, I understand. Anyway, I'm sorry I thought you were a spy."

"Don't mention it. I'm sorry I thought you were a killer."

They both chuckled.

CHAPTER ONE HUNDRED TWENTY-EIGHT

HOW SWEET IT IS

The month of June sped by quickly. Between Pattie's bridal gown fittings, shopping for a trousseau in Pattie's new, even larger size, along with wedding arrangements and preparations, it was a blur to both Pattie and Jordan. Pattie didn't think she needed any household items, so on Saturday July 3rd, Miranda threw her an intimate lingerie shower which was attended by Pattie, Miranda, Edie, Cheryl and Cheryl's mother. Her gifts all reflected her new proportions and they included a black silk thong and matching bra, a translucent, white dotted swiss thong and matching bra, sheer black stockings, complete with seams and a black garter belt with embroidered red roses to hold them up, white marabou slippers, a pair of fetching red baby doll pajamas and a red silk thong and matching bra. The most respectable item was the ice blue silk garter for Pattie to wear under her wedding gown, which came from Cheryl.

CHAPTER ONE HUNDRED TWENTY-NINE

WEDDING DRESS

On July 29th, two days before the wedding, Pattie found herself in Madame Rosalie's atelier for her final fitting. Clad only in a white bra and pair of white underpants, she inhaled deeply and tried to wiggle into the delicate, white silk and point d'Alençon lace wedding gown Madame Rosalie had so painstakingly hand stitched for her. When Madame Rosalie zipped it, Pattie nearly fainted. Madame Rosalie shook her head and clucked her tongue.

"Quel désastre! Oh well. If I hadn't made zees gown in such a way that I could alter eet, eet would never 'ave fit you at zees point. I'm extremely grateful for zees type of lace, because eet's going be our saving grace. But I swear, zees is the last time I can alter zees gown for you. I'm not a magician, you know. Anyway, let's take eet off carefully and step onto za scale," she said.

She helped Pattie remove her gown and checked Pattie's weight against the weight she had previously recorded in Pattie's file. The scale registered one hundred twenty nine pounds. Pattie gasped, while Madame Rosalie noted the weight gain, shook her head again and wagged her finger at Pattie.

"You mean to tell me I've gained over thirty five pounds since Christmas? How in the world could such a thing have happened?"

"The same way eeet always does. No exercise and unhealthy eating 'abeets. You know Cherie, you're still jolie, but you're really not in a position to gain any more weight if you want to stay zat way. You must seenk about what you stuff down your mouth," Madame Rosalie warned.

CHAPTER ONE HUNDRED THIRTY

UP ON THE ROOF

It was July 31st and Mother Nature had decided to be very cooperative. It was a bright, clear, summer's day; one of those warm, sunny days when the weather wasn't too humid. Finches chirped from inside the shady shelter of the London Plane Tree outside, which caused Pattie to stir. She opened her eyes and looked at the unfamiliar walls of the strange bedroom. It was large and masculine. She closed her eyes and tried to think. She blinked and then it finally dawned on her where she was. She stretched, sat up and slid out of Ryan's bed. She pulled her cellphone out of its charger and checked the time. It was shortly past seven in the morning. She ran to her overnight bag, fussed around in it until she found her shampoo, conditioner, body wash and razor. Then she brought it all into the bathroom. She turned on the shower, darted in and after luxuriating under the warm, steady water pressure, she washed her hair. She rinsed and conditioned it and while the conditioner was soaking in, she scrubbed her body from head to toe. Then she rinsed herself off, got out of the shower and whipped a towel around her hair. Afterwards, she patted her body dry with the other towel, put on a new pair of jeans and a large, new tee shirt. She unwound the towel from around her head, rubbed her hair dry with it and carefully combed through her tangles. She remembered the hair dresser telling her she wanted no products on her hair.

"Just shampooed, conditioned and rinsed," she said.

Once Pattie finished combing her hair, she left it to hang loose and air dry. She breathed a sigh of relief that after many months, some of the original luster had finally returned to it. She scrambled for her black sunglasses, tiptoed out the door and climbed up the stairway that led to the roof. It was a five story building that occupied the corner lot of Ninth Avenue and West 54th Street and it was occupied solely by Ryan and his family. She looked up at the bright sky, whose baby blue color reminded her of a primeval lake. It was dotted with little white puffs of cumulous clouds. She smiled at its beauty.

What a wonderful day to get married, she thought.

She walked toward the ledge of the roof, clutched the railing and looked down at the garden in the courtyard below. The summer foliage on the trees dappled the sunlight on the ground. The slow moving traffic murmured as the finches continued their song. Pattie could hear the rich cheerful noises, as one by one, members of the Pilgrim Family came to life in their separate apartments. She tilted her head back in order to let the warm breeze caress her neck. Then she looked out into the distance. The view was different from what she was used to seeing from Jordan's terrace, yet every bit as lovely. As she looked to the Southeast, The Empire State Building formed the crown jewel in the jagged skyline. The rooftops shone like a pearly acropolis in the sunlight. She turned and looked north, toward the green of Central Park South and then further north, where the George Washington Bridge stood out sharp and gray against the cobalt hue of the Hudson River that glittered below it. She deeply inhaled the air of a city that at times could be harsh, but no matter what, it was HERS. Her city. Her hometown. Her birthplace. And she thought to herself that before this night was through, she would no longer be a nobody, a lost soul, a fish out of water, but rather the happily married, unconditionally loved wife of Dr. Jordan Armstrong, the man she adored. She congratulated herself on finally finding her happiness. She wrapped her arms around her upper body and hugged herself with glee. Then she dropped her arms and squinted in a northeasterly direction in the hopes of catching a glimpse of L'Abbaye's magnificence.

Just then, the door to the roof squeaked open. Pattie turned and saw Ryan carrying two mugs of steaming coffee. She stepped back from the railing and made her way over to a pair of folding beach chairs. When she sat, he winked, handed her mug to her and took his seat. They smiled at each other.

"Yum. Coffee. Thank you. And thanks for giving up your bedroom so I could borrow it last night. I really appreciate it. It means a lot to me that your brother Zachary took you in as his roommate for a night. I thought it was best not to be around Jordan, since they say it's bad luck for the bride and groom to see one other on their wedding day."

Ryan smiled.

"Well, at least until the ceremony begins," he said.

They both chuckled.

"Cheers," Pattie said, as she held her mug up and took her first sip.

"Also, just in case I forget to bring this up in the future, you have been the most amazing friend I've ever had. You've always been there for me, through thick and thin," she said.

"Thanks. But I want you to know I feel the same way about you. YOU have been a true friend to me too. So, old chum, old buddy, old pal, that being said, I think the least I could do for you would be to ensure you start off your wedding day with a decent breakfast."

"You mean you're going to fix me something?"

He chuckled and shook his head.

"No. I said I wanted it to be decent. That's why I'll ask my mother to fix it."

They both chuckled.

"Thanks, but believe it or not, I'm actually not very hungry. Besides, if I gain one more ounce before it's time for Madame Rosalie to stuff me into my gown, she'll probably send me off to the guillotine."

Ryan smiled and watched, as Pattie took another sip of her coffee. They gossiped about some of the people they worked with at the courthouse, joked about Annie and ruminated about some of the more memorable defendants who came through the Arraignment Courtroom, until the door creaked open again and Ryan's mother appeared.

"Good morning, Dear. I just wanted to let you know your limousine driver is downstairs. He's ready to drive you and Ryan any time you're ready, but he emphasized that there's no rush," she said.

Pattie smiled, thanked her and quickly drained her mug. When she stood, Ryan took the mug from her. She went back downstairs, returned her toiletries to her overnight bag and made sure her newly issued passport was in her black velvet tote bag. Then she slung the tote bag over her shoulder and went downstairs. The white stretch limousine was parked in front of the building. The driver, a trim, neat, silver haired man who was dressed in black, opened the rear door. He ushered Pattie in and made sure she was comfortable. Then he disappeared into the building. A few minutes later, Ryan joined her. His formal attire and shoes were in the garment bag he held.

When he climbed in and sat across from Pattie, she smiled, reached out and patted his arm. He flashed a smile back at her and tapped the pocket over his heart to make sure Jordan's ring was in place. Then the driver returned with Pattie's overnight bag and suitcase for her three week long wedding trip to Scotland. He opened the door, took Ryan's garment bag and stowed everything in the trunk.

CHAPTER ONE HUNDRED THIRTY-ONE

THE OVERTURE

Edie looked like an old war horse as she stood sweating outside the entrance to "L'Abbaye." She wore a cheap, midi length, orange taffeta and tulle gown, with coral colored feathers around the hem. Sadly, because her dress fit her just like a slip cover, it actually did nothing to conceal the ever growing rolls of fat around her midriff and upper arms. Furthermore, it hid most of her shapely, albeit slightly heavy legs and her bust. Her "almost" matching hat looked like a poor woman's attempt at emulating a Royal Ascot fascinator. That, along with the four inch spike heeled, peau de sois pumps she had dyed to match her gown were off by enough of a shade to create a serious clash. And sadly, the pumps were too narrow for her puffy feet. She had paid for acrylic nail extensions which were painted orange and during one of her trips to the Dollar Store, she found a lipstick she thought matched. The entire ensemble could have easily won her First Prize in a "Worst Dressed Mother of the Bride Contest".

Worse than her appearance was her state. Even though it was early in the day, she was already three sheets to the wind. Her lower lip was curled under in her infamous drunken snarl and the mean glint was already in her eye. She was flanked on one side by Chet, who looked dapper and buff in his black formal evening clothes, complete with his black and silver striped tie and white rose boutonniere. On Edie's other side, stood her rat faced cousin Rory, who had arrived the previous night from Allentown, Pennsylvania. Rory was decked out in a red gown that was made from the same synthetic material as Edie's and which was in even worse taste. Its puffed sleeves and layers of ruffles overpowered her scrawny frame. The "R" she had personally embroidered with hot pink thread over her heart made it look even worse. Plus, she sat on it wrongly in the back seat of Chet's '94 Ford Festiva. As a result, by the time she reached L'Abbaye, it was wrinkled. At least it hid the ugly, heavy, support stockings that she rolled up just above her kneecaps.

She grinned, which inadvertently showed off her huge, dull grey, buck teeth. And what made everything about her even uglier, was her misconception that because she was thin, it automatically meant she "had a good shape." But she was more "scrawny" than "thin" and her long, pointy nose with its broken blood vessels and her beady eyes ensured she would never be considered "sexy." She had tried to jazz up her thin, baby fine, dirty blonde hair by putting streaks in it, with an at home frosting kit and she wore ice blue metallic eye shadow. Her nails, like Edie's, matched her dress in color, except hers weren't acrylic. She had given herself a home manicure before she hit the road. If someone were to close one eye and squint through the other, her left hand was passable, but her right hand was a mess.

Lou, Cheryl and Cheryl's mother stood across from Edie, Chet and Rory. Lou was dressed identically to Chet. Cheryl was dressed in a plain pair of jeans, one of Lou's plain black tee shirts and a pair of sneakers. Since she was a member of the wedding party, she dressed comfortably, because she knew she would be changing into her bridesmaid's gown later. Her mother looked more like one of the maids just finishing an eight hour work shift at L'Abbaye, rather than one of the wedding guests. She appeared as if she needed a long, hot bath and a thorough hair washing. She wore an outdated, wheat colored, sleeveless, unlined cotton summer shift that was little more than a glorified house dress. She hadn't even bothered to put on a slip. And she had a straw hat and a laminated straw bag that had seen better days. Her bare legs and her off white open toed Naugahyde sandals showcased her revoltingly thick, yellowing, unpolished toenails. And her toenails matched her thick, tobacco stained, unpolished finger nails. Cheryl had thoughtfully plucked the lone stray hair from her chin the night before, so she could "look her best."

Edie fished through her orange, plastic beaded bag and pulled out a cigarette and the plastic lighter Jordan had returned to her. She tossed the lighter to Lou and held out her cigarette, until he lit it for her. The minute she inhaled, it broke the ice for Rory and Cheryl's mother to fish around in their own bags and retrieve cigarettes for Lou to ignite. Within minutes, the entire area where they stood was enveloped in a thick, grey cloud of smoke. As if on cue, Chet sniffed, wheezed and began gasping for air.

When Edie finished her cigarette, she flicked the butt onto the cobblestone courtyard and mashed it with the pointy toe of her pump. When she lifted her dress over her thigh, everyone's eyes popped open. No one could believe she was concealing an antique pewter flask in an old, faded blue garter. She cursed and fumbled with it for a few seconds until she was finally able to get it free. Chet sniffed again and squinted.

"Do you really think you should be drinking like this before the wedding?"

"Yes, Chet, I do. After all, this is like a medicine to me," she said, as she fought to unscrew the cap.

She took a huge swig, wiped her mouth with the back of her hand and held the flask out to Rory.

"I got jugs and jugs more of this in the cooler, so

drink as much as you want," she said, bobbing her head in the direction of the parking lot.

Rory looked at her quizzically.

"It's my usual Margarita mix," Edie said.

Rory smiled, nodded and took a swig. Like Edie, she also wiped her mouth with the back of her hand. Then she burped and handed the flask back to Edie. Edie guzzled some more and handed the flask back to Rory. Rory chuckled, gulped some more and burped again. Then she took a final swig before handing the flask back to Edie. Edie chug a lugged until the flask was finally empty. This exchange took place without either of them ever offering so much as a drop to anyone else. Chet, Lou, Cheryl and Rory were used to Edie, so although they weren't thrilled, they also weren't too surprised, but Cheryl's mother was both shocked and disappointed. She too would have liked a taste. After all, she was hot and thirsty and this was a wedding for God's sake.

Edie handed the flask to Lou.

"OK, go fill 'er up again," she said.

"I don't get it. I always remember when Pattie was a kid how she had these high fallutin' ideas of becoming a big deal lawyer. But just because she had a setback, it don't mean she should throw in the towel and settle for being a dumb hausfrau," Rory said.

Edie bristled self-righteously. Both she and Chet glanced at each other and then shot Rory a dirty look.

"Well, I'll tell you what, Rory. A hausfrau is better

than a revolting, obsolete Flower Child from the sixties. Besides, she'll never be dumb no matter what she ends up doing. In fact, in a couple of hours, she'll actually be sitting on top of the world," Chet blurted out, in a momentary fit of indignation.

Edie shook her head and laughed bitterly.

"Yeah, but I doubt her luck will hold out. As a matter of fact, I get the feeling she's going to fail at this marriage the same way she's failed at everything else she's ever tried. It's a shame really. I mean, in the past her other fuck ups only involved herself, but this time it will be two lives she ends up wrecking," Edie ranted in a voice loud enough for all and sundry to hear.

Lou returned with the flask. After Edie took a good sized swig from it, she strapped it back onto her garter and rooted around in her bag. When she retrieved another cigarette, she held it out for Lou. Lou lit her cigarette, as well as Cheryl's mother and Rory's.

"You're wrong Edie. She's only twenty six and she's already tooling around Manhattan in a brand new BMW. It doesn't get much better than that, now does it?" Chet said.

"Oh, she's a real bitch on wheels, all right. And when you stop and think about what we're forced to drive—"

Before she could finish her sentence, Pattie's limousine rolled up the driveway like a chariot and stopped in front of the entrance. The smiling, uniformed valet, who had been eavesdropping on the entire conversation, sprang to attention and opened the door to let Pattie and Ryan out. As he escorted Pattie through the haze of second hand smoke, Ryan trailed behind. Edie squinted, took a long drag on her cigarette and scrutinized Pattie and Ryan. She made sure she exhaled her smoke just as Pattie walked past her.

Pattie knit her brow. One look at Edie told her all she needed to know about Edie's condition. Anxiety replaced Pattie's good mood, as she fought off the billowing grey tentacles that were already burning her damaged lungs. She broke into splotches and her stomach filled with butterflies for the first time that day. But she kept walking. Ryan stepped up his pace, in order to keep up with her. And as she wiped the beginnings of tears from her eyes. he reached for his handkerchief and carefully dabbed them away. When he was done, Pattie shook her head and kept on walking.

"Poor Jordan, having to marry into such a family," she said.

Ryan shook his head.

"NO! Don't think like that. Always remember, he's marrying YOU, not them," he said.

"I know, but seeing the shape my mother is in right now, makes me nervous. I mean, what if she does something terrible during the ceremony? Or the reception?"

Feeling disgusted with Edie and Rory, Cheryl decided to join Pattie and get ready, so she sprinted until she caught up with them.

"Since you're one of the bridesmaids, I thought you would be riding in the other limousine, with Miranda, Clint and Laurie," Pattie said.

"Your mother wouldn't let me. She insisted I ride in the Bronco, with my mother and Lou."

Pattie nodded vaguely, as if somehow that explanation made sense, even though it didn't. As she reached for the door handle, a doorman opened the door. A hostess and Bridal Suite Attendant smiled and greeted them.

"Hi, I'm Cassie. Please allow me to escort you to the North Sanctuary," she said.

CHAPTER ONE HUNDRED THIRTY-TWO

OVER THE RAINBOW

After Cassie dropped Pattie and Cheryl off at the North Sanctuary, she turned to Ryan and smiled.

"Come with me. I'll lead you to the South Sanctuary," she said.

Ryan turned to Pattie and looked at her with an exaggerated expression of helplessness. Pattie chuckled and blew him a kiss, so he blew one back at her. When she closed the door, she turned to find Madame Rosalie fussing in French and carefully liberating the bridal gown from its heavy waterproof, duck cloth garment bag and layers of purple tissue paper. Then she painstakingly undraped it from its two padded, scented hangers, scrutinized it and plugged in the steamer.

On the other side of the room, trays of melon balls, bagels, cream cheese, lox and raspberry cookies, along with pitchers of coffee, orange juice, water and iced teas awaited them. A few minutes later, Cassie returned with Miranda and Clint's new wife Laurie.

They all snacked and chatted and about an hour later a team of hairdressers, makeup artists and nail technicians arrived to beautify them. Pattie's hair was gently swept back into a romantic, curly chignon, reminiscent of Scarlett O'Hara in "Gone with the Wind." It was fastened with an antique pearl comb that Chet's mother had bequeathed to her in her will.

Several hours later, after Pattie, Miranda, Laurie and Cheryl were all manicured, pedicured, made up and coiffed, Madame Rosalie dressed Pattie. The bodice of her silk and d'Alençon lace wedding gown was close and form-fitting. The front dipped into a gentle "V" and the back dipped into a deeper "V", exposing her flawless ivory skin. The lower half of the gown trailed the floor and fanned out in the shape of a trumpet, which gave Pattie a regal look. Her long dainty sleeves caressed her arms and tapered to showcase her slender, elongated fingers and elegant pale lilac nail polish. Her toenails were polished to match her fingernails and when they were completely dry, Pattie slid her feet into her delicate, handmade silk and Carrickmacross lace bridal slippers with their three inch, silk, wine stem heels. And there was not one hint of anything Gothic about the way she looked. She gazed at herself in the mirror and for once, even she could find no fault with her stunning reflection. And her stunning reflection sparkled its approval right back at her.

She was not the type of bride who believed she had

to make her bridal attendants look ugly in order to enhance her own image. Miranda, Laurie and Cheryl were dressed in sleek, lovely, wisteria colored floor length halter style bridesmaid's gowns. Their petite floral crowns were miniature versions of Pattie's bouquet. It was obvious the beauticians and aestheticians had done an exquisite job on all of them. They looked in the mirror and admired themselves and each other.

Cheryl beamed at her own reflection. The hairdresser had softened her pixie haircut by sweeping her bangs slightly to the side and making them wispy. And her makeup artist did a lovely job bringing out the best features on her face. She had no idea that once they finished working on her, she would be transformed into such a beauty. After the women all complimented one another, the hairdressers ensured their floral crowns were secure. Then Pattie looked down at the tops of her slippers and wiggled her feet back and forth.

"You know what my biggest fear is? That I'm going to trip in these," she said, to no one in particular.

Laurie shook her head.

"Don't worry. Every bride feels that way. That's why we're all going to take turns walking with you," she said.

She held out her arm and slowly promenaded around the sanctuary with Pattie.

"I know your gown, veil and shoes are something

new to symbolize you and Jordan beginning your new life together," Laurie said, as they walked together arm in arm.

There was a knock at the door. Pattie knit her brow and hoped it wasn't Edie. The attendant opened the door. When Chet stuck his head in, the attendant turned to Pattie. Pattie nodded and the attendant let him in. He was holding a box. He greeted everyone, then he focused his full attention on Pattie. Pattie broke away from Laurie and approached him.

"My! Don't you look handsome," she said.

He blushed, smiled and handed her the box. She brought it over to one of the dressing tables. As soon as she opened it, she gasped. Her face lit up at the sight of her Grandmother's salt water pearl necklace. Each individual pearl was large and matched all the others perfectly. She looked at the delicate play of color that shone on their iridescent surfaces. She looked up at Chet, smiled wistfully and gently ran her fingers over them.

"Oh my! Grandmother's pearls. They're exquisite! As you know, I've always loved them. Thank you so much," she said.

Chet nodded and smiled back at her.

"Well, they're yours now. She specified in her will that you were to have them on your wedding day. So this is it," he said, as he gently removed them from the box.

Pattie turned around. With shaky hands, he

fastened the pearls around her neck. When she turned around to face him again, he beamed at her and kissed her on the cheek.

"Are you happy?" He asked.

She nodded.

"At first I was nervous, but now I want to be Mrs. Jordan Armstrong more than anything in the world. I love him deeply. And it's a fine thing living in a wonderful apartment and exchanging deep thoughts on many subjects with a gentle, intelligent and loving man."

He nodded.

"I am proud of you. Not only because you are a good lawyer. Not only because you survived that ordeal you went through with courage. Not only because you look so stunning on the day you're marrying a good man. And not only because you have a bright future ahead of you. I am proud of you just because you're the girl you are and always have been. You are the best daughter anyone could have ever hoped to have."

After he left, Miranda, Laurie, Cheryl and Madame Rosalie inspected the pearls. Cheryl said nothing. As hard as she tried, she could not feel happy for Pattie. Longing for something nice, she simply glanced at them jealously and wished Chet had given them to Lou to give to HER instead of handing them over to Pattie. Miranda gave the pearls a double take, looked at Pattie's hair and smiled. She picked up the hand held mirror and held it behind Pattie's head.

"Looking at how perfectly they match your comb, I have to say, they were probably a set," Miranda said.

Pattie looked in the mirror, pondered that notion and smiled.

"You could be right, because she bequeathed the comb to me, with instructions I receive it on my eighteenth birthday."

"Anyway, now that we've figured out what's new and we have the pearls and the comb to signify something old, we need something borrowed and something blue," Laurie said.

Pattie carefully lifted her gown to reveal the light blue garter on her left leg. It looked identical to Edie's garter, except it was new.

"Great. We've got something blue. Now the only thing left is something borrowed," Laurie said.

She looked at Pattie's ears and realized they were pierced. Since Pattie was wearing no earrings, Laurie removed her own diamond earrings and carefully inserted them into Pattie's ears. Pattie smiled and thanked her.

CHAPTER ONE HUNDRED THIRTY THREE

PROCESSIONAL

A beautiful fragrance filled the summer air and the wedding garden looked elegant. The fountain in the swimming pool was lit and the several hundred candles burning tastefully in gleaming lanterns gave the leafy nook an enchanting glow. The sun was setting in immense smears of red and yellow in the azure sky and its brilliance was reflected on the surface of the pool. The organist arrived and began to play a soothing, traditional, pre-wedding medley. A handsome young piper in his "Black Watch" tartan carried his bagpipes into the garden.

Kyle and April were the first guests to arrive, with Justin, Thomas and Bonnie in tow. April was dressed in a silver grey silk gown with a scalloped neckline and a matching, silk lined cape. Her bejeweled Judith Leiber clutch was shaped like a dove. Kyle wore a navy blue suit. Although Justin, Thomas and Bonnie were a bit old for their roles, they too were part of the wedding party. Justin and Thomas were pages. They were dressed identically to the groomsmen and Bonnie looked beautiful as a combination junior bride's maid and flower girl. April had pinned a small tiara into Bonnie's updo and her corsage went nicely with her lilac dress. Lou escorted April to her seat, while Kyle brought the three teenagers back to the rear holding area. He warned them to remain quiet, wait for the rest of the bridal party and just do whatever they were told. When he left, the trio stood around shuffling nervously.

Thomas looked at the pool and wondered what it would be like to swim in something that luxurious. He continued to obsess about it until Frank Bernard and his wife arrived a few minutes later. When he spotted Frank, he nudged Justin in the ribs with his elbow and pointed.

"Hey, that's the guy who used to persecute me in the Family Court," he whispered.

Justin looked at Frank and nodded. Then, when Pattie's highest connection in the world, Judge Bender, arrived, Thomas gasped.

"Oh my God! You mean they let that God-awful judge in here too? HE'S the one who let Frank persecute me the way he did," he said.

Dressed in a brand new rose colored designer silk suit with shoes and a fascinator to match, the slender, glossy Mrs. Bender would, without a doubt, turn out to be the best dressed wedding guest. As she hung on her husband's arm, the diamonds that hung on her ears, throat and wrists sparkled. She smiled mechanically and looked around to see whether anyone noteworthy was there. When she spotted Frank Bernard and his wife, the two women smiled and waved at each other. Then they quickly turned away, since they basically hated the sight of one another. In spite of that, though, it was uncanny the extent to which Mrs. Bernard was a junior version of Mrs. Bender. Younger, prettier and certainly more bubbly than Mrs. Bender, she grabbed attention. And like Mrs. Bender, Mrs. Bernard was also slender. But her blonde hair was a few shades lighter and it hung down her back, a few inches longer and sleeker. And although her spike heels were an inch higher than Mrs. Bender's, the diamonds that glittered from her earlobes, wrist and fingers were smaller. Her frilly, billowing sage green silk dress with its three quarter length sleeves, was almost as expensive as Mrs. Bender's suit, but not quite.

A few minutes later, Clint entered the alcove, carrying a basket of lavender, white and purple rose petals. He gave them to Bonnie and showed her how to gently scatter them when she walked up the white runner in front of Pattie. He reviewed with Justin and Thomas what was expected of them and he reminded them that they would be walking behind Pattie during the ceremony and carrying her train. The fact that Pattie had entrusted these important tasks to all of them, made them feel important.

Shortly thereafter, Lou and Ryan emerged from the South Sanctuary, looking handsome in their identical black formal wedding attire. Not knowing what to say, Ryan smiled at Lou. Lou nodded and managed to smile back at him, for the first time ever. A few seconds later, Cosmo arrived, accompanied by the dwarfish, egg shaped Dante. Lou frowned, nudged Ryan and pointed at them. When he asked who they were, Ryan explained.

"The taller one is Cosmo, owner of Cosmo's Astral Plane Café and I'm actually surprised you don't know who the shorter one is. That's Dante. He runs the lockup down at the courthouse."

Lou shook his head.

"I never get as far as the lockup. I take them all the way to Central Booking and then they become somebody else's problem," Lou said.

Ryan nodded and chuckled.

"Yeah. Eventually mine."

Shortly thereafter, Edie and Rory entered the Wedding Garden. Lou had the job of escorting Edie and Clint escorted Rory. Edie unsteadily made her way up the path, but because Lou wrapped one arm around her waist and used his other arm to hold her arm securely, he ensured she wouldn't stumble, trip, or stagger off of the white runner. Once Lou and Clint reached the first row on the left side of the path, they gently helped Edie and Rory into their seats. Then they returned to the alcove.

Jordan peered in from the right hand side of the garden, smiled and took his place. He looked debonair in the traditional green, blue, black and red Armstrong Tartan kilt, with the same style jacket, dirk and sporran his ancestors had worn for centuries.

Reginald Reese arrived alone. He wore a black Armani suit. His black silk tie had genuine tiny diamond chips interwoven throughout. When Mrs. Bender and Mrs. Bernard spotted him, they both waved enthusiastically at him and he cheerfully waved back.

Like Reginald, Toby Barnett also arrived stag. He wore a dark brown suit he had outgrown fifteen pounds ago. Even though he too had prosecuted Thomas in the past, Thomas didn't have an opportunity to comment upon his arrival, since he and Justin had already left to meet Pattie at the North Sanctuary.

Following Toby Barnett were Pattie's former neighbors, Gus and Martha. Martha wore a knee length, yellow chiffon dress. Then, Dr. Farnsworth and his wife arrived. Mrs. Farnsworth was dressed in an ice blue silk cocktail dress. The short, plump, red haired Nancy Speck and her husband arrived a few minutes later, followed by Jordan's golf pro Kevin Gordon and his date. Behind them were Jordan's neighbors, Miltie and Kay.

As the Wedding Garden filled up, muted murmurs of small talk filled the air, along with a sense of solemn anticipation. At eight o'clock, even though a violet twilight was quickly settling in, it was still easy for the guests to appreciate how Mother Nature had provided an endless riot of colors for the wedding.

Madame Rosalie gave Pattie's gown, veil and train one final going over, to ensure everything was smooth. When she was confident Pattie looked perfect, she carefully draped the veil over Pattie's face. With an air of satisfaction in a job well done, she smiled at Pattie and patted her hand. After that, the Bridal Attendant opened the door to the sanctuary, where Justin and Thomas were waiting. The attendant led Pattie, Cheryl, Miranda and Laurie out of the North Sanctuary to the alcove, while Justin and Thomas walked behind Pattie and practiced holding up her train.

When Lou spotted Cheryl, he looked at her as if it were the first time he had ever seen her. He smiled and walked up to her. When he told her how beautiful she looked, she blushed.

"Thank you," she said.

The Reverend Thomson came out in his black vestment and white wedding officiant's stole. He took his place facing the rows of guests. The whispered conversations dwindled to silence. Lou escorted Cheryl up the path and they stepped into place. Then Ryan escorted Miranda and Clint escorted Laurie. Jordan looked worriedly at Clint and Ryan. They both smiled, patted their vests and pointed to their ring fingers. Reassured about the rings, Jordan was finally able to relax. He smiled back at them and gave them the thumbs up sign.

Pattie remained in the alcove with Chet, Bonnie, Justin and Thomas. Her eyes were bright with excitement and her breathing was heavy. Chet was sweating and his boutonniere was crooked. As nervous as Pattie was, she pulled herself together and asked Chet to hold her bouquet, so she could fix his boutonniere for him. When he returned her bouquet afterwards, she held it close to her nose and inhaled its heavenly fragrance. Then she turned her attention to the Reverend Thomson.

The Reverend Thomson nodded at Chet, who signaled to the organist to begin playing the "Lohengrin Wedding March". Pattie took hold of Chet's arm. Bonnie walked up the path, sprinkling the runner with the rose petals, just as Clint had instructed. Doing his best to conceal his limp and with tears welling in his eyes, Chet slowly and majestically guided Pattie up the white runner. Justin and Thomas followed, each solemnly working in tandem to hold up the train.

Pattie pushed all thoughts out of her mind, except her goal of staying on the runner without falling or flying into a cartwheel. Not only did she succeed, she managed to walk past the dim mass of faces so gracefully, she actually looked like a goddess floating on a brilliant white cloud. When the guests all turned and stretched to see her, they gasped. She could hear their murmurs of approval over the sound of the organ music and she was surprised when she realized the collective look on their faces was one of stunned admiration. When she reached the end of the runner, Bonnie, Justin and Thomas stood to the left of the bridesmaids. Bonnie looked at Clint for his approval. When he smiled and nodded at her, she breathed a sigh of relief.

A limousine pulled up to the entrance. The valet smiled and opened the door. Gripped in a combination of obsession and deadly wrath, the vengeful Anne Carey sat in the back seat alone. She was dressed in a stunning jacquard off white on white pleated gown, with three quarter length sleeves and an elegant scoop neck. Her grandmother's hand tatted, white lace mantilla muted her red hair. Her eyes were well hidden behind her white, cat shaped designer sunglasses and her cell phone was on her lap. She clutched the wedding announcement in her sweaty palm. On the seat next to her was Jordan's "rejection letter." Both the wedding announcement and the rejection letter had been upsetting her for weeks. Every time she happened to glance at either of them, she felt sick to her stomach.

"Oh my God! You're going to be late for your wedding! Hurry," the driver chided, when he heard the music.

She stared at him through her sunglasses and

flung the wedding announcement on top of the rejection letter.

Late for my wedding is right, she thought.

"Forget all that. Just remember what I told you. Don't get out of the car. Just wait right here for me, no matter what else happens," she said, as she wagged her finger in his face.

He nodded.

"Sure thing," he said.

Holding her cell phone in her left hand and her white clutch evening bag in her right, she slid off the seat and smiled at the valet. Once he helped her onto her feet, she pushed him out of her way, ran past him and followed the sound of the music.

As Pattie took her place next to Jordan, the music stopped. A hush fell over the Garden. Chet's hands shook as he carefully lifted Pattie's veil and draped it away from her face. Then with an expression of pure joy, he looked into her eyes, smiled and gave her a quick hug. When she smiled back at him, he kissed her on the cheek.

"Dearly Beloved, who has the honor of giving this woman to this man to be wed in Holy and Lawful Matrimony?" The Reverend Thomson's cultured voice rang out.

After Chet gave Pattie away, he took his place in the seat next to Edie. Pattie turned toward Jordan. He was already admiring the extraordinary way in which her curves filled out her wedding gown. He had always known she was lovely, but he had never seen her looking quite so gorgeous. Standing there, smiling at him, she looked like a resplendent queen in all her glory. And with her skin reminding him of pale white lilacs, she dazzled him to the point where she actually took his breath away.

Just then, he noticed the slender silhouette of a latecomer against the glow of the candles. The straggler tiptoed over to the last row on the groom's side of the garden, as far away from everyone else as possible. Then she quickly darted into a seat on the aisle, so she could make her getaway quickly and quietly. Jordan squinted in order to see who it was, but it was too dark for him to tell.

Feeling self-conscious because she thought Jordan was squinting at HER, Pattie wondered what was wrong with her appearance. As a result, she began to worry. She cleared her throat and finally decided to distract herself by focusing on the pageantry.

Morbid curiosity consumed Annie. She craned her neck and cocked it to one side, so she could absorb as much of the doings at hand as possible. She had to admit, Pattie looked less ghoulish than usual. However, it gratified her to know that Pattie was fatter than ever before. She spotted Ryan in the wedding party. When she saw Toby Barnett, Frank Bernard, Judge Bender and Dante seated among the guests, she froze. Their presence certainly put a damper on her goal of disrupting the wedding. She wondered what they would think if they saw her there, uninvited. Since she definitely didn't want to get caught doing anything that could jeopardize her job or her license to practice law, she swallowed a sigh, sat up tall in her seat and abandoned her plan.

"Dearly Beloved, we have gathered here, at this happy time, in the presence of God and under His proud watch, to publicly declare and witness the commitment on the part of Jordan Charles Armstrong and Pattie Anwald, as they join in this sacred Covenant of Holy and Lawful Matrimony. Understanding that God has created, ordered and blessed the gift of this union, let us all give thanks for it."

When he asked Pattie and Jordan whether they affirmed their desire and intention to enter into this Covenant and to pledge their troth to one another in love and honor, they both assented.

"Pattie and Jordan, since it is your intention to marry, please turn to one another and join hands."

As Pattie and Jordan complied, they stood there, smiling and gazing deeply into each other's eyes, as if they were the only two people in the world.

"It is my understanding that you have each written your own unique marriage vows, to be read and exchanged for the first time today. Pattie, would you like to begin?" The Reverend Thomson asked.

Pattie nodded and cleared her throat.

"Dear Jordan, I thank God every day for having brought you into my life. And I now vow before God and these witnesses, to become your lawfully wedded wife, for richer or for poorer and forsaking all others. I vow to give you my loyalty, my support, my laughter and my tears, along with my unending friendship and my undying love. I will cherish you all the days of my life."

Annie rolled her eyes.

"Dear Pattie, the doors to my heart had been frozen shut for a long time, but the minute I met you, they miraculously sprang open. And I know why. It's because YOU are the person I was destined to spend my life with. It took both of us an entire lifetime to get to this marvelous, most perfect place where we are standing right now. But here we are, ready to make each other whole. There are a million reasons why I love you. You're sweet and caring and you make me laugh. You are beautiful, kind, generous and wonderfully quirky. I want you to know you are my one true love as well as the best friend I have ever had. Your love has transformed me into the luckiest man in the universe. Every day with you is an absolute adventure and I can't imagine not sharing my life with you. I now vow before God and these witnesses to become your lawfully wedded husband, for richer or for poorer and forsaking all others. I vow to give you my loyalty, my support, my honor, my respect, my honesty and my protection. And I will cherish you as long as we both shall live."

He looked over at Clint and Clint handed Pattie's

pink diamond and ruby studded wedding band to him. When Pattie lifted her hand so Jordan could slip it onto her finger, Annie caught sight of Pattie's matching engagement ring shimmering in the candlelight. She bit down on her right thumb nail, tore at it and spit it out onto the lawn.

"With this ring, I thee wed," Jordan said.

Pattie cleared her throat and handed her bouquet to Miranda, while Ryan gave her Jordan's eighteen karat gold wedding band. Her hands shook as she slid it onto Jordan's finger.

"With this ring, I THEE wed," she said.

"By your blessing, oh God, may these rings be to Pattie and Jordan symbols of their unending love and faithfulness. May they remind Pattie and Jordan of the sacred Covenant they have just entered into. Remember, on this day, before God and in the presence of this congregation, Pattie and Jordan have confirmed their commitment to one another by the joining of hands, by the exchange of vows and by the giving and receiving of these rings."

Edie, who desperately needed a drink and a cigarette, was finding the ceremony boring beyond belief. She leaned back, closed her eyes and fiddled with her hair.

"Joining together in a lawful, wedded union that embodies the ideals as expressed in your vows, is not something to be entered into lightly or unadvisedly, but rather, reverently, discreetly, advisedly and soberly. Therefore, If there be anyone here present who knows of any just cause why Jordan and Pattie should not be lawfully wed as husband and wife, I require him or her to come forward and make it known by speaking now or forever holding his or her peace," the Reverend said, as he looked around at the congregation.

Suddenly, Edie came to life. She opened her eyes, cleared her throat and struggled to make it onto her feet.

"Padre," she called out, in a drunken slur.

Annie started to snicker and Chet shot Edie a look of horror. He yanked her back into her seat.

"Oh hell, never mind," she said, as she hit the seat with a thud.

Then, just for spite, she mustered as much force as she could in her drunken state and kicked Chet's bad ankle with the pointed toe of her pump. When the pain startled Chet, he groaned. The Reverend looked over and glared at both of them. When he was confident they had settled down, he pronounced Jordan and Pattie husband and wife, Annie made a gesture of sticking her two fingers down her throat, as if she wanted to force herself to vomit.

I'd be getting a lot more out of this wedding if I were the actual bride, instead of THAT freaking zombie, she said to herself.

"Whom God has joined together let no one tear

asunder. Dr. Armstrong, you may now kiss your bride," the Reverend said.

Just as Jordan kissed Pattie, Annie lifted her phone and snapped a picture of them. No one noticed the flash, since the photographer also took a snapshot of them at that exact same moment. Jordan patted Pattie's arm and smiled ecstatically at her. And Miranda looked at her watch and checked the time, in case Pattie ever needed to consult an astrologer about the wedding. It was 8:22 pm.

As the organist played Mendelssohn's Wedding March. Pattie and Jordan turned around. Pattie hooked her arm through Jordan's and they took their first stroll as husband and wife. Followed by their bridal party, they walked down the path, under the blaze of the stars that had popped out during the ceremony. Their guests threw handfuls of rice at them for good luck.

With an impending fear of getting caught and a dread at having no control over how much longer fate would force her to remain single, Annie skulked out of the Wedding Garden. She made her way into the main lobby of the Abbey, scurried off to the ladies' room and closeted herself in one of the stalls. She opened her clutch, removed a small makeup mirror, a rolled up twenty dollar bill and a glassine bag she had tucked away. She placed the mirror on top of the toilet paper rack and poured a line of cocaine across it. Not having a razor, she used her fingers to fashion the cocaine into as neat a line as she could. Then she hurriedly snorted it through the twenty dollar bill. A second later, she quivered as though an electrical charge surged through her. She smiled, wiped her face and licked the residue from her fingers. Finally, she stuffed her contraband back into her clutch and unlocked the stall.

I plan to be at their divorce too. And that's when I'll snap Jordan up on the rebound, she thought, as she raced out of the ladies' room. She glanced around. Grateful no one had noticed her, she opened the door and got into her limousine, before either the valet or her very confused driver could help her. Then, she began to sob, as she ordered the driver to step on it.

CHAPTER ONE HUNDRED THIRTY-FOUR

SHUT UP AND DANCE

After the ceremony, the night still remained warm and windless. The Maître D'hôtel led Pattie, Jordan, Chet and Edie to an area where they could form a receiving line. Chet shot Edie a look of venom that served as a warning for her to be as pleasant and polite as possible. And because she had been able to sneak a cigarette and a drink beforehand, she was able to pull herself together. She acted agreeable and good natured, as she, Chet, Pattie and Jordan greeted and shared genuine smiles and firm handshakes with all the guests. Meanwhile, the piper played "Amazing Grace", "Highland Cathedral" and other traditional songs. Pattie was less shy than usual. She laughed, hugged and kissed people. Gus and Martha thanked her for referring them to Reginald and mentioned they were renting a brand new luxury townhouse in Riverdale, as a result of the settlement he had obtained for them.

After the receiving line, the photographer took

pictures of Pattie, Jordan and members of the bridal party, while the remaining guests drifted into the Grand Ballroom, one or two at a time. The room was illuminated throughout with opulent chandeliers that hung from forty foot high ceilings. The elaborate crown moldings and joists intersected with one another and created an intricate pattern. Closer to the floor were romantic, antique lanterns identical to those in the Wedding Garden. The table settings consisted of fine white damask tablecloths, lovely lavender linen napkins, delicate Villeroy & Boch China from the Artesano Lavender collection, elegant Baccarat stemware and shiny Towle silverware. The centerpieces consisted of glittering, pure, silver candelabra. Encircling them were lavender, white and purple roses, which matched both Pattie's bridal bouquet and the flowers that bedecked the entire room. The Omnia University String Quartet was playing tasteful, classical music to sweetly welcome the guests, while waiters milled around, bearing silver trays laden with imported salmon canapés, lobster mousse in bite sized Phyllo shells, caviar and other assorted hors d'oeuvres.

Chet, Edie and Rory were the first to walk in. Chet approved of the majestic ambience, so he smiled and nodded proudly. Even Edie smiled and nodded along with him. Rory was so impressed by the grandeur, her mouth and eyes popped open. When she finally caught her breath she remarked at how romantic it all looked. The other guests filtered in and engaged in small talk, while they happily nibbled away and sipped cocktails or the Dom Perignon which ran freely from several fountains.

When the photographer finished shooting the bridal party, he came in and took pictures of the guests. As Pattie and Jordan strolled into the Grand Ballroom, she looked ecstatic and she was stunned by the scent of the flowers.

Rory nudged Edie in the rib cage.

"Keep your hands off my side, creep!" Edie snapped.

Rory gasped.

"Sorry. Anyway, all I was going to say is that Pattie appears to be genuinely happy," she said.

Edie waved her hand in dismissal and went to find their table. Eventually, all the guests found their tables, via engraved place cards and once they were all seated, Dom Perignon flowed freely into everyone's champagne flute. The only exception was the teen-agers. They were served unlimited refills of freshly squeezed lemonade in Waterford Crystal Goblets. Bonnie's came with a shot of grenadine to color it pink.

When the Reverend Thomson noticed every glass was filled, he stood, picked up a fork and used it to gently tap on his flute. Once everyone was quiet, he said grace. After grace, he raised his flute in a sim-ple toast to Pattie and Jordan. Everyone else lifted their flutes and toasted the couple. When he sat, Clint stood. Edie sighed and Chet gave her one of those withering glances he had been giving to her all evening. She ignored him and slumped down in her chair with her arms locked across her chest. Her lip was curled under, in her customary snarl and the mean glint in her eye gained strength with each passing second. Pattie stared at her anxiously from across the room and when Jordan realized what was going on, he frowned.

"I happened to be talking to Jordan on the night he met Pattie. I had telephoned to let him know I had just gotten engaged that very morning. Anyway, after having assured me that he, personally, would never fall in love, much less get engaged, a miracle occurred. He described this lovely, raven haired waif who had wandered into his office, drenched from a rainstorm."

Pattie and Jordan looked at each other, smiled and nodded.

"And even though it was obvious Jordan was smitten, he argued and tried to debunk the notion of 'Love at First Sight.' Well, his vows tonight serve to remind us all that 'Love at First Sight' IS a reality. Love in and of itself IS a reality. In fact, Love is the ONLY reality, because in the end, 'Love Conquers All'. And seeing Pattie tonight, resplendent in all her radiance, I can certainly understand why Jordan was so love struck. So, here's to you, Jordan and your charming bride, Pattie. Let's hear it for the happy couple, as they begin their life of wedded bliss together. Cheers," Clint said.

He lifted his flute and everyone toasted and sipped along with him. Then Pattie stood. Jordan remained standing. Edie stood and pointed at Lou. Pattie cleared her throat and quickly turned to Jordan, but before he could react, Chet had already pulled Edie back into her seat.

"Oh Jordan, I'm so grateful to have you in my life. You are my one true love and my soul mate, not to mention my own personal Prince Charming. I love you," she said.

Jordan smiled and lifted his glass. He decided to keep his toast brief, because he felt uneasy about Edie. The only thing he said was, "here's to you, Mrs. Armstrong. Tonight and always."

Pattie blushed.

"Thank you, Jordan. And cheers right back at you," she murmured, coquettishly.

Jordan thanked her. They clicked their flutes and sipped. Then Jordan turned to everyone and thanked them all for joining them in their celebration. They clicked flutes again, then turned back to the room and held their flutes up. Everyone raised their flute and joined in the toast. When they sat, Jordan squeezed Pattie's arm and they gave each other a quick kiss on the lips.

A few seconds later, the staff served a velvety

smooth shrimp bisque. While the guests enjoyed it, the quartet left and the band came in and quietly took the stage. They started their set list with some easy listening songs. When everyone finished their bisque, busboys quickly cleared the tables and served a sublime ballotine de fois gras. At that point, the music gradually grew more animated.

"Oh my God! This is absolutely the best appetizer I've ever tasted!" Pattie exclaimed.

Although Anne Carey was long gone, she was not the only interloper that night. Another intruder lurked in the shadows of the flickering candlelight. He had started to grow a mustache on the day he read the wedding announcement in the newspaper. By the night of the wedding, his mustache was so long it actually curled at the ends. His hair was slicked back with a pomade that made it look darker than it was. A diamond earring glistened in his left ear. When he walked past the Benders, he leered at Mrs. Bender's cleavage, stuck his tongue out at her and wiggled it. She recoiled, looked away and shivered. Then he walked over to the teenagers' table. He noticed none of them had even bothered to touch their appetizer. When he reached over to clear Bonnie's plate, he leaned in very close to her, stared at her breasts and flashed her a Cheshire cat grin. When she looked at him in horror, he threw her a sly wink and blew in her ear.

"Looking good, BONNIE. Meet me outside after dinner," he whispered.

When he saw her wince, he chuckled and twirled his mustache like Snidely Whiplash. Then, as he reached over to clear Justin and Thomas' plates, Justin caught sight of his diamond earring and gasped. It winked at him, as if it were mocking him.

Justin touched his own earlobe where he had worn that very diamond until the day Leland LeRoux kidnapped him and stole it from him. He nudged Thomas and pointed at the waiter's ear. Thomas squinted and gave the waiter the once over. That's when he caught sight of the name "HUD" stitched above his jacket pocket. Then "HUD" slipped back into the kitchen with the plates.

Thomas leapt to his feet, so he could to run to Pattie's table and warn her. In the excitement, he knocked over his goblet of lemonade. Kyle, sensing a potential problem, put his fork down, stood and walked over to block Thomas' path. Just as he demanded that Thomas tell him what was going on, a busboy came to clean up the spilled lemonade and "HUD" reappeared to serve the salad course. Thomas pointed at "HUD" and whispered that "HUD" was actually their janitor, Willie Hudson; that "HUD" just HAD to be short for Hudson and oh by the way, "HUD" was now wearing Justin's stolen earring. Kyle quickly glanced at the waiter, dismissed the notion and placed his hands squarely on Thomas' shoulder. Then he spun

Thomas around, directed him back to his table and pulled his seat out for him.

"Now you just sit yourself right back down and stop imagining things," he said, as he tried to force Thomas into his seat.

Thomas shook his head and used all his might to resist Kyle, but Kyle dialed up the intensity of his grasp. In the end, his strength enabled him to firmly but gently plant Thomas back in his seat.

"You know, Thomas, if you really liked Pattie as much as you claim, you wouldn't ruin her wedding by trying to create drama when there doesn't need to be any. Shame on you. And I'm warning you to just stay in that seat and eat your damn salad," he said, as he pointed at Thomas' salad plate.

Even though it was a lovely salad, which consisted of a mixture of maiche lettuce, mixed baby greens, radicchio and arugula, with generous portions of halved grape tomatoes stirred into it, Thomas couldn't have cared less about it. All he could think about was "Hud." He got out of his seat, walked over to Kyle and pointed his finger at him. Then he screamed at Kyle, accused Kyle of never believing anything he had to say and added that he was "sick and tired of it!" His outburst was so loud, it grabbed everyone's attention. All eyes were on him, so no one noticed when "HUD" crouched down and disappeared.

Kyle didn't answer Thomas. He simply got out of his seat, re-directed Thomas to his own seat and warned him to stay there. In the meantime, the leader of the band, having been to many weddings, saw trouble brewing. As a result, he tested the microphone.

"Ladies and gentlemen, please enjoy your delicious salad and while you do, let me announce Dr. and Mrs. Armstrong's first dance together as husband and wife. They have chosen this song in honor of their special day," he announced.

He turned to the band and they began to play "Endless Love."

Not expecting to dance quite so early in the evening, Jordan nevertheless stood. He turned to Pattie and gazed deeply into her eyes. She stared back at him with a lazy, hazy, flirtatious twinkle. They smiled at each other. Then Jordan bowed ever so slightly and gallantly extended his hand to help her out of her seat. Once Pattie was on her feet, he led her onto the spacious, dance floor, with its walnut parquet squares.

When Kyle was confident that Thomas would not attempt to defy him again, he returned to his seat and leaned over to April. In a whisper, he repeated everything Thomas had told him. Everyone else was busy staring at Jordan and Pattie on the dance floor.

Jordan smiled at Pattie, stepped toward her and reached for her hand. When she nodded and took hold of his hand, he wrapped his other arm around her waist and pulled her close to him. She nuzzled up to him and kissed him on the cheek. Then he moved her back and forth, pausing and turning in perfect time to the music. She followed his lead easily. They looked beautiful as they happily twisted and turned. Pattie's gown coiled and uncoiled around her. It seemed to her as if she were standing still and the rest of the world was spinning. And with each rotation, it seemed to her as if she were spiraling free from the shackles of her past. And just as the song ended, Jordan punctuated it by dipping her. Once she was upright again, she beamed at Jordan, gently ran her hands through his hair and kissed him on the cheek. He smiled, did his best to smooth his hair into place and calmly led her back to their table.

Things were on an even keel for a while. The music gradually grew louder and the tempo got faster, but when the seafood course arrived, more difficulties cropped up at the teenagers' table. When "HUD" vanished in the wind, L'Abbaye, suddenly found itself short staffed. However, the Maître D'hôtel quickly figured out a way for the other staff members to fill in the gap. They all rose to the occasion and by the time they served the sorbet, service was back on track and flowing seamlessly.

Eventually, the head waiter wheeled in the main course, which consisted of racks upon racks of delicately seasoned roast New Zealand lamb. It sizzled on a grill over a spirit flame. As the head waiter carved it, the other servers rushed over so it would still be piping hot by the time it reached the tables. It was accompanied by wild rice, thick white asparagus with a Hollandaise Sauce and julienned, roasted, sweet red peppers. Rory looked at the generous portion and pushed her plate away.

"You know, if I try to eat this now, I'll lose my wonderful champagne buzz. And since I never drank champagne before, I don't want THAT to happen. So, I'm hoping they'll just let me take everything home in a doggy bag," she said.

Chet shot her the dirtiest look ever.

With each course, the music got livelier and more fervent. By the end of the entrée, the band leader announced that Chet and Pattie would be taking the floor in a traditional father daughter dance. Because Edie had kicked Chet's ankle earlier, Chet was in more pain than usual. As a result, he had difficulty concealing his limp. In spite of that, though, he made his way over to the bridal table, gently took hold of Pattie's hand and helped her onto her feet. Before Pattie left the table, she turned to Jordan and blew him a kiss.

When Pattie and Chet took the dance floor, the band began to play "I Hope You Dance", a song which Pattie had handpicked several weeks before. Chet was very tense and he broke out into a sweat.

In the meantime, Thomas was nursing his grudge against Kyle. He couldn't believe the way Kyle dismissed everything he had to say. He was insulted and he resented it. He finally came to the conclusion that no matter WHAT Kyle thought, he WOULD tell Pattie after all. Since all eyes were on Pattie and her father, he decided it would be an opportune time to go to the men's room. He figured by the time he returned, the dance would be over, Pattie would be back at her table and he, Thomas, would be standing there, just waiting to break the news to her.

Halfway through the dance, Chet's left knee buckled and he faltered. Pattie pulled him up and as he struggled to regain his equilibrium, he accidentally stomped on her right foot. She groaned in pain, looked down at her wedding pump and decided not to react to the ugly smudge mark that marred its beauty. For the rest of the dance, Chet took tiny, shuffling steps while clinging to her for dear life. When the song ended, he kissed her on the cheek and escorted her back to her seat.

The band broke into "Brick House". The bandleader clapped his hands and invited "all the pretty ladies" to take their place on the dance floor. Edie's face blazed. She squealed with delight, as she struggled to get out of her seat. It was finally HER turn to dance and she was sure when the bandleader mentioned "all the pretty ladies," he specifically meant HER. And as most of the couples began to stream onto the dance floor, she found Chet hobbling back to their table. She waylaid him, blocked his path and dragged him onto the dance floor. Even though he was dying to get off his feet, he didn't want Edie to make a scene, so he acquiesced.

They were an interesting pair. Chet stood in place and moved his arms around self-consciously. In the meantime, Edie staggered, stomped, shimmied and cavorted, all to no particular rhythm. When the band got to the part where they sang "she's letting it all hang out," she emitted a war hoop. And from that point on, she sang along with the band until the song ended. By that time, beads of sweat had broken out all over her, from her scalp, right down to the soles of her puffy, fat feet. And when the song was over, her eye liner, mascara and foundation were melting and her cheap, imitation fascinator was loose on one side.

The band leader goaded everyone into dancing to "The Electric Slide". Once again, Edie shrieked with glee. She didn't care that she was falling apart. All she wanted, was to keep dancing. When Chet turned to limp back to their table, she followed him. With every step she took, her fascinator flapped back and forth. When she reached Chet, she grabbed him by the back of his collar, spun him around and shook her finger in his face.

"Listen Buster, me and you have an appointment with destiny out there on that dance floor, which means we're gonna dance 'til we drop," she screeched.

Even though the music was loud, Edie's voice was louder. As a result, everyone in the Grand Ballroom heard her. Chet sniffed and turned away from her without saying anything. She grabbed him by the shoulder, locked him into a half Nelson and pulled him toward the dance floor. He jerked away from her and turned back toward the table. In the scuffle, his boutonniere dislodged from his lapel and landed on the floor. Edie waved her hand in dismissal and turned away. Embarrassed, she overcompensated for it by staggering back onto the dance floor and confidently planting herself right next to Mrs. Bender.

On his way back from the men's room, Thomas saw that April and Kyle were dancing, so he made his way over to Pattie's table. Out of the corner of his eye he happened to spot an endless supply of champagne, flowing from one of the fountains. Eager to try it, he walked up to the fountain, grabbed an empty flute and filled it. Then he poured the champagne down his throat. He liked it so much, he did it four more times. When he was done, he scratched his head and tried to collect his thoughts. He was supposed to do something, say something to someone, but he couldn't remember what. Or even who, for that matter. He filled the flute again, one last time and drank it down. Even though "The Electric Slide" was half over, he decided to join the line. He staggered over to the dance floor, stumbled onto it and positioned himself right behind Cheryl's mother, who was huffing, puffing and struggling to keep up with everyone else.

Edie was in front of her. She slid, gyrated and

grooved with the spirit of the dance. Her eyes looked glassy and her face was beet red, but her naked legs worked overtime as they whirled and kicked out from under her orange feathers. And as the band played on, she swayed, rotated and swiveled her hips. Mrs. Bender used her peripheral vision to study Edie as if she were a grotesque type of prancing circus horse. At the same time, she silently prayed they wouldn't collide. At one point, Edie slipped. She didn't careen into anyone, solely because her spike heel got caught in one of the seams between the parquet squares.

"Oh for fuck's sake," she screamed, when she realized she couldn't move her foot.

Mrs. Bender looked aghast, as a string of epithets tumbled out of Edie's mouth. Edie struggled and tried hard to twist her heel out of the seam. When she pulled back, her heel finally dislodged and her ankle wobbled, causing a cramp in her calf. At that point, she lost her balance and cursed some more. She hobbled away from the dance floor, in order to regain her bearings.

Even though Cheryl's mother looked like a frump, Thomas was mesmerized when he became aware of her underpants and the way they undulated against the flimsy fabric of her dress. When Edie's cramp subsided, she strutted back onto the dance floor and rejoined the line, but a minute later her heel got caught in the same seam. She twisted, turned and cursed, but in spite of her struggles, she couldn't break free.

With all eyes on Edie, Thomas had an opportunity to surreptitiously pinch Cheryl's mother, as hard on her buttocks as he could manage. Cheryl's mother lurched forward, at the exact moment when Edie tugged with all her might. Edie's heel broke off, which caused her ankle to twist. She lurched backwards. Her arms circled frantically like a whirly bird and she slid backwards, headlong into Cheryl's mother.

Cheryl's mother screamed. Her eyes glazed over and her legs flew out from under her. When Thomas saw her body rise from the floor and sail backwards, he stopped dancing and leapt out of the way, just in time to see her land on her left hip. Her face and head weren't injured, only because she had the presence of mind to stretch her arms out to brace herself for the fall. She moaned in agony and crumpled into a heap. Mrs. Bender recoiled in horror and Cheryl gasped as her mother lay there, panting, sweating and glaring up at Edie. Edie merely stood helpless and red faced, batting her bloodshot eyes. Cheryl, Judge Bender, Lou, Chet, Pattie, Jordan and the head waiter all ran over to her, while the band played on. Mrs. Bender took long, graceful strides back to her table. Pattie's face and décolletage broke out in hives and she wheezed as she bent over Cheryl's mother.

"Are you all right?" She shrieked.

When Cheryl's mother shook her head, Lou frowned and knelt next to her. The head waiter bent down and whispered in her ear.

"Can you tell me your name?"

"Sure. Sadie Mae Zadfrack," she answered.

The head waiter looked at Lou wildly, as if she were delusional, but Lou nodded.

"That's her name, all right."

Then Lou turned to her and asked whether she thought she could stand. When she nodded, he and the head waiter helped her sit up. She leaned on both of them for a few seconds. Once she felt steady, they helped her onto her feet. She dusted herself off in indignation. Lou, Chet and Cheryl escorted her back to her table and everyone else returned to their own table.

"Really! Such common riff raff you expose me to sometimes. You just love it, don't you? I hardly expected to attend a wedding where the waiters act lascivious and the mother of the bride is three sheets to the wind before the damn ceremony even begins. There's something radically wrong with these people and I find them all simply appalling. I've had enough, so can we PLEASE just go home?" Mrs. Bender whispered to her husband, trying to stifle the anger in her voice.

Judge Bender shook his head.

"No. We can't 'just go home'. That would be rude. We have to wait until after the bride and groom cut the cake," he said.

She sighed and shook her head back at him.

"You're always too damn polite for OUR own good and it's becoming a real problem."

"Well, even if I weren't polite, I'd hate to let them down, because, in spite of whatever you're thinking, they happen to be good people."

Edie decided she desperately needed a cigarette and a drink. She kicked off her shoes, ran barefoot toward the exit and ended up trampling Chet's boutonniere in the process. Rory, having watched everything while chuckling and downing flute after flute of champagne, stood, grabbed her handbag and followed Edie. Once Edie made it outside, she only stopped running when she literally bumped into the valet parking attendant. He gripped her squarely, stopped her in her tracks and held her in place for a few seconds.

"How may I help you?" He asked.

She lifted her dress and patted her flask.

"Well for one thing, you can get your big, fat paws off me, so I can go fill THIS up with some of my own fucking booze. I'll have to get it out of the cooler in my trunk, because I have no intention of paying jacked up prices for any of YOUR watered down crap," she said. Her speech was slurred.

The valet gasped.

"Didn't you even notice it's an open bar?" He asked, as he released his grip on her.

"Well then get me a shot of straight tequila, you stupid lout and bring it to me down by my car!

Pronto!" She snapped, as she pointed at Chet's faded, old Festiva.

The valet shook his head and simply stepped out of Edie's way. In the meantime, Rory had been rifling through all the keys on his pegboard. When she found Chet's key ring, she yanked it off the hook. Several sets of keys fell to the ground. Not stopping to pick any of them up, she ran past Edie all the way to Chet's car. Just as she opened the trunk, Edie caught up to her, shoved her out of the way and broke into the cooler. She refilled her flask, guzzled from it until it was half empty and breathed a sigh of relief. Then she ordered Rory to unlock the front passenger's side door. Once Rory did, Edie fumbled around in the glove compartment until she found her pill bottle. She grabbed it, opened it and shook three pills into the palm of her hand. Rory's eyes popped open in shock.

"Hey don't YOU judge ME, Miss Two Beer Annie. Anyway, want one?" Edie asked.

When Rory shook her head, Edie chuckled and waved her hand in dismissal.

"That's because you're a lightweight," she said.

She shoved the pills into her mouth, chomped down on them and crushed them with her back teeth. Then she took a deep gulp from her flask and flushed them down her throat.

"I left my bag back at the table. Give me a cigarette?" Edie asked.

Rory reached into her hand bag, handed Edie a

cigarette and lit it for her. Then she lit one for herself. The two of them stood by the car, smoking and drinking. When Edie finished her cigarette, she didn't even bother to grind it out. Instead, while the butt was still lit, she tossed it onto the silver Toyota Rav4, which was parked next to them and which happened to belong to Kyle and April. When Rory did the same thing, they both started to laugh. Then they drank, smoked, threw some more cigarette butts onto the car and laughed some more. Rory fished through her bag and found a Granola Bar. She broke it into two pieces and gave one to Edie. Then they both crumbled their halves and hurled the nuts, seeds and dried pieces of fruit onto the top, hood and windshield, laughing uncontrollably the entire time.

"They're gonna think it was squirrels," Edie said, when she saw their handiwork.

Suddenly, Edie spotted Lou coming toward them from across the parking lot. Even in her drunken state, she could see he was fuming. That caused her to crack up even more. She jostled Rory in the ribs with her elbow and pointed at him. Rory felt intimidated at the sight of him and immediately stopped laughing. He was glaring at them and when he got close to them, he pointed at Edie's bare feet. He demanded to know where Edie's shoes were and she shrugged.

"How the hell should I know? I must 'of lost 'em in the shuffle. Get it? Shuffle? Dancing?" She said in a drunken slur. Then she cackled at her own wit.

Disgusted, Lou ordered her and Rory to pull themselves together. Then he spread his hands out, pressed them against both of their backs and physically ushered them across the parking lot and into to the Grand Ballroom. Edie bobbed, weaved and staggered every step of the way. They made it just in time to see Pattie and Jordan cut their three tiered purple, lavender and white ombre butter cream wedding cake. When Pattie and Jordan fed each other their first piece, everyone except Edie and Mrs. Bender applauded.

"I'd like you all to know, Pattie designed this very cake to match her bridal bouquet. The buttercream icing was kissed with a subtle hint of culinary grade lavender extract, according to Pattie's exact specifications. The cake inside is a white cake infused with champagne and the same lavender flavoring. The fillings are layered with chocolate butter cream, a seedless raspberry spread and lemon curd. In addition to the cake, we also have a Venetian table and a chocolate fountain, so please be sure to enjoy all of it," Jordan announced.

When the waiter placed Edie's slice in front of her, she sneered, shook her head and used the back tines of her fork to bulldoze it all the way to the edge of her plate, as far from herself as she could get it. Then, she pushed the plate toward the centerpiece. Finally, she rested her elbows on the table, cradled her head in her hands and started to cry. Ignoring her, Chet dug into his slice. When it was gone, he reached for Edie's plate, slid it in front of him and polished off her slice.

After the dessert course, it was time for Pattie to throw the bouquet. Kevin Gordon's date, Sadie Mae, Miranda, Cheryl, Bonnie and Rory lined up. And when the bouquet was in the air, Cheryl reached as far as she could, in order to catch it. However, her efforts were in vain. Kevin Gordon's date jumped in front of her at the last minute and snatched it. After-wards, Reginald Reese, Kevin Gordon, Toby Bar-nett, Thomas, Justin, Dante, Cosmo, Ryan and Lou lined up. And after Jordan removed Pattie's garter, in time to "You Sexy Thing," Pattie threw it over her left shoulder. Much to everyone's surprise, Reginald Reese, the confirmed bachelor, seized it.

It was one o'clock when the reception finally wound down. Baskets of fruit, nuts and after dinner liqueurs came out. Jordan gave Clint, Lou and Ryan diamond studded tie clips and Pattie gave Cheryl, Miranda and Laurie, diamond studded hair clasps. Then Pattie returned Laurie's earrings. When the Honorable Judge and Mrs. Bender realized Pattie and Jordan were about to leave, they were the first guests to approach them. Judge Bender conveyed his best wishes, then he and his wife hurriedly said their good byes and disappeared.

As soon as Pattie and Jordan walked into their suite, Pattie stepped out of her bridal slippers. She removed the pearls from around her neck and the matching clip from her updo. Then she shook her curls loose. Jordan stepped up to her. They embraced and engaged in a long, passionate kiss.

"Oh my God! I feel so bad," Pattie said, when they broke the embrace.

Jordan knit his brow.

"Why?"

"Because my vows sounded so shabby compared to yours."

He shook his head.

"Nonsense Your vows were wonderful. Always remember, we're not in a competition. We're on the same team. Here, let me help you out of your gown," he said.

She smiled and turned around.

Meanwhile, back at the Grand Ballroom, Thomas felt frustrated. Nothing was working out for him and on top of it, he didn't even catch Pattie's garter. Plus, he was overheated from all the champagne and dancing, so he decided to go outside and cool off.

As April and Kyle were getting ready to leave, April bent down to pick up her evening bag. When she couldn't find it, she frowned and asked Kyle where it was. He shrugged, shook his head and asked her where she last remembered having it. She shrugged and shook her head. When she and Kyle questioned Justin and Bonnie, they also shrugged and shook their heads.

"By the way where's Thomas?" April asked, almost as an afterthought.

Again, the two teenagers shrugged and shook their heads.

Thomas let the glow from the lanterns serve as guideposts to help him locate the swimming pool. When he finally found it, he shed himself of each item of his clothing and flung it into a heap on the ground. When he got down to his jockey shorts, he decided to leave them on. With a loud splash, he took a swan dive into the deep end of the pool and treated himself to what he believed was a well-deserved moonlight dip. When he was done, he swam over to the fountain, came up for air and clung to it. He opened his mouth and let the flowing chlorinated water cascade down his throat. As he positioned himself underneath it, he urinated, farted and laughed hysterically, while the water beat down on his head.

Lou told Chet he was taking Cheryl and Sadie home to Jersey City. Once he left, Chet waited, while Edie and Rory scrounged around each of the tables. They seized every remaining centerpiece and hospitality gift and Edie also hunted down and stuffed every loose piece of silverware into her hand bag. Afterwards, with the aid of one of the busboys, she and Rory toted Rory's doggie bag and the rest of their booty out to Chet's Festiva. Like ants bringing food to their hive, they trotted back and forth as fast as their legs could carry them. Embarrassed beyond belief at their antics, Chet sniffed and sighed, as he jam packed, angled and forced everything into his trunk. After their last trip, he slammed the trunk shut.

"OK, we're loaded and locked, so let's get the hell out of here," he said.

Without even bothering to tip the busboy, Edie and Rory got into the car. After Chet pulled away, the busboy stormed back to the Abbey. Before he reached it, he heard splashing and laughter coming from the pool area. When he walked down to investigate the disturbance, he spotted Thomas. He was so shocked, he stopped dead in his tracks.

"Hey you! What the hell do you think you're doing?"

Thomas gasped and cupped his hands around his eyes. He wanted to find out whether the busboy was "HUD." When he realized it wasn't, he stuck out his middle finger and grinned.

"Listen, there's no swimming here tonight, so you'd better haul your ass out of that pool right now," the busboy yelled.

As the busboy ran toward the pool, Thomas ducked under the water, swam to the far end and climbed out. Clad only in his wet jockey shorts, he sprinted off into the darkness. When he was out of sight, the busboy ran over to the pile of clothes and shoes, picked them up and rifled through the pockets. When he didn't find any money, he cursed, carried everything off and tossed it into the nearest dumpster.

CHAPTER ONE HUNDRED THIRTY-FIVE

CRUSH ENDO

Chet pulled his old clunker into a parking space as close to his brownstone as he could. He, Edie and Rory made several trips unloading the trunk. They carried the cooler, their booty and Rory's doggy bag into the house and placed it all on the kitchen counter. After the last trip, Edie watered the centerpieces, while Chet locked the front door for the night. He and Rory went upstairs. He took a shower and Rory undressed and went straight to sleep in Pattie's old bedroom. Edie stayed downstairs. After she removed the stolen silverware from her bag, she hurriedly washed, dried and stashed it away in the sideboard in the dining room. After that, she returned to the kitchen, collapsed into one of the Naugahyde chairs at her cheap Formica kitchen table and lit a cigarette. Staring into space, she took a deep drag. And then it hit her. The brainstorm. She pondered for a few minutes about whether or not to go through with it. In the end she decided she would. She let her cigarette burn in the black plastic ashtray, while she stood and lined her favorite jumbo Margarita goblet with her usual mixture of ground rock salt, pain killers, tranquilizers and antidepressants. Then she filled it with crushed ice. She removed the flask from her thigh, poured the contents into the goblet and gulped ninety percent of the drink. Then she licked the salt mixture from around the rim and put the glass down on the table. She walked over to her red dial telephone and called 911.

"What is your emergency?" The dispatcher asked.

Edie kept it simple. No sense in camping it up by panting too heavily, so she breathed normally into the receiver.

"Hello? Hello? Hello, is anyone there?" The dispatcher pressed on, impatiently.

Edie let go of the receiver. As it dangled on its cord, it occasionally bumped against the wall. She walked back to the table, took a long last drag on her cigarette and replaced it in the ashtray, where it would die a natural death. Then she picked up her glass, took it into the bathroom in the hallway and closed herself in. She turned the water on, shook her head and giggled with delight at her impishness. And when she stopped laughing, she pulled a bottle of sleeping pills out of the medicine cabinet. She opened it, grabbed three pills and stuffed them into her mouth. Then she washed them down with the last little bit of her drink. She laid the goblet sideways on the floor next to the sink. Then she left the water running and staggered into the hallway. She made it to the front door, unlocked it and opened it, ever so slightly. Then she gently lay on the floor at the foot of the stairs with her arm reaching out toward the door. Once she was face down on her stomach, she sprawled out like a star fish. And waited.

Chet got out of the shower, reached for a towel and patted himself dry. When he heard the knock, he frowned. He knew there was no way Lou could have made it back from Jersey City so fast. Then he heard the sound of boots in the foyer. He wrapped his towel around his waist, limped over to his night table and grabbed his .38 out of the night table drawer. Then he limped out to the landing and hobbled down the stairs as fast as he could. Two paramedics were already in the process of strapping Edie onto a stretcher. Edie smiled weakly at Chet and gave him a pathetic finger wave, just as the paramedics lifted the stretcher and carried her out the door.

Chet's heart raced and he broke into a sweat. By the time he got outside, the terrier who lived next door was already standing by the fence and barking at the top of his lungs. Lights went on in the houses all around. Helpless and confused, Chet watched as the paramedics loaded Edie into the back of the ambulance and called out to them to find out what was going on.

"We're taking her to Bellevue's Emergency Room,"

one of the paramedics said, as he slammed the door and closed Edie in.

Rory heard the commotion outside, got out of bed and raced down the stairs. She ran out into the street in her nightgown and bare feet and watched with Chet as the ambulance sped away. Chet turned to her and shook his head.

"Just for once, I'd like to know what the hell is going on under my own roof," he said.

They looked at each other in confusion, ran inside and threw on some clothes. Then a few minutes later, they were back in Chet's Ford and on their way to Bellevue.

Edie was fully conscious, already being treated and sprouting a band aid on her left arm where they had just drawn blood.

"All right. In your own words tell me what went wrong," the handsome, middle aged, psychiatrist asked Edie.

Edie liked him. Unlike Chet, he spoke to her in a kind voice. Plus, as far as she was concerned, he was distinguished looking. She liked the way his thick, black, wavy hair was just starting to turn gray at the temples. She looked up at him demurely, smiled and then arranged her lips in what she hoped was a coquettish pout. And for several seconds, that was her only answer, until she was able to come up with something she thought he might fall for.

"Well, when I got home from my daughter's wedding tonight, I was all keyed up. I just couldn't get to sleep, so I thought I would unwind by taking a sleeping pill. I didn't realize what a mistake THAT would turn out to be. Because I probably had a little too much champagne at the reception and I forgot to keep track of all the toasts," she simpered.

The nurse bristled in, handed the doctor the results of Edie's blood work and disappeared. He read the report and looked up.

"Well, the good news is your blood alcohol levels are low enough that we won't have to pump your stomach. Thank God you called 911 though. It's always better to be safe than sorry in these instances. I'll be back to check on you later," he said.

He headed straight for the nurse's station and prescribed unlimited amounts of black coffee for Edie. Chet and Rory were standing there and when they overheard him mention Edie's name, Chet limped over and introduced himself.

"As it turns out, she's going to be all right. If you don't mind though, I'd like to keep her for the next day or so. Once I'm certain she's stable, I'll discharge her. Provided of course someone will be there to take care of her. Although she's blaming it on an accidental overdose, I'd prefer that she not be alone for the next couple of days. You know. Just in case," the doctor said.

Chet frowned and sniffed, but Rory figured a few

extra days of free drinking with Edie in New York would certainly beat drinking alone in boring old Allentown, so she poked the doctor's arm.

"Hi, I'm the patient's cousin. I came from Pennsylvania to attend a family wedding, but I don't mind staying around to help look after Edie," she said.

The doctor looked at her, nodded his assent and made a note in the chart. Not owning a cell phone, Chet stayed by the nurse's station and asked whether he could use their desk phone to call Lou. Rory walked down the hall to Edie's room, where she found Edie drinking black coffee from an oversized mug. She walked up to Edie's bed and grimaced.

"Ouch. I'll see if I can find a way to get my hands on some Kahlua so you can at least spike that shit up," she whispered.

CHAPTER ONE HUNDRED THIRTY-SIX

BRUISES

Lou pulled his Bronco in front of Sadie Mae's apartment building. He opened the passenger's side door and helped Cheryl out. Then he opened the back door, so he and Cheryl could carefully guide Sadie Mae out. Once she struggled onto her feet, strong gusts of wind blasted her from the river and blew her dress over her hips and thighs. That's when Lou and Cheryl noticed the beginnings of the huge black and blue mark that was already forming. Cheryl shook her head sadly as the dress fell back into place. When she gingerly hugged Sadie Mae, Sadie Mae winced.

Lou's face was red with embarrassment. He looked down at the tops of his shoes and shook his head. As soon as Cheryl draped her arm around her mother, he instinctively flanked Sadie Mae on her other side. He gently took hold of her elbow and helped Cheryl slowly walk her toward the apartment building.

"You know what? The worst part of injuries like these is that they sometimes get worse as time goes on. But at least you didn't break your hip. In any case, once we get inside I'll set you up in a nice, warm Epsom salt bath," Cheryl said, when they reached the stoop.

Sadie Mae nodded and rested there for a few minutes.

Once they were inside the apartment, Cheryl led Sadie Mae into the bathroom, while Lou waited out in the foyer. A few seconds later his phone rang. When he picked up the call, the first thing he heard was a sniff. Chet was on the line demanding to know when he was coming home.

"I just got here, for God's sake," Lou said.

When Chet told him he had to turn around and come home right away, he sighed.

"Why? What's going on? What did Pattie do now?"

"It's not Pattie. Your mother accidentally OD'd on some booze and pills. We're at Bellevue's emergency room now. I don't want to leave her, so somebody's got to head over to the house and get her night gown, robe, slippers, reading glasses, current crocheting project and her book of cross word puzzles."

"Why can't Rory do it?"

"Because she's as drunk as your mother. Anyway, once you get everything together, bring it all over here. Besides, I don't know why you even had to drive the two of them home. Between the PATH Train and that New Light Rail system they've got going on over there, why couldn't the two of them have taken THAT to get home?" Chet snapped.

Lou frowned. Before he could even respond, Chet had hung up. Lou sighed, called Cheryl out into the hallway and explained what was going on. Then he apologized one more time for Edie's behavior and said goodnight to Sadie Mae through the bathroom door. Afterwards, he kissed Cheryl on the cheek and left. Cheryl went back into the bathroom and told her mother what was going on.

"You know what struck me as weird? She never even apologized to me for almost crippling me. And believe me, it WAS all her fault," Sadie Mae eked out the words in painful bursts of syllables. She carefully omitted the part about having lurched forward as a result of being pinched.

Cheryl nodded.

"Yeah, well, at least from now on when I tell you what an awful old lush she is, maybe you'll believe me. In any case, I'm sorry she hurt you," she said.

Meanwhile, on the other side of the river in Manhattan, Chet tried to call Pattie from the nurse's station. Since Pattie's cell phone was on "do not disturb," all he got was her voicemail.

CHAPTER ONE HUNDRED THIRTY-SEVEN

SHOCKED

The following morning, a severe Charley Horse in Pattie's left leg jolted her out of her sleep. In an effort not to disturb Jordan, she squeezed her eyes tightly, slid down on the bed and wrapped her toes around the footboard for leverage. Keeping her screams to herself, she somehow managed to power through the pain. When, it finally subsided, she slowly worked her way up to a sitting position. She crept out of bed and went into the bathroom. Hoping the jets from the double jacuzzi would relieve some of her residual soreness, she ran the water.

The rush from the tap interrupted Jordan's sleep. He reached for Pattie. When he realized she wasn't in bed, he got up and knocked softly on the bathroom door.

"Come in," she called out.

He opened the door and stuck his head in. The jacuzzi was already filled. Pattie was leaning back. Only her neck and head stuck out.

"I had a Charley Horse, but I'm sure I'll be fine. After all, this is the beginning of our beautiful, new life together," she murmured.

She turned the jets on. Jordan went into the other room, popped open the bottle of Dom Perignon that was chilling in an ice bucket and put it on a tray, along with two flutes. He carried the tray into the bathroom, poured the champagne and handed her a flute. He placed the tray on the wide ledge of the tub, climbed in and sidled up to her. He picked up his flute and they toasted each other. She swirled the champagne around in the flute and took another sip. Then she reached over and placed the flute on the tray.

Entwined in each other's arms, they reveled as the hot bubbles surrounded them. Pattie closed her eyes, leaned her head back and arched her spine like a cat. She moved her leg around until she found the position where the gushes of water could best soothe her aching calf muscles. A few minutes later she opened her eyes and looked up at the skylight. Just as the daylight was turning the heavens bright, there was a knock on the door. Jordan got out, threw on a fluffy white terry cloth robe and hurried to answer it. Pattie closed her eyes and continued to relax, while a waiter wheeled a breakfast cart into the room. Jordan pointed to the porch that enveloped three sides of their suite. The waiter wheeled the cart out onto the porch and set up their breakfast. After he left,

Pattie stood, drained the water and quickly patted herself dry. She wrapped herself in a robe identical to Jordan's and joined Jordan out on the porch. She marveled at the Mimosas, Eggs benedict with Hollandaise sauce, Grand Marnier French toast made with brioche and the bowls of mixed berries and Mascarpone. Jordan filled her cup from a hot carafe of freshly ground gourmet coffee. She helped herself to two slices of French toast, spread a pat of butter on them and poured maple syrup over them. Then she topped off her coffee cup with heavy cream.

They ate at a leisurely pace. After all, there were many hours left until their flight. After they showered, Pattie made herself up to look as beautiful as she could. She arranged her hair into big barrel curls and changed into a brand new white linen dress that accommodated her voluptuous new size. After Jordan fastened her pearls for her, she draped a pink, white and lavender silk scarf around her shoulders. She slipped into a pair of plain, white leather pumps and inspected herself in the mirror. She decided she liked what she saw and smiled at her reflection. Jordan wore black pants and a light grey button down shirt. Hand in hand they went outside to peruse L'Abbaye's grounds for the last time. They walked to the highest point on the property and looked down at the Sound below.

"I feel like I'm standing on top of the world. It's

such a shame we can't spend more time here," Pattie said.

He nodded.

"We'll come back again soon," he said.

After they returned to their suite, Jordan got their luggage in order, rang for the bellman and left to pay the bill. While he was checking out, Pattie removed her phone from her charger and played her messages. The only one was from Chet. She listened to it, hit the return call button and waited. When it said her request could not be completed as dialed, she tried her parents' land line. It rang and rang. Exasperated at this point, she reached out to Lou. He had long since returned from delivering Edie's belongings to the hospital, so at that point he was asleep. When the phone rang it woke him up. He forced his eyes open and answered the call in a groggy voice. When he realized it was Pattie, he explained Edie's situation to her and went back to sleep.

About ten minutes later, Jordan walked through the door and found Pattie hyperventilating and covered in splotches. He frowned.

"What could possibly have gone wrong since I left? I was only gone for a few minutes,"

She answered him by relaying the information about Edie. When the limousine driver picked them up, they asked him to make an unscheduled stop at Bellevue Hospital.

CHAPTER ONE HUNDRED THIRTY-EIGHT

I THINK I'M GOING OUT OF MY HEAD

After hearing Lou's description of Edie's situation, Pattie was surprised to discover Edie had been admitted to the general part of the hospital, rather than to the psychiatric ward. When she and Jordan got off the elevator, they rushed down the hall. Edie was sitting up in bed, alone in a private room and her door was wide open. She wore a black translucent nylon negligee, which was partially covered by a black quilted bed jacket and she was busily crocheting a black shawl.

When she heard Pattie and Jordan enter the room, she dropped her handiwork in her lap, slid her tiny black, rhinestone studded reading glasses down toward the tip of her nose and peered over them. The malevolence in her expression was unmistakable. Without taking her eyes off of either Pattie or Jordan, she reached for the huge mug on the bed stand next to her and sipped.

Edie reminded Pattie of a black widow spider. Not knowing what to make of the entire scenario, Pattie and Jordan glanced at one another, shook their heads and remained in the doorway. Pattie wanted to break the silence, but she just didn't know what to say. In the end, Edie was the first to speak.

"I hope the two of you haven't come to kick me when I'm down. After all, no matter what you may think of me, I'm still a force to be reckoned with. And if you don't believe me, you can ask that old dingbat I gave flying lessons to on the dance floor last night. Splat and happy landings to the old wretch," she said, as she broke into raucous laughter.

Pattie and Jordan both gasped. What made Edie's comment even more unnerving, was the fact she had spoken it in an uncharacteristically sober tone of voice. Pattie cleared her throat.

"And I might as well tell you, I'll do even worse to whoever's handy if I don't get my hands on a cigarette soon," Edie added.

Just as with all Pattie's other life's emergencies, she could feel the heat rising on her face, neck and décolletage. She knew they were the harbingers of the inevitable splotches and hives that were to follow. Suddenly, a strong wave of nausea overtook her. Knowing she only had seconds to spare before she started to throw up, she whipped the scarf from around her neck, shoved it in Jordan's hands and raced into Edie's bathroom. She slammed the door, lifted the lid on the toilet and leaned over it, just in time to throw up the entire contents of her delicious gourmet breakfast. Jordan waited for her on the other side of the bathroom door, while Edie rang frantically for the nurse.

When the nurse saw the flashing buzzer, she looked up from the computer screen where she was entering data and hurried down the hall. Pattie flushed the toilet and glanced at her reflection in the mirror. Her eyes looked glassy. And even though she was pale to begin with, her face looked even whiter than usual. In an attempt to regain her composure, she turned on the tap and ran her wrists under the cold water.

The nurse ran into the room and found Edie trying to stifle a gag. She knocked on the bathroom door, barged in and looked at Pattie. And Jordan was right behind her. Pattie turned the water off, dried her hands on a paper towel and then ripped off a couple of squares of toilet paper. She wet them gently under the tap and dabbed her tears. And Jordan put her scarf back in place.

"Are you Mrs. Anwald's daughter?"

Pattie nodded.

"Well, try not to be too upset. The good news is she's going to be all right. And if everything goes as planned, she'll probably be discharged tomorrow."

Pattie nodded again.

"My husband and I just got married last night."

The nurse smiled.

"Well, Congratulations and Best Wishes."

"Thank you. We're scheduled to fly to Scotland for our honeymoon in just a few hours," Pattie said.

"Your Dad, your brother and a cousin of hers have all stepped up to the plate to keep her company. You know. Just in case. So that means the two of you shouldn't have to cancel your trip. Just go and enjoy yourselves. And above all, don't feel guilty."

Without looking at or even saying good bye to Edie, Pattie thanked the nurse, turned on her heel and walked out. Jordan and the nurse followed her as she made her way down the hall. When they reached the nurse's station, the nurse asked her to wait a minute. She walked over to a supply closet and returned with a small bottle of mouthwash, a plastic cup, a toothbrush and a small tube of toothpaste. She handed the items to Pattie, then led her to a visitors' bathroom. Pattie went in, used the items and re-emerged a few minutes later. The expression on her face told Jordan she was embarrassed. He gently took hold of her arm, squeezed it and led her down the hall toward the elevator. Once they were outside, Jordan thanked their driver for waiting and asked him to take them to the British Airways First Class Check in Counter at JFK Airport.

CHAPTER ONE HUNDRED THIRTY-NINE

WEDDING BELL BLUES

Thoughts whirled around Willie Hudson's brain as he stared through the grime of his window at the fleabag motel where he lived. Summer days were just too long as far as he was concerned. He really disliked daylight savings time. He wished he had a cold beer to wrap his hands around. He was proud of himself for having come into a windfall of thirteen hundred dollars. He couldn't fathom the idea that April Higgin's stupid clutch bag was worth eleven hundred dollars.

Well, If the pawn broker was stupid enough to pay that much money for it, that's his problem, not mine, Willie told himself, as the thoughts continued to assault him.

The other two hundred dollars was easy pickings. It was the cash April had stashed in her wallet. And as happy as he was for pulling off that caper, at the same time he was disappointed in himself for still having failed to finish off that menace Pattie Anwald last Thanksgiving,

In any case, he knew it was time to get out of Dodge. The new and improved game plan was to catch the next Amtrak train to "Destination Anywhere". He figured once he was "all aboard" and comfortably seated he'd have plenty of time to strategize a way to blow Pattie Anwald AND her husband out of the water. AND her lawyer too. He hadn't forgotten him shooting off his big mouth and blah blah blahing on the news. Putting the blame on him for Leland's murder. And while he was at it, he'd kill Justin and that nitwit Thomas Amissah too. After all, that lousy bastard almost blew his cover last night, making today's impromptu change in plans necessary. As for Bonnie? Well, he'd keep her around for a while and only get rid of her after she'd outlived her usefulness.

He shook his head, chuckled and walked over to his closet. Then he pulled every piece of clothing from the hangers and put them on, one layer on top of the other. He walked out of his room, headed toward the lobby and told Donna at the desk he was going to get a six pack. He even asked her if she needed anything. When she said "no," he nodded, told her he'd catch her later and simply walked out the front door. Of course he had no intention of ever returning or paying his outstanding balance. He made his way down Eighth Avenue, threw the room key and April's wallet in the first available trash can and turned the corner to head for Penn Station. As he sauntered down the street, he could have sworn he spotted yesterday's "Man of Honor" from that damn Anwald wedding. The guy seemed like he was walking right up to him. He squinted, turned his leathery face away and clenched his fist, in case the "Man of Honor" recognized him. But he didn't, so they both just kept on going their own way.

Annie stared at the picture of Pattie and Jordan with sheer, unadulterated hatred. She was repulsed by their wedding; she reviled their wedding kiss and she despised the two of them. She forwarded the photograph from her phone to her computer. Then she printed it. And before the ink was even dry, she thumb tacked it to the wall over her toilet. She spit at it and then looked up at her bathroom ceiling.

"Please God, just tell me WHY you're forcing me to play rhythm guitar behind that loathsome wretch," she screamed, as if somehow God was ready to make His appearance on her ceiling.

She looked out the window at the harsh glare of the sun beating down on the Palisades and burst into tears.

CHAPTER ONE HUNDRED FORTY

LEAVING ON A JET PLANE

Pattie and Jordan boarded the aircraft and fastened themselves into their seats. Jordan had a strange thought about his father's recent plane crash, but he decided to pay no attention to it. He was too concerned about Pattie. He looked over at her. Her grandmother's pearls and her scarf perked up her skin tone a bit and she seemed calm enough, considering she'd had a rough morning, had never flown before and was loathe to travel anywhere outside of New York City. He put his arm around her and pulled her to him. She pressed her head against his shoulder, snuggled up to him and grabbed hold of his forearm. Their eyes locked and they smiled at each other. When the pilot started the engines, she clung onto his arm for dear life. He kissed the top of her head, just as the plane lifted off the runway.

"I love you," they murmured to each other in unison, as the plane soared into the clear twilight.

The pilot made a wide circle and spiraled over the airport towers. Pattie and Jordan looked out the window at the ocean shimmering below. They watched the planet shrink beneath them. The spectacular sunset splashed the sky behind them, until they were so high, the earth looked like nothing more than an orange colored line.

The End

Did you know *It Can't Rain This Hard Forever*
is set in Georgia, a serif typeface designed in 1993
by Matthew Carter as a font that would appear elegant,
yet still legible in small print.

DAWN'S UNOFFICIAL BIOGRAPHY (IN A NUTSHELL)

DAWN DITTMAR is a contemporary American crime novelist. A lawyer by profession, Dawn is the author of *Pattie's Best Deal* and this sequel *It Can't Rain This Hard Forever*. Dawn is also a teacher and a Reiki Master. She has appeared on radio and television shows throughout the tri state area.

She lives on the Jersey Shore. When she is not writing, teaching or meditating, you might find her relaxing on the beach or by her pool, (with a good book in hand, of course). And no matter where she may be, if you listen carefully, you can sometimes hear her lapse into legalese when she feels the need to help someone fight injustice.

Dawn is grateful for her writing and she views it as an important sanctuary in the middle of each day. She believes tapping into her creativity gives a higher purpose to her life. It means a great deal to her that you are reading this book and she would sincerely value your feedback. Feel free to visit her at Dawn Dittmar on Facebook or contact her with your thoughts and comments at Dawndittmar@aol.com.